One Sweet Quarrel

Also by Deirdre McNamer

Red Rover
My Russian
Rima in the Weeds

One Sweet Quarrel

a novel

Deirdre McNamer

Introduction by Nancy Pearl

This is a work of fiction. Characters and events portrayed in this book are either products of the author's imagination or are used fictitiously

Printed in the United States of America.

Published by AmazonEncore
PO Box 400818
Las Vegas, NV 89140

ISBN-13: 9781477807644
ISBN-10: 1477807640
Library of Congress Control Number: 2013904880

Introduction

Many years ago now, my husband's cousin Bob called me to talk about a book he'd just finished. Our conversation went something like this:

"Nancy, I just finished reading a terrific thriller and wondered if you've read it yet." (I could hear the enthusiasm in his voice.)

"What's the name of it?"

"*The Da Vinci Code*. It's by someone named Dan Brown. Did you read it?"

I paused—a long pause. I think of myself as a promoter of reading, someone who recommends good books to read. I'm not a book critic, and if I don't like a book I'd just as soon not talk about it at all, but Bob had, unfortunately, asked.

"Well, actually, I began to read it because so many people were talking about it, but the writing was so abysmal, so clunky, that I couldn't get much farther than the first page. There are so many terrific books available. I just can't bring myself to read the badly written ones."

Silence on Bob's part. Then, in a tone of great amazement, "Really? I thought it was wonderfully written."

A few months after that conversation, a woman I didn't know approached me at a party and asked if I could suggest a book she might enjoy. (This happens more than you might think.) When I asked her to tell me about a title that she'd liked, she didn't respond directly, instead saying that she liked only well-written books. Without questioning her any further, I suggested Arundhati Roy's *The God of Small Things*. About two weeks later I got an e-mail from her to say that she'd loved the Roy novel and wondered what else I would recommend for her to read.

"Well-written" is a phrase that comes up often when people talk about books, be they editors, reviewers, blurb writers, or ordinary readers. But what does that phrase mean exactly? For some, it might bring to mind the dazzling paragraph-long sentences and the languid and lush narrative to be found in the transporting novels of Gabriel García Márquez. Or the writing style of William Faulkner, which my cousin Stephen, a retired English professor, describes as "complex, dense, challenging, innovative, and filled with rich, subtle implication." For others, perhaps, it means the simile-laden prose that characterizes Raymond Chandler's work. Others might believe it refers to the pun-filled humor of Terry Pratchett's novels, or the witty writing that's found in Jasper Fforde's Thursday Next stories. And then there's Stephen King (*The Stand*, among many others), a master of providing his readers with the delicious tension between feeling compelled to turn the page to find out what happens next (or, in the case of the "complete and uncut version" of *The Stand*, to turn well over a thousand pages) and terror at the thought of exactly what that might be. His books are certainly effectively written, but are they well-written? (Bob is a big Stephen King fan.)

Or what about, for example, *Dinner at the Homesick Restaurant* (Anne Tyler), *Pale Fire* (Vladimir Nabokov), *The Storyteller* (Jodi Picoult), *The Other Side of the Story* (Marian Keyes), *Bleak House* (Charles Dickens), *Beloved* (Toni Morrison), *Midnight's Children* (Salman Rushdie), *The Poisonwood Bible* (Barbara Kingsolver), *Emily, Alone* (Stewart O'Nan), *Ulysses* (James Joyce), *Safe Haven* (Nicholas Sparks), and *The Maytrees* (Annie Dillard)? I know which of these I'd consider to be "well-written," but what about you? Based on my experience from talking with readers of all kinds, we're unlikely to find ourselves in strong agreement on many of these titles.

Too often, I think people rather casually (and carelessly) equate a "well-written book" with "a book I enjoyed." When Bob said that *The Da Vinci Code* was wonderfully written, I think he meant that it delivered the reading experience he was looking for: a fast-paced and exciting page-turner of a novel. He'd never describe himself as someone who read "well-written" books; that isn't what he wants from a novel. But when I use the phrase "well-written," I associate it with a particular kind of reading experience, one that focuses on the pleasure received from the way in which an author uses language.

Whenever people want me to help them find a good book, I always begin by trying to ascertain the kind of reading experience they're looking for. I ask them to tell me about a book that they've enjoyed. Often they'll talk about how they couldn't put a certain book down because it was so exciting, or they'll say that they cried when they finished a novel because they didn't want to leave the characters behind. Sometimes, though, people will describe a favorite book like this: "I kept reading and rereading sentences because they were so beautiful;" "I savored the writing, constantly amazed that someone could have put words together like that;" "I kept copying down (or underlining) paragraphs so I could go back to them;" "I love books where the sentences sing;" or "I didn't care what happened in the end; I just wanted to find out how the author would describe it." For these readers, the way the author uses language goes a long way toward determining whether or not they'll enjoy, or even read, any particular book. Readers like this will frequently preface or conclude their description of a book they've loved by saying, "I love well-written books."

I'm one of those readers. And Deirdre McNamer's intricate and beautifully written second novel, *One Sweet Quarrel*, is one of my all-time favorites. It spans the lives of three siblings, Carlton, Daisy, and Jerry Malone, during the first three quarters of the twentieth century. Carlton becomes a businessman, Daisy stays home to care for her ailing mother, all the while yearning to move to New York and sing professionally, and Jerry heads off to homestead in north-central Montana. Much happens to these three over the course of the novel, including marriages, deaths, lost loves, and a major boxing match, in which heavyweight champion Jack Dempsey takes on Tommy Gibbons in Shelby, Montana, in 1923. (You can actually watch a video of the bout on YouTube by googling Dempsey Shelby.) While I enjoyed the story that McNamer tells, what drew me in from the first sentence and kept me reading to the very last page of *One Sweet Quarrel* was her skill at weaving real events and real places into the lives of her imagined characters. (Or are they imagined? They seem so real to me that I can't help but wonder about the extent to which her novel is taken from her own family's history.)

I've now read *One Sweet Quarrel* four or five times (twice in the last three months as I prepared to write this introduction). It's one of those novels that rewards rereading. Each time through I find more to admire about the way it's written: how McNamer can take ordinary words and turn them into sentences and paragraphs bursting with meaning and emotion, sentences and paragraphs that perfectly fulfill the task she gives them. The first time that Alan Turkus, editor of the Book Lust Rediscoveries project, and I talked about this novel, he was about halfway through reading it, and the first thing he said to me was, "It's so well-written." Indeed it is. The language is miraculous and meticulous. Even minor characters become living and breathing people.

Indeed, I could have filled this whole introduction with quotations from *One Sweet Quarrel*, but I'll limit myself to these three.

In this one paragraph about the death of Carlton, Daisy, and Jerry's father, McNamer tells us all that's important for us to know about the man and his death:

> The Reverend Franklin Malone died in the spring of 1912 after he cut himself with a dirty penknife while repairing a hinge on the cellar door. The poison set in, and he was gone in four days. When he realized he would not continue to live, he had an attack of pure panic and had to be tied for a few hours to the bedstead before he found acceptance.

Here's a description of the morphine-addicted doctor who's caring for Daisy's mother:

> He had the addict's grandiosity, which says that a drug in the bloodstream does not represent a weak person's intolerance for pain; it represents a strong person's willingness to look honestly at real pain, to acknowledge the terrifying whimsy and heartbreak of this life.

Writing about the terrible five-year drought (1915 to 1920) in Montana, McNamer makes this striking comparison: "Drought, like a slowly dying marriage, is only a growing absence, and it can take a long time to believe."

If "well-written" is an accolade that makes you perk up your ears when you're in the market for a new book, then I recommend *One Sweet Quarrel* to you. And if it's not, well, try it anyway. It might broaden your horizons about the pleasures to be gotten from reading. In either case, I hope you enjoy *One Sweet Quarrel* as much as I have.

Nancy Pearl

To My Parents:
Hugh and Patricia McNamer

To the Memory of Theirs:
Bruce and Lucie McNamer
John and Jean Owen

And to Bryan

The sergeant sang a ballad through a megaphone, turning from side to side that his voice might carry out into the skimpy crowd. He stood there bareheaded under the hot sun, in those surroundings, a pair of blue glasses over his sightless eyes and singing away.

—Damon Runyon, *New York American*,
reporting on the Dempsey-Gibbons world heavyweight boxing championship in Shelby, Montana, July 4, 1923

I

MORNING

July 10, 1973

As SHE aged, Amelia Malone spent an ever larger portion of each day preparing for it. First, she drank three cups of tea in her dim, low-ceilinged kitchen, while her cat, Verdi, caught a sunbeam under the window. Then they both moved into the bedroom and Amelia stood for a long time at her mothball-scented closet, deciding what to put on. She wore a chenille bathrobe and metallic gold mules.

Amelia was quite old. Her bluish scalp was plainly visible through the last of her colorless hair. Her flesh yearned downward, resting in rolls at her belly and hips, hanging in sleepy flaps from her upper arms. Her legs were short and sticklike, and her toenails, poking through her toeless slippers, were horned and yellow.

Her eyes were the eyes of two people. One eye was brown, alert, surrounded by crinkles. The other was larger, and milky as the moon.

Once she had chosen her dress for the day—she had four—she repaired to the bathroom for a lengthy session at the sink and mirror. She inserted her teeth. She combed her curly black wiglet and anchored it to her own wisps with many bobby pins. She put on her face.

When she emerged—all this could take an hour or more—she had a vermilion mouth, stately pink circles on her cheeks, new eyebrows, the hair, and rhinestones on her wrinkled earlobes. Often, at this point, she wore the concentrated, gathered look of a performer waiting to go on.

The rest of the job was mostly a matter of redistribution. The armorlike girdle was pulled upward, pushing flesh before it, until it was braced in place around her midsection. Now she had a bosomy pigeon silhouette. Stockings and shoes—she was gasping a little by now—brassiere, slip, and, finally, a print dress with a fluff of lace jumping from its throat. Sparkly bracelets and a good dose of Chanel No. 19. Then she had to sit awhile dabbing beads of sweat from her upper lip with a small linen handkerchief. It would be late morning, perhaps noon.

Amelia lived in a small house halfway up a long shallow hill in a little town called Shelby in northern Montana. Her house was two homesteaders' shacks that had been moved to town back in the twenties, then added to. It had a porch now and a room off the kitchen that doubled as a laundry room and music studio. The yard was bare of trees or shrubbery, and the grass was sparse and dry. A big blue Buick, almost thirty years old, waited in the driveway.

Amelia's first plan today was to drive the Buick seven blocks down the long hill to the post office, where she occasionally received something with her name on it from the Baha'is or the government, or, every month or so, from her friend in the Montana State Prison.

That's when people in Shelby saw Amelia—when she drove her huge blue car to the post office or the grocery store. She wore a hat with a small veil attached to it that shaded her eyes, and she drove in fits and starts. Almost everyone knew her. Some had taken piano or voice lessons from her when they were growing up. More recently, of course, there had been the incident with the convict on the run.

He smelled like outdoor smoke, like a campfire, and that's how she knew he was there. Even before the cupboard squeaked and set her heart knocking so furiously it pinned her to the bed. Smoke first, campfire smoke on dirty clothes, and then the sound of drawers sliding open. These are my last moments, she thought, amazed.

The drawers closed. Bold feet moved across the floor toward her bedroom, then stopped. They moved away—why?—and out the back door, and sweat broke through all her pores at once, drenching her.

Twenty minutes later, smoke poured from the sagging storage shed behind her house, and by the time the fire truck got there, two flames were licking out of the roof. Amelia clutched her yellow bathrobe and watched the shed until she realized that half a dozen neighbors, including her brother Jerry, were staring at her. She was more shocking in her unconstructed state than the fire was, or the fact of a criminal from the state prison who had left a burning cigarette or something more deliberate in her shed, then crept through her house opening drawers.

The day after the fire, she sat at her kitchen table—wigletted, toothed, dressed, made up—and picked through a large box of charred and soggy letters, newspaper clippings, narrow leather diaries, a few photographs. The box was Jerry's, and it had been in the shed, forgotten, for years. Some of the letters were in her own handwriting, her handwriting of half a century earlier. She studied it, trying to remember a time when she had lived somewhere else.

On her way to the post office, she stopped at Jerry's to see if he wanted anything mailed. He sat watching the television news with T.T. Wilkins, a man to whom Amelia had been briefly married in the twenties.

Both men were in their eighties. Wilkins had a drooping white mustache and was asleep on his hand. Jerry was listening to Nixon, and he looked cranky. The last time Amelia had stopped by, he told her the cleaning girl had stolen a bunch of his mineral lease documents. This time, he handed her his subscription renewal to the *Oil & Gas Journal* and told her he'd be ready for the banquet at six. He went back to the TV, leaning forward a little. He had a wild shock of whitish hair, large eyes in a narrow fallen face. His skin was mottled, and his fingers were knobbed. He wore a starched white shirt and slacks and old-fashioned high-top shoes.

She and the prisoner corresponded about the Baha'i faith. After he was captured and returned to the prison, she had refused to press burglary charges because her religious beliefs demanded forgiveness and tolerance. This had prompted the prisoner to convert to Baha'ism himself and to begin a correspondence with her. A week before, he had written to ask her to tell the parole board about his religious sincerity. He suggested that she send the board his letters to her from the previous year. That's what she was doing today.

The prisoner's letters were the only personal mail she got as a rule, though she had also corresponded recently with a man in California who said he was a former piano student of hers. This man was named Michael Cage, and his parents still lived in Shelby. He lived in Pasadena and did something so important with the television industry that he had been invited to be the guest speaker at the banquet tonight in honor of Shelby's pioneers. He wrote to her to say that he particularly hoped she would be at the banquet because he was pegging his speech to his memories of her. You are, he said, the hook.

Amelia wrote back to say she would be most pleased to see him again. She had no idea who this person was.

For forty-one years, they climbed the long shallow hill to her studio, their music under their arms. The studio had a wooden floor, then a linoleum floor. A wringer washer and some drying racks stood in a corner.

An old upright piano with small gouges in the paint of the black keys. A music stand. Two folding chairs. Bare wooden walls, then plaster and calcimine, then, in the fifties, blond wood paneling. A wood stove, then gas.

In the early twenties, her name was Daisy Lou Malone, though she called herself Amelia. Then, briefly, she was Mrs. T.T. Wilkins. Then she became, in permanent ink on a courthouse paper, Amelia Malone.

Knickknacks. Samplers with quotations from the New Testament, Coué; then Kahlil Gibran, Aimee Semple McPherson, Bahá'Alláh. A small tattered Bible. A blue stoppered bottle with a faded label wrapped around it. Two shelves of phonograph records. A gramophone, then a Victrola, then a hi-fi, then a modest stereo.

In this room, listening to her students, she had held her arms close to her sides, the tips of her fingers stretched outward as if they rested on the heads of tall hounds.

When Michael Cage took piano lessons in the fifties, Amelia was still allowing her students to play for her. She hadn't taken over completely. She required a routine of scales, arpeggios, Czerny exercises. She would seem to be listening carefully, but the student she heard was never the student before her—not Michael Cage, for instance. She listened always to the perfect student trying to push through.

In the sixties, she began to play along with one hand. Then she began to scoot the pupils aside and play the piece herself, the best she could, her face pinched and rapt.

She did the same with her voice students—listened to them with an expression on her face that grew increasingly distracted, until finally she was joining in, then singing the passages herself. And not just passages, finally, but entire songs, entire arias.

Her last few students spent the full hour on folding chairs, leafing through comic books, picking their skin, while Amelia played the piano or sang to them in a wild and quavery voice.

No mail. She made her way carefully back across the post office vestibule to her car, which she always left running in the No Parking space closest to the door. Her heels clicked—she wore black suede pumps—and the clicks were echoed by the tongues of two girls, nine or ten years old, who marched behind her imitating her diva's prance, their hands propped like flippers on their scrawny hips.

Amelia didn't hear or see them, because she was thinking about a speech she wanted to give at the banquet. She hadn't been requested to speak, but she felt she should have some remarks ready in case Michael Cage had his version of her all wrong. What made her think about this was an item she'd seen in the *Great Falls Tribune* a few weeks earlier about an elderly man who had decided to go on a train trip without notifying his only relative, a son who lived four blocks away. After three weeks, the old man was declared missing. Two months later, disembarking from the train to return to his house, he picked up a newspaper that contained his obituary. They found him in a fatal coma, the newspaper clutched in his hand.

Amelia felt it probably wasn't the fact of the obituary that had killed him but the way they had worded it—leaving out the important things, putting in the trivial. The shock of seeing your entire life reduced to five statistics and a hobby. She didn't want that to happen tonight, so she went home to gather her thoughts and take a long nap, hoping for the wherewithal to amplify herself if Michael Cage made it necessary. Also, her eye had begun to ache, the worthless one. It had never seemed to go entirely dead—she thought sometimes of hands beating against a wall—and she needed to give it a rest.

1

It would have been a hot green day around a pond of stagnant water. The high drone of mosquitoes. Steamy Minnesota air and the smell of everything overripe. Boys, five of them, in the stiff Sunday shirts, the heavy trousers and chunky boots, of their time. Small-town boys with dull, badly cut hair, their sweat pushing the smell of soap and starch into the air where it hovers like their mothers.

They stand on the rim of the brackish water, searching its buggy surface for the slow shadows of pike, of pickerel. It is the aimless time between church and the long midday meal.

A girl in a white dress comes through the trees, a huge bow in her hair, dolls in her arms. She sits herself on the grass, booted feet straight ahead, and arranges two dolls, torso to torso, so that they appear to be having a conversation in bed. One of the dolls tells the other that she has been bad and must be punished. This time, the punishment will be worse than it has been before. Legs will be pulled off. The other doll pleads for mercy in words she has used before.

One of the boys, the loudest and beefiest one, heaves himself up a tree and untangles a rope. It is tied to a branch that stretches over the waiting pond. The boys strip to their underdrawers. The girl on the grass looks up; returns to her dolls.

The boys take turns swinging from the bank on the rope, dropping with heavy splashes, flailing back to shore to do it again. Their faces, necks, and forearms are deeply colored; the rest is white.

The girl on the bank is Daisy Lou Malone. She is eight years old. The beefy boy is her brother Carlton, who is thirteen. One of the frailer boys, the one who seems to be studying the water, is her brother Jerome. He is ten.

Jerome had knobby squared-off shoulders, big hands and feet, enough height for his age. But there was something wispy about him; his reedy neck perhaps, or his large girlish eyes, which had already the squint of a person who is not surprised by pain. And he *had* suffered, Jerome had. He had nightmares in which ordinary things—the back of a person's neck, an unblinking house cat, an empty barn—became holy terrors. He had days that began with sun and oatmeal and possibility, then developed sudden holes of bleakness that he couldn't seem to leap or step around.

Sundays like this were particularly bad for Jerome, because he had to listen to the sermons of his father, the Presbyterian minister, a kind but over-innocent man who would have been shocked to know that his homilies could settle on his younger son like a vest of lead. A vest of lead, which is what Jerome's attacks of asthma felt like too. A vest with laces that tightened each time he took a breath, so that he couldn't exhale. All the old air built up, and he couldn't get it out. And then his whole body felt broken and sealed. He got on his hands and knees to breathe. A couple of times, he spent hours like that on a cold floor in the middle of the night, crouched like an animal, trying desperately to get rid of the old breath while all the tall shapes around him released air easily, sipped it in again.

It wasn't always terrible for Jerome, not at all. He did ordinary things, had ordinary days like anyone else. He laughed and did schoolwork and played boy tricks. He had a dog named Captain. Many nights, he slept straight through. Even the asthma seemed something he might outgrow.

Jerome hated his brother Carlton. No one else seemed to know this, though Carlton might have suspected it if he cared to wonder. Carlton was a completely different manner of boy than Jerome. He didn't fear his dreams; didn't even remember most of them. He was a stocky, auburn-haired, high-colored, round-faced boy who snored softly at night, his heavy limbs splayed. He was, in many respects, already the man he would become—a jovial bully; a red-faced hustler. A man who would never, in his prime, be prone to melancholy or scrupulosity. No, his trip wire would always be greediness; a need especially for things he could get sooner rather than later. He would always want more, and what he would want would be obvious things like clothes and money and, when they became available, an automobile. He would want the well-fed, smooth-browed look of a man who could want nothing because he had it all.

Even when he was a boy, most people didn't like Carlton very much. His parents had for him a certain respect—the wary respect of the religious for the unapologetically worldly—and they would have told you that they loved him. But they didn't particularly like him. Not at all. Maybe he knew it and that's what made him so grabby.

See? Carlton is doing it again. He is pretending to throttle one of the boys, his joyless adolescent laugh barking across the water.

He releases the boy and hitches up his soaking underwear, his belly shaking a little as he does it, and looks around for his favorite victim. Jerome stands at the edge of the pond. Carlton smacks water at him with the flat of his hand.

Then, with tumultuous splashing steps, Carlton lunges at his brother and swoops him into his arms like a farmer lifting a sack of oats. He wades off the sandy shelf into the deeper water, where he can dunk him; hold him down there in the thick water for a few seconds so he'll come up sputtering and gasping and the other boys will laugh.

Carlton knew Jerome's fear of not breathing. He had seen him crouched like a dog on the floor at night. But he put that out of his mind, or perhaps he told himself that he had the job of making his little brother tough enough for the world. In truth, Jerome scared him sometimes. That desperate gasping for something so ordinary. The possibility that Jerome would die while he was gasping, and the way that made their mother love him and brush back the hair from his damp forehead, the way she would never think of brushing back the thatch of her eldest.

Carlton stands thigh-deep in the water, holding Jerome's angular body to him. Jerome feels a great weariness beneath his fury. This has happened so many times before, some version of this. His role in life is to oppose Carlton in a way that entertains others.

This time, though, he begins to feel detached from his legs. They kick and flail with a vehemence that is removed from his head or heart. He is a chicken whose head on the block can seem to gaze on the body that is running away.

The boys in the middle of the pond stretch up their thin arms as Carlton wades in deeper with his prey. "Red rover, red rover, throw him on over," they chant.

Jerome dutifully begins to kick his way toward the end of this, to the dunking and the draining rage. But he is visited that moment with a vision of his father in the pulpit. He hears his father's sonorous voice. And the vision, the voice, stop his legs. They fall silent.

The Reverend Franklin Malone, father of Carlton and Jerome and Daisy Lou, was a tall, gentle man with a deep voice and the rawboned, intelligent look of a Lincoln. He was the pastor of a Presbyterian church in a wooded little town that would someday be a suburb of Saint Paul.

Shortly before the children went to the pond that day, the Reverend Franklin Malone gave a sermon on hope.

It was stifling in the white frame church, the men fidgeting in their hard collars and scratchy wool, rivulets of sweat running down their sides; the women cinched tight at the waist, swaddled with corsets, petticoats, chemises, dresses, stockings, gloves, shoes, hats like sleepy crowns.

The Reverend Malone was not fire and brimstone. He loved his flock—that would not be too strong a word—and he wanted to leave them encouraged. He quoted the Bible as he always did; mentioned Lazarus and reminded his sweltering congregation that hope is a high virtue and that the prophet says to be of good courage. It was a theme he circled back to every month or so, as if he wanted to convince himself and his listeners that their picket-fenced, end-of-the-century lives required battleground gallantry.

He always tried to finish his sermons with something less ornate than Scripture, something more friendly, something to relax his people and put them in the mood for the big noonday meal. He liked to encourage a collective chuckle—the kind of chuckle that acknowledges the futility of human fussing.

"A friend told me a story the other day, and I'd like to share it with you," he began in a comforting voice. "A little boy suffered a terrible accident in a threshing machine. The doctors worked over him night and day, but the poison set in and they were unable to save his legs. So they did what they had to do. It was the boy's life or his legs.

"When the boy awakened from the ether, his little legs had been taken away. His parents held his hands, tears in their eyes, waiting for his head to clear, dreading the news they must give him. His name was Bobby.

"'Bobby?' his father said softly, confronting the most difficult job of his life. 'Son? I have some bad news.' The little boy lifted his pale face to his father's.

"'Son, the doctors had to cut off your legs,' the father said, his voice choking. 'It was the only way.'"

The Reverend Malone raised his hands then and extended them toward his audience, palms up. He smiled serenely.

The three Malone children sat in the front row with their mother, Mattie. Jerome's breathing had acquired a wheeze on the edges.

"Now, my good people. What do you think happened next?" his father asked. "Did that little boy hide his head in the bedsheets? Did he turn his head to the wall? Did he panic and scream?"

Jerome closed his eyes and tried to think about the way Captain had learned to catch a thrown stick with his teeth while running.

"No he did *not*!" his father exulted. "Do you want to know what that little boy said?"

A few people smiled as if they'd heard the story before. Jerome bent forward to try to ease the tightening in his chest.

"This is what that little boy said. He turned to his father with shining eyes. And he raised first one little white arm and then the other, and a smile broke across his face and he said: 'But, Papa! My *arms* are all right. Papa, my arms are *all right*!'"

He let that sink in for a couple of beats while his audience rustled complacently.

Carlton yawned, then clapped a stub-fingered hand over his mouth at a stern look from his mother.

Jerome. Thin and alert and wheezing.

Daisy? All dressed up like a summer package, the big bow stuck in her lank hair. A heart-shaped face made somber by her lofty eyes, the kind of eyes that don't crinkle or disappear when a person laughs but seem somehow to sit in judgment upon the rest of the face. She thought about legs and arms. About the arms of her doll Annabelle and how long and white they were. How she wished she had Annabelle on her lap right now so she could move the arms and legs and Annabelle, in her ballerina dress, would appear to be bowing.

So there we have them, some long time before the real story begins, the lineaments of their adult selves already present. Carlton thick and unheeding. Jerome aghast, resistant. Daisy in a dream.

"What did little Bobby have?" the Reverend Malone said with a broad shy smile on his face. "He had faith in our Father's plan for him. Faith that he was put on earth to serve our Maker's designs, though he could not—as we cannot—know with certainty what those plans are. Bobby had his spot in heaven, you can be sure of that. And, here on earth, he had his faith. He had his trust and his hope. He did not give up. He did not turn his head away."

He raised his long arms above his head, the hands clenched in a gentle fist. "And that, my dear friends, is *better* than two legs. It is better than a hundred legs."

Jerome's head snapped up.

"It is better than a *thousand* legs," his father insisted.

He raised his arms over the congregation now and inclined his head. "Heavenly Father, may each of us find within ourselves the wisdom of young Bobby. And may we go forth now, serene in the knowledge that the path is marked and we have only to grasp Your hand and walk it well."

He smiled gravely, the signal for their release.

A loose collar now. A big chicken dinner.

A thousand legs? An endless centipede of a smiling boy? How could that be better than *anything*?

That was another of Jerome's problems. He got a picture in his mind and it took over. Swallowed up everything else. He thought about a boy who tried and tried, who lived a mutilated fighting life though the outcome, his place in heaven, was the same, legs or no legs, fight or no fight. There was something horrible in the idea. There was cruelty and terror in the idea.

Jerome goes absolutely limp in Carlton's arms. He can feel the back of his head skim the surface of the pond. It is the last thing Carlton expects him to do, and a look of slow curiosity moves across his grinning face. He bends to examine his brother. Jerome's eyes are closed. He has thrown it all in.

The other boys laugh loudly at the surprise of this. Carlton doesn't know exactly how to capitalize on the situation. He could go ahead and dunk Jerome, but without his resistance, the fun will be out of it.

He examines his brother's face again, the dangling body, then pretends he'd had nothing in mind at all. He places Jerome upright in the water, shrugs his shoulders, and dolphins himself toward the other boys, kicking hard so his brother gets a good splash.

Jerome stands in place. He shakes water out of his hair. He wears a small new smile.

Daisy has stood up and holds one of the dolls, the ballerina Annabelle. She is making the doll clap for Jerome. Tick tick, go the little china hands.

At the big midday meal, Mattie is crisp and impatient with Jerome because he has an uncustomary vitality that worries her. Jerome and Daisy Lou have a stifled laughing fit at the table and are sent to their rooms for an hour. Carlton eats much more than usual and gets a stomachache and has to lie on the porch swing for a while, flies droning around his head. The Reverend Malone unbuttons his vest and reads the newspaper while his wife and the Anderson girl clear up.

The walls of the house breathe like an old dog.

2

New York City
New York
May 18, 1910

...t out there? The newspapers ... the face of the sun in the ... but did you see them? This ... ot, I must say. First there ... n across the river in New ..., you remember her from ...ngements for a guest artist (me) and ac...panied me on the piano. A man from the church with a very deep and dramatic voice gave two readings, "Knee Deep in June" and something else I fail to recall at the moment. My voice I believe has reached a new level in the past two months from a program of very vigorous exercises that leave me nearly prostrate.

This visit to New York has confirmed my desire to pursue a musical career in this city. As I was singing in the church this afternoon, the knowledge came over me that *this* is where I am meant to pursue my musical path, and so I now plan to take up residence in New York within one year at most. I will return to St. Paul to complete my preparations, Italian lessons and etc., and then I believe I will be ready.

Well then no sooner did we return from the church and take a rest and it was time for the comet! We walked to Riverside Drive where swarms of people were already facing toward the West. We took umbrellas and it soon began to rain lightly due to comet dust and Lelia almost went home right away because a group of people were praying loudly and a scientist was talking to some people about deadly Cyanogen gas from the comet's tail. There were only one or two very ordinary stars visible and then they fell behind the clouds, but we stayed anyway and didn't see anything tho I must say I felt the comet's presence.

A boy was selling small blue bottles with stoppers in them. A scientist who accompanied the boy told us to hold our bottles high into the air for four minutes. I did so and then stoppered it at the scientist's signal. The purpose was to seal up the comet atmosphere for future analysis.

Your loving sister,
Daisy Lou

It is a damp, flatly lit evening with a thin cloud cover that breaks only here and there and steadily threatens rain.

Daisy and another slim young woman make their way toward the river, pool of lamplight to pool of lamplight.

Daisy's brown hair is drawn up in the plump look of the time. On it, a large hat that has undergone a number of refurbishments. New net here, a ribbon there. The lofty eyes. Beautiful teeth. She is very proud of her teeth and scours them with baking soda three and four times a day. Forgoes black tea.

There is already, at nineteen, something concocted about Daisy. Yes, there it is. Her friend has said something to her and Daisy Lou has tipped her head in a way that looks both innocent and contrived, like a child in a school play. She has fixed her gaze in such a way that she appears to be listening less to her friend's voice than to the emanations around it.

In other places, Halley drew its electric tail across the sky a number of nights running. Employees at the Mount Wilson observatory in southern California applied glycerin to the tower struts to collect the comet dust. Professor K.M. Colquhoun in Great Falls, Montana, set up his big telescope and ran a newspaper advertisement inviting the public to call at his lodgings at 3:30 a.m. for viewings.

The king of England died suddenly. Ten days earlier, he had been in the pink. Now he was dead of something quick like pneumonia, and the book was closed on the peaceful Edwardian age, the Pax Britannica. An earthquake killed thousands in Costa Rica. A dirigible mysteriously lost altitude over Kansas and two unconscious men were found inside, the notes on their shirts alerting the *New York Times.* Troops were rushed to New Mexico to check on a possible Indian massacre of white ranchers. A woman in Santa Ana tried to murder her children to spare them the comet. Revolution commenced in Mexico. A rancher in Albuquerque drank poison. Spiritualists clenched their eyes tighter and let their pencils move across paper on their own. A mill explosion in Canton, Ohio, sent arms and legs aloft among the flying boards.

It all built up to May 18, the night the comet drew closest to the earth, flicking its tail right across our earnest and blindered path in a manner that seemed audacious if not disastrous. A cosmic taunt, a flirtation. Scientists refused to rule out the possibility of an outright collision.

The comet watchers on Riverside Drive include a man in a top hat who holds a large black umbrella over his newspaper.

"'Scared by Comet,'" he reads aloud. "'Crazy Sheepman in California Attempts to Crucify Himself on Rude Cross.'

"'San Bernardino, California. While brooding over possible ill effects of the comet's visit, Paul Hammonton, a sheepman and prospector, became insane and crucified himself, according to mining men who arrived here with him yesterday. Hammonton was found where he had nailed his feet and one hand to a rude cross he had erected near a gold claim last Friday.'"

The reader pauses, scans the crowd, raises his voice.

"'Although he was suffering intense agony, Hammonton pleaded with his rescuers to let him die upon the cross. Since the visit of the comet, Hammonton has been much alarmed, and when he learned that the earth was scheduled to pass through the tail of Halley's Comet, his mind gave way and he believed that the end of the world was at hand.'"

This brings some laughs, though a few in the crowd bend their heads and pray harder.

"Well," says Lelia, grinning, "I guess it would be a job to nail down *two hands* all by yourself!" She is long-limbed, bright-eyed girl wearing a rust-colored dress that works against her coloring. She is a musician, like Daisy Lou. In fact, they had several of the same teachers back in Saint Paul. Lelia is a music tutor for the children of a wealthy family that occupies an entire floor of a large building near Central Park. Her brother, the Presbyterian minister in New Jersey, is always warning her about the perils of the single woman's life in New York, but Lelia has a group of the finest sort of friends and her own small flat, and she thinks he is a terrible fusser. Old-fashioned and small-town. Like Daisy Lou Malone.

Daisy Lou shoots Lelia an irritated look. She has no idea what Lelia thinks is so funny and thinks her laughter unseemly. She's also angry that the clouds are blocking the view of the comet. She had wanted to see the blazing arc while she was here in New York. It would have seemed a blessing on her own aspirations. She might have watched the comet and whispered, "A change in times and states," and thought of roses raining onto a stage, onto her shoes.

She holds her blue bottle toward the lightless sky, looking around anxiously to make sure she is pointing the opening in the right direction. Should she move the bottle to scoop up something invisible? Should she let whatever it is, this comet dust, let it float on its own into the bottle's emptiness? She is a little chilly. The scientist, the one who is calling out orders, is distasteful to her, though she doesn't really doubt that he knows about comets. He has mutton-chop whiskers, which she thinks unattractive on a man, and is somewhat unkempt.

She looks around at the others, for the most serious-looking people she can find, to see how *they* are holding their blue bottles, and she picks a well-dressed lady in her thirties, with a lovely filmy shawl, a very expensive-looking shawl, and watches how this woman holds her bottle and does exactly as she does. Four minutes.

Daisy thinks that if she could see the comet dust it would be wonderful-looking, like electric light perhaps. Slow, cool, steady. Maybe it is the sort of substance that needs long darkness to show itself.

When the time is up, Daisy stoppers her bottle firmly. She shakes it; thinks of Aladdin's lamp, Pandora's box, and vows never to yield to the temptation to unstopper the bottle before it seems time to analyze the dust. But how will she know when that time has arrived, she wonders. Will the newspapers say?

She hands the bottle to Lelia so she can fix the pin on her hat, and Lelia does an extremely rude and shocking thing. She unstoppers the bottle and pretends to pour its contents down her throat as though they were water.

Daisy is so shocked and angry that she slaps Lelia hard on the arm and grabs her bottle back. Red-faced, her expression tight, she stands absolutely still for some moments, gazing at her shoes. Then she lifts her bottle into the air and stands there like the Statue of Liberty. Lelia apologizes, tries to convince Daisy to come along home. The crowd is dispersing. The professor, the scientist, whatever he is, has disappeared.

Daisy won't budge. She consults her watch in her waist pocket, grimly waits the four minutes, then stoppers her blue bottle briskly. They begin to walk back to the flat in silence.

They pass an old lady. She leans on a gold-knobbed cane and gestures impatiently to someone who isn't there, mumbling to herself. Brilliant stones cover her gloved fingers. Her hair is a large wig the color of rust. She has rouged her mouth with an unsteady hand. An ancient actress? An ancient prostitute? Who knows? Daisy has never seen anyone like her, and she glances at Lelia for verification.

Lelia smiles, shakes her head, links arms with Daisy Lou. They make their way back to the brownstone, pool of lamplight to pool of lamplight.

Before bed, Daisy presses the stopper deeper into the bottle. She wraps the bottle in paper and string and labels it in her large impatient hand. Comet Dust, she writes, and tucks the package in a corner of her water-stained suitcase.

Then she writes a letter to her brother Jerome, who is playing the land game out in Montana. He lives in a tar-paper shack that rides the prairie like a small boat.

3

Bluebunch wheatgrass, Indian ricegrass, tufted hairgrass, slender wheatgrass, blue grama.

Junegrass, squirrel tail, foxtail barley, prairie cordreed, sand dropseed, rough fescue, little bluestem.

The grass in 1910. It wasn't high everywhere. People like to say that, but it isn't true. It was deep in places, though, and it had a silvery sheen to it. The texture was different than it is today—very smooth and dense; not bunchy and harsh. You could walk it barefoot.

The buffalo, of course, had been gone for thirty years. Entirely. The last of the unshot were traveling the country, mangy and punch-drunk, in Wild West shows. But you could still see their wallows in the grass that spring, caves in the grass, big as rooms. And their big white bones too.

Somewhere in eastern Montana, passengers in a westward train huddled at the windows to watch two children ride a sled down a hill of that grass. The sky had no ceiling.

A solitary homestead shack, the sledding children, the hard clean sunlight, nothing else.

They rode the tawny grass slowly to the flatness, their small backs very straight. Then one of them waved a brown arm at the train, and it was as if the wave sent something to the people in heavy clothes who crowded around the windows, and the ones who stood smoking at the rail of the caboose, because they all laughed happily and at the same time.

This is how we are now, they thought. This is how we get to be.

They came in droves that year. Some of the train cars contained entire transported farms, minus only the land. Bundled and stacked fence posts, a flanky milk cow, a dismantled house. Stoves, dogs, washbasins, children. And soon, very soon, land to put it on—320 acres of it for the asking, the taking.

Other parts of the trains carried other kinds of homesteaders, including the ones in city suits and dresses and hats. Young men, young women, from Minnesota, Illinois, Wisconsin. Teachers, clerks, realtors, maiden ladies, who had all decided to be farmers now because the railroad had told them they could. The only illness in Montana comes from overeating, the railroad said in the brochures it sent to Europe. Bumper crops, year after year. Land for the asking.

Someone made a survey of the previous occupations of fifty-nine homesteaders in a northern Montana township. Twenty-three had been farmers. The rest included two physicians, three maiden ladies, two butchers, two deep-sea divers, and six musicians.

Which one is a deep-sea diver? The ruddy squinting one with the dirty shirt?

Six musicians?

Many of these were second sons, unwed daughters, the ones with dimmer prospects, more to prove. More than a few had spent the Sundays of their childhoods in lace-doilied parlors with heavy dark furniture, growing up during those musty decades that flanked the year 1900 like large black-skirted aunts.

Now they had brilliant brochures in their vest pockets and valises. A smiling farmer glided his plow through loamy soil, turning up gold pieces the size of fists. The farmer's house on the edge of the field had a picket fence and bushes and a garden. Everything was unblown, well-watered.

Get it now before it's gone; your own free home! They came in waves. Olly olly oxen, all home free!

And the big aunts speaking too: Child, improve yourself.

Jerome changed his name to Jerry the day he stepped on the train. He rolled up his long white sleeves and made notations in a small leather diary with his new fountain pen, looking up from time to time to watch the grasslands flying past.

On that day in 1910, he wrote a sentence about the weather. *Fair and warm.* A sentence about the terrain. *Much land for the having and the grass appears to thrive.* He was, after all, from a generation that logged the days in dry one-sentence reports. It was as if they recorded some ideal emotionless self; a self not subject to despair or transport. Maybe they thought if you could write it neutrally, you could keep living it, keep stacking the days.

Sometimes, though, a small cry broke through and it all seemed to tumble. On September 11, 1952: *Vivian slipped away today, 4:15 p.m.* On Christmas 1952: *One long day since Sept. 11.* And then he would put down the pen and try to make his own body go as quiet as hers.

What must they have felt when they looked back on those dry little sentences piled up for a big fall? When they saw the entries on the days *before* unexpected disaster. *Bought two dozen chicks at Halvorson's. Strong wind from the east.* Did they read the words later and feel tricked?

A young man in a dirty black suit began to play "Red Wing" on a mouth harp. He had colorless patches on his skin, flat eyes, and filthy hair. He was slumped in the corner of his train seat, one thin leg crossed over the other, his entire upper body a tent over his harmonica. Still learning the tune, he played it over and over, repeating phrases, stopping, starting again.

Jerry knew the melody, and it gave him a queasy feeling he tried to shrug off. The other passengers seemed to like the sound of it. One man whistled quietly along. A mother with a child in a blanket hummed it to her baby's head.

The Reverend Franklin Malone and his wife, Mattie, gave a tea for their son before he ventured West. The deacon's twin daughters—teenagers with orange hair in ringlets—sang "Red Wing." They sang without harmonizing, so they sounded like one person with a very loud voice. It was raining. His kindly Calvinist father presented Jerry with the fountain pen, telling him proudly what it had cost. Mrs. Ritter passed a plate of her famous lemon swirls. All the women commented on the lemon swirls. All the men and children chewed quietly. Jerry could have wept for the deadness of it.

Everyone at the tea was careful with him because of the problems he had developed the last time he left Saint Paul—a bad, dark time that brought him home from a small college weeping, and then silent, and then refusing for a few weeks to leave his room because he had, in every way, come to a halt.

He doesn't know, as we see him on the train, precisely what went wrong, what shut him down. It had to do with tall doors opening wide on a cosmos that was not being made; it was finished. Fixed and airless for all time.

A membrane away from horror, that thought. What was the point of doing anything? What protection did a person have from the most terrible of fates or the most mundane?

Hints of what might lie behind those slowly opening doors had come upon him early. Maybe that is why he developed a habit of refusing, in the small choices of childhood, to do what seemed to be expected. He resisted. He bent his response.

But the world began to fill up with people who expected things of him—first family, but then teachers, coaches, friends, girls—and to refuse to cooperate became an increasingly vast and complicated undertaking.

By the time he went to college, the expectations of the entire world seemed laid at his feet, and all he could do, finally, was stop. He could not move an inch without cooperating. And he could not cooperate with a plan that wasn't his.

Sometime during the third week in his room at home, he had a simple thought: If I can feel myself to be at real risk, that may be evidence that free will exists. If I can feel myself chancing something, perhaps that means the outcome is not fixed. Perhaps that is a pale clue.

And so he decided to behave *as though* he were making real choices. He would measure the success of the effort by feelings of being in danger. It didn't feel authentic at first, this pretending. It felt like putting on a costume to see if he could fool himself in the mirror. But for much of his long life he would continue to do it. He would pretend he was a gambler, an adventurer, a person given to hazard. He would pretend that life was not accomplished, that it could still be made. It was the only way to feel hope.

And so, naturally, when a friend handed him pamphlets from the Great Northern Railroad—get it now!—Jerry Malone did not think long. He felt what he felt, and he got on that train.

As a young man he had reddish unruly hair, pale-blue eyes, a full mouth; an unconscious glower to his eyes and forehead, which perhaps made others more brusque with him than they might have been otherwise. The brusqueness stung him and deepened the glower he didn't know about, and so it circles.

He was still new to his life, though, and the wary expression wasn't constant. Sometimes he looked soft and hopeful, as he does now, resting his head against the chair seat while the train pounds west, the thin sound of a sentimental song from the previous century wafting from its open windows.

The harmonica player raised his head to look carefully at the tawny, unpeopled, unfenced place they were pushing through. A place that seemed to own itself.

By now, he had been playing "Red Wing" for hours; starting and stopping and starting again; ignoring requests for something new or for silence. Whenever the train stopped, everyone in the car looked at him hopefully. He didn't leave.

In a twangy Appalachian accent, he spoke his first words of the trip. "*This?*" he barked, throwing an arm at the prairie. "Why, this ain't nothin' to be *satisfied* with!"

They looked around them.

Somewhere the train had pulled away from towns, from roads, from rivers, hedges, and people. Somewhere it had reached a point—at night perhaps, when no one really saw—where it had catapulted onto some taller place. A place that was scoured and glowing and as ferociously innocent as a new-laid egg.

They passed through Shelby almost four days after leaving Saint Paul. Clouds had moved in and given the sky a ceiling. It was late afternoon and drizzling.

Almost the end. Twenty-five miles to Cut Bank, and then the fence that began the Blackfeet Indian reservation. Then the Rockies. This was it. Jerry got off in Shelby, thinking he might get located there. Then he thought, I choose to go on. He felt the verifying trickle of fear as he stepped back on the train and went on to Cut Bank, to the very edge of the available plains.

Shelby had looked too provisional and unlit. The previous evening, a large fire had started in the outhouse behind a barbershop and spread to the warehouse and mercantile of one James A. Johnson. Johnson's store was destroyed, though the contents were saved. It would have been worse, far worse, without a snappy bucket brigade and the beginnings of a soaking rain. As it was, Johnson lost thousands.

Smoke mingled with drizzle in the flat afternoon light, giving little Shelby the look of a kicked-out campfire.

It did not look like a place that would be famous throughout the entire country in thirteen years. And James A. Johnson, resilient and flamboyant as he was, even then, did not seem like the kind of man who would be on the front page of the *New York Times*.

These are some of the names they would give their twelve-by-sixteen-foot shacks and their quarter sections or half sections of land: Kubla Khan, Scenic Heights Farm, Peace Valley Ranch, Dulce Comun, Experimental Farm. The publisher of the *Cut Bank Pioneer Press* asked them to name their new homes and send the names to the paper for the record. Clonmel Ranch, Meadowbrook Heights, Boomers Retreat, they would write.

Only a few seemed to guess what might be coming: Grasshopper Ranch, Locust Hill, Bluff Arcade.

The shacks had tar-paper roofs, most of them, and you could buy the pieces precut at the lumberyard in Cut Bank—homestead prefabs for all those young people, men and women, married and single, who didn't know the first thing about building a building, farming a farm. Most of them had never set plow to earth at all, much less earth that had never been turned.

How was it possible for them to look around at where they were—treeless wind-strafed prairie—and call a shack Kubla Khan? Maybe they were wittier than we give them credit for.

The walls of the shacks were papered with newspapers. You could read your walls for recent news. The Unitarian Church Quartet, seventy-five miles to the south in Great Falls, had performed "In a Persian Garden" by Liza Lehmann. A man who claimed to be a dentist from Bozeman had been arrested for joyriding. Peruna was the medicine of the day for puny girls, Clemo for arthritis, Electric Bitters for female troubles, and Dr. King's New Life Pills for those times when a lazy liver and sluggish bowels made a man so despondent he wanted to die.

In San Francisco, Jack Johnson, the Negro with gold teeth and a scarlet racing car and white women, trained for his Independence Day prizefight with James Jeffries. Poor Jeffries had been coaxed out of retirement to pummel his three-hundred-pound body into something white that could silence the yappity cuckolding black man, but it wouldn't work. He would lie bruised and bleeding at the end, and his fans would race out all over the country to redress the insult by spilling blood.

In Colorado, a fifteen-year-old white brawler named William Harrison Dempsey was bathing his face and hands in a secret putrid brine, making them into leather for the days ahead. This wasn't in the newspapers.

When Jerry stepped off the huffing train at Cut Bank, the first person he spoke to was Vivian McQuarry, the woman he would live with for forty-one years.

She stood near a tall democrat wagon, the locator's wagon, in a white shirtwaist and long slim skirt. Her chocolate-colored hair was in a puffy chignon, and she had a flat straw hat perched atop it. The clouds had lifted and scattered. Vivian held her hat against a stiff little breeze. A slim-shouldered man wearing wire-rimmed spectacles bent with her over a map.

"Are you here to be located?" Jerry asked them. They looked up. The man nodded. The woman gave a happy ironic smile. "I'd give a lot to be located," she said. She had rosy skin, a wide smile, grave black eyebrows.

They laughed together at the strange new word, made introductions all around. Vivian McQuarry and her brother George, from Cleveland. Jerry Malone from the outskirts of Saint Paul.

The locator was a rabbity man with a big official plat book. He wore a suit and gumbo-crusted work boots. He collected their twenty dollars, made pencil notations, explained that tomorrow's trip would be north of town. Prime country.

A decade later, during the bad time between them, Jerry and Vivian would wonder if they would have been so instantly alert to each other had they not been new people in a new place.

They would think that they had, perhaps, been predisposed to be exhilarated by each other because they were travelers then and were seeing everything with the seizing eyes of adventurers.

Jerry became, the moment Vivian saw him, as enchanted and familiar to her as her engraved dream of her long-dead father, which was actually just two impeccable images: one of him lifting her laughing aproned mother a few inches off the floor; the other of his strong young hand on a straight razor, drawing the edge along his stretched jawline.

Vivian struck Jerry—as she stood with one hand on her hat, the other on the wagon that would take her to her own land—as the very antithesis of the ordinary; a ravishingly odd woman who could keep him surprised the rest of his life.

It would occur to both of them later that the secret to the kind of love that beats the heart is to somehow keep yourself, in your mind, a traveler. That way, you don't make the mistake of wishing for an earlier version of a husband or wife, when what you really want is yourself when you were in motion.

In creaking voices, homesteaders tell their stories to earnest young people with tape recorders. Sometimes you will hear in the background, as they pause to pick their words, the restless whine of someone down a carpetless hall.

Will they tell you what the countryside looked like, or the train station, or how many people were at the train station, or what the weather was? No. That is for us to imagine. They will tell you instead about the smell of a neighbor woman's perfume at a country dance, about a Gros Ventre man in braids and a city hat at the Havre station, or the smell of burning cow chips on a fall day. They will remember the glowing newness of a neighbor's hand pump, the pretty pink gums of their young dog, a hamper filled with the bread they had baked in Minnesota. And a hot plate wrapped in woolen underwear for a father's rheumatism, the way a cook spit on a restaurant stove to test it, oil of cloves on a wound, strung cranberries on a Christmas bush, thousands of tiny red bugs in a pail of reservoir water, the taste of a rabbit pie.

They would write in their diaries: *Planted twenty acres of flax with help of Johnson boys.* Or, *Copper wash kettle arrived today.* But a woman might recall, most vividly of all, the way a neighbor kissed her before he went back East to retrieve a young wife. A man might remember digging a well and going so deep that stars appeared in the tiny circle of sky above.

The sound of a wolf. The uncanny greenish color of oncoming hail. The smells: raw lumber, tar paper, cut flax, the exhaust of the store owner's automobile. The wet warmth of a chinook emerging from an arch of dark clouds.

For Vivian and Jerry, it was bare ground that finally stood still, a wide vault of sky, some small new buildings with large spaces between them, the smell of raw lumber, and a cartoonishly high wagon with two long wobbly benches.

The locator pointed north toward the line that separated vast ground from vast sky.

"I'm here to locate you," he promised.

The locator's horse nudged Jerry hard in the back as they all huddled over a map and knocked him against Vivian and George. Jostled them all for a minute. The map crackled. Jerry smiled and gently pushed the horse's head back. "Beasts," he said gallantly. "Brain the size of a gopher's."

They ate at the Beanery, a long raw building near the station. Long-cooked stringy beef, mashed potatoes, beets from jars, bread, pie. Jerry and George bent their heads over the maps again. George's face was flushed with excitement.

They all took rooms at the new and boxy Metropolitan Hotel, where they put all their luggage and crates, and then in the morning the three of them met the locator at his high-seated wagon with its wheels that were almost as tall as they were and its two long seats, placed high for the long view.

The cart lurched and moved, and the horses quickly fell into a brisk walk that kept everything bobbing and moving. They headed north, leaving the scramble of Cut Bank's buildings behind. North and north in the bleached light for six miles. They kept to the grass along rutted wagon tracks. Occasionally they passed or caught sight of a shack out there on the grass. Occasionally they passed a field of blue flax. But mostly they saw prairie, prairie, tinged green, moving blankly in the breeze.

They stopped and the locator affixed some stakes to the ground and made a notation in his book. And they moved farther east and he affixed some more. One half section for Vivian. One half for George. One half for Jerry. They looked at each other and burst into full laughs.

Jerry had brought bread and cheese and dried beef, and they had dinner in the growing dark in the grass. The wind had stopped, a moon would be out, there were lanterns for the wagon, there seemed no huge hurry. They were located.

They traveled in the silver-lined dark toward the tiny winking gaslights of town. Not a dense line of them. Just there, there, there.

The homes of their childhood had been planted and close. Old brick and painted wood. Shade trees. Canaries in draped cages.

Here, the moon rode the sky, the stars shivered, Halley's leaped across the horizon. The wind rippled the grass; the clouds moved in small, liquid herds, breaking and re-forming. Small animals flickered. All of it was light and silver and moving.

They trapped rainwater and bought more in Cut Bank for fifty cents a barrel. George hauled it out once a week in a wagon. It was straight from the Cut Bank River and the color of pale rust by midsummer. A Russian thistle grew by the back door of Vivian's shack. She thought it was handsome, so she drew a cupful of her precious water every day and watered it—the tall spiky purple-topped thistle that would make all the farmers so miserable in another few years.

Looking back, Vivian would see that she had been a fool about a simple weed. But at the time, the thistle was a discovery. Bending to trickle copper-colored water over it, she thought to herself, I shall make the prairie bloom!

George got a typesetting job at the *Pioneer Press* and spent weeknights in town at the Metropolitan. He brought Vivian a cat she named Manx. Manx had begun his life as a cat named Cotton. A year earlier, Cotton's nine-year-old mistress had cut off the cat's tail with her mother's butcher knife. Not all at once either. In inches. He left the house shortly after that and hung around the Beanery, where they fed him, and then he went to live with Vivian in her little ship on the grass.

She strained her fifty-cent water, boiled it, boiled her clothes and rinsed them and blued them and wrung them and hung them to dry. The boards of her shack began to shrink, and she stuffed the cracks with catalogues and rags against the winter. She cut up the rabbits George brought her, cooked them, canned them. She made soap in the early mornings when it was still cool.

She helped Azalia Newcombe, three miles north, thrash her crop of navy beans. They stood on the roof of the chicken coop, two women in their twenties, and poured the beans into a tub on the ground below so the wind could comb the chaff away.

She named her homestead Flax View because Jerry Malone had planted a field of flax and she liked to watch it waving blue in the sun.

They didn't know anything then—had no idea what the soil and the weather and the fates had in store for them. They lived in their shacks on the edges of great patches of soft-blue flax, a shade of blue that would always be, for Vivian and for many others, the color of possibility.

On the last weekend in August, George and Vivian McQuarry, Jerry Malone, and scores of other homesteaders and townspeople drove their buckboards and wagons to Round Lake, north of Cut Bank, for a big picnic. The lake was the only substantial body of water for many miles in any direction. It was perfectly round without a bush or tree on its banks. It glimmered blankly, naked and prehistoric.

These were the kinds of people who looked at such blankness and saw something green, planted, producing. There was talk of building a pavilion for shade, and it wasn't hard to imagine that pavilion on a summer night not so many years thence, when the sky would be the color of lilacs and the band would be playing and the sound would carry through air made windless and soft for the occasion. They would have earned something like that: music on a soft summer night.

The air held the smoke of burning pine trees a hundred, two hundred miles west in the mountains, and of the grass fires in the eastern part of the state. The fires would burn themselves out, out of sight somewhere. No one was panicked. Today was a picnic. It had been a good summer, and the crowd was buoyant.

Look at them. How young they are! How rosy and cheerful. The men still have their city slouches. They wear the suits they wore on the train west. They don't know how to handle their horses or their farm equipment. Everything is still an experiment. Some of them politely scan the crowd for possible wives; for someone's sister who may have come out on the train. Everyone, man and woman, wears a hat.

Ten miles to the west, a fence runs along the Blackfeet reservation. The Indians have been put behind it somewhere.

A few children duck between the adults, ice cream smeared on their faces. A six-piece band sets itself up. Blankets are spread on the slick grass, the corners anchored with hampers and rocks. The women carry parasols. Their hands are still smooth.

Roderick Adams has brought a couple of cases of his homemade beer, and some of the men are drinking it. One of them climbs onto a buckboard and offers a toast to the first summer in God's country. Beers and hats and parasols lift skyward.

The band is a little rusty at first, but smooths out. It's the first music most of the crowd has heard in months. They play all the familiar tunes.

When they start "Red Wing," a few people raise their heads quizzically, trying to think why it makes them pause. Then someone mentions the boy on the train and his infernal harmonica, and a small cry goes up. Stop! they plead with the band, laughing. We've heard enough "Red Wing" to last us the rest of our earthly lives. The sun is red.

Jerry Malone stands with two other men, smoking. Vivian watches him. He lifts his head to watch her too, and they wait a few moments to turn their heads away.

They look around at the crowd and all the space stretching beyond them, the wind-ruffled lake and the children wading at its edge. They keep their eyes away from the sun, which looks like a wound through the smoke, and concentrate on the people around them. On how happy everyone is.

4

The Reverend Franklin Malone died in the spring of 1912 after he cut himself with a dirty penknife while repairing a hinge on the cellar door. The poison set in, and he was gone in four days. When he realized he would not continue to live, he had an attack of pure panic and had to be tied for a few hours to the bedstead before he found acceptance.

For a man of the cloth, he held surprisingly substantial savings. His three children—Carlton, Daisy Lou, and Jerry—each got $2,000, and Mattie, his wife, got $3,000. Carlton sent Jerry's share to him out in Montana and gave Mattie's to her, but he appropriated Daisy Lou's to invest in stocks and bonds, at first with her blessing and later without.

For two years, she had been making plans to move to New York and embark on her musical career—her old friend Lelia had even offered her a cot in her small apartment until Daisy could find a room of her own—but she did not want to go, to face all those auditions, until she had a repertoire of four arias and six recital songs and a better grasp of French and Italian.

Then her father's unexpected death and her mother's need of her made a definite departure date impossible to fix. Also, Carlton would not hand over her inheritance, so there she was, stuck in a sleepy tree-canopied town on the edge of Saint Paul.

Carlton, at twenty-six, was a businessman, a drinker, and a gambler. He had a wife and two young children, but spent many of his evenings with a Minneapolis actress who had a taste for clothes and travel.

There is a photograph dated August 4, 1913, about a year after Franklin Malone's death. The names are written on the back in

Daisy Lou's looping hand. The people in it—there are seven—appear to be propped up by the starches and trussings of their clothes. You could faint and your clothes would keep you upright. It looks that way, doesn't it?

Taking a photograph was such a formal and lengthy undertaking that the subjects felt called upon to present a self that was not frivolous or ephemeral. And so they did, and that is what is touching. That they felt it was possible to do that. It's in their faces. They believe, absolutely, that there is something of them that outlasts the moment, runs under it like a river.

Mattie Malone feels a deep heaviness in her chest as she holds herself unblinking for the camera's shocking flash. The absence of her husband makes her heart ache badly on family occasions like this. Without him, she has difficulty identifying the version of herself that belongs to posterity. What we get is a short, round, dark-haired lady with a mouth that is set and petulant. Her plump hands grasp a dark folded fan.

Since her husband's death, Mattie has suffered from vague and frequent seizures of the heart and stomach. She is having one at the moment, in fact, and will go to her high-pillowed bed immediately after the photographer is finished.

There are cousins in the photograph. An uncle too, and an aunt. And Carlton, large and vested, and Daisy Lou, her eyes focused theatrically on something distant and off to the side. Jerry is not there. He came home for his father's funeral, then left again.

Daisy Lou still looks like the girl who went to New York three years earlier to see the comet. The only difference is a faint new line of tension between her eyes, barely discernible in the photo, which stems from her mother's attacks of heart and stomach and from her own artist's nerves. Also from the absence of her father, who doted on her and whose death sometimes feels to her as if a supporting hand has been removed from the small of her back.

When she is particularly taxed or tired, Daisy tends to get pale and teary, and then she has to rest immediately or she gets the sweats or female troubles, which she treats with Electric Bitters.

March 14, 1914

Dear Jerry,

Well happy birthday and many happy returns! Your nice letter came two weeks ago and as Mother is in bed with another heart attack, I'll answer. She fainted after church meeting and has been in bed three days this time and I have been nearly wild with cooking meals, carrying trays & etc.—and then my concert Sunday afternoon at the new concert hall, I was nearly beside myself. Sunday morning Mother no better so Mrs. Sayer said she would stay. So suffering from extreme exhaustion, I went to sing. We had a crowded house both concerts and I had so many curtain calls that finally Mr. Daseli had to call a halt. Helen & her husband sent me gorgeous roses about three dozen and took me to dinner at the Windsor Room afterwards, but I was so weak they were afraid I'd faint before my food arrived. Eloise Ketchum told Mr. Daseli she considered me one of the very finest artists of the Twin Cities. I finished the program with "A Spirit Flower." Do you know it?

My heart was frozen, even as the earth
That covered thee forever from my sight.
All thoughts of happiness expired at birth.
Within me naught but black and starless night.
All shimmering like to silver butterflies,
They seemed to whisper softly thy dear name.

Can you see why my voice cracked when I thought of poor Papa and I wondered for a moment whether I would finish?

Virginia Winterbourne, Dr. Winterbourne's eldest daughter, accompanied me on the piano, she is a dear and musically talented to her backbone. I have taken her on as a voice student on the insistence of her father and hope to inspire her to become more well-rounded artistically. That makes four students I have. I teach them in the parlor and it is difficult at times because Mother's attacks come at unpredictable times and then she rings the bell by her bed and I must run tho I am giving a voice lesson. I must remind myself at those times to pray for greater patience for, after all, how much longer will Mother be with us and this is the time for me to refine my character and complete my preparations for a Musical Career.

Carlton and an actress (!) came by auto a few days ago and stayed to supper. He says he has three good investments for my money but I wonder when I will see a nickel. Oh! he is a dreamer I fear, and poor Ruth and the little boys.

This is four heart attacks Mother has had in two months. She says she hopes to be all right and not to worry. She says to tell you this one was like the attack she had in church that time when she fell over.

At first she didn't want me to tell you, thot it might worry you & you would come home even if you couldn't afford it, but tonight she thinks I had better tell you. Well now, Jerry, I just can't begin to tell you how much I admire your character, the way you are carving out your life in grand and distant country, and of course your example helps me too.

Your loving sister,
Daisy Lou

In those days, the term described a variety of occurrences in the heart region—the big seizing killers, but also flutterings, transitory nips, even just a vague leaden wrongness that could settle in the solar plexus for hours or days, refusing to lift or move on. Heart attacks of one kind or another had become as familiar to Mattie as her children. "My heart attacks," she called them. "These pesky heart attacks." They could put her to bed for an afternoon, a day, the better part of a week.

Daisy Lou in 1914. Her audiences loved her. The Schubert Club, the Minnesota Club, the various churches in Saint Paul and even beyond were constantly requesting her. She had a way of making the familiar seem insightful because she sang as if she were discovering something instead of insisting on it. Eventually that quality would become stylized in her, but during her twenties she was able to seem freshly amazed whenever she sang.

She was something of a chatterer in conversation and used her hands to whisk the words away. When she sang, she used her hands too, though in a more conscious way, as if she were drawing a picture.

She took Italian and French lessons in Minneapolis on Tuesday and Thursday afternoons. And then there were her voice students and three new piano students as well. Her own voice she kept at its best by daily practice. She sometimes sang the vocal prologue at a movie theater and took part from time to time in big recitals, like the one at the Art Institute in which the Ensemble of Fourteen from the Little Symphony Orchestra of Minneapolis played and then Daisy Lou sang three songs with piano accompaniment—"Iris," "The Spirit Flower," and "There Are Fairies at the Bottom of the Garden."

Often, her day would be so busy that Daisy wouldn't find time for her own voice practice until the hour before she started the evening meal for her mother and herself. Then she might position herself near a curtained window in the silvery old house, her hands folded in the concert position and pressed lightly to her midriff. Occasionally, as she sang, she reached up to touch a forefinger to the hinge of her jawbone, making sure she had created the hollow that ensures proper resonation.

The sun through the curtains burnished the outlines of her slim figure. She looked gallant and solitary. Her voice was sweet, but it sometimes wavered a little, just on the edges.

The residential streets weren't paved yet, and the wheels of buggies and phaetons and Fords released clouds of dust, making the late-afternoon light, sometimes, as filmy and golden as we imagine it now.

Jan. 4, 1915

Dear Jerry,

Mother and I thank you and Vivian and little Francis for the lovely box of Christmas presents. Mother loves her pretty hankies and the stationery set for me is dear. We had the Ketchums and Winterbournes to punch and cookies, and Vivian's fruitcake "brought the house down."

My most promising voice student is Virginia Winterbourne. Did I mention her before? She is fifteen, a young lady now and has a lovely natural voice, tho she don't know the proper way to use it. She also has a reckless temperament which makes me despair that she will develop a well-rounded artistic approach and the necessary discipline. Oh! it is a challenge. She is a dear tho. I invited her to a lecture on Culture at the College Club and she said afterward that she had never heard anything so inspiring and she was grateful she had me for a teacher and gave me a hug. She is very impulsive, and I only hope I can guide her according to the best lights.

Your loving sister,
Daisy Lou

Mattie outlived her own doctor, Virginia's father, who was not an old man and was in fact a perfect example of the heavy-bellied, bully look that was taken to mean physical health in the early part of the last century. Spiritual health too, for all those predestinationists. Your eternal fate might be decided against you, they knew, but if you looked well-fed and prosperous on earth, that was a grand and godly hint in your favor. (The ragamuffins swarming in from Europe, many noted, looked wildly unsaved.)

In actual fact, the robust Dr. Winterbourne smoked black cigars and wheezed like an ancient walrus on his sweaty bedcovers, and he departed this earth one morning in a brief noisy rush.

His successor was a disturbing young physician named Daniel Sheehan.

On Sheehan's first visit, Daisy took note that he was quite handsome and wore no wedding ring. She had begun to automatically scan the left hands of young men she met—though, of course, many married men are ringless—because she hadn't had much luck finding a beau and her school friends were getting married right and left. Marriage wasn't Daisy's goal—she considered herself an artist, a keeper of the sacred flame—but she would have liked an opportunity to say no. At the very least, she would have liked an escort. She would have liked to dine after her recitals with someone besides her friends and their husbands. She had a sense of missed signals—that something about beaus, and fiancés, and, for that matter, men in general had been made clear to her friends and contemporaries in a way that did not include her. She could not understand the casual way they got married. It seemed to her like sitting down to dinner at a friend's, then inexplicably promising to stay there the rest of your life.

In the mid-teens of the century, Daisy was still girlish and pretty. She had a willowy figure and delicate hands and an air of purpose, of severity even, that went well with her piquant face.

Though she was curious about Dr. Sheehan—he seemed instantly mysterious—her manner with him was identical to her manner with most other young men. She practiced a stylized coquetry, which has the opposite effect of what it seems at first to intend. The recipient soon knows that it is not directed in any real way at him. The motions of it are like accidental punctuation. You notice it, but it means nothing, alters nothing. Even the rapid little gestures that referred other eyes to her body—the impatient flick of a crumb off a sleeve, an overattentive straightening of a blouse cuff—all those gestures seemed to pass through a screen that neutralized them of real intent. In this way, Daisy kept herself single.

As she moved through her twenties, she thought herself to be in love from time to time, but the object was generally someone who was not possible. He turned out to be married or to have an unsatisfactory character, habits of drink or gambling, for instance.

When America joined the World War, she sometimes pretended she was in love with a handsome young man who had gone off to Europe to be killed; to be stopped forever in his firm and glossy youth, eternally desirable and out of reach. That is not such an odd fantasy for an artist, after all. Artists are yearners. She made him up and then she killed him, so he would be with her, perfect, forever.

July 1, 1916

Dear Jerry and Vivian and little Francis and Maudie,

My but we are having a heat wave like you would find hard to believe. Baking must be done before midmorning or it is no use trying to stay in the kitchen. I would prefer no baking at all, of course, but the Ensemble of Fourteen has its ice cream social at Furness Park this weekend and we must all bring goodies. I made Midge Ritter's famous Lemon Swirls and they are delicious if I may say so myself.

Virginia Winterbourne, the girl who usually accompanies me on the piano, has her own voice solo this year at Aberdeen Hotel's musicale. I perform too, of course, so have had to find another accompanist. Virginia has been my star student for several years now, and she has grown in so many ways that she is a regular young lady, tho still flighty. I worry so about her. We have developed a friendship and are very congenial most of the time, tho she is very headstrong, more since her father died, and doesn't practice her music as she should. Virginia and I plan to hear John McCormack in Chicago together in two weeks' time. We shall go by train. I am so looking forward to it.

I pray for Virginia daily, as I do for you and Vivian and the kiddies, and for Mother, especially during this recent trouble with Carlton. Oh! it pains me to even think about it much less commit it to paper, but here goes. Sunday, note from Carlton to say he is delivering my money at long last. "Investments have yielded return." Tuesday no Carlton. Wednesday, he shows up in a new Hudson Town Car, fawn-colored with luxury tires! Well! you could have knocked me over with a feather. I knew when I set eyes on it that it was my money from Papa right before my eyes! And of course I wasn't wrong, tho Carlton says I will have it within three months and that he needed a new car to show his business clients they were not wrong to put their trust and their money with so fine and secure a fellow!!! He says he expects a promotion from home office in a month maybe and then my money will be handed over in a lump sum. Meanwhile, he says I am making a needless fuss because Mother has said she will send me to auditions in New York if that is what I feel I must do. I do, but I will never take her old-age money to do it. I will go with my own money or not at all, which Carlton knows perfectly well and so he is just keeping me in St. Paul indefinitely with his tricks. Oh! he is a rogue.

I wish you were here to advise me how to deal with him. Mother is no help because of her attacks which are more frequent with the heat. Dr. Sheehan has been here three evenings in the past two weeks to check her and adjust her medication. He is very well-dressed but I sense something tragic about him. Mother says it's only his eyes, which are different from one another, one wide open, one squinting. She says eyes that don't match are no reason to suspect tragedy and she is probably right. I do know he is unhappily married.

Well, I think of you in your frontier town and try to imagine all that space and grandeur and those cool breezes too! It must feel wonderful, at the end of a long day, to watch the sun sink behind the purple mountains and know again that you are part of a grand American enterprise. Yes you are! And I admire you for it.

P.S. Do you have Christian Scientists in Cut Bank? I met a lovely woman two weeks ago who is a Christian Scientist and we talked for two hours after the lecture at the St. Paul Institute. They believe that the limitations of our mortal state can be overcome if we come to understand our true spirit nature, and I am inclined to agree. I am coming to know that I have unconventional, unorthodox religious tendencies, which doesn't surprise me a bit with my sensitive temperament.

P.S. again—Mother's birthday is the 24th, so I'm sure you won't forget to send her a greeting. She misses you sorely and says, I only hope I am not taken unexpectedly without seeing Jerome and my grandchildren, and of course she includes Vivian too. She would make the trip to Montana, but Dr. Sheehan advises against it in this heat and with her heart.

Your loving sister,
Daisy Lou

From the beginning there was a shadow attached to this Sheehan. Rumors that he drank spirits; that his wife had been seen weeping or was too pale; that he accepted German immigrants as patients. Within weeks of his arrival in Saint Paul, it was remarked upon that the young doctor was sometimes noticed sitting by himself after evening rounds in the hospital ward where the sickest patients were. The ones who were very quiet. He simply sat there on a wooden bench, very quiet himself, sometimes with his eyes closed.

Daniel Sheehan was at that time a lanky man in his early thirties, dressed so impeccably and conventionally that his clothes seemed a conscious antidote to the edginess that showed itself in his wild shock of black hair, his parson's forehead, and the eyes that looked unmatched in a way that often belongs to people apart.

One fact about the natty and troubled Daniel Sheehan was that the chaos and noise of his daily life had come to seem intolerable to him. Everything seemed to conspire to bowl him over with sound. The screech of the baby, the sharp scolding exhausted voice of his wife, the ringing metallic sounds of the hospital.

Another truth was that he did not love his wife. Did not even like her and could not remember why he had promised to go to the death with her. Could not remember himself as he was when he made that terrible vow.

Another fact: He was addicted to morphine. His wife would realize later that she had never seen his arms in the daylight without sleeves. He was a controlled and knowledgeable person, and so he timed his injections and remained mindful of dangerous doses and the necessity of masking the symptoms of bliss.

He was not ashamed. He had the addict's grandiosity, which says that a drug in the bloodstream does not represent a weak person's intolerance for pain; it represents a strong person's willingness to look honestly at real pain, to acknowledge the terrifying whimsy and heartbreak of this life. No fully conscious person could do that unaided. Morphine aided. It was his shield against the sad and answerless. He could either acknowledge the sadness, see it, and take morphine. Or he would have to seal himself off, become sober and not care. He felt he had made the nobler choice.

When did he put the needle into his arm? On occasion. Not daily. But regularly. Often at dusk on the evening before another doctor took night duty. When newborns weren't due. Then he would lock himself in his office, which was next door to the hospital, and he would lovingly and ritualistically prepare the needle, lovingly wipe his arm with alcohol, tenderly press the veins. Take his time.

He would take a deep breath and insert the needle, gently press the drug into himself, withdraw the needle, apply the cool-hot burn of alcohol on a wad of cotton and close his eyes.

The feeling was one of utter well-being and warmth. A person who loved him beyond all telling had wrapped him in a fleecy warm blanket and insisted that he never worry about anything again. That he had done all he could and it was enough and the deeper secret of life ran joyous beneath its tragic and stupid and jarring surface. Now he could float down there for a while where it was sweet and real.

Sometimes, at this point, he took himself to the death ward next door. He went to the ward and sat with the people he and others had been unable to help. It was all right. It didn't matter. All was understood.

5

On the day Vivian and Jerry were married, the long tablecloth flew up at the corners, ladies grabbed for their big hats, a hawk floated across the sun, a meadowlark on a fence post made a sound like gurgling water.

Everything moved then.

The stars spiraled and the moon stalked the sky beyond all hearing.

Rippling flax like blue water. The howl and clatter of the trains and their cargoes of the disembarking—it all moved. Raw little buildings sprouted overnight.

The galloping sun stirred the air. Everyone was young and they moved with the quick bright motions of young people. Each day leaped up new.

In 1915, the rains didn't come.

In 1916, the Russian thistle—those tall purple stalks Vivian had tended like flowers—spread like prairie fire, grabbing moisture and soil from the wheat, mocking it with their fat nodding flowers. That was the second rainless summer.

And then a third. Stunted scorched wheat during the World War, when prices were higher than they'd ever been.

This had to be an aberration, a test, they all said. An accident, a hailstorm, is a presence. Something happens. Drought, like a slowly dying marriage, is only a growing absence, and it can take a long time to believe.

They waited.

You want to hope. It can't stay like this, they said as the tops of the wheat turned brown and fell off; as they dipped rags in an inch or so of rusty pail water to plaster over their faces at night so they could breathe. It can't.

They said it in 1917, 1918. And then the summer of 1919 arrived, and it was as if a face of pure malevolence turned itself full upon all those town kids from Minnesota and Wisconsin and Illinois. The sun beat down on them. The wind chiseled at them and blew their fields into great clouds of dust that rolled away like breakers. A purple cloud formed on the horizon, moved toward them slowly. Slowly it moved over their heads, darkening the sun. Slowly it moved on and away, leaving a few drops of moisture or none. And then the cloudless idiot sky again.

On a July day in 1919, a traveling preacher drove into Cut Bank in a sheepherder's wagon and stopped in front of the Metropolitan Hotel. His pink and watery eyes looked out from a face the color of old cowhide. A silver shock of hair fell over his forehead. He wore a tall black hat with an eagle feather in the band. His bony horse leaned unmoving into the traces, head bowed to the heat.

The preacher erected a dusty umbrella over his head and sat for a few hours on the wagon seat, reading a small thumbed Bible and paring his ragged fingernails. Sometimes he spoke briefly to himself, nodded in polite agreement.

When the white sun was directly overhead, he collapsed the umbrella, wiped off his forehead with a piece of tattered gingham, and stood. He drew himself up to his full lean height and began to shout in a shockingly melodic voice. He shouted about the day of judgment, the invasions of locusts, the trials of Job, and the devil's due. About valleys of darkness and pinnacles of redemption and the stubbornness and blindness of sinners in the face of all the clear signs.

He pointed a knobbed finger at the vengeful sun, then stopped to cough the dust out of his throat.

Businesses along Main had shuttered their windows against the sun and the dust and the hot-grease sound of grasshoppers, and when the traveling preacher stopped yelling, the town had no human voices. The cook at the Metropolitan threw a pail of slop out the side door and made a weary, batting-away motion at the preacher, who kissed his frayed Bible and steered his horse into a scant patch of shade.

The town baked. The prairie beyond quavered lakelike in the heat. In another month, most of the last of the beaten ones would arrive in town with the clothes on their backs, a few tools, their old faces. In the corners of the wagons would be outlandish remnants of other lives, what they'd had and hoped for—a hand-painted soup tureen, a lace wedding veil, a book. *To Violet on the occasion of her high school graduation, from Aunt Mary. June 1904.* Violet, aged thirty-two, is now an old woman on a buckboard seat.

By August, some of them would be begging for food, for a roof against the sun while they figured out how to leave this hell for good. But it was still July. There was the slimmest chance of rain. Everyone waited, moving in a trance.

The town pulled itself in to its bones. Shrunken wooden doors ticked, ticked in the harrying breeze. This waterless world? It was gravel through a child's listless fingers; food turned to flour in the mouth; an inch of drinking water with the metal aftertaste of blood; clothes gummy with unrinsed soap; teeth grinding sand; dull hair, dull fur; the wheezing of an old horse that would one day forget to draw the next breath.

Two figures emerge from the rippling air at the far end of Main. Two bent men leading horses with sagging heads and bladed flanks. One of the horses carries a few bales of miserable overpriced hay, just off the train from Minnesota.

The men draw closer. T.T. Wilkins and Skiff Norgaard. They are young men who look older than their fathers back in Wisconsin. T.T. is thin and dark, with a flamboyant mustache and a beetled brow. Skiff is weathered Scandinavian, his eyes too blue for the harsh sun. Everything about him looks blistered.

They live with their families on adjacent half sections east of town. Four days ago, T.T. lost a four-year-old child to diphtheria. The other child, the two-year-old, has a fever.

T.T. and Skiff led these same bony horses, this morning, down the side of the rim to the river, which is only inches deep and beginning to pool. A stockman they know sets nets. He pulls the nets every morning, dumping suckers and goldeneye on shore. Mostly suckers. Then he rides back to his house on a tall spotted horse, never glancing at the people who wait up above.

Dry-land farmers, broke honyockers like Skiff and T.T., wait until the rancher is out of sight. Then they crawl down the long ridge on horses, in wagons, on foot—a half dozen or more men a day—to pick up the stockman's already stinking fish, jam them into already drying burlap sacks, and take them home to be ground, canned, eaten. Because there is nothing much else by then.

The preacher begins to shout. The grasshoppers crackle and hiss. The breeze stirs up columns of dust that skitter down the street like dervishes.

Skiff and T.T. raise their heads in tired curiosity at the black, hatted figure on the wagon. They draw closer and begin to hear what he is saying.

"Lord God," the preacher screams in his boy's voice. "Where are you?" Then he shouts something about the dark fires that burn a thousand times hotter than the noon sun. "Sinners!" he shrieks. "The day is at hand! Ignore not the signs! Cast off your human folly and avariciousness. A man's life consisteth *not* in the abundance of the things which he possesseth. Therein lies ruin. Turn your face from the blandishments of the devil before it is too late!"

Still shouting, the preacher eyes the two men walking toward him with their bent sick horses carrying charred-looking slough grass. They stare back at him. T.T. Wilkins brushes his hand over his eyes to clear away the grit so that he can see the man more clearly.

They might have kept walking, T.T. and Skiff. They might have been able to ignore the raver in black. But as T.T.'s hand came to his face, the smell of putrid fish settled on him and made him gag, the way the feel of his little daughter's cooling feet had made him gag. He had tried one day to feed her a mash of the warm fish and, because he was her father and trying to help her, she had let it sit for a moment on her unmoving tongue before tipping her head so it would fall out. His bright-eyed girl, who hadn't asked to be born and had looked so engulfed at the end.

He turns to Skiff. As one, they drop the lead ropes on their hay-heavy horses. The horses sink their heads. As one, T.T. and Skiff walk up to the preacher and they pull him off the wagon. And then they beat him until he doesn't move.

They work speechlessly, kicking ribs, breaking an arm, pounding the head onto the baked dirt of the street, splitting skin to release the bright blood.

At the finish, he lies sprawled like a broken crow, collecting flies. And there is a stretch of time when nothing about that changes. No one comes out of a building. Nothing on the man moves, not even the blood. He lies black and crumpled in that halted place, looking like his own pronouncement.

Oh, those years! The war in Europe, the killer influenza, seemed nothing to compare to the absence of water. Clouds of grasshoppers came that blotted out the sun. Talc on your tongue, your teeth. The world turned to ash. Even the hoppers were parched. They followed the moisture a working man left in the air, his trail of sweat.

One farmer over east was targeted by a locust cloud as he furiously harvested the crisp remnants of a crop of oats. The invisible spray of his sweat drew them whirring and clacking, and they reeled the moisture into themselves and landed all over him, already chewing.

They descended on him and ate his shirt off. Everything they could get to. The collar, the sleeves, the sides—all but two strips beneath the heavy denim of his coverall straps. They chewed the hair on his head, the finer hairs inside his ears. They crawled bony inside his overalls, and they popped and jumped and chewed as he stumbled, shrieking, back to his shack, arms bare, neck bare, raped.

In 1915, the first year the rains stayed away, Jerry and Vivian moved to town. They had proved up—the homesteads were theirs—but their farming was a bust, even before the drought. Rain at the wrong time. Two demolishing hailstorms in two successive years, just before they would have cut their crops. Lack of farm machinery and the necessity of cumbersome sharing arrangements with those who had it. Their essential ignorance about all that was agrarian, and then the arrival of one child and then another.

Vivian's brother George married Emily Mainwaring, the mother of the girl who cut off the cat's tail, and they moved to Seattle, where George got a job as a printer.

Jerry got a clerk's job in the Cut Bank post office and decided to go into real estate. They moved into town to wait out the worst.

By 1917, with the drought and the grasshoppers and worms, they couldn't even get anyone to lease their adjoining homesteads. The shacks of Jerry and Vivian and George—so new and audacious seven years before—stood neglected on the parched prairie, strips of newspaper curling off the inside walls.

As the moisture went away and failed to come back, a great slowing began. The days began to blur, each one more like the one before. Those who stayed walked more slowly. The animals walked more slowly, and some of them lay down on the ground. The stalks of wheat and oats bent over, then lay on the ground. The air hissed.

Vivian pulled aside the curtain and saw T.T. Wilkins and Skiff Norgaard walk past in the heat, stately as a dream, leading their two old horses. One had a few bales of bad hay on its back. The other had hay and a man in black, slung like a sack of grain so that his arms dangled off one side, his feet off the other. His trousers had ridden up, and the exposed leg between pant and boot was maggot white.

They moved slowly, the footsteps of the men and horses puffing up clouds of dust. They looked calm. T.T. had a stain on his shirt. The man in black raised a bloody face, dropped it again.

Was that what made her sure they must leave: the sight of that? Or the harrying wind that was coming up again? Was it the whimpering of her two small flaming-cheeked children in the heat and stillness? Or the news about the Wilkins children? The prospect of bringing more children into a place so singed?

Low voices that night, her own and Jerry's. They talk about Seattle. About some night work Jerry might get at the railyard to begin to save money for a move. Their voices are papery in the dark. There is decision and relief in those voices.

They will go to another place. They have done this, and now they will do it no more. They will go west again, to Seattle, as far as they can go. Rain. Taxis. Babies in a city park.

It is time. This country is not what it seemed. This country is a fraud. It blows away before your eyes.

6

On an autumn evening in 1918, just before the end of the Great War, Mattie Malone began her serious dying. A crisp evening that smelled of wood smoke. Darkening skies and the sound of red leaves clattering in a small breeze.

After supper, as she sipped tea with Daisy Lou, her hand fluttered across her chest. Her heart felt squeezed, as it had so many times before, but there was something more this time. Some feeling of numbness, though it was not on the surface of the skin but far inside her. A deep numbness creeping upward.

She anticipated her next day in bed. She lectured herself. You *must* take care of yourself, Mattie, she thought gratefully. No arguing! She was a child ordered back to a cool-sheeted bed.

When she spoke to Daisy Lou, her voice slurred a little. Everything about her—her voice, her movements, the tracks of her eyes—slurred a little. This was new.

"A heart attack?" Daisy Lou inquired solicitously. Mattie was unsteady on her feet. Her toe stubbed the bottom stair. Her face was pale, and she was docile as a tired child when Daisy dressed her for bed.

"Best make the pies early tomorrow," Mattie said very slowly. "And watch the meringue. You know you and meringue."

Those were the last casual words Mattie ever said to her daughter or anyone else. A half hour later, Daisy Lou heard a loud thunk and ran down the hall, to find her mother curled in on herself, silent, on the floor.

Now everything changed. When her mother was stricken, it was, to Daisy Lou, like the dismantling of a tableau vivant. She realized she had felt for some time like the frozen explorer scanning the horizon. And now the curtain was drawn closed and everyone in the tableau was moving, scurrying back into life.

The presence of a crisis made her realize that a kind of timelessness, not unpleasant, had infused her for years; that she had stopped expecting major change in herself or anyone around her. Her mother would always be mildly ill. There would always be a war on some far continent that took all the young men, thus obviating the need for questions of marriage and romantic alliance. Her fame would always be waiting at a fixed distance from a fixed present.

But now the present had become unfixed. The trance was over. The war was over. Her mother lay in bed, beginning to die. Men walked the streets, some with missing limbs. Hearses carried the victims of influenza. Some of them had literally toppled in their tracks.

Daisy woke up and darted her head around and felt panic. A tooth began to trouble her. It was linked to all this somehow—that urgent throbbing on the side of her face, as if someone had yelled in her ear. She felt assaulted and without information.

Virginia Winterbourne, Daisy's star student, was now eighteen years old and had the new look that a number of girls were putting on, and a slangy way of talking. She had become quite wild since her father died, and Daisy was afraid she would become common as well. Virginia's hair was tied up to look bobbed. Her skirts were short enough to show most of her high boots. And she did have a reckless manner.

Daisy knew that Virginia had a herd of friends that she jumped into as soon as she stepped out of doors. She could almost hear them milling around outside, breathing like dainty animals, waiting for Virginia to join them. All of them were young and pretty and slangy like Virginia.

Sometimes a young man came by in a motorcar to pick up Virginia after her lesson. Daisy straightened her sheet music and watched through the lace curtains as they roared away. She thought then about words and phrases Virginia had let drop. Words like B.F., which stood for best friend. Entire plots of moving pictures. Which actresses she loved, which leading men. "There were a lot of white kisses in it," she said about a new picture show. "And a few red kisses too!"

White kisses. Red kisses. Daisy Lou turned the terms over in her mind and wondered what it must be like to say the words so blithely.

The most unsettling aspect of Virginia Winterbourne, however, was that she had developed a beautiful voice. Encased in that flighty young person was a singing voice that cracked your heart. It was a soprano, with a husky undertone that suggested recent weeping or shouting, though, of course, she had done neither and tended to wear an insipidly cheerful look on her face most of the time.

Virginia had only to open her mouth and out came that voice, high and rich and true, beautifully inflected, as confident as the lope of a young athlete.

Hearing it, Daisy felt anger at the mismatches of fortune, at how this voice had mistakenly inhabited the wrong instrument, one that didn't deserve it, didn't keep itself in tune; didn't try. She thought of Virginia's voice as a lovely animal, a lioness, forced to jump hoops in a fly-by-night circus.

At least she, Daisy, could try to make the instrument, the conveyance, more worthy. So she was hard on her student. Drilled her. Criticized her attacks and made her sing arpeggios over and over.

She would show Virginia the proper way to fold her hands while singing, and the girl—lanky, careless, good-natured, heedless—couldn't seem to do it in a way that didn't look like a simper, an affectation. She seemed to mock her teacher in the act of imitating her.

This made Daisy Lou furious. You throw away your gift! That's what she shouted inside. Outside, she tightened her mouth and recited her directions again or sang a phrase slowly, methodically, for Virginia. Giving it its full articulation and importance. Her voice wobbled at the edges.

Like this, Daisy Lou would instruct. Place your hands like this, your chin tilted, so and thus. And Virginia would try again and burst out laughing, and then an auto would honk and the young man would be out there to take her back to her group—"my group" she said to Daisy—and they would both be relieved the hour was up.

The auto chugs loudly down the street. Daisy Lou impatiently straightens the sheet music, her clothes. She brushes a crumb off her skirt as if it has attacked her. She draws her hand across her damp forehead and takes a spoonful or two of Electric Bitters for her nerves before she goes to tend her mother.

The voice won't leave. It stays in the room, high in the room, a red and unblinking bird.

Mattie's hair turned white by leaps. Each day, it seemed, another stripe of white appeared. She wanted it loose. She wanted it unpinned. She asked for a summer straw hat that had belonged to her husband, Franklin, and she kept it next to her on the white bedspread.

Now it had been six years since his death. She was aging rapidly beyond him, becoming his older sister, his mother, his white-haired grandmother. He lagged further and further behind, a boy kicking up gravel.

For two weeks after her stroke, Mattie did not speak. Then some words began to come, but they were very slow and in a deep register. She seemed to search for them, so that by the time she arrived at the point of utterance, anything she said took on weight and importance.

Before, she had been a talker. Even to herself. You must take care of yourself, Mattie, you must take a rest, she would tell herself when she had heart attacks and stomach attacks. She talked to the cat and the caged canary. She talked to herself about daily chores, fidgety details. She talked like fingers picking at nothing.

When she was seized, the chatter stopped. And when she resumed speaking—one side of her face drooping, one arm useless—you had to listen. Sometimes the words came out in a rational way. Other times not.

"I would like a husband," she said, pushing her fingers toward the pitcher of water.

Carlton brought her a posy once. "Carlton is in jail," his mother told him after a long search for the words.

On another day, when Daisy Lou asked if she wanted an extra pillow behind her neck, the words seemed especially long in coming. "You are a blear," Mattie finally uttered.

Daisy gently corrected the words in her mind. "You are a dear," she said to herself as she ran a comb slowly through her mother's tangle of fading hair. "You really are."

Dr. Sheehan arrived at twilight to check on Mattie. His stride was calm and stately. At the door, he took Daisy's hand in both of his and pressed it warmly. She was shocked. He looked at her with something that resembled love. The smell of lilacs rode the soft air.

Most times, Dr. Sheehan was a stern, even cold young man, snappish sometimes, and now suddenly there was this new person, and he seemed—how did one read that look on his face?—he seemed to see her fully and to embrace what he saw. She had the feeling something very untoward was happening, but she couldn't say what it was.

Maybe, she thought, it's me. Perhaps I am the peculiar one today. I am the one who is altered and strange.

He walked up the stairs ahead of Daisy, slow and complacent as a husband, and he listened to Mattie's heart, then put his arm lightly around her shoulders to lean her forward when he urged her to cough.

He took out his beautiful pocket watch—it was larger than most and had scrolls on the silver like figure eights on ice—and he timed Mattie's pulse. Daisy watched them from the door. Her mother's streaky hair hung loose around her colorless face.

He sat on the edge of Mattie's bed, urging her to cough. Something about that—the sight of the young ardent-eyed man with his arm around her mother's stooped shoulders—produced in Daisy Lou a sense of such sharp mourning and nostalgia that she had to leave the room.

Back in the kitchen, she offered him a glass of iced tea, and he sat at the table, his eyes like fingertips on her face. They talked a little. He asked her what she was reading. She read him part of "Endymion," a long poem by Stephen Phillips, her favorite poet.

Selene, the dark moon goddess, has removed blitheness from the shepherd Endymion and left him with something riveting. Daisy spoke the words: "But now what melancholy sweet / Steals over me, what magical distress, / Distant delicious trouble and new pain!" She read in a shy, fervent voice. "Ah! Ah! What hast thou done? for I begin / To grieve for ancient wars, and at the thought / Of women that have died long, long ago / For sea-tossed heroes…"

She looked up. Dr. Sheehan nodded gently, seeming to recognize the truth of it.

He had a look of vivid relaxation that she had never seen before. It was not drunkenness. Despite the rumors. She knew drunkenness when she saw it, from Carlton. It was loud and without judgment or discretion.

"Those then who bear the torch may not expect / Sweet arms, nor touches, no, nor any home / But brilliant wanderings and bright exile," she finished softly.

He asked Daisy some quiet questions. How she taught voice lessons. How one went about coaxing the best from someone else. She recited some of the technical aspects and also addressed the importance of creating a picture in your mind to instill the proper feeling. She told him one must learn to place the tone properly.

She talked about pitch and resonation and training as if the voice were a rambunctious pet. It was a matter of patience and discipline, she said, and perseverance above all else. And then there was the artistic component. She found it helpful to link every piece of music with a certain emotion. She thought Sorrow, she thought Spiritual Yearning, and so on. She thought of the difference between a shepherd girl's adolescent pinings and a queen's grief, for instance.

She had never talked this much to a man to whom she was not related. Never come close.

So how do you imagine a queen's grief? he asked. Well, she said, you think of someone with a natural dignity, a natural gentility, and a high degree of sensitivity. And, like most queens, she is isolated. She is behind walls. She lives a rarefied existence. And then she has lost something upon which her heart was set. The king, or a son perhaps. Or a kingdom. Whatever made being a queen worthwhile. The loneliness worthwhile. She has lost it, and she must spend the rest of her life expressing that grief.

And how is her grief different from that of the young shepherd girl?

Well, it isn't different in kind, Daisy said. The pain may feel the same for them both. But the queen's grief is more noble because she doesn't have the freedom of the shepherd girl to wash the pain away with new experience. No. Because the way she responds to it has to be an example. She is not free to be undignified or confused or changeable. She is an emblem. An example of how to be sad. Her music is lasting.

He listens. He nods. He consults his beautifully scrolled pocket watch.

He looks up and he tells Daisy that she is an artist and she is a queen, and she should never listen to anyone who says otherwise. He rises to leave.

They stand face-to-face. He extracts an immaculate handkerchief from his vest pocket and draws a corner of it along Daisy's damp hairline. And then he is gone.

Hot. The parlor shaded. Sweat beads on Daisy's upper lip. Mattie upstairs in bed, eyes closed, her old black fan moving the air past her old face. Otherwise, nothing moves. Not even the leaves on the trees. Not a quiver.

Daisy knows that she should be studying her Italian, but she can't seem to do it. She has reclined on the horsehair sofa behind the thick paper shades of the parlor windows. She sips iced lemonade and blots her face with a batiste handkerchief.

She finds that she is crying a little for no reason at all. She dabs at her eyes. She dips the corner of her white handkerchief into the cold sticky lemonade and sucks the liquid out like a child. It is faintly salty with her sweat and her tears. She dips it again, sucks it delicately, sighs.

How long she has waited! That's what she feels on a day like this, this unmoving kind of day that seems the essence of waiting. And for what has she waited? For a sea-tossed hero. For distant delicious trouble. For someone to imagine her because she cannot seem, yet, to fully imagine herself.

She waits in the heat. Her mother's small cranky cough floats down from the upper floor. She dips the handkerchief again and dabs her forehead with the sugary cold liquid, squeezing the cloth so that the stickiness runs in small rivulets across her closed eyes down her nose and cheeks, onto her tongue. She licks her fingers. A few more tears; not a torrent, just a few. A fragment of a hymn in her head and then the fragment of an opera she heard on Eloise Ketchum's Victrola and then a fragment of her student Virginia's wild light laugh. I have a pain, Doctor. Her hand resting now on her waist. It is here, a dull pain that came on this morning. Fingers press. Here? The pain?

Just tea and a piece of toast, and then there it was. The heat perhaps. Here? The fingers firm and knowing. Locating. Placing. Moving in from the outer reaches. Tell me when it hurts. She stretches her arm, her sticky hand, to its full length. Moves it. Here? Anything here? No. No. Her white-stockinged leg tips outward. Her hand moves, the stickiness catching slightly on the material of her long skirt. Here? She licks the lemonade daintily from her lips.

August 16, 1919

Dear Jerry,

Just time to dash off a quick note as I am so busy with Mother I could drop. She must have constant attention and so I am always on the run with her trays and so forth, not to mention total responsibility for the upkeep of the house. Elmer Donlan came over to look at the porch and I have a girl to help me with the shopping but it is very difficult and I must pray constantly for the strength. I know there is a reason for this, that it will put steel in my character, but oh! I am so tired sometimes I could drop. You asked, Does Carlton help out. He and Fitzi the Paramour come every Sunday to visit and he has made contributions to the food and doctor bills, says he is going great guns as regional manager and home office plans to give him an award.

I have to say I have grown to like Fitzi tho she is not so pretty or stylish with a good figure. But her disposition is fine, easy going, efficient, always good natured, never ruffled. We are quite congenial. Needless to say Carlton is crazy about her & I believe altho I may be too innocent to live, that it is an honorable alliance & I believe they intend to keep it that way until they are both free. Her husband has offered her separate maintenance if she will sign an agreement never to divorce him & she & Carlton refuse any such compromise. Husband says she can have any number of sweethearts & do as she pleases only he will never consent to a divorce. (!)

Carlton says he will give me Papa's money in a month but I will believe it when I see it. He was very upset about Mother because of her difficulty in speaking but now he is used to it, as am I. Doctor Sheehan comes twice a week now and he says Mother has a tough road to full recovery but her constitution is on her side.

Mother is so beautiful now, it is as if some sort of an atmosphere surrounds her all the time and I think of that Bible verse, about the path of "growing brighter and brighter, onto the perfect day." She speaks very slowly and deeply and must often search for the words, but when she utters them they sound as if she has been thinking about them for her whole life. Her hair has gone white.

I am so thrilled that you are coming for a visit and I can tell Mother is too! There is no reason to come before October, though I thank you for asking. Doctor Sheehan said her condition has stabilized wonderfully and he said, You're the one I sometimes worry about, Miss Malone. He said, Miss Malone, What about your own life? And I answered him that I consider it a privilege to care for Mother in her hours of need, and I do. I have been reading Mr. William James on the subject of how the religious temperament is allied to the artistic temperament and I think this is all preparation, and I only hope I shall be worthy of whatever is meant for me. If my vocation is to care for Mother for some years to come, then so be it. Doctor Sheehan is a comfort to me in this. He is a man with a secret sorrow in his life I believe, and we have become quite congenial. Mother did not like him at first but now I believe she is glad to see him.

This long crisis has certainly put me "out of the swing of things." I have temporarily canceled my Italian and French lessons and have told my own students that I must stop teaching for a period of time. I miss my girls but see no help for it. Virginia, my star student, has asked me to accompany her to Chicago to attend "Aïda." I shall, though I shall have to get Mrs. Spooner to stay with Mother, because I believe Virginia is ready for exposure to a different level of performance. She has a wonderful gift but lacks discipline and drive.

Lelia Todd came home to visit her parents. She has now been in New York City for almost ten years and she has made a career as a whistler. She has a contract with Aeolian and has two recordings already. One is called "The Bird and the Clarinet" in which she performs the whistling solo, and the other is "A Woodland Flirtation." In that one, she is both of the birds.

She says she could get me a contract with Aeolian but I don't know. She says no one in New York is interested in art songs like mine anymore, but that's probably what a whistler *would* say, don't you think?

I got a tooth pulled at the dentist and took gas.

I am so very sorry to hear about the grasshoppers and the crops and the poor animals. How terribly dispiriting, I thought.

I must run now as Mother needs me. Kisses to Vivian and the kiddies. We'll see you soon and won't it be grand after all these years!

Your loving sister,
Daisy Lou

7

The first snow of the season, a flagrant temporary October snow, had already melted to bright patches. The street was a muddy mess. Jerry walked the three blocks uphill from the streetcar, picking his way through the wetness, his shoes beginning to seep. He seemed the only person about, though it was midmorning.

The towering old maples dropped their last leaves silently at his feet. They arched over the street and the houses, sturdy frame houses with porches and newel posts, their ample backyards running into one another. Lawns made for iced tea on a hot day and lazy hand fans against the damp sweet heat. No wind. No trains. A cat sat unmoving on a porch and blinked at him. Piano music, very faint, from somewhere through the trees and the quiet houses. Porch steps swept. All of it bright, quiet, dripping. Only the clouds moved, and when they passed over the sun, the day and the place became muted as an old photo. The way he remembered it. A place that was cupped, neat, ritualized; all the people good people in small and steady ways.

There was embedded grime in the seams of his fingers, and he rubbed at it. Three months, and the switching job had already burrowed into his skin. He had a quick vision of himself atop a boxcar at night. How the wind came up in the blackness and blew out the lantern as he squatted, and then he heard, felt, the wheels begin a slow roll because the yard was uneven and anything could move that wasn't tied down. Frantically twisting the brake wheel, squinting into the lanternless night, the wind grabbing at him, the coal chute looming four stories high at the side of the tracks, a black column in the blackness—and was that another car just ahead?—and then the stopped car and his jumping heart.

More than once that had happened, and now, in this place, he felt like a sailor who had been set on land, trying to recall the mannerisms of gentility, the conventions of the fixed. He felt uncomfortable; awkward and shabby in his old suit. He carried visions of deserts and dark shapes into this bright drip, drip of melting snow and the sound of a piano exercise, melodyless and steady; carried them up the steps of his own house, the house of his childhood.

A broom was parked near the door. A corner of the porch sagged perceptibly and sent him a pang of guilt. Daisy in this small structure with their mother for all these years, trying to be steady and good. His own seven-year absence, the years suddenly biblical to him in length and import, though the time had contained invitations and near-visits and temporary delays. Still, there it was. Seven years since he came home for his father's funeral and left again. He felt his chest begin to tighten in the old way.

Daisy ran toward him, arms like a diva's. They embraced quickly and awkwardly, then she propped him at arms' length, examining him. She had a brittle birdlike aspect to her that seemed new, and dusty blue circles under her eyes. She brought a faint scent with her that was deeply familiar. Not perfume, but the smell of old cedar dresser drawers, a rigorous smell that made him six years old again, waiting out a Sunday in this soft interior gloom among the dark furniture and half-pulled shades and the tock tock of the clock—that clock—on the mantel.

He made a movement toward the stairway, thinking to greet his mother in her bed, but Daisy stopped him with a light touch on the arm. A cup of tea first, she said. Mother was sleeping. A new doctor had come and given her something that finally made her sleep. She had been so agitated. It wasn't like her, but, of course, her son didn't come every day. Her long-gone son.

She didn't know why Dr. Sheehan, the regular doctor, had sent a substitute. She had thought nothing of it at the time, but now she had a strange worried feeling and planned to make inquiries.

Their teaspoons clinked in the tea. He listened to her talk. The new doctor had seemed quite stern. Judgmental. That was not too strong a word. As though Daisy wasn't doing everything humanly possible to make her mother, their mother—hers and his and Carlton's mother—comfortable and happy. Carlton was coming. He had been delayed by an important meeting. He was very anxious to see Jerry too. Everyone was.

She sometimes slept an hour, never more. And then the bell would ring and that would be the end of conversation. So talk now, while you can!

Mattie's regular doctor, Dr. Sheehan, was beyond reproach. He was an unhappy man—it was in his eyes, there had been gossip—but his only problem was that he was attuned to the sufferings of others. Even the small sufferings, the passing ones like irritation and small-mindedness and loneliness.

She hoped Dr. Sheehan did not have the influenza. She planned to make inquiries.

It had not been easy. And because it had not been easy, Jerry listened. Tamped down his own impatience and weariness and listened. Because he had been gone seven years.

The porch, he had doubtless noticed, had begun to sag on the near right corner. Elmer Donlan was looking into it. Digging and cement would be involved. Carlton said he would pay, but then Carlton always said he would pay.

They got the news about the porch, the full extent of the trouble, that is, last Saturday. That, plus certain other developments, made it the worst day in memory since Papa's passing and then Mother's troubles. Certainly one of the very worst. Virginia Winterbourne had sent word that morning, the morning of the news about the porch, that she was simply not going to attend *Aïda* in Chicago, for which Daisy had purchased reserved seats two months in advance. Virginia had a beau and she simply preferred to spend the day with him and his motorcar. It was an opportunity to learn and to be inspired, and Miss Virginia Winterbourne simply preferred to do otherwise.

Jerry listened, unfathoming. Virginia Winterbourne's name sounded vaguely familiar, but he couldn't begin to know why the mention of it produced such a wronged, pinched look on his sister's face. It was as if he had missed a whole packet of letters, an entire story, detailed and heartbreaking. He nodded as he if knew, shrugged as if to say, What can you do about people like that? He glanced at the mantel clock.

She's catching up on her sleep. She's exhausted from waiting for you.

He had a quick vision of his mother in a white nightgown, floating supine above his head.

The new doctor, the one who came two days ago with no explanation at all, by the way, he exhausts her too. He is not, how to put it, congenial. That would be the word. He is cold. He doesn't care.

It is a shame when a person loses the capacity to care.

She had perfected several new mannerisms. He didn't remember them, at any rate, though they now seemed habitual, ingrained. She would tip her chin up a little, the point of her heart-shaped face, and drop her lofty eyelids very slightly as if she had refocused on a far horizon. Then she would say something that had a formal, rhetorical cast to it. I should like to take him to task, she said of Carlton. I should truly like to do that. She also had a habit of hitching her skirt a bit so that her crossed ankles showed, and they were pretty ankles in pretty polished shoes.

She crossed her ankles, tilted her head, dropped her eyelids and talked. The words, the recitation of small troubles, came out calm, flat, delicately aggrieved. He thought of Cut Bank, of the clouds of grasshoppers and army worms, of the red sun, as he listened to this catalogue of an old house's ailments, of his mother's symptoms and medications, of her daughter's contained fury. And it was, indeed, anger. He knew it, could hear it beneath the words like the tick of a pencil on a tabletop. I have been here, been here; and you have not. Have not. I have been in this house, these years. And that makes me a serious person and you must somehow find a way to say so.

Light filtered through the lace curtain onto the tabletop. It dimmed periodically, briefly, like a slow signal.

You've been a godsend for mother, Jerry said. Daisy inclined her head and smiled slightly. She thanked him. Not exactly a godsend, she said. I've been here all the time.

In his old room, Jerry opened his valise, the one he had taken to Montana a decade earlier. He changed his shirt and sat on the edge of his old narrow child's bed, breathing. On the dresser was a cross he had carved as a nine-year-old for a Bible class. It was crude and grudging. Great gouges out of the wood. Frayed twine to bind the two parts. It rested on a lace doily. He remembered how pleased his father had been to get it, and he buried his face in his dark hands.

The teapot began to whistle two rooms away. He heard Daisy's footsteps. The teapot continued and the whistle grew. Take the teapot off the fire, he said in a low voice. It climbed, the sound, and he heard a drawer open and close. Another drawer. He clenched his eyes. The sound had grown to a shriek. The clouds passed again and the room turned bright.

He leaped to his feet. Threw his jacket onto the chair and walked rapidly into the kitchen. Daisy had squatted before a low cupboard and was reaching far back into it, her gaze concentrated on the ceiling, her arm moving in the recesses. The teapot was deafening.

Jerry grabbed a towel, grabbed the handle, held the pot for a moment while the sound trailed down, tapered off into quiet.

He slammed it onto an iron trivet. He was breathing fast and wheezing a little. I'm going up to see Mother, he spit out. I'm sure she's awake by now, Daisy mildly agreed.

What had she expected? She asked herself that as she followed him up the stairs. She had expected the clean glow of a pioneer, the look of someone who stepped out of a crude log cabin each morning onto a wide place of sun and crops and horses. Sunsets that lasted, maroon and gold, for hours.

He had written about the grasshoppers and the heat. He had said there was a need for rain. But it had all seemed settler chitchat. Now she saw that it was not. This Jerry before her did not look radiant and calm. He seemed scrubbed, as if the top layer of his body and soul had been taken off with a wire brush. His dark-red hair had become thin, light, and dry. Like cured grass. His blue eyes had faded and become narrow and wrinkled at the corners. His skin was mottled and patchy, bleached here and there of its color, and there were black creases around his fingernails like a hobo's.

He wore suit pants, white shirt, and starched collar, of course, but his clothes looked thin. There was something faintly neglected about his entire person. That discolored front tooth, the lifeless hair and scraped-looking shoes.

He had a snappy, impatient, nervous aspect to him too. Talked faster than Daisy remembered, and bit off his sentences and his laughter.

Perhaps Mattie's life had slipped away as soon as Daisy had covered her for her afternoon nap and descended the stairs. Perhaps then. Perhaps when Jerry still rode the train, or as he walked the edge of the wet street toward the house with the sagging porch. Or while they talked over tea, the sister and brother, about sagging porches and faithless students and money.

Perhaps that shrieking kettle had been a pure alarm. It would always seem so, later, to Jerry. And he would never again hear the sound without a wash of the deepest self-doubt.

They pushed open the door to her room, obedient smiles on their faces, and found her marbleized and for the ages. Her long hair—plump, pinned-up, and dark when Jerry last saw her—was pure white. It fanned across the white linens and the sleeves of her white gown.

Shouts. The thud of heels down stairs. Daisy flying out the door to the neighbor who has the telephone.

Jerry shaking his mother's arms. Gently at first, then so hard her head begins to rock. Shaking to start her, as if she were a balky pocket watch. A sour smell rising up to him from his own skin and the vise now around his ribs.

Daisy back in the room. Where is Dr. Sheehan? she cries. Where is my mother's own doctor? She whirls upon the body. I can't find the right doctor! she shrieks.

The cold floor of his room, and himself like a dog on all fours, his ears and eyes dead to the world, only trying for trickles of air, watching the hot tears fall out of his eyes on the floor. He puts his mind someplace else. Does everything he can not to care, not to feel, so that he will simply be able to live and to breathe.

The funeral is over and they all mill around in the social room of the church. A row of high windows and in the windows red leaves swirling. The last big gusty day—the wind sounds like water from inside the wall—and then the big trees will stand bare.

There are the Malones—Daisy, Jerry, and Carlton. They stand in a half circle and shake hands, accept pats, incline their heads to hear murmured condolences. They don't look like siblings, do they? Well, perhaps Jerry and Daisy share a certain contained, trim look. A certain solemnity of the eyes and mouth. Both look very pale—Jerry bleached somehow and Daisy just drained of blood. The black cloth makes her skin almost translucent. She wears a brooch of her mother's, a cameo. She is speaking slowly today. She seems a little glassy with grief. She took a double dose of tonic, but it isn't working as well as she'd hoped on her nerves and she wants badly to go home.

Carlton is a large man, upholstered, florid, loud-voiced. He is already rather pear-shaped and has odd womanlike hands. He shakes hands vigorously. A gleam of tears comes easily to his eyes.

When he arrived in his Hudson Town Car, about an hour after they found Mattie; when he came booming into the house, pulling his vest over his large girth, and then looked up, smiling, to really see their faces—well, then he had actually thrown his big body across the foot of the bed. Pounded his fist on the wall, every movement extreme and heavy. But he was soon done, and all that was left of that was the pinkness of his smooth face, the easy tears.

What has returned to him, in this little gathering, is his manner with the public. He had a certain surface finesse, always. He mastered, early on, the gestures of authority—the crisp signals for cabbies and waiters, the guiding hand on a woman's elbow or back, the satisfied flip of a white napkin as he embarked on an expensive meal.

Carlton loves deals. In fact, he is talking at this moment—light hand on a shoulder—to a neighbor who might be interested in a new kind of fire insurance policy that Carlton sells. Not real business talk, but he wants the man to know he is available, and they will arrange a time to talk. His job is with Minneapolis Fire and Marine, but he has side deals going all the time. The stock market, a share in a mining venture, a large bet on a hot-air-balloon race. This all puts him daily at some risk. Most days, that is, hold the potential for dramatic loss or gain, and that gives Carlton an aura of peril and extravagance that draws certain women to him. Quite a few, to tell the truth.

He is also beginning to be in thrall to alcohol. It gives him an infusion of confidence and gusto. Confirms him in his energies.

Those women who stand near the table with the tea and the cookies, that little clot of them speaking so furtively? They are talking about Dr. Sheehan. They are saying he let a baby die. They are saying he had been drinking liquor and did not notice that the baby could not breathe, and he let it die.

They are saying a nurse defended him. A nurse vowed the baby had been born dead and said the mother's grief had blinded her to the facts. The nurse was insistent. But Dr. Sheehan did not defend himself, and so it seemed she was making a fool of herself out of misguided loyalty or more. He did not say, himself, that the baby had been born dead. He did not deny that he had been drinking liquor, but he did not confirm it either. He did not say anything.

His wife went to the chief of the hospital and pleaded for him. This was known through a sister of one of the staff doctors. Mrs. Sheehan said she would have to take the children and go back to her old parents in Boston if her husband's overseers allowed him to be wrongly disgraced. She wept.

Dr. Sheehan was called in again, and again he did not defend himself. He did not say anything. The baby was buried. His patients were transferred to another man, Dr. Colfax by name.

The women's voices drop another notch. They are saying now that some local men, the father of the dead baby and some of his friends, dragged Sheehan out of his house last night. They called him terrible names—Bolshevik, slacker, fiend, rummy, murderer—all in front of his wife. They bloodied his face and ripped his clothing and threw him on a freight that was headed west.

They are nearly whispering now, and that is what they are saying. That all of that happened and Dr. Sheehan, through it all, didn't say a word.

They are saying someone should tell Daisy Malone, in as vague and kind a way as possible, of course, because she has to be wondering where her dear mother's personal physician is. Why he has been so absent.

None of the other doctors will say anything yet. It is an official secret. But it seems Daisy, at least, should be told. In the kindest way possible at this difficult time.

Jerry has been at his childhood home for three weeks, a lifetime. He leaves tomorrow. He and Carlton went to a burlesque show last night. It was business, Carlton said. A chance for Jerry to meet some men who were interested in the uranium business and had a prospect in Montana they wanted him to check out. A small mine up by the mountains somewhere. One of the men had an interest in the mine and wanted Jerry to arrange for testing of some ore samples. For a cut of any proceeds, of course.

The woman at the burlesque hall was at least six feet tall, with white-blonde braids wrapped around her head. Broad white shoulders and a dress with no top or bottom, just fancy red stuff with lace from breasts to thighs and a long train. Not enough cloth there to wad a shotgun, Carlton announced, and all the men laughed and bought expensive drinks and the woman's husky voice floated over their heads and her large white hands, her long fingers, coaxed whatever was in the air to come into her lace-covered arms.

Carlton's life. Smoke and men and deals. Prospects. A long discussion about a uranium mine in Idaho and how rich someone had gotten overnight. The ore involved. Extraction methods. Markets.

Carlton's world. Cigars and premium brandy. A dollar bill in the shoe of a woman who floated in the footlights undressed. Easy laughter. Prospects.

Jerry didn't tell them he had been switching trains. He mentioned land. He said the key was to buy now, after a stretch of bad years, and wait for values to rise. For demand to increase. As it was sure to. The key to the land game, he told Carlton and his friends, was timing. He heard himself say those words. The key is timing. Knowing when to hang on. When to bail out. What to hang on *to*.

He didn't tell them he had promised his wife they were leaving that country, moving to the city of Seattle when they got together the money to move. The very instant they had the money.

He didn't tell them his shack on the prairie was in tatters and that all the topsoil had blown away. Or how slowly everything moved. How stunned the place seemed. How Vivian strained the orange water through cheesecloth to filter out the tiny red bugs.

He thought about that, and his children.

He thought, for a shade of a long moment, about the way his mother used to brush back the hair from his sweating forehead as he gasped for breath. Her cool hand and how it had helped.

The air had grown very close.

He didn't tell Carlton's friends how his impeccable sense of timing had caused him to miss his own mother's death.

The woman sashayed to the edge of the stage, her arms still beckoning, her red satin flickering. I need air, he told Carlton. I need a walk.

Daisy had waited up because it was Jerry's last night. Her eyes were red. She looked at them reproachfully and cut cold beef for sandwiches. The three of them sat at the table. It was after midnight. They had made the decision that morning, and now they all felt like transients. The house would be put up for sale.

For a week after her mother's death, Daisy had been volatile and inconsolable. She had fainted while talking to a group of women at the funeral. She had burst into tears and slammed herself in her room when Carlton handed over her inheritance with interest. (He had unloaded some stocks at a profit.)

But then she became very quiet and calm. Brisk in movement. Matter-of-fact about the disposition of the furniture and so on.

It is time, she announced to her brothers. It is meant. I have had a dream that confirms it beyond any doubt. I have the money. I shall go to Manhattan and pursue a musical career. This has all been, these years, an important test of my character. It has all been a preparation.

She made them clasp hands in the dim light then, and they tipped their heads over the remains of a midnight supper. They said a prayer for their dear gone parents, and then they said another one for themselves.

8

There are four of them gathered around a table with a red cloth on it and a small roast duck at its center. It is Christmas 1919, the one they believe to be their last in Montana. It is the pause before the beginning of their highest venturing. Four Malones in a three-room house at the beginning of the worst winter of all, the one that will finish off all who still hang to this country by their fingertips.

Part of the main room has been sheeted off to make a bedroom for Francis and Maudie. Another room is just large enough for Jerry and Vivian's bed. The kitchen and wash area is the biggest room, and that is where they all are now, seated around the table with the red cloth. The stove is stoked. It is bitterly cold. Rags are stuffed at the bottom of the door; blankets are tacked across the windows.

There is a small tree over on the hutch—the train brought a stack of them one day from the mountains—and it is draped with chains of paper rings and topped with a battered angel. The bare electric bulb that hangs from the ceiling is dark. There are candles on the table and in one corner the kerosene light. The light is fluttering and warm on their faces.

Francis is now five. He is an alert child—hearty, high-colored, bright. His emotionality, his exuberance, are attributes Jerry never remembers having in himself as a child, and he welcomes them in his son. And Francis's generosity too. He is the kind of child who will in a few years buy birthday flowers for his mother with money from his newspaper route; who will like beautiful places and things and wonder aloud, more than once, why the family doesn't live across the mountains where there is water and, in the spring, acres and acres of cherry blossoms. But he doesn't brood—not as a child. There is nothing furtive or shadowy about Francis.

Already, at five, he is known for his fits of laughter. There will be times when something strikes him as funny and he will laugh in such a helpless extended way that everyone around him will have to start laughing too.

The duck, slick and gaunt, was brought to them by a friend who shot two on a lucky day. He kept one for his family and gave the other to the Malones. Vivian stuffed it with lots of seasoned bread and cooked it carefully, making a gravy with a tablespoon or two of some old brandy she saved for holiday cooking. They sit around the table in the warm light. They say their prayers. They listen for a few seconds to wind throwing new snow against the door, the snow so cold it is sand.

There is a quacking sound. A very accurate quack. Francis is making a near-perfect duck sound he learned from an older boy, and he is doing it with barely a change in the shape of his mouth.

Maudie's head jerks up. She is four and has a small, avid face wreathed by flossy hair. A large bow bobs on the crown of her head. She glances sharply around the table, at her parents with their eyes cast down and small smiles on their faces, at her brother whose eyes are off on the far side of the room. She squints at the glossy hot duck; hears the sound again.

Her eyes dart around the table once more. Then she stands up and reaches over to the duck and slowly lifts its wing, twisting her head with the big floppy bow to see under it—and everyone bursts out laughing, Francis loudest of all. He can't stop. He stands up and doubles over and falls to the floor, laughing and kicking his heels until his laughing mother pulls him up.

Maudie is clearly about to cry, so Jerry calls her over to his side of the table to help with the duck. He slices it—she still looks dubious—and puts the pieces on a plate for her to offer around. Her mother gives her a long hug.

They eat peach preserves sent by George and his wife in Seattle; wild rice from Aunt Mina and Uncle Charles in the

Twin Cities; cheese from Vivian's mother; tinned crackers from Daisy Lou.

"In Seattle, we'll have a big pink salmon for Christmas," Vivian announces happily. "Oysters. Oyster stew."

"We'll take the trolley down the big hills of the city"—her hand swoops—"and see a Christmas tree as tall as the coal chute. With small electric lights all over it. Thousands and thousands of them."

"Will there be firemen in long motor trucks?" Francis asks. "Will there be stores with toys clear up to the ceiling?"

Jerry is quiet during this conversation, these questions. He has visited Seattle, he has a picture of it, but it does not hold glamour or release for him. It strikes him as a realm that is, more than anything, familiar. Despite its surface differences, there is something of it that is the kind of place he left ten years ago, making the boldest, most exhilarating decision of his life.

East or west of these plains—he pictures the sweep of them from the Rockies to the Mississippi—east or west you ran into the city scramble; noise and old stone and the agendas of the established.

But they've made the decision. It's time. And he tries once again to convince himself that it will be another adventure, another move west. But it isn't. It is a move to a place with firemen in bright city trucks, and thus it is a circular motion. He doesn't like the idea of circularity. It gives him that old hopeless trapped feeling. That foolish feeling of being someone who thinks himself to be advancing when he is really walking a treadmill like a donkey.

On the other hand, there is something about Cut Bank, this country now, that is like an abandoned battlefield. Beneath the weather, there is a great quiet. The place is ravaged. Young faces are exhausted, and if this winter turns out to be a long one, and not just cruel, then you will begin to hear gunshots in the air, there, then there, and animals toppling to the ground.

The presents were always opened Christmas Eve so the house would have a day's warmth in it and the children would sleep through the night. Such meager gifts this year. Everyone so broke.

Maudie had yearned for a new doll with a nightgown and a traveling dress that she had seen in a neighbor's Sears catalogue. She got a small, cheaper one, and Vivian made all the clothes for it from scraps. She didn't like to sew, and it showed. There were signs of impatience on the little dresses, undone hems that made her ashamed when she saw them, though she had spent hours on the tiny scraps at night when she was half asleep.

Francis got a wooden replica of a World War airplane, made by Foster, a young guy who worked at the mercantile. Each child got an orange. And pencils from Daisy with their initials on them. And a one-dollar bill from their uncle Carlton, which made the biggest impression of all and caused their parents to feel, for a bleak few moments, like bystanders.

The children got their mother a 1920 calendar from the mercantile. They had loved its size and color and had insisted on it, though Jerry had suggested a muffler instead. The calendar showed slim young women in fur coats, fur muffs, ice skating on a pond surrounded by pines. Thatched English cottages with chimney smoke like treble clefs. Lawns. Croquet. Parade horses with red plumes. A girl in a swing under a huge spreading maple, her blonde hair brushing the ground.

Jerry got from the children and Vivian a small cardboard case to hold his pens and pencils and silver letter opener.

Vivian's mother had sent handkerchiefs for everyone and a packet of well-wrapped fudge. Four pieces of it sat on a saucer like a prize.

They eat the fudge slowly. Francis remembers the quack. He does a small quiet one just for himself, eyes on the ceiling, and Maudie slaps him on the arm. Vivian leans back in her chair, her hands resting on her stomach. She is two months pregnant. She and Jerry are the only ones who know.

He puts a hand on her arm and does something then that startles them all because he's never done it before. He clears his throat and, in a hearty tuneless voice, begins to sing. He may have been trying to dispel the quiet of his mother's home and her quiet white form. He may have been listening to the billowing wind and how it covered all other sounds outside their windows and doors. Whatever the reason, he now sings "Sailing, sailing, over the ocean blue..." Quite loudly. The children join in raucously, still chewing their fudge. After a moment of disbelief, Vivian sings too. They belt it out—each rather surprised at the rest—and they feel, for a few seconds, like they are indeed in a tight ship on wild seas.

Vivian's hands stay lightly on her belly and she catches Jerry's eye, and they both see the strange night that caught this baby. How passion flared up like a dust devil, so unexpected and engulfing, after such a long time gone.

Jerry had just returned from Saint Paul and his mother's house and her funeral. He was angry, agitated, low on sleep. Whenever he drifted off he saw his mother floating over him; floating over his head while he talked trivia with his sister. After three days hunched in a crowded, cold train, he wasn't even given the chance to walk up the stairs and say good-bye. She drifted above him as he talked porches and money and Carlton with his sister. And the worst of it was that the whole missed chance felt like a manipulation—a heartbreaking manipulation because the perpetrator paid with her life and thus you could not accuse. She was beyond reproach, and there was only anger thrown at a corpse.

He came home with that to Vivian, who had spent a month with two small children at the end of the worst summer and fall in memory. No railroad pay for that time, and then he had come home from his mother's funeral to talk about his brother Carlton and Carlton's high-roller friends, his schemes, the way Carlton handed Daisy her money after all these years. He mimicked the very gesture, bowing like a prince. He scarcely mentioned his mother. He did not request the details of how she, Vivian, had been getting along.

But he had suffered his mother's death and so she could not accuse. She could only be angry.

She told him about how the Iversons had lost their little boy Delbert to diphtheria. How the doctor was out of town and nobody knew the symptoms soon enough to send for another. She had given him the news in a letter, but now she told him the details and how bitter and scared it had made her feel. How fearful for their own children.

Jerry nodded thoughtfully, gave her shoulder a tight little pat. Then, after a pause, he told her about a bet Carlton had put on a balloon race. A winning bet, and then Carlton did the same thing on a prizefight they took in together, and lost exactly the amount of money he had just won on the balloon.

She knew he was simply giving words to the images that floated closest to the surface of his mind, though it wasn't, of course, the surface images that he cared about. It was something else, which he couldn't talk about. So he would speak in non sequiturs, the words having nothing to do with what he was feeling or what he was puzzling about.

She knew he was speaking around his thoughts, but she was still infuriated. Nothing about their talk was a conversation.

Just three days earlier, little Delbert was fine, she said.

Neither Daisy nor I thought Carlton would ever have the money, he said.

The Jones brothers left town, she said. One of them knew your mother and sister back in Saint Paul, did you know that? They had a coal business and delivered to your mother.

Daisy Lou plans to go to New York City, he said.

It went on like that for three days, and then it all broke or melted. The children were in bed. A new burst of polite dead phrases went back and forth, but this time Vivian felt her face change. It flushed, then seemed to drain, and she threw a hot pad at him and there was not the shred of a joke in it. It caught the corner of his eye and he winced, blinked hard a couple of times, then he grabbed the top of her arm. She clasped his wrist and their fingers trembled with a fury that seemed to take the covers off their eyes. And when they looked at each other then, they were absolutely avid and ungentle, hurt and without rules. They gave themselves up in a kind of terrifying relief.

The look between them now is mostly gentle, mostly familiar, but there is an edge of wariness in it, the memory of how much anger there was in a night they never wanted to end. How close their bodies seemed to run, in pantomime or not, to murdering and being murdered.

The kids are doing something. Francis has his airplane by his plate. Maudie is flipping up her doll's dress to look under it, showing Francis. Their oranges, one for each, sit side by side on the cupboard with Jerry's cardboard pencil case and Vivian's calendar. January is a red velveteen parlor and a man with a handlebar mustache in a brocaded wingbacked chair smoking a pipe, a fluff of a dog at his feet, two starched and ruffled little girls peeking around the corner, fingers on their rosy lips.

When the dishes are done, they bundle the kids and themselves into vests, sweaters, coats, mufflers, and hats to have dessert and cards at the McClintocks'.

As the children let themselves be dressed, their faces as detached and patient as ponies being saddled, their parents look at them and love them. They love their particular kind of fortitude, their immediate investment in the new—how they took long wild sniffs of the oranges; how they examined the doll's crazily sewn clothes. The way they seem to have emerged out of these acid, wormy, scathing years with clear eyes and beautiful skin and helpless laughter at the drop of a hat.

There was a carpenter's kind of truth in children, they thought. They trued the corners.

The McClintocks were the young Methodist minister and his wife. They were rather modern and adventurous, childless, very handsome and clean-browed and only in town for the previous three years. They liked to have people over, like Vivian the Catholic, who didn't belong to the congregation. They were liberal that way.

There was something about them that said money. Money somewhere. The evidence wasn't in their clothes or their home, which was modest, though there was good china and a small painting or two in a silver frame. It wasn't their possessions, though they were casual toward their nice things in a way that made you know such things had always been abundant in their landscapes.

No, the signal was their freshness. They had a kind of heartiness that made you know they had the freedom, emotional and financial, to leave. They were, in some psychic respect, tourists. They were buttressed. On safari.

They were great fun to be with. They always had an activity at their home when they had desserts—charades or cribbage or auction bridge. Very unlike a preacher and his wife. But it went with her prettiness, which didn't fit either.

What did she look like? Very thin and modern-looking. Blonde hair that was not bobbed—her sister's was, but she said she was afraid to take the leap. She wore it pulled back in a style that looped over the ears and somehow *looked* bobbed. Her hair was very shiny, clean, and light. And her eyes were dark—dark eyebrows, dark eyelashes, dark-blue irises. The effect was startling—the coloring was natural but it looked artificial. And so there was a kind of innocent artificiality, an unplanned tartiness that was immensely attractive.

Her name was Suzanne. It had the sound of an adopted name, but she never offered another, a former. She was constantly in touch with her sister of the bobbed hair in Chicago and always knew the latest games, fads, and so on. Somehow, she could offer them in Cut Bank at the end of 1919, the worst year anyone had known, because she was fun and kind and she was a minister's wife too. Her looks conferred raciness. Her husband conferred seriousness of purpose. And Suzanne—who knew? She didn't choose. She was just friendly and lively and a little eccentric, as some put it, in the most harmless kinds of ways.

The Norgaards were there too, and the soldier who had jumped off the train a year earlier, half frozen. The tips of most of his fingers were missing. The McClintocks had befriended him—he lived alone in a lean-to by the depot—and had hired him to do some carpentry on the church.

Late into the evening, the adults played bridge. The Malone children and the three-year-old Norgaard boy, Thomas, played with an elaborate fort and soldier set that belonged to the minister and then they had cake and fell asleep on the big sofa.

George McClintock, the minister, didn't play but preferred to stand behind the chair of his pretty wife. He had a long handsome face, curly hair, and a kind of innocent goodwill that might have been insufferable if he hadn't backed it up with good hard deeds—which he did. He visited the sick and the dying and sat with them for hours. He gave money to those in the direst need. He was kind in his sermons, urging patience and tolerance. He invited people like the soldier to his house, his table.

He pointed himself toward what he knew to be good and tried to conduct himself so that he moved toward it. Suzanne, though, was what he adored. She was his delight, and that is why he hovered around her; because anything she did seemed more interesting than himself.

She was not going to commit a sacrilege, Suzanne announced with a dramatic folding-up of the cards, but her sister in Chicago had described to her in detail how to tell fortunes from tea leaves—it was hardly a matter of a swish and a guess, as they might think—and she planned to tell theirs then, on the spot. In Chicago, almost every party included a fortune-telling session. Suzanne believed she had a gift for it.

Her husband stoked up the stove, sat back down. They all peered in the bottom of their thin china cups at the remaining leaves of good black Ceylon.

A blast of wind shuddered the house, seeped cold at them, gave them quick visions of horses leaning into it, racks of bones, hay flying out of their mouths; grim small visions that hovered always inside the black wind and made them jump eagerly on the homeliest diversion.

Fortune-telling in a warm room. It seemed the kind of thing that people would be doing who didn't live on the Sahara, the moon, the back of God's head.

Suzanne swished the remains of Alice Norgaard's tea, a little liquid, the lazy black leaves, and then she turned it all over on the saucer, swished it again, closed her eyes, and put her fingertips dramatically to her temples.

"A trip," she said. "A trip to the south. No, not Great Falls. Farther. A trip to Denver in the not too distant future. A happy event. A..." She squinted her eyes at the leaves. "A christening? A visit with a young woman, a dear friend?"

Alice nodded, a little bored. Someone had surely told Suzanne about Alice's brother and his wife in Denver and that they were going to have a baby and there was worry because they'd already lost three at birth. This pregnancy was thought to be twins.

"A christening?" Alice asked innocently, as if for verification. Suzanne studied the leaves again, tilting the saucer slightly.

"Yes, I would say a christening or some other important event. An important birthday?" She looked up at Alice sharply. She threw her beautiful dark eyes around the table. Stared closer at the leaves. "A *double* christening?" she asked, incredulous.

They all laughed at her antics. She was such a ham. Two pink spots had appeared on her cheeks. Her husband gave her a look of the purest affection.

It was Vivian's turn now. She had only a couple of leaves in the bottom of her cup. "Are there enough to tell anything?" she asked. "Maybe I swallowed all my secrets."

She gave Jerry the slightest sideways look, a brush with her eyes. And there was the brief presence again of their dark people.

"Too few?" said Suzanne. "I think not." Her diction was becoming more formal. She had taken on a slightly hollow, out-of-time-and-earth voice. "I think, for the purposes of the future, there are not too few."

Suzanne rocked the china cup. It had a small garland of pink roses around its rim. English. Four or five leaves floated in the last of the tea. She turned the cup over on the saucer and the leaves rested in a perfect half circle. Suzanne studied them, looked back into the cup as if there had to be something else.

"Half," she said. "A half that wants to be whole. Or"—she turned the plate so that the leaves arched—"a small mountain. A small mountain to be climbed." She was flailing a little. She turned the saucer again and examined Vivian, who felt for a startled moment that Suzanne foresaw her billowing nine-month profile in the leaves.

But if she did, she did not say so. She made a pronouncement: "The year holds for Vivian a mound of treasures, the extent of which she has no reason, at present, to suspect."

Vivian smiled at the bland little pronouncement, nodded her head in thanks. She allowed herself a brief vision of the curve of Seattle's Puget Sound, the arch of its Queen Anne Hill.

During the silence between fortunes, they heard, through the hiss of the stove, one of the children—Francis it was—murmuring something in his sleep. "Put on my swimming costume," he said. "I'm going to take a splash."

That broke them up for a few minutes, even the soldier, who had seemed to be by himself and not given to hilarity.

Suzanne turned to him and suggested that he be next. He handed her his teacup with his blunted fingers. He was a man in his twenties, he'd have to be, though his cheeks had long furrows in them and the whites of his eyes had a yellowish tinge. The hair on his head looked dead. He didn't seem to say much, and what he did say seemed slightly off the beat of the conversation though it was spoken in a pleasant, gravelly voice. When dessert was passed, for instance, he gazed at the cake and said, "Sugar." And then his eyes blinked and he began to eat.

Suzanne studied his tea leaves with a very intent look on her face. She said, in a softened voice, "These suggest that the low point of your life is behind you. You have passed the test and the rest of life now stretches before you, productive and rich." She paused and resumed. "The miseries of war will soon fade and it will come to seem a dream of hardship that tempered you but never again has to be lived."

George McClintock's eyes gleamed with compassion as he watched the soldier take in her words.

"It *was* cold out there, I can tell you," the soldier said with more energy than he had shown all evening. There were sympathetic, somewhat uncomfortable looks all around. Here will come an intrusion of horror. Why do the McClintocks bring these people in? Small shameful thoughts like that. Someone had said the soldier had circulatory problems that could cost him a foot. Was that why he limped?

"It was cold, sure enough." His voice was reckless. He had a faint Scotch burr. It occurred to Vivian that he might have come to the evening slightly drunk.

"Some of those boys were just sick with Christmas grief," he said. Christmas grief, as if it were a term everybody knew. "They wanted new socks and their mamas."

Some murmurs, some quiet bracing for the worst of it.

"I was in the forward trench. Not a hundred yards from the German forwards. We had two fires going, it was so cold. Two fires because that wool always seemed to be damp and lousy and if you stood close you felt you were driving out the water and the bugs and maybe even your own putrid smell. That was the idea." His voice was cheerful.

"Suddenly, straight ahead, a white flag pops up. It was a bright night with a big icy moon, and up pops this flag. Then up pops this soldier beneath it, and he's holding some kind of tree in the other hand. Well, a bush. But they'd put some kind of little flames on it. Twigs, maybe, or paper that they'd lit. And this fellow walks forward a few steps, flag flying, and if it had been a few more he would have been a goner, but he stopped and planted that thing. Already it was half burned out.

"Then he just stood there, arms at his sides, and sang that 'Tannenbaum' song. He sounded about fifteen years old.

"So it turns out this fellow Walter in my trench became moved to sing. In German, if you can believe that. Would have brought the home guard down on him back home, you can bet. And then some other fellows sang it too. 'Oh Tannenbaum.'"

He paused, squinting at a grease mark on the tablecloth.

"And when Walter and the other boys stopped at the end of a verse, you could hear that they were singing over there too, more than just the one fellow out in the open.

"By this time the Christmas bush, or whatever you want to call it, was out, all the lights on it. So all you could see was the bare outline of that German and the white flag kind of fluttering as he moved away. And then it just dropped into the earth like a dead moth."

No one said anything.

Maybe they all just listened for a few moments until the sounds of the present world came in. A murmur of a child in the next room, a slam of a shed door, frozen snow breaking loose to slide down the roof, the oceanic wind.

And, closer in, the clink of silver. The feel of the warm stove and the air full of sugar and tea. Cards on a green tablecloth. Teacups with garlands of baby roses around the rims.

"That would have been two Christmases ago?" Suzanne finally asked solicitously.

"Yes, 1917," he said. "We had quite a march ahead of us."

The children were roused and bundled in their coats and hats to walk home. The adults were all a little agitated, a little brisk.

The soldier seemed a stray person again, on the outside of things. He sat quietly, making no move to go, hands folded on his lap.

Vivian and Alice seemed to be taking a long time with the children, so Jerry, to lighten the night again, handed his teacup to Suzanne.

It would, of course, be a happy fortune. Her happiest. The minister passed the candy again. Suzanne swished the leaves eagerly.

"Ah," she said. "Real details!" Six or seven of the leaves clumped on the dish. A small line of stray ones stretched out from the clump.

Francis came over to peer sleepily at the dish, scan the faces of the adults quizzically. "What's she doing?" he asked.

"Telling the future," Jerry said noncommittally.

"From those?" Francis's voice was loud with sleepiness. "Looks like a lump of something to me, and two, three little lumps of the same thing. Looks like spit tobacco!"

"I see," said Suzanne, "I see that your luck is all ahead of you. It's dazzling luck. Perhaps a lucky guess, a fortunate hunch. What could it be? It's the mother lode. Your peers will hold you in the highest esteem. Does this mean a run for public office? Does this mean fortune and fame?"

Vivian broke in. "No fortunes to be had in the Malone household, I'm afraid. Bad fortune if we keep these children up too long." And they moved out into the night with thanks and Merry Christmases and went off into the whiteness, the preacher and his wife waving from the warm window, the soldier aiming toward his lean-to by the depot.

"What were the other fortunes?" Francis asked. Maudie whimpered sleepily in her father's arms.

"Mounds of luck," Vivian said softly. "Mountains of it."

II

AFTERNOON

July 10, 1973

Jerry had two armchairs angled at the television. T.T. Wilkins sat in one of them, finishing a little speech about fuel shortages and the state of the world. Arabs. Cartels. Oil about to climb sky-high. And on, in a voice gravelly and aggrieved.

Jerry had the sense that he had been responding, nodding at least, but he wasn't sure. It seemed to him that something was happening to his mental arrangement of time. Often, these days, he felt doubled back on himself, scrambled. He seemed sometimes to hear his whole life at once, and it sounded like the anarchy of an orchestra tuning up—all the individual voices shooting off on their own, pirouetting, refusing to take part in the whole.

And then someone like T.T. Wilkins will be sitting across from him—an old man with a dipping white head—and he will think for a moment that Wilkins is his father or even a figure from a childhood Bible story. It will take a moment to place him in the lineup. And while he does it, he feels a flutter of panic, the mad scramble.

It is similar to the frozen panic he felt when he left college to sit at home in his room and time had seemed nothing but a many-stranded knot.

In going west, he had unraveled it, made it linear again, a series of events reaching out like a long string of boxcars to the horizon. Comprehensible and in motion. His diaries were reminders, verifications of that vision. One thing and then another. Year-end recapitulations. This happened and then this happened and I stand at the forward end, the engine.

This happens. The two of them are out of the weather in a long room that smells of pine and lamp oil and gravy; also the smell of the coal in the crevices of the skin of the railroad men who have wet-combed their hair and come in for a bachelors' Christmas Eve.

She is wearing a good winter dress and not a nightgown at all, as he had thought at first when it fluttered into his sight on the edges of the room. A medieval kind of gown, it had looked, with black jewels on it that flashed colors. And then she walked fully into the light and the gown was now a modest red wool, a port-colored wool, and the buttons winking in the lamplight were jet. Rainbow black.

The wind batters the windows. They have just arrived, he and Vivian, and their clothes and hair smell like the snow-combed wind.

Her arm in his as they leaned happily into it and made their way along the tracks and the small hunched buildings of town, the lights widely spaced and small in the moving dark.

The railroad hotel and its oilcloth tabletops, the jet buttons flashing and her laugh so beautiful and strong the bachelors lower their voices to hear it.

Someone has fetched a tree, brought one from the mountains, and it leans candlelit in a corner, swathed in paper chains, hung with butcher-paper angels and a collection of fancy silver spoons that float lazily and blink. The cook sings and coughs in the kitchen and delivers the plates himself, everything under gravy and a sprig of evergreen on the edge. A tumbler with a finger of port for everyone and it glows and is the color of her dress.

They each get a whole orange on a small plate that is placed ceremoniously on the oilcloth. The No. 44 pounds and shrieks past them on the windowless side of the building and they mouth laughing words and the oranges rock. And then the quiet again, like a still face beneath long flying hair.

They exchange gifts, quietly so the bachelors won't watch and feel hungry. She gives him a silver letter opener engraved with their full names and tomorrow's date, Dec. 25, 1911. And he gives her a small book of Shakespeare's sonnets, covered in red leather and inscribed in India ink with their names and the date and the place.

She takes him to a midnight mass in a small piney building behind the livery. Calcimined walls, raw wooden pews and kneelers; the warmth of her against his arm; the room all flickers and small bells and the smoke of the pope.

The silver bell rings one last time, and it is no louder than a fork on crystal. The tiny sound wavers up through the heat. And then the dark arm is hoisted to the sky, lifted like an animal just dead, and the Blackfeet cry once again, this time for the champion, that long warbling war cry that can make the hairs on your neck stand up, whether it is real war or a Wild West show or the boxing championship of the world.

Sweat down the face, down the ribs. The smell of vaporized pine sap lifting faintly from the new boards. Then the dark arm held another time against the sky, and cheers, and some boos, and a bottle landing on the edge of the ring to roll slowly toward the feet of the referee.

The movie men like buzzards on the parapets, small in the distance. Gargoyles making film, a record, to send down the ages, to send down to now. They don't want the edges. They don't turn their cameras around to the empty prairie or move them slowly across all those empty seats. They want only the two men down there on the white square. A killer with a high voice and pimples on his legs. His true-hearted and gritty challenger. Just two men panting after a fight that no one suspected could ever last so long.

T.T. Wilkins, the T.T. Wilkins of now, sat in a chair talking about Nixon getting railroaded, about forty-dollar oil. And then he drifted into a small nap, chin on his hand. And then T.T. Wilkins's brief and long ago wife, Daisy Lou aka Amelia Malone, knocked at the door and pushed it open.

This happened. Then this happened. Mail call, she sang in her fluty cracking voice. T.T.'s head swiveled rustily and he held his eyes on her until she arranged herself in them, and then he greeted her—Hello, Madame Malone—as he always did.

She left T.T. because of the pocket watch. Because of a pocket watch he had bought cheap, the summer of the big prizefight, and she found it in a drawer and left him. But why? Why was it the pocket watch that caused a divorce and, of course, a brief scandal because she'd been in town only three, maybe four years?

The pocket watch and her injured eye. They went together, and Jerry knew the connection as well as he knew his own name. But now, for this moment, it was all gone. He couldn't remember.

He was talking normally to Amelia and T.T., he realized. He felt like his own impostor.

He didn't want to talk or remember. He had a job to do today and he wanted to get on with it. Amelia and T.T. suddenly seemed glacial to him, so slow to move. Amelia with her huge car running outside—one front wheel up on the curb, as usual—and T.T. sitting there as if he had come to stay the day, the week, a life.

Jerry stood up, clapping his hands briskly. They hurt when he did it, the finger joints did. Off, he said to both of them. Out of my sight. Sayonara. See you later. I've got work.

They looked at him, surprised. But he could see that the announcement cheered them too. Well, yes. They were people with things to do. The day was for the business of the day.

T.T. wanted to go to the library and look something up. Amelia said she would give him a ride. They would all regroup at six to go to the banquet.

And so they departed, leaving Jerry to his business, their heads small as children's in the springless blue car.

The plan was to lay a trap for that Sharleen. To get the goods, the proof.

Sharleen Norgaard, granddaughter of his old enemy Skiff Norgaard, came to clean the house and make Jerry a hot meal twice a week. Did the same for Amelia. His children had hatched the arrangement over his objections, but he hadn't raised a huge fuss because he knew it eased their minds, being so far away, to think of the old people fed and orderly.

Then the helper turned out to be a Norgaard.

She was a slack woman in her early twenties with flappy trousers and a slow, casual way of talking and moving. She kept a cigarette steadily lit in an ashtray as she moved around the house, stopping for puffs in a way that seemed an afterthought. Casual. But she didn't fool Jerry. The Norgaards had always had that bovine slowness to them, white eyelashes blinking lazily while they ticked like Swiss watches underneath.

The old man, Skiff. He had exactly that kind of way of moving and the same thin-lipped mouth and big-fingered hands. The pale eyes on the lookout for the main chance, always, and never mind if a friend happened to be in the way. Mow 'em down. Stab 'em in the back. That's Skiff. Ask T.T. Ask Jerry. It had been a half century since either of them had given him the time of day.

And now Skiff and his son, Tom, had fifteen thousand acres of strip-farmed wheat reaching in shallow waves to Canada and beyond. A couple Cadillacs. Cruises in the winter.

Tom's daughter, this Sharleen, was a black sheep. She had married some bad drifter for a few months and run with him until he rolled a car somewhere in Louisiana and got himself killed. And now she was back, of course, and lived in town with her divorced black-sheep sister, a teller at the bank, and cleaned houses and supposedly didn't speak to her parents or vice versa.

There was a look to her that was pure Norgaard, though, disowned or not. A look that said, I'm not always going to clean houses. I'm waiting. She thought she hid it behind those bleached eyes, but Jerry saw it the second she walked in the door. She was on the lookout for some way to weasel back into the good graces of her dad and grandpa. Back into their pockets, anyway.

He watched her as he knew he had to, though he pretended indifference. Left the house for walks so she'd get the idea he was absolutely unconcerned.

Her first ten visits, he walked for exactly a half hour. The eleventh time he came back after ten minutes, and there she was, going through his records. She was lifting a big pile of papers—papers that just happened to include the manila folder with his latest calculations and maps, the ones he planned to show to the oilman, that Henderson, when they met for a business lunch next week.

Henderson was sinking test wells right and left and had come up with a good producer just ten miles south of town. No one knew much about him except that he apparently had the money to explore. He wouldn't talk to the newspaper or much of anyone else. He was, the newspaper said, "hunting for something."

Jerry knew what he was up to. He knew Henderson was playing out a hunch that Jerry shared—a hunch that the big deposits were along a horizon where no one had thought to look. The top of the Madison Lime.

Henderson would follow the Madison Lime up north into the Sweetgrass Arch. That was what he was sure to do. He would want the mineral rights on some parcels Jerry just happened to own.

And he would pay a pretty penny for them.

And Jerry would reserve a hefty percentage.

And Henderson would drill. And hit. And they'd both be rolling in the dough. Rich in a day!

She said she was dusting; was moving the papers just to get at some dust. Bald-faced. Said no, she didn't know the Arabs would be pushing oil to forty dollars a barrel, maybe higher. Acted as if she had no idea what he was talking about.

She said Amelia had told her to do the whole house, not just the parts Jerry pointed at, and so that's what she was doing. Bald-faced.

Forty dollars a barrel.

He has studied this oil field for half a century. He has kept track of discoveries, year by year; plotted countless versions of the structure and done it scientifically because he learned the ropes from the earliest and best geologists in the field. Not the doodlebug men. The real scientists.

A person could argue that, on the whole, it turned out to be a factory field—a fair number of dependable, modestly producing wells spread out over many miles. Steady. Low drama. For many years, Jerry, too, believed that to be its nature.

Now, though, he has a strong hunch that everyone has been wrong, including himself. That the field still hides its best secrets. That a few of those secrets are spectacular. And that any of them, in a summer when the entire country is wailing for fuel, are worth pursuing.

He tried to read Sharleen's face for evidence that she had been poking through his files; knew his best guesses. It was flat. She shrugged. Put out her cigarette and moved with her duster to the other room.

She was a perfect spy. She was the one who had told him she didn't speak to her parents or grandparents. Made a point of telling him that, now that he thought about it. Perfect. He had her number. The knowledge gave him a little thrill.

Tom Norgaard came back from the second war and told a poker group at the Elks that he had run into Jerry's brother, Carlton, in a bar off Times Square. Struck up a conversation with an old boozer in a tweed coat, and the guy turns out to have a Shelby connection. The old boy told Tom how he had been to Montana during the oil boom in '21, how he had sent two sons to Dartmouth, how he was the author of a book and had owned a number of fancy cars. What a rummy wreck. You had to feel sorry for him.

No you didn't, said Jerry, who had walked in and overheard. Everything Carlton said was true. It was also true that he was a drinker, Carlton was. Lost everything to financial misadventure and then the Crash. But he wasn't a liar and he wasn't a *particularly* pitiful creature. There were more pitiful creatures anywhere you might want to look, he said straight to Tom's face.

He would booby-trap that Sharleen. He would rig up some kind of detection system that would confirm her spying. He would plant false information and see if she grabbed the bait.

The system might involve marking old maps in a misleading manner. Or concocting false notes to himself for her to find. Perhaps the use of something nearly invisible—thread or fishing line—to measure whether particular documents had been disturbed. Disturbed and copied by Sharleen the spy.

He got out some paper and pencils and began to jot down a few ideas, a few diagrams. He saw soon enough that a good plan would take him the rest of the afternoon.

9

It is thirty-eight degrees below zero, the kind of cold that wants your breath and runs away with it. Hinges shriek. Leather saddles become iron. A hidden bottle of hooch turns to slush. Ping! A jar of preserves in the back room of the mercantile shatters of its own accord.

This is the day Jerry and Vivian see T.T. Wilkins and five others chopping hay from a freight car. It is blackened hay, strands of marsh grass frozen hard in blocks of mud. They chop it to feed their starving plow horses and milk cows. The hay is abysmal and not enough. Three of the men, including T.T., will sell their farms in the spring to pay for bad hay they fed to animals already half dead.

T.T.'s buyer will be his friend and neighbor Skiff Norgaard, who promises to sell the land back, cheap, when T.T. gets on his feet again. Skiff has somehow survived these years in slightly better shape than most. He planted a strain of wheat that was not so vulnerable to the worms. He got some spatterings of rain that skipped most everyone else.

The hay costs sixty dollars a ton, six times the normal price. They chop it out, split it six ways, and cart it to their shacks and their starving livestock. The animals chew it slowly, crunching ice.

Both of T.T.'s young children have died. His wife has stopped speaking and has gone away, silent, to her sister's in Pennsylvania.

Horses are turned loose and chased off if they return. Some of them survive to wander the prairie like mild derelicts, gnawing on fence posts, gnawing on their own long manes. Railroad tracks snap. Humans freeze, freeze and starve both.

Over west, up by the mountains where the trees are, five Blackfeet are sledded, board-stiff, from a shack in Heart Butte to reservation headquarters, half a day away. Two of them clutch frozen potatoes. They are sledded to headquarters, where their clothes are replaced with dark-blue business suits. The suits arrive inside the government coffins that are stacked against a wall of the big store.

They will be buried in the blue suits in the government cemetery. It is the law. With the ground too cold to break, they will lie for some days in the coffins in a shed. In the blue business suits. White shirts. Bow ties. Hands made to pray.

There was something as final about that winter as there was about the Great War. Some knowledge of how much loss there was to be borne; an end forever to easy sentiment. Now it was down to the last of those who were down to their last—and if they had someplace to go, they went.

When spring came, the farmhouses, the shacks of those once-young people from Minnesota, Illinois, Wisconsin, Canada, stood empty in the season's first mud, doorways agape.

A tongue of a wagon. A spool of rusted wire. The carcass of a pet who had to be shot.

They were called relinquishments, those abandoned homesteads, and they could be bought for a song.

The spring thaws finally came and the small sounds of running water and returning birds were loud against the stunned silence of those plains. The sun shone full and melted the last of the ice, and those who were still there looked around and blinked.

The baby is due in July. Jerry is working full shifts at the railyard now, switching. Good fortune, that job.

He owes his brother Carlton $600, so he works any extra hours he can. The switching is dirty, sometimes difficult, work. Some days he looks greasy and hollow-faced, but there is, in general, a new quickness to his movements and he has gained bulk in his shoulders and upper arms. His hands, battered and blackened around the nails, are not the hands of the man Vivian married, and she is sometimes oddly captivated by the change. She will find herself studying his hands at the dinner table, tantalized. Then she chalks her driftiness up to the baby inside her and does something practical and brisk.

She knows they are leaving this place as soon as they have the money for a move, and that seems part of some new calmness in her head and body. She writes frequently to George and Emily—Emily's daughter, the one who cut off the cat's tail, is now a pretty teenager and engaged to be married to an optician—and she has accumulated hundreds of possible details about a future life in Seattle. This is, in fact, what she did over the brutal winter as the baby grew. She built a whole vision of herself and her family in that city on the coast. Down to the placement of the candles on the mantel.

They would live in a white frame house with green trim and a Japanese maple in the yard. It would be fifteen minutes by streetcar from her brother's, not so close that they'd all be on top of each other. The kitchen looks out on a small backyard that has a lawn, a stone bench, and a trellis for roses. The roses are a mixture of American Beauty, Black Prince, and Paul's Scarlet Climber. It was roses during the worst of the Montana winter, in late January, but then as spring came on, the trellis went away and raised beds of poppies—Peacock, Helen Elizabeth, Sultana—were what Vivian saw from the kitchen window. A wilder, more exuberant, less tidy sight. The poppies were linked to the sounds of streetcar bells. That is, she would see a bed of bending red flower heads, gemlike in the wet sun, and always hear, at the same time, the brisk pinging of the climbing streetcar, so bright and clean it looked lacquered.

At three in the afternoon there would be a soft rain shower, and that's when the children would have their naps. She would brew herself a pot of tea while they slept and would read one of the magazines George had brought over, a *Literary Digest* or a *National Geographic*, or perhaps a chapter or so of a novel she had bought in an old store with mahogany floors and a Tiffany lamp. She would read the novel while the rain washed the city and flowed down the leaded windows of the modest sitting room. And then the rain would stop and a sunburst would push through and the skies would fold back again to blue.

Jerry would come home around six from an office. He would be relaxed and would carry a thick newspaper and an umbrella. He would laugh about some bit of business, a prospect, some small unexpected development regarding a piece of real estate, and she would laugh with him. And then he would talk to the children and read the newspaper in a chair by the grate. The chair was new and had a matching footstool. The material was moss green with a thin brown cross-grain stripe.

Occasionally, not often, Jerry stopped off at the card room of the Metropolitan Hotel after his shift at the depot. He had a smoke and a cup of tea, which the waiter sometimes made medicinal if the day was raw. There were usually a few men he knew in there, and he found the sound of their voices consoling. Vivian had grown quiet. She seemed to speak only to the children, and then only about the practicalities of dressing, eating, school.

One day at the Metropolitan, Jerry struck up a conversation with a couple of fellows he'd noticed driving around in a big Ford truck. Their names were McCloud and Stone. They spoke in soft Texas accents and wore khakis and high boots. Field geologists, they had come to Montana to investigate the Cat Creek field, 150 miles east of Cut Bank, where several gushers had come in. Now they were conducting a reconnaissance of the larger area. They were not young men, but they seemed fresher, more alert, than anyone else around.

The card room was dim and low-ceilinged, with mud-tracked floors. The new men sat at a rickety table by the window, the setting sun lighting their map. Jerry sat with them and watched their fingers move across the paper.

"Oil," he would say as an old man. "Oil has long been my ruling passion."

It began, that long passion, in the late dripping spring of 1920 in the card room of a bare-bones prairie hotel. It began with a chance conversation with a couple of geologists named McCloud and Stone.

They were rather unprepossessing representatives of the breed, not like some of the flashier ones who would show up before long. They weren't hustlers or doodlebug men divining oil with willow sticks and flashing gizmos. They had not consulted fortune-tellers or the boy down south with the x-ray eyes. No, McCloud and Stone were men of science, low-spoken fellows whose instruments of divination were topographical drawings and core samples and exhaustive, detailed logs.

They had thin scholarly shoulders, both of them, and skin that was burnished by the outdoors, weathered, with deep lines fanning from the corners of their eyes.

They had both been in Texas for Spindletop. Stone had gone to Persia in 1908. McCloud had watched the Alamitos No. 1 blow in. And now they were in northern Montana because oil was clearly the coming thing and there clearly wasn't enough of it in the world.

Jerry visited with them casually at first. Then he began to stop almost daily at the Metropolitan, and he began to ask for explanations of their maps, their language. He began to absorb some of what they knew. And as that happened, an odd little urgency grew in him like an important word on the tip of his tongue.

It was a quickening. He became quickened.

He began to see that the parched, scraped ground he walked upon was only the shallow ceiling of another realm. There were layers beneath his feet that descended in stairs and rooms and tunnels to the fiery liquid at the center of the earth.

Sometimes the risers heaved and thin seams of gas-oil-water fell off to the sides and pooled themselves according to the laws of lightness.

The risers, the layers, were called horizons—a term that charmed Jerry with its sweep and hope. "Producing horizons," the geologists said casually, and it seemed the perfect term for what a person might want above all. "Pay horizons," they sometimes said.

He saw black lakes, liquid fortune, resting against chalky walls that displayed the imprints of clams. Lakes that lapped against the slopes of domes. Domes that wore swirling, misty caps of gas.

He studied a well boring that held on its surface the lacy indentation of a sea scallop. McCloud said the scallop was part of a "suite of fossils." The fossils, he said, were "markers for horizons." Domes. Anticlines. Suites. Horizons.

All this beneath the blowing dirt, the crackling grasshoppers.

The structure. Folds and rooms that held or waited for oil. Because oil, they told him one day, is not always fixed, indigenous. It can move. Forced by water or gas, it will move through porous strata until it is caught in a structural trap.

Moving oil. Immigrant oil sliding lazily toward the borders of all those abandoned homesteads, those relinquishments.

And how do you guess where the stuff might be?

"Underground folding is reflected at the surface," McCloud told him in his professor's way. "This is what we know now. This is what we must not forget. No more willow sticks. No more gizmos."

The informed eye will see in broad stretches of land some evidence of the unseen arch, the hidden dome. "Oil on the flanks," they said. On the flanks of the Rockies perhaps, where the Blackfeet Indian reservation lay. Or east and north. North of Shelby near Canada, near the Sweetgrass Hills.

The geologists McCloud and Stone rumbled onto the prairie with their Brunton pocket transits, their hand levels and aneroid barometers, their hand magnifiers and flap hats like Conan Doyle's sleuth. On one of their trips north, they identified surface signs of a shallow dome. They called the hidden dome a name that seemed, to Jerry, the essence of promise—the Sweetgrass Arch.

Oil. Fuel. Blue-black as a crow's wing and warm to the touch. Oil that sends signs of presence to the surface for anyone with an informed eye to see.

They warned him about the false signs. How glaciers a thousand feet thick had moved across northern Montana and how that monstrous plowing ice could crumple shales and sandstones into sharp folds that appeared to be evidence of heavings underneath but were really only fancy frosting. Deceptive glacial squeezes, they said. Beware.

Jerry saw glacial ice as tall as the Woolworth Building scraping across the floor of an ocean gone waterless. He saw the layers, the horizons, gathering themselves in slow arches beneath that ocean floor. He watched the convulsive lift, the curve of the spine, and the way that lovely movement slid oil into the lower regions, where it waited. Pagan lakes of it.

All this beneath the hooves of horses who had chewed on their own manes.

He borrowed a book called *Practical Oil Geology* from McCloud and pored over it, though he pretended, when Vivian asked, to be only casually interested in these men and their theories and the books they loaned out. He began, after the baby was born and all the chaos now of midnight feedings and three children in a small house, to wake himself at five in the morning to read and make notes.

Vivian made her own notes. She made lists from the Sears catalogue. They were inventory lists—detailed listings of household furnishings, garden tools, clothes for a family of five. She was not an acquisitive person by nature. This was something else. She was not planning to order these things. How could she, after all? They were still broke and it looked like another year before the move.

It simply felt good to be going through the motions of a life that wasn't yet onstage. Rehearsing new surroundings.

She would leaf through the catalogue, checking things briskly with a sharpened pencil, coming back with the baby in her arm to make a new decision and write it down. She had headings on the paper for various rooms. The list of contents went under each heading, numbered. Piano, sofa, phonograph.

Jerry asked her once what she was doing—he was puzzled, a little nervous—and she brushed him off. She was tired in her very essence. Her skin seemed to have lost its firmness and color, and she had a faint steady cough that she couldn't seem to shake. They were hers, those lists, that catalogue. She kept them at the back of a cupboard, where the children couldn't get at them.

So she did her lists of furnishings and Jerry did his oil reading. Occasionally they read and made lists at the same time, on those rare evenings when all the children were asleep early. It was as if they were holding conversations with separate groups of people in widely separate rooms.

McCloud and Stone told Jerry they were going to set up a base in Shelby, twenty-five miles east of Cut Bank. The play, they said, was likely to be north of Shelby on the Sweetgrass Arch. They came no more to the Metropolitan card room. Jerry stopped going there too.

Instead, he began to go to Shelby on the one-car train shuttle—the skidoo. Several times a week, after his shift, he climbed aboard the skidoo just to move across land he hadn't really seemed to see for a decade.

He thought about oil. About the structure. He began to imagine himself as some big gun from out of state who might be interested in an oil venture in northern Montana, and he was amazed, then, to realize how cheap this stricken land was, how empty, how so many homesteads had simply been abandoned. And some of them, he now saw, were on the very edges of the possible strikes.

Flying along through the summer evenings, he felt something like joy ruffling up his spine.

He went to Shelby after working ten hours at the railyard, simply to be closer to the idea of oil. To hear the talk. To visit with the geologists, the land men, who drove around the countryside, stalked in their big boots through the café, the hotel lobby. Not so many, that year. But a buzz was in the air. A geologist named Campbell was sinking wells all over the place—practice for his huge verifying hit in the spring of 1922. The one that would turn the country upside down.

Toward the end of the summer, Jerry got a tip and he put his entire paycheck down on two parcels of land near the Sweetgrass Arch.

Two weeks later, $600 was on its way to Carlton with a small flamboyant note of thanks. A week after that, sniffing telegrams from Carlton began to arrive. He wanted to know exactly what Jerry had bought. He wanted to know about the reservation land too. He and some other fellows had the idea of loaning money to the Indians, money they knew wouldn't be paid back, and getting some properties that way. Would Jerry be the intermediary, or should Carlton come out himself and check out the situation? Respond soonest.

He is making a campaign sign and his son Francis is helping him. Vivian looks gray and angry. The signs say Jerry is running for city treasurer in the November election. It would be a modest but steady salary and would get him away from the depot to an office. He would simply resign when they moved to Seattle in the spring.

In an office, he could store information from the land office. His title searches. His list of best bets. His purchase agreements and bills of sale. His records from the reservation loans.

The winter of 1921, and Jerry spends his days in a business suit in the treasurer's office, the railroad behind him forever. He does the city's work. Before that, he does his own work. *At office*

5:30 a.m. And it is his own work he pores over. Maps with pins. Notations. Charts. Reminders to meet with so-and-so. *Favorable wire from Carlton about 320 oil land.*

At home, Vivian sits into those same evenings with George's wife, Emily, who has come from Seattle to help out for a few weeks because Vivian has been so run-down.

Jerry comes home about eleven. *Vivian not well.* The two women are heads in the window.

10

311 W. 88th Street
Apt. B
New York, N.Y.
June 21, 1920

Dear Jerry, Vivian and kiddies,

Greetings to you all from the new song bird of New York!

I am all settled in with Lelia Todd now, and she says I may keep a cot in the parlor while I search for my own lodgings. She is a dear and we are very congenial for the most part, tho she has of course become a professional whistler and has many demands on her time so she occasionally becomes impatient with me.

Thank you so much for the handkerchiefs. They are lovely and it was sweet of you to remember my birthday, though I try not to remember it myself because of the "Spectre of Advancing Age" and so much to accomplish yet before I can launch my singing career the way I should like to.

I met this week with the Aeolian-Vocalian record people and they said they will send for me and I will make a test record shortly! They charge $20 for the test record because they are taking a chance on an unknown voice, but the manager told me, Miss Malone you have an absolutely *lovely* voice and it is very possible we will sign a contract with you. I have to sing several times for test records so they can find out what I can do.

I am practicing very long hours, and my voice is much rounder and less hard than it was last year and I sing with much more finish of course, hit a High C now with perfect ease and real beauty. For the test record I shall sing "The Volga Boat Song" by de Gorgoza. I have recently added to my repertoire three new songs: "Life" by Curran, "Vale" by Russell and "The Star" by Rogers. In the past month I have learned five French songs, five arias and a group of English songs. I am taking a test tomorrow for church work and will probably have that as a settled thing. Sang for a church in New Jersey a week ago because a girl became ill with the grippe and got $5 and expenses and could have had another church if I wanted it. I expect to learn the score of six operas this year. If you think English is hard to memorize, imagine memorizing a whole opera in Italian! Quite a task, believe me.

Lelia and I both practice in the mornings though it is sometimes very difficult because whistling can be heard very well from behind closed doors. I could almost believe that a country meadow full of larks existed in Lelia's bedroom. She is very enthusiastic in her practice. Also the people above us are a "merry band" and have gin parties day in and day out. They do not rise before one p.m. on many days and then they start in. As Lelia says, This is not the outskirts of St. Paul, Daisy Lou, and I have to agree. There is every kind of person here you can think of, and many of them very smart-looking and fast. To be perfectly truthful, St. Paul has begun to seem like a dream. Shall I tell you a secret? I feel as tho my real life is just beginning and it is such a comfort to know with certainty that my life's path is an Artistic Career.

That is interesting news about the oil explorations. I shall keep my fingers crossed!

Your loving sister,
Daisy Lou

She waits in the shadowy wings with six other women who look her age but are certainly younger. The air is stale with cigar smoke and the dust from the huge old curtain; the wooden floor is scuffed and gouged. All the young women except Daisy Lou are hatless—modern and smart with their bobbed hair and red mouths. Something in their light agitated voices sounds like too many glasses carried on a tray. Daisy Lou wears a hat and cloth gloves that smell of rose water and talc.

Those who aren't talking appear to be mouthing words silently. One stops to gargle water from a small paper cup. They all clutch sheaves of sheet music.

Daisy stands at the end of the line, a little bit apart. She watches the others and feels like a governess, all muted and tucked; long hair rolled and pinned; conscious now that her clothes are a few years out-of-date. Her face is unlined, pretty but unadorned. No rouge on that mouth. She closes her eyes from time to time as if in prayer.

They hear the final triumphant chirp of a soprano on the other side of the big curtain and then the girl is scampering back among them, her face flushed and hopeful. A brief bleak patter of clapped hands somewhere out there. They move up a notch. Daisy and five others in the dim wings.

Daisy is thinking about her hair and about God. She wonders again whether she should get a bob; whether a bold and light-hearted look would help her musical career. She is asking God to be at her side during the coming ordeal and trying to wipe out the accelerating ripples of panic by concentrating fiercely on her song.

To encourage the proper emotion in her voice, Daisy likes to conjure a small story or a picture to go with the words. A tableau vivant. Strange images come to her. When she sings "A Spirit Flower," for instance, she sees her mother's white hair like a fan, and then the young Dr. Sheehan on a block of marble, an iris sprouting from his chest. And then she has the appropriate feeling of beautiful grief.

This will all have to be conveyed with her voice alone, without the usual help from gestures and movements, because those men down there in the smoky auditorium have their eyes closed. She sees that as soon as she begins to sing. They won't watch but will simply listen, trying to imagine how the singer will sound on a phonograph record. She could be a Hottentot for all it mattered to a phonograph record.

Shafts of light from three small oily windows at the far end of the high room hold moving dust and smoke, make it gold, and stretch it dusty, smoky, and gold onto the heads of the three men who sit at the foot of the stage, legs crossed, fingers weary around the stubs of cigars. It is the end of the day.

"Okay, doll," one of them calls up in a high gravelly voice. "What'll it be?"

"I should like to sing 'A Spirit Flower,'" she announces in the mellifluous speaking voice she's been practicing for the stage.

"*Parrot* Flower!" His voice is a squawk. He appears to be interrogating the man next to him.

"Spirit." Her voice echoes in the big room. "Spirit."

He heaves a sigh of capitulation. "Belt it out, my girl," he says. "Let's get outa here."

She clears her throat and clutches her gloved hands to her midriff for support, fixing her eyes on a point far behind their heads, on the windows that let in the dirty light that fills her eyes, pushing everything else—the room, the barking men—away. The pianist begins. The men close their eyes. Daisy sees Dr. Sheehan on light-filled marble, an iris growing from his lovely cold chest.

"My heart was frozen even as the earth / That covered thee forever from my sight," she sings, articulating each syllable perfectly, placing her tone so that she will not quaver.

She imagines that she is placing the song directly on a phonograph record, to be preserved for posterity—her voice as it exists at this very moment. What a thought that was! It was a way of stopping time, the way a painting or photograph did, while somehow keeping it still alive and moving too. A person hearing her on the phonograph record for the first time—her brother Jerry in Montana, say—would not receive her all in a piece, as he would in a painting or a photograph, but would hear her step by step, the way you knew a person in life. Gradually unfurling.

"All thoughts of happiness expired at birth. / Within me naught but black and starless night." She drops her voice to a hush. Her eyes close. She could almost weep.

Someone is talking. Two of them are talking. The mumbles make their way into her thoughts, like taps at a window, and give her a little jolt. Her eyes fly open. The voices march in and push her song aside with dirty hands. They are talking, these men, while she sings for them! Huddled, talking among themselves, they share murmurs, a laugh. She could be the charwoman. A burst of louder laughter comes from beneath their tipped heads.

The one with the tiny bow tie waves his arm suddenly, as if he is hailing a cab. "Whoa there, doll. You're in the wrong place. This ain't a temperance meeting. Enough spirit we got already. Stop with the spirit. You got anything from musical comedy?"

Sept. 30, 1920

Dear Jerry and Vivian and dear children,

Well, the Aeolian people sent for me again yesterday, and I shall soon have a test record at last! My friend Lelia, the whistler, will be on it as well. I have been to a number of auditions and oh! it is a grueling business. At one audition, I sang "A Spirit Flower" by Campbell Tipton because I feel it is absolutely right for my range and also it is so very moving. The man who ran the machinery told me my voice was the most natural sound he had ever heard. However the men who decide about the test records were very difficult and I discovered they were looking for selections that were more frivolous and cheerful. One of the men said to me, "Miss Malone, my fear is that you are too spiritual for musical comedy." I believe he is right and I am not ashamed of the fact.

Lelia and I performed "The Nightingale's Lament." It is such a good study to hear your own voice, because then I can see all I want to undo and perfect. I do hope I shall have a test record soon and my voice will be coming to you in Montana in the form of a phonograph record.

I am taking stage dancing and learning how to bow, do you know it is an art all its own, and how to pose and I have to stand before mirrors and make myself look artistic. If you were here, you would laugh me to noon, but believe me, you can't go on the stage and be *natural*, my entrance is timed, my exit, every detail studied. Of course I should have had this training years ago, but didn't get the opportunity with Mother's illness.

I sang at a Congregational church in Summit, New Jersey, yesterday. My selections were "The World Is Waiting for the Sunrise" by Seitz and two Schubert songs. A pianist played "Grande Polka de Concert" by Bartlett. I had numerous ovations and they have asked me to return at my earliest convenience.

I shall cross my fingers for your election, Jerry. When you are treasurer, could you send me a small pile of money? (That's a joke.)

Love to all of you,
Daisy Lou

A neatly dressed young man sold liquor to the people upstairs in white ribboned boxes, the kind that might have held dozens of long-stemmed roses. Daisy sometimes spoke with him on the front steps of the brownstone if she happened to be going or coming at the time. His name was Brendan Furey and he was a man in his middle twenties with springy dark hair and innocent eyes and the continual blue shadow of a beard. He held the boxes as if they were light with flowers.

One day he told Daisy Lou a story about four girls from White Plains who drank bay rum and perfume, anything they could get their hands on, for the alcohol; drank such lethal stuff that one of them died and the rest were taken to the hospital half blind. Then he told her how Volstead had wreaked so much disaster and heartache you couldn't believe it. And then he lifted the lid of one of the boxes and showed her the rows of brown bottles inside. Bona fide Canadian Scotch, he said. No poison in these.

She felt for a moment as if he had said something lewd to her, shown her dirty playing cards. And then she looked at his young blue-shadowed face and thought, He's Irish and an immigrant scrambling for a foothold. He does what he must. His face was so handsome and open and alert.

Just then, a long Packard rounded the corner and drove slowly down the street, window open and in the window a man with a hat pulled low. All they could see of his face was a chin and a cigarette. Brendan Furey gave an amazing little jump—the same large twitch that would, not so many months later, mean he'd come to his bad end—and it rocked the length of his body and made the bottles ping softly against each other.

"Smell these," he hissed through a tight smile. "Smell these and smile. Give me a kiss on the cheek."

Startled, Daisy Lou simply stared at him. Then she stared at the man in the slow car. She could hear Furey's fast breath, smell its sudden sourness. She bent her head like a queen and inhaled deeply. "*Tea* roses!" she said loudly, delightedly. "For *me.*" Then she stretched up to kiss his cool blue-shadowed cheek, and as she did it, as the car slowly disappeared around the corner and Brendan Furey's eyes blinked blankly and she heard the faintest trembling of glass, she had the sudden instinctive knowledge that this particular combination of danger, adrenaline, and pantomime was what people meant when they said they were madly in love.

Jan 2, 1921

Dear Jerry and Vivian and children,

Happy New Year to you, and thank you so much for the little writing kit. It is dear.

I imagine you all in a cozy cabin in the swirling blizzards of the plains, with a crackling fire and the scent of holiday food! I hope you are warm and happy with one another.

It is raining and snowing here. Very gloomy today, the autos throwing up huge piles of dirty snow and the horses sliding around. I saw one lorry with a fallen horse and it broke my heart. Lelia has gone to St. Paul for the holidays so the flat is mine. She is suffering from a bad romance. He was a young florist who came often to our house. A little more than a month ago, he simply disappeared. He told Lelia he was going to the corner for cigarettes and never returned. I did not know they were sweethearts, but Lelia insists they were, and she fears he has come to a bad end. She does not keep the best company, has become very interested in jazz and goes to clubs with young men, a different one every night. I fear she is squandering her musical talents. She is a disappointment to me. However, she wants me to stay on in her flat indefinitely because she needs help with the rent, and so I shall.

So now it is another year, and time for reflection.

Our test record is out and it is fine. I will send you a copy when they give me one. There are three different whistlers on it, including Lelia. Our selection is "The Nightingale's Lament." It seems after all my talk and all the promises from Aeolian Co. that there will be no contract for three more months. It is a continual disappointment to have to wait and to fight here, every step. I have had to learn so much and take all kinds of disappointments, they promise and then don't live up to the promise, etc., but slowly, I am getting along. I am a better woman for it.

Some of the people in this profession are pretty bad. Mister Ward at a company that shall remain nameless called me in his office presumably to sign a record contract, locked the door and tried to kiss me. I looked him straight in the eye and told him, Mister Ward if you are buying voices, mine is for sale, but if you are buying bodies mine is *not* for sale. He got terrible red and said maybe I wasn't hungry enough yet and I turned on my heel and walked out. Oh! I get sick of the whole business sometimes but something *makes* me keep on. Advice from me, having no kiddies. Don't shield your girl from hard knocks. I only wish I had been compelled as you boys were to face life when I was a child, it wouldn't be so hard now.

The people upstairs have been at it now for three days. You would not believe what you see right on the streets here from poison alcohol, people losing their eyesight or the use of their nerves. I saw a young woman, blind I believe and shaking, drinking spirits out of a Mason jar in a corner of Pennsylvania Station. What would Mother and Papa think if they were alive, I wonder! This world would shock them and break their hearts I think and they are better off out of it.

My this is a gloomy letter. Don't let the kiddies read it! I am just blue because it is the holidays and I have no home it seems and my record contract is so long in coming. But I have not lost hope, don't worry! I *will* keep on. (Perhaps I won't mail this after all.)

Your loving sister,
Daisy Lou.

P.S. Someday I will get a break and some money and then I will visit you in Montana.

If the church was out of the city, in Queens or up the Hudson, say, she wrapped a roll and perhaps some chicken left from dinner, or a hard-boiled egg, and put it in her small valise with her music. She also carried several folded rags to remove mud or dust from her shoes when she got to whichever church wanted her that day.

She had bobbed her hair but wore a hat over it and she still reached up, suspicious, to make sure her new hair had not become mussed or disheveled in a way that would make her look flyaway or cheap. Dressing, she fixed her belt in exactly the right position and draped the bodice just so over the belt, stretching to see the back of herself in the long mirror.

When she tended to her physical self in a slow and detailed manner, she felt tended by someone else. She adjusted her collar, her hat, in a proprietary and loving way, pretending that her hands were a mother's hands. She smiled in the mirror for her father.

Whenever she bought a piece of clothing, she made it a very long and involved process, even for something minor like a camisole. She would find clerks who liked to fuss and take time. When she had a dress made, once a year, many fittings became necessary because Daisy craved the feeling of someone attending to her. Seams had to be ripped out and done again. The hemline went up an inch, down two. And the ripping and resewing only stopped when the dressmaker lost all patience and called a halt to Daisy's fussing.

The test record was all whistlers, with an occasional soprano as accompaniment. Three different whistlers, including Lelia, and then Daisy in one song, and another soprano in another.

She and Lelia drew wooden chairs close to the machine. The man who operated it lowered the stylus gently to the heavy disc. Rhythmic scratchings first, and then the wavering sound of violins coming to them, it seemed, from the past or a faraway room. A waltz. Then a bell, like a church bell in a distant green glade. Through and around all this floated the traffic from the street outside, a cop's shrill whistle, the shouts of lorry drivers. Lelia squinted her eyes and bent closer to the phonograph as the sleepy flutter of her first whistled warblings began.

This kind of whistling, this bird mimicry, was a skill. It required that the whistler pucker, blow, and flutter the tongue all at once. Now the soprano voice, Daisy Lou's, began the refrain, "Once again… Once again…" And the bird grew ecstatic—warbling in and out, over and under the tune, its voice like burbling water. Daisy was entranced.

The Woodland Flirt. The Bird at the Waterfall. The Bird and the Saxophone. Beyond the Clouds. Warblings at Eve.

Lelia had become a full-fledged flapper who wore makeup, smoked, drank spirits, and loudly espoused free love. Though Daisy wouldn't have put it in so many words, aspects of Lelia now appalled her. Aspects of both her personality and her musicality. After the florist-bootlegger disappeared, Lelia got fast and edgy; couldn't slow down and smelled like begonias and gin. When she whistled, she got a very businesslike look on her face, a tough little foot-out stance, blotted her lips and wetted them and warmed up, cutting eyes at the technicians, stubbing out a cigarette.

A few practice trills. Then the soggy little orchestra and Daisy Lou singing "once again," in a frail nineteenth-century parlor voice, and this tough Lelia doing a fierce warbling bird for all she was worth and asking the man afterward when the thing was going to come out for crying out loud.

Which Daisy Lou wondered about too, because she was running out of money. She needed a contract, more church work, something. She was certain that her fortunes would take an upward turn if she could just discover the proper mental attitude; tap her subterranean layers.

11

Carlton arrived on the No. 2 with a woman, the tearoom hostess named Fitzi. They had been together two years now. His wife, Ruth, wouldn't give him a divorce; wouldn't charge him with adultery or abandonment.

Fitzi was a tall blonde and wore a very stylish city suit and lip rouge. Jerry had somehow expected a delicate cold little thing, not this rather formidable lazy-eyed woman with a deep, extravagant laugh. Ruth was much prettier. But this woman, as soon as you began talking to her, gave off a wry worldliness, a calm and sexy modernity. Was that what Carlton couldn't live without?

Carlton is made for the twenties. He loves this decade already. The hedonism and hope of it.

He looks much the same as he did two years ago—was it only that long ago?—at his mother's funeral. Perhaps a bit more slim, more assured. He gives the impression—in his dress, his imperial manner, the edge of dissipation in his face—that he is always in the thick of it. He has become a heavy, steady drinker. At this point in his life, alcohol actually confers exhilaration and has not yet become a ritualized summoning of it and then compensation for its nonappearance.

He is, after all, a young man still. Thirty-five years old.

Here he is with the Paramour, as Daisy refers to her.

They stay in the Metropolitan in separate rooms, and Carlton introduces Fitzi to Jerry's children as his friend and business partner. He has become worldly enough not to be flagrant.

They play Daisy Lou's test record that night for Carlton and the Paramour.

It arrived a few months earlier and the children were waiting for it. They couldn't contain themselves as Jerry removed the packaging with great deliberation. Their aunt on a phonograph record! Will it be her real voice? Will we be able to hear it whenever we want to? They pawed at their slow father.

It arrived broken. The children's faces emptied, all the eagerness blasted away. Francis, the one who had been most excited, broke into frank sobs.

Jerry fixed it with glue but it sounds, the crack, like a schoolmaster's cruel yardstick.

The children have to explain to Carlton that the voice, running faintly behind the rampant bird whistles, is his sister's.

Two days after Carlton arrives, he and Jerry and Fitzi take the train east to Lewistown, where they catch the spur north to the Cat Creek field. A long trip over scrub prairie, but the surprising thing is the number of automobiles they see making their way along a muddy track in the distance. A dozen at least, carrying people to see the field.

It is odd, contorted country, shallow hills and gullies dotted with low jack pine, the black tree line of the Musselshell River a mile or so away. They travel over emptiness, the train rumbling into a big silence, as the sun turns red and slowly falls.

On the other side of one last shallow rise, a full-blown little city, bright with lights, sits there under the first stars.

Jerry thinks of a walk he took years ago, during the time when he had to come home from college, his mind paralyzed.

He walked out to the edge of town where it was heavy and lush, full of the roar of frogs and crickets, that thick Midwestern screen of sound. He walked along the path they took, as children, to the pond to swim.

The air that evening made him remember a time when he was very small, almost a baby, digging in the dirt with a large silver spoon in a beam of such gentle warmth that it seemed to melt him to the dirt he sat on. It had touched the back of his neck and moved through his back and through his hands and flashed off the silver spoon and made all the smells mix—the dirt, the sleepy air, the hollyhocks along the porch, his full diaper. That is how the air smelled as he walked in the heavy-lidded evening to the pond.

And then through the trees a flicker, much larger than a firefly, and a distant frail shout. Walking slowly around the last bend, he saw an entire glowing party on the far side of the pond. Carts festooned with lanterns, a half dozen small campfires, a trickle of guitar music, a high-pitched laugh, all of it crisp and dazzling, all of it in some way its own little fire bursting from the fading day. A traveling road show. Gypsies. Vagabonds of some banded and colorful kind. Fairies.

Well, there is something of that at Cat Creek. Derricks as tall as buildings are lit up bright. Fires burn in shallow barrels and the firelit figures of men move among them. Straggly rows of tar-paper shacks throw light from small windows, sounds from open doors.

There is a long building that seems some kind of headquarters. A post office with a frayed flag. The scattered shacks. All of it is lit up and alive and dirty.

Children dart here and there, nocturnal and shadowy. Two women pass by, arm in arm, bright-clothed and languorous. A tall horse with no saddle or bridle wanders among the bustle like a bored constable.

And around and among all this, the clank and groan of moving iron, the sound of oil being pulled from the earth. And beyond the moaning machinery, more derricks, spectral sentinels, blazing on the border between the rowdy little camp and the huge dark night.

Jerry gazes around at it all and feels his blood jump.

He led Carlton and Fitzi around the place, giving an excited little lecture to them on the kinds of equipment these people used; how they kept drilling-depth records, how they classified samples; what kinds of oil they were finding in the area, and what the relative merits of the oil types were. He mentioned his long and detailed talks with McCloud and Stone, and when he did, he could imagine the geologists' surprise at how much information he had managed to absorb.

Jerry wanted Carlton to know that he, Jerry, had some expertise. That he knew the oil business. That he knew where to put the money Carlton seemed to have. He and Carlton would be partners. Carlton was Jerry's ticket to the coming boom.

As if on a whim, Carlton buttonholes a young fellow who turns out to be the head of a drilling crew. The fellow invites them to the combination saloon and store and school, and they drink with him and his friends far into the night. Fitzi is directed to a family home that takes overnight guests.

With two drinks in him, Carlton takes charge. He portrays himself as a fellow from back East with some money burning a hole in his pocket, someone looking for a venture; and so they all pay attention to him.

Jerry, of course, knows much more about the field and about oil in general and he asks detailed questions that occasionally cause one of the company men to look at him with surprise. One of them asks if he is a geologist.

And Carlton picks it up in true Carlton form. My geologist, he says, with a small knowing nudge in Jerry's ribs. My field man, he says. Carlton has appropriated the place. He buys drinks, makes jokes, alludes to itchy money and city friends. By the time they stagger off to a dormitory, exhausted and drunk, Carlton is calling the men by their first names, their nicknames. See ya, Ross! Remember what we talked about, Red!

Jerry feels as if he has missed something—some part of the conversation, the exchange. As if some kind of transaction occurred before his unseeing eyes. They have talked through the evening about where the next drilling will be. What kind of capital an independent guy needs to raise to drill. What kinds of syndicates are being formed and how they are looking for investors. All of this Jerry understands.

There was a quart jar of oil on the table and someone brought up the subject of viscosity, and Jerry was able to illuminate the table on that score. He understands viscosity.

What he doesn't understand is how Carlton can still make him feel so furious; so bleary and unreal. How Carlton can, in a few strokes, seem to gulp up Jerry's life; take it over; drown it.

On his cot, Carlton already snoring beside him, Jerry takes long deep breaths. I choose to ignore him, he thinks. I choose to let his voice fade, his presence. I give him up. I give up my own poison, let it drip out the ends of my fingers, and think instead about that jar of oil. About the way it slides back and forth, the essence of richness. The emollient of the ages. The balm of Gilead. He hears the thick dark river before he sinks into it, and it is his river and it carries him wherever he wants to go.

12

SHE CAME awake the way that country did after the bad years.

Jerry arrived from his office one day and found Vivian sitting on the front step, shelling peas with a neighbor. She looked up and, for the first time in months, seemed rested and alive. There was a slight crackle to her—a look on her face that was hard to read. Part humorous, part relieved, part angry. She was fully present.

Sometime during the summer, her cough had finally disappeared and the color had come back to her face. Tip, the baby, was amiable and a sleeper, and perhaps that was part of the reason.

Also, she had begun to go to mass at dawn several mornings a week, and maybe that had something to do with her new energy. It was a mystery to Jerry, the sight of his wife's back in the early morning, her solitary walk to the little church. He sipped coffee and watched her out the window in the limpid morning light. He tried to imagine what she prayed for, what she got.

What did he really know about her? What did she tell the priest in that dark box? What did she feel on her tongue when she took the host? He would never really know—only that something in it seemed to lighten her, to relieve her of herself.

On the day he found her shelling peas and giving him that crackly here-I-am look, they had a long argument about Carlton.

"Carlton is a hustler and a con man," Vivian said, two points of red appearing on her cheeks. "And his scheme to get land out from under the Indians is despicable. After those hard years they went through, the same way anyone went through them? To make them loans they won't repay?"

"It's money," Jerry said. "They don't have to take the money."

"It's a trick," Vivian snapped. "It is playing on their hopes in order to take everything they have left. Carlton and his high-roller friends!" She spit the words out. "How can you be part of anything like that?"

It went on for some time. And though Jerry felt the vehemence in his own voice, his impatience with her swift and easy sentiments, he felt relief running beneath their sharp voices. Relief. They were exchanging something.

He agreed to detach himself from Carlton's loan scheme. Carlton could handle his own loans if he felt compelled to make them. Carlton would not be part of their life.

That evening, she showed him a letter from her brother George in Seattle. The letter said that his hours had been cut back at the print shop and they would have to move to a smaller place. A flat. That he was having some trouble with his eyes and prospects weren't as bright in Seattle as they had seemed.

She showed Jerry the letter with no comment and put it on the sideboard, where she cast worried looks at it from time to time.

She was awake. The children picked up on her mood and argued roundly with each other, fervently, and were sent to bed. All day, the house had been louder, janglier, and Jerry was so lightened by it all that he had to take a long walk before sleep.

He walked the paths of little Cut Bank, dark between the scattered houses. There was a fitful warm wind. He thought about the night he and Vivian and George ate their picnic on the prairie, the stakes of their homesteads fresh in the ground. How the brother and sister, children of a widowed mother clear back in Cleveland, had seemed orphaned in some way. They had four brothers and sisters back East, but Vivian and George were the only wanderers, the only ones who left. A sister once referred to them as Hansel and Gretel, and the others picked it up.

Jerry knew a few details like that, but little more. His wife and her brother seemed cut off, set adrift, in some manner even more irrevocable than his own break from his childhood home.

Maybe that was the source of the great quiet that could sometimes overtake Vivian—that she felt herself to have no other home than Cut Bank. No place to go back to, should she want to. Maybe the fact that she had adventured, had taken a large chance, was also the source of her exuberance when it appeared. Her flashes of generosity and wit and anger. Her ability to laugh until the tears appeared in her eyes.

After supper, her fingers impatiently repinning a strand of hair, she ventures one more comment. "Carlton," she says, jabbing the hairpin, "is a horse's…"

Maudie wanders into the kitchen, wanting milk.

"Is a horse's," Vivian says, "head."

And she and Jerry both burst into laughs because of the clumsy feint, and then because the image makes them remember the night Vivian refused to sit on the head of a horse that was fallen and tangled in its own harness.

They were courting. The horse ran away with the buggy and turned it over and got itself all tangled in the tack. Not injured badly, just fallen and knotted up.

Jerry and Vivian ran up to it. Some bit of bad wisdom came upon Jerry, the town fellow, and he drew himself up and pointed at the animal. "Sit on its head while I get this harness off," he ordered her. "That is what you do. Sit on its head so it can't see."

"I will not sit on that animal's head," Vivian replied, quite calmly. "That is not what a person does in a situation of this sort."

And she walked off a ways to watch Jerry dart at the fallen horse, pull a strap, pull another, dart away, until finally the sweaty animal shook itself to its feet and loped off to town, three miles away.

"It is not what a person does…" Jerry mimicked her gently, in a high voice. And she pushed at him, then took his arm, and the two of them walked back to town in the night, very slowly, happily dragging the sweaty harness.

The day after their argument about Carlton, a Canadian offered Jerry a decent price for their homesteads. Jerry invested the money in property north of Shelby, near the area where the geologists were now scouting around, and resold it a few weeks later for $3,000.

That evening before dinner, he handed the entire amount to Vivian and told her it was hers. They could move to Seattle right away. They could stay and see what this country was going to do. The decision, he said, was hers.

She gave him a long, unreadable look and put the money in a sock, far back in a drawer. She did not talk about it. For three days, she said nothing.

On the afternoon of the third day, she sent Francis and Maudie out to play and bundled the baby into the big buggy. She negotiated the rutted paths to Jerry's office, parked the buggy, retrieved the baby, and went inside. She wore her best hat.

Jerry greeted her quizzically, shoved his papers aside, and invited her to sit. She removed two packets of money from her pocketbook. One had a letter around it, which she unfolded and slid across the desk. The letter was to her brother George. It said she was sending him a money order for $500, to use however he wanted. It was a no-interest loan, repayable at his convenience. She and Jerry were having a run of luck, the letter said, and they could afford the loan and were happy to do it. The tone of the letter was light and easy.

She gave the rest of the money to Jerry and suggested he get it into the bank. She suggested that they might want to invest some of it in land, since the land game—she used those very words—seemed to be picking up.

He knew, the moment she said it, exactly what he would buy. The geologist Campbell was drilling holes all over the place, north of Shelby. Campbell was after something. He had a hunch.

Jerry would buy two farms he knew about. He would resell them, reserving the mineral interests, which he'd lease to Campbell or one of the others who were sinking money and drill bits into that land. He'd reserve twelve or fifteen percent for himself. Who knew when someone was going to hit? Who knew which day a millionaire would be born?

He took the money from Vivian and pretended to adjust the little cap on the baby's head, because he felt overwhelmed and without words. He looked at his wife. There was a sheen of moisture on her broad forehead. She brushed her fingers along her hairline, smoothed her grave eyebrows, tipped her head at him as if she'd just asked a long question.

13

THEY DRIVE north and east from Cut Bank, the roads following section lines—four miles, then a right angle, four miles, another ninety-degree turn—and so they zigzag their way across the countryside. The day is rain-washed and smells young. The sky is the color of flax.

The Ford keeps threatening to slide off the drying road, has done it more than once already, so Jerry and Skiff Norgaard have mud-caked shoes, mud on their pants, flecks of mud on the sleeves of their stiff white shirts. The women, Vivian and Alice, wear their motoring costumes—large, light-colored coats, men's hats with veils drawn down against the assault of flying dirt. The men wear goggles.

Alice and Skiff are a rather solemn couple most times—young and blond, with straight Norwegian mouths and hair, a slow way of talking—but today they seem given, both of them, to shouts, even laughter.

A hawk wheels above them. Two hawks. They wheel above the bullet pops of the auto as it creeps across thirty-five empty miles on that wayward, hard-cornered road, the laughter and shouts of its riders floating up through the blue.

The countryside from Cut Bank moves in long flat undulations for ten miles, say, as the hawks fly, and then you're at the shoreline of an ancient sea, and the prairie drops down to the floor. Where the oil is—Campbell's discovery well and the others now, the derricks popping up all over the countryside. At one of those derricks, a young couple will be married today, and that's where the Ford is aimed.

The ocean. A sea. Its floor. Covered with glacial debris and then soil and scrub grass, true; but a real ocean floor it now seems to Jerry, and to Vivian too, with the heartbreaking shell marks of clams pressed into the sandstone. Seashells scattered through the sediments of the Sweetgrass Arch. And in the traps, in the deformations, in the folds and the faults—yes it is possible, yes it is true!—the now and future richness of big-time oil.

They have launched themselves off the rim, the shoreline. Lots of smoke from the brake, a sashaying motion of the car, small screams. The gumbo is tacky on its surface, there is a little grab; but a few inches down it's still grease. Their movement is headlong, too fast for comfort, because the road takes a hard left at the bottom, a hard corner north. Miss the corner and you end up, in twenty or thirty yards, at a fence and some outbuildings belonging to a bachelor farmer named Wally Swenson.

More than a few drivers have plowed through the fence. Swenson has a big wooden sign tacked to it with a yellow arrow pointing left, as if anyone might wonder.

Why is the solitary track placed so that the turn occurs just at Swenson's? Who knows? But there goes the auto, careening, sending out small shouts, the brash sun flashing off its fenders. The driver makes a strategic decision to leave the road for the grass just before the curve, and they get a grip and make the turn.

They stop, giddy, and take a break. The ladies shake out their veils, the men scrape their shoes again, and they all have a glass of cider from a big jar wrapped in a blanket against the shock of the road. Skiff sits on the running board and pulls a happy Alice onto his knee.

The latticed tower against the sky. Two figures climbing it and a crowd below, chins tipped up. Jerry and Vivian, Skiff and Alice, greet their neighbors, their acquaintances of a decade and more. Some new people here, some oil people, but not so many. Most of these people they know—the ones who came in the land rush and remained after the worst.

At the Round Lake picnic last summer, Vivian watched her children, Francis and Maudie, throw rocks in the water. They stood by a boy with a fishing pole. When the boy turned sideways, Vivian jumped a little. He is an old man, she said to herself. The boy's chest was sunken; his shoulders were stooped. The way he held himself was closed and stoic; brutalized. He had none of the extravagant energy of a child but was already hunched and guarded. Francis skipped a rock far out onto the water. The sunken-chested boy watched it the way an old cat fastens her eyes on a jumping piece of yarn, no longer able to care.

You saw that look on others after the worst years. But not today. Not this early summer of '22. Today it is as if these people have been dipped in something that makes them young again.

It's a slow climb with many stops for the nuptial couple—the Donlans' daughter, the wilder one, and a young geologist with an Oklahoma twang and oil-field stories that make you see money on trees. Eight million paid to the Osage Indians down there, for their ground, for the oil. Indians! And who's to say this land didn't hold the same and it wouldn't be Indians with the bills dropping out of their pockets, it would be you, and you.

Look at Flanagan over there with his vest open. He hung on. He shot his horses and ate canned fish and rabbits and wormy flour, and Standard Oil just made him, two weeks ago, a rich man. That sorry piece of land was just a lid over what they wanted, and they paid a bundle to see the contents.

There is an excited pitch to the conversations. Laughter. A new lightness. With each long step the bride and groom take up the wooden crossbars, the spirits of the crowd lift like helium balloons. All the little clots of people in their driving costumes and muddy suits are talking excitedly. Everyone has had a blast of luck, or expects to. Someone begins to play a clarinet.

That group of men there? They were there when the Mid-Northern Howling No. 1 came in a few weeks ago, a gusher. And the story gets told all over again. Three more feet—no, two and a half—nothing really, the bit down just a notch and then, Glory! all that gas-compressed oil fuming out of the top. That second or so when it plumed against the sky, an emblem of pure release, and then the viscous black rain dropping on their hats, their faces, the palms of their outstretched hands.

They tell it over again, lovingly, in second-by-second detail. And someone chimes in with a bad British accent, mimicking a big gun with one of the companies. "Nasty business, fellows. Nasty business." He flicks the phantom oil off his face. "A nasty business." Then they all chime in, the line countlessly retold: "But all in the game, what!" And they laugh just as hard as they did the first time.

And then their voices move into the realm of sober delectation, secrets, reverence. The Ellis formation. The upper Ellis. The Sweetgrass Arch. The Structure. Glacial squeezings. Domes. Commercial deposits. Producing horizons. Strike and dip. Flanks. Penetration. Flow.

There are the motoring costumes and the suits, but there is also khaki. Khaki everywhere. It is the look. Even for women. Khaki breeches with laced bottoms. Here they are on some of the women. Everyone suddenly an explorer, a geologist, on safari.

That group over there talks radio with Nate Zimmerman. What else? He has the only radio receiving set for miles. Made it himself, and he says he's going to construct a portable one that can go in an auto!

A few weeks ago, Jerry spent most of a day in Shelby, shouldering through the crowds of oilmen, land men, leasehounds; through the lines at the land office, the lines at the Gingham Café, the Log Cabin. Everything crowded, jumbled; wayward autos and someone standing out in the street once in a while to try to direct.

The actual physical town was still just a scramble along the tracks, a scattering up on the hill. But it had taken on the roiling quality of a carnival midway. Shouts. Men in suits flying out of meeting rooms, the "card and soft drink" room at the Sullivan. A deal done, a hot tip, these men running down the street to the land office to file.

Groups of men fresh in from the fields, dust-covered, huddled over maps.

A day of that, then a few hours to kill before the skidoo back to Cut Bank. And so he joined a couple of others at Nate's for a demonstration of the crystal set. They said he had caught radio waves from Los Angeles and, on one splendid night, a phonograph concert from Denver.

This night it was KDYS from Great Falls, just new through the air to Zimmerman's rectangular box with all the wires sprouting out of it. Black steel plates on it with knobs and dials, three electric light bulbs, a group of big batteries, and, on his rooftop, silly-looking wires stretched between a couple of poles.

They had a drink of good Canadian Scotch brought over by the Williams kid and sat in a half circle around the box while Rachel Zimmerman made them sandwiches and cast long patient looks at the thing and at her husband, whose face was absolutely alive. They heard Eddie's K.O. Orchestra come wavering through the air and two xylophone numbers by an eight-year-old named Harold Nichols, who played "Homesick" and "Thru the Night." Then Miss Gladys Spooner sang "Smile Through Your Tears" and "For You Alone," and a man came on to read a paper titled "The History and Uses of Copper."

Jerry had to leave before the copper man was finished talking, and he did so quietly. He left the three men, and now Rachel too, with their heads dipped toward the receiving set, their faces touched by the small steady electric light of the bulbs, mesmerized. They murmured good-byes but kept their eyes on the sound.

And what did he think about as he rode the skidoo back through the night to Cut Bank? Was it some sense that he had been surrounded by something—voices, people, ghosts—all this time and they had just been invisible and now they could be pulled out of the air?

Did he feel intruded upon by all those voices in the air? Too crowded? No. Not then and not for quite a long time.

As he flew through the cool June night, he felt that the presence of the radio confirmed, somehow, the presence of oil. The thought came clear and gave him a trickle of joy.

One couldn't just believe in the surfaces, whether it was a section of scrub grass or air that looked empty or even the way another person seemed to be. There was something below, within, that could, with luck, be coaxed to reveal itself. He heard again the man's ponderous voice, moving in, moving out to the edge of hearing, pushing its way back through a roar of static—"copper-bearing conglomerates or gravels which occur near disseminated or porphyry copper deposits"—and, earlier, the same frail here-now-gone presence of Miss Spooner singing something about bravery and smiles. He thought about all of it and felt like a child who has opened a new cupboard.

Nate is telling Jerry and Norgaard and several others about going back East to New Jersey and how he heard the first radio broadcast of a boxing match. Not just any match, either, but Dempsey and Carpentier at Boyle's Thirty Acres, and he heard it—*it*, the sounds of the blows themselves—more than ninety miles away at the Metropole Theater in Morristown. The sounds came floating out of tulip speakers strung across the stage. Every seat full. It was wonderful, all of it. Straining for the crackling announcer's voice; joking that he was probably tricking them from the wings. And then the unmistakable sound of an audience, a crowd, thousands and thousands of voices cheering and booing. It was as if the air itself cheered. And then human fighting sounds too. The slap of leather on skin, a body hitting the floor, breath expelled in a grunt, a reverberating bell.

His face lights up again as he remembers it, and he is patient with the questions, the doubts. What was the point? Didn't he feel like a blind man at a prizefight? No, he says, he felt like a kid who had snuck in, had sandwiched himself down there among tall obscuring adults where he couldn't really see. But actually at the fight. There. Purely thrilled.

That's the last time Dempsey looked like anything, someone says. Hollywood. He's gone soft. Lost the hound in the belly.

Nate tells them the cities are sprouting radio towers. They poke up into the sky everywhere. Like this, and he flings his arm at the wooden derrick and the two figures clinging to the criss-crossed beams.

They have stopped climbing and they wave down at the crowd below, at the judge, who holds a megaphone.

He calls out their names. Their voices float back, faintly, faintly, through the sky. And Nate watches the faces around him become the same faces he saw at the Metropole. The eyes refocus on something distant. The face forgets itself. It's the listening look that is coming onto the faces of people everywhere in the land.

The bystanders stand in a loose circle around the greasy legs of the big derrick. A small breeze puffs among them, across the patches of soaked-in oil on the ground and the clumps of heavy tools and pipes, greasy with work. The breeze brings them the June smell of sage, the smell of fresh mud, all of it infused with the ancient odor of oil.

Vivian slips her arm through Jerry's. He covers her hand with his. They are partners, lovers, on the move again, the way they were the first couple of years. They have held on and now they are here on this good day. The land game has begun to pan out, and they have $1,000 in the bank and notes for three thousand more.

Next week, Jerry will meet with four people about leases, royalty shares. He will have a conversation with the man over there in the leather puttees, the one with the little terrier. He's a big gun, a big field geologist with Standard, and he has looked up a place near the rim and discovered that Jerry owns it, and he wants to talk about a lease. It is on the furthest edge of the possibilities, but he is interested. And his company, of course, does not underpay.

Vicissitudes. Ups and downs. Folds. Anticlines. Up one side and down the other and the luck was in the pockets and sometimes where you'd least expect it. Jerry is permeated with the lingo. He loves it. He glances at his wife, her sweet face tipped up, her brow furrowed with listening, her shiny hair under a smart new hat.

The voices float up out of the megaphone, back down to the ground, intersecting. Would they for the rest of their lives? And they did and they would, and now a hat flies into the air from the derrick and it wafts down to the ground, where everyone is clapping.

Fried chicken and your face aching from laughing. A discreet drink out of the sight of the judge, who doesn't care anyway. And that prompts a story from Jed McKenna, one-legged from the war. A good-humored young man with a voice made gravel by gas.

McKenna has relatives up in Edmonton; in fact, his cousin Bernie is a member of the Royal Canadian Mounted Police, and Bernie let him in on a new plan to apprehend bootleggers running the border.

That means you, Williams, someone calls good-naturedly. Williams is a small, alert man in his late twenties who moved to town with his mother when they lost the place in 1919. He runs Canadian whiskey in a new Maxwell with cord tires and a motor-driven horn. The Williamses have been poor as church mice, so no one judges the young fellow's line of work and no one begrudges him the new car it's bought him.

Picture this, McKenna says. High-powered motorcycles with machine guns attached to them. Tear gas bombs too. War planes on the ground is basically what you have. Same stick steers the motorcycle and points the gun. Those Mounties are basically riding a gun. They just point themselves at the quarry and fire whenever they please. For backup, some of 'em have sidecars and they stick a Mountie in there with his own gun.

The men are laughing at the thought of it. Canadians! They rib McKenna. They say his memory is maybe addled by his medicines.

I saw the demonstration, he sings above the laughter. Put an old car up on the bank of the Saskatchewan River last winter, got one of those motorcycles going down the ice toward it, firing to beat the band, must have been going fifty, maybe sixty. They counted the hits. Sixty-nine out of eighty-two.

They always get their Ford, someone intones, and this brings new hilarity.

The bride and groom are on the ground. He licks the tips of his fingers and wipes a small smear of grease from her face. They roar off in a field truck toward Shelby and a party in the new dance hall, and everyone else soon follows. Four white ribbons flutter from the legs of the derrick.

Jerry, Vivian, and the Norgaards drive in to Shelby across the alkali flats. Here, a farm with sagging fence, abandoned. There, another, with a crop that will need rain in the next few weeks, and maybe it will come and maybe it won't but that is not the thing now to hang your hat on. Not wheat, not flax. That is not the thing.

Shelby, late afternoon, late June of 1922. Still just a straggle of small buildings along a street, a branch of that street with more small buildings, a corridor of rails. No trees to speak of. No plan. No shelter. Fewer than a thousand locals still, but look at Main Street! Look at Division!

The boardwalks are crammed with men in khaki, men in leather puttees, a clump of men bent over a map that's spread on the hood of a car. Women no one has ever seen. Some of them look like city women. It's their shoes, which aren't made for the mud. The fashion sense of Shelby women stops at their ankles. Shoes are made for mud, for snow, for ice. Some of these new women look like respectable city women with nice shoes, but no one has ever seen them before, so what are they doing on the main street of Shelby?

Others are more decipherable. Paint on their faces, lace on their sleeves, the flimsiest shoes of all.

It's five o'clock, and the supper lines have already started at the Log Cabin, the Gingham Café, the Sullivan. Someone dug a cesspool in the lot behind the Gingham and put up a privy, and there is a line there too. Lines, men, more autos than Shelby has ever seen, meandering, idling, roaring off.

The hack hack of hammers. This time, this particular year, will always contain the hack of hammers—energetic, earnest, then faltering, then angry—but always the sound until the day, a year and a week from now, when it is all over and everyone, everything falls silent.

The hammers are loud in the falling light of a summer day. They will go until dark. And the town will stay alive far beyond that. A new dance hall has opened and the men will be there and the women too. There is recklessness abroad.

They drop off the Norgaards, who catch the skidoo up to Cut Bank. Jerry waves to a man wearing a cape. He is said to be a Russian count.

Their friends the Iversons live in a modest porched house over by the school. Jerry and Vivian pull up to the house. A couple of kids run behind the auto, keeping up with it, just for something to do. Jerry and Vivian sit for a few moments after the machine has quit popping and talk about Main Street, the scene, who they saw. The woman in the red skirt. The count in his cape. The safari men—that's what Vivian calls them—the oilmen, the explorers. Some of them board at the Sullivan. Some move cots into the half-finished Rainbow each night after the workmen leave. Some sleep on Pullmans their companies have leased and parked on the sidings. Some of the poorer lease-hounds spend the nights in their automobiles.

The looks on the faces of people. Maybe that's what strikes Vivian and Jerry more than the clothes, the elaborate compasses and other ferreting gizmos, the new women, the snake boots and swagger.

What is that look? Gritty-eyed. Not so much sleep for these people. But avid too. Eyes open. Heads moving around, trying to pick up the latest tip, the latest theory. There had been a museum-guard look creeping in before this boom. Patient. Ritualistic. The look of people who don't see anything new. And now there is the exhilarating shock of all this action and hope, all these fast people with plans and contingencies and fallbacks and money. All eyes are wide open.

You try to be skeptical and well-reasoned, make your plan, but there is a headlong quality to this town now, and reason doesn't much enter in. You look around you and get hungry and see the meal coming your way.

Ann Iverson calls them in. Instead of sitting them down in the front room, she leads them straight through it to the low-ceilinged kitchen in the back.

A stranger sits in the front room on a cot, paring his fingernails. He waves casually. There are other cots in the room, half a dozen of them, with boots on them, valises, map cases.

All six of the Iversons are in the kitchen. A couple of kids and Walter at the table, the smaller children rolling around on the floor with a kitten and a wooden top. The room beyond them, an unheated lean-to lined with shelves, has wall-to-wall bedding on the floor.

We live back here now, Ann says happily. We sleep there, all of us. The men rent the cots, get the use of the outhouse, eat down at the Log Cabin or the Gingham and pay us for the privilege.

The seven-year-old pipes up. A lot! he says. Piles and piles of gold!

They shoo him and the others outside and the adults sit around the table eating warm cherry pie with cream. The day is still lovely and warm, peach-colored now, and a beam of the sinking sun falls through the open door and across the floor.

Walter says he is thinking about going in with some other fellows on a rooming house. Move a couple of old homestead shacks to town and open for business in a couple of weeks. He is considering the advisability of it. But on the other hand, who knows how long this excitement is going to last? Who knows how accurate those boys are, out there mapping the field? They're as susceptible to mistakes as anyone else. Still, if it keeps going until the end of the summer, this boom, why, a fellow could make some money on some shacks. Hard to know what to do.

Jerry listens to him, bored. The carefulness, the hedging, the doubts. This is not the way to be in these times. The way to be is extended, fast-hearted, ready to go all in. If he knows anything, Jerry knows that.

The Iversons' oldest girl, the sixteen-year-old, comes in. She and two of her friends have housekeeping jobs at the Sullivan.

She is a tall, gawky girl with eyeglasses and a beautiful rare smile. She hunches. She's "broody," her mother says, but she seems to like the hotel job even though she protested so much at first.

The girl, Charmaine—all the Iverson children have exotic names—eats her pie slowly, says she's fine and the hotel is jammed as ever. Then she lifts her head and addresses them as if she just woke up. "That Standard man, the field geologist? That one with the high leather boots and the cane? And the little terrier?" They all nod.

"He wears silk pajamas. Embroidered silk pajamas. And he leaves them on the floor. Two pair. Sometimes red ones and sometimes, um, purple. Or kind of a dark bluish purple. Like blueberries. With sewing all over them."

They all digest this information.

"What are you doing bothering with the man's pajamas?" Walter finally remarks grumpily.

They all chew their pie.

"On the floor?" Ann asks.

Most of a full moon is rising, a melon-colored disc with a rough bite off one edge. It is a warm night. They will drive home to Cut Bank, they decide. Clearly their friends have no space, and clearly there are no rooms to be had in town. They will make a lark of it. Mrs. Callan and the children don't expect them until tomorrow, so a late-night arrival won't worry anyone. It seems like the perfect day, the perfect time, to do it.

They start out, taking the southerly road, which doesn't have to climb the rim, though there will be a few wide gullies to contend with. They point the auto toward the red seam at the far edge of the earth.

To the north, they see the winking of dozens of autos making their way back to Shelby from the field. And then, when they are farther west, the darkness arrives and they are alone with just their own headlights arrowing narrowly onto the track. One other car on the road and then nothing.

Sometimes the road runs close to the railroad tracks. They hear low thundering over the industrious yammer of their auto, and it grows upon them, the blaze of the engine lamp, pounding steam, and the white of it lighting the sky. Then it flies past, all the cars sealed and dark and faster than anything else that moves on the ground. The silk train from the coast. Sixty, seventy miles an hour, and it has a deadly mysterious look that, with its speed, draws people in the scattered towns just to watch. Loaded with bolts of silk from the Orient, bound for the factories in the East. Sometimes a stop for water or coal at Cut Bank, and then children and their parents will gather around it, dart forward to touch its windowless cars, listen to it breathe, and even its breath sounds as if it comes from another part of the world. The men in the small engine window do not step down or even wave. They are ghosts! a little kid shouted once, and no one laughed. They are the headless horseman! he shrieked, calling upon more of the ghouls in his arsenal, and still no one laughed, and his mother grabbed him and took him home because he'd been like that all day.

It roars past Jerry and Vivian in their secondhand flivver, and its red taillight rocks and then it is gone and they are alone and sputtering along.

It takes them an hour to fix the first flat tire because one of the tools seems the wrong size and won't do the job. And it is dark. When they finish—both of them with black hands—they steer the auto off the track, the frail little road, and they retrieve blankets from the back and simply camp out there on the ground.

Why? Because they are sleepy and it has been such a good day. And they are also thinking, both of them, about the couple high on the derrick, their faint voices calling down their vows. And so they don't want to go home yet.

"I may quit my job and go into the oil game full-bore," Jerry says lightly. "Move us to Shelby." They spread the canvas and the blankets on a patch of spongy long grass. Vivian holds the lantern. She knows he is saying it just to test the sounds of the words, see how easily they form themselves, how casual or desperate or decided they sounded.

He likes the sound of them. They seem springy, hopeful. He can't really read Vivian's face to see whether she thinks so too. But she doesn't take exception, either, or say that's too rash or that he is too caught up in all this. She seems to know that he is testing the sound of the words and that no response is called for.

It does no harm for the words to hang there. They might wink out. Or they might stay and become something to look at, like all the icy lights spread across the sky for them tonight, the solitary glittery ones, and the filmy veil of the Milky Way.

14

311 W. 88th St.
New York, N.Y.
June 19, 1922

Dear Jerry, Vivian and kiddies,

Well, that is wonderful news about the big oil strike and the boom. And since you have bought some of those relinquishments, perhaps the "black gold" is beneath your land and someone will discover it and you will be a big oil tycoon.

You and Carlton have the right attitude about boldness and taking the main chance. I find I am getting braver every day, but it has been a long struggle. Now I am using Coué, New Thot and common sense. So I ought to get a break, had I not?

Monsieur Coué you no doubt know about, he has been in the newspaper in all parts of the country and no doubt even in Montana. He is a Frenchman, a pharmacist and a philosopher of the common man, and he spoke last week here in New York and I went to his lecture. Oh! he is the *most* wonderful man, a mixture of common sense and higher thot such as I have never before heard of. And I think you should try to find out as much as possible about him for your efforts out there and your self-confidence and the chances you ask yourself to take. He is a big help.

The basic message is that we cannot *try* to do something, such as sing a concert without stagefright, etc., because our subconscious which is the Imagination is what controls us. And it fights the Will. So if I say I *must* go to sleep, well then I will not because my subconscious is saying Perhaps I Will Not Go To Sleep. And the subconscious always wins the battles with the

Will. Now the point is to learn how to control this subconscious, this Imagination, and to substitute new ideas for the old ones. And it is so easy! This is what you do. Every morning before rising and every night before bed, you shut your eyes and repeat twenty times in a monotone, "Every day and in every way I am getting better and better." And you do not think of the words, you keep track by tying twenty knots in a string and just moving your fingers along the string. You speak like a child and do not think about the words. That way, they will slip past your Will and settle straight on your Imagination and then you have planted the Idea that improvement is happening at all times and then it becomes a Reality.

And of course this applies to all things, such as stagefright and tightening of the throat when singing. My throat is loose! you say. I *can* sing as I should! And then, there you are, singing away!

And do you know, this wise wise French man reminded me of old Silas Tooey back home, he is that humble looking, rather short and thickly built with white hair and beard.

Lelia went to the lecture with me and she said, My, he doesn't sound as smart as I heard he was, he is so much like a child, and I said, Lelia, that is exactly the point. His philosophy is simple, so simple, so it is only right that he is too! And I said, Lelia, you might try it with your whistling before you scoff too much. Because Lelia has the thought when she is whistling sometimes that she will burst into a laugh or even a smile, which makes it of course impossible to whistle, and she has done this in a recording situation. And of course the more she thinks, I *must not* laugh while I whistle, well that's what she does! And this problem is exactly what Mr. Coué addresses.

Well, I must stop for now. Oh! I must tell you another thing. I have been praying for one friend, a real spiritual friend to come into my life. I feel that I have had marvelous spiritual experiences myself during the years since Mother took ill, have perfected my spirit in a number of ways, but I seem to find no one who speaks that language with me and who is congenial. Certainly Lelia is not. So of course I have slipped and fallen a number of times and gone way out of tune. Well, just a week ago, I met a woman at a meeting of the Theosophical Society. I knew at once we were kindred spirits and we are. Her name is Mrs. Wexner and she is independently wealthy but very idealistic and not worldly at all. She says I have a truly rare voice that should be cultivated like a hot house plant.

What about the OIL!!!
Lots of love,
Daisy Lou

They met in a large room of the Genealogical Hall on West Fifty-Eighth Street, where Dr. Hereward Barrington was scheduled to discuss "Latest Developments in Psychical Research." It was a dim room that looked, before the people arrived, like a sepia-tinted photograph of itself. Twenty rows of folding wooden chairs and a wooden podium and glossy wooden floors lit here and there by dull light from the tall windows. Then the audience arrived in twos and threes, talking, stirring the air, the lazy dust motes. Someone pulled back a curtain, and all the shadows ran away.

One of the arrivals is Daisy Lou Malone—she has come alone—and another is a tall, broad-shouldered woman wearing the newest style of Egyptian dress. She takes a seat just ahead of Daisy's. She is a woman in her early thirties perhaps, with a strong, almost sphinxlike profile that is reinforced by flared straight-bottomed hair and the dress. Her voice is deep. She smells faintly of something like sandalwood.

Daisy studies this woman while she waits, and it occurs to her that style, real style, is not the dress, the makeup, the expensive bob, even the odd bold touch, like this woman's hatpin, an alligator with stunned emerald eyes. No, it is the ability to trust in your accoutrements, whatever they are. The insight makes her feel she has moved the last small piece of a Chinese puzzle box so that the lid opens. Remember that small truth, Daisy instructs herself as she relaxes into a slightly more insouciant posture.

The lecture, it turns out, is a virtual repetition of one Daisy attended two weeks earlier, but, unlike the other, there is an intermission during which punch is served in an anteroom and some mingling goes on. Daisy is introduced to the tall woman with the alligator pin—her name is given as Mrs. Penelope Wexner—by a polite, forgettable man who says he met Daisy at another talk on the psychical phenomena. Here is a little veering of fortune, Daisy thinks as she shakes Penelope Wexner's hand for the first time.

Daisy considers herself a spiritual explorer. She has gone to rallies by Miss Aimee Semple McPherson, she has read the Book of Mormon, but she is particularly interested, recently, in clairvoyance and precognition. Trance states of various kinds interest her, as do theories about the seven astral planes. It seems to her that Theosophy has enlightening things to say about the various spiritual dimensions and an enlightened and searching attitude toward the mysteries.

Daisy continues to attend the Presbyterian church, to sing the songs Presbyterians expect her to sing at their churches, and she sees no essential conflict between that allegiance and her explorations. As someone said at a lecture on the topic of religious tolerance, "It discredits the Creator to say he belongs in one jar with one label."

She also likes the aura given off by the people who attend spiritist gatherings. Well, some of them. Often there will be a person in the front row, absolutely grim-faced, who asks too many questions in a voice too desperate. Or an audience member or two who keeps blinking back tears. But on the whole, she feels a sense of imagination and exploration that she likes. She feels that, if she knew some of the people in these audiences, she would find them highly congenial and would perhaps make some spiritual friends.

Daisy and Mrs. Wexner stand for a moment without much to say. Then Mrs. Wexner says, very calmly, "Would you mind removing your hat?" She seems to have her eyes fixed on Daisy's forehead, as if a spot or a stain has appeared there and she is trying to determine its nature. Startled, Daisy obeys. Mrs. Wexner pushes back the loose curls that frame Daisy's face, pushes them off her forehead, and continues to study the same spot. Her fingers are long and cool. She wears a square onyx ring on her right hand, an oval opal on her left. ("The light, the shade, without which the other does not exist," she would proclaim to Daisy once, holding the ringed fingers aloft.)

She places the first and second fingertips of both hands at a spot in the center of Daisy's forehead, then slowly moves them apart, tracing a circle around her head and moving back again to the middle. Daisy's eyes are level with Mrs. Wexner's chin. She glances to the side and sees, to her surprise, that no one is regarding them with any special interest. The others are in small clumps, absorbed in their own conversations.

"You have," says Mrs. Wexner, "a somewhat unique cranial topography." She drops her hands to her sides but tips her head to look once more at a spot in the area of Daisy's ear. "You have extraordinarily well-pronounced areas here..." She taps a point above Daisy's left temple. "And here." She taps the right. "This indicates well-developed brain organs of Ideality, Wit, and Tune." She places Daisy's hat back on her head.

"What caught my eye first, however, was the bumps on your forehead. Feel them?" Daisy runs her own fingers across them. She has never thought them more pronounced than anyone else's. "They, of course, indicate an ability to detect causality in human affairs," Mrs. Wexner says. "The silver ribbon that links cause and effect.

"Well!" she adds brightly. "Shall we go hear what else the wise man has to say?"

They began to meet on Thursday afternoons for tea at Mrs. Wexner's flat on West Eighty-Third Street. It was a rather opulent suite of rooms, in which Mrs. Wexner lived alone. She had a husband, Mr. Theodore Wexner, who was her second cousin and some twenty years older than Penelope. He was in stocks and bonds and lived two blocks from his wife in rooms that looked like a club—all leather wingbacks and decanters and manly silence. They went to social affairs together and were on the best of terms, the best, said Mrs. Wexner, that they could hope to be, given the disparity in ages and interests. Separate residences, she insisted to Daisy, were the only way for married people, with the means to do so, to preserve a shred of what she called "the necessary mystery." In another year, Fannie Hurst, the novelist, will be putting forth the same argument in the pages of the *New York Times*—what a furor!—and Mrs. Wexner will say that Fannie, whom she'd met a time or two, got the idea from her.

On a rainy Sabbath in April, Daisy returns from a singing engagement at a Congregational church in Queens, to find Mrs. Wexner disembarking from a Packard at the steps of Daisy's building. She wears fawn-colored stockings and thin, fawn-colored shoes, and that's what comes out of the auto first, long fawn-colored limbs and then the ducked Egyptian head and a green umbrella whipping into full sail.

They shake hands as they always do, smiling at their synchronicity, pleased but not surprised.

Daisy is tired and a little light-headed because she is trying to save money and has not eaten. This is the first time Mrs. Wexner has come to her flat, which Lelia has abandoned because she has gone to be a singer or hostess in a summer resort in the Adirondacks. Daisy doesn't believe for a second that Lelia is coming back, and the prospect of finding another person to share the rent makes her more exhausted. She realizes she does not have any friends except Penelope Wexner. She has many acquaintances, some lovely people among them, but she does not have the faintest idea what the living situations of her single acquaintances are.

Both women are in rather pensive moods. The rain is relentless, saturating. The trolleys and wagons and automobiles move through it like specters. Veils of rain whip down the canyons of the city, bend the trees of the park. A drenched terrier, trailing a leash, trots through it at an angle.

They make a fire in the stove. Mrs. Wexner looks quickly around the spartan room, imperiously draws the curtains and lights candles. It is, she says, a candle sort of day.

They are both drifty. Perhaps it is the rain, the way it seems to engulf, seems to want to obliterate, the world. They sit with each other in the dimness, listening.

Mrs. Wexner, rather out of the blue, tells Daisy that phrenology, the science of the brain and skull, has been unfairly tainted by money-grubbing charlatans, the ones who charge money to read your skull. They say anything they want; they don't know the demarcations. But a student of the science finds it to be uncannily accurate, she says. A real student does.

"My own skull, for instance," she says, shaking her full bobbed hair so that it falls over the top of her bent head, revealing a long naked neck. "You see these," she says from under the curtain of hair, her fingers placed at protuberances at the base of her skull. She throws her hair back.

"Amativeness," she says wearily. "And these." She takes Daisy's hand and touches it to a spot high on the crown. "Ideality. Like you." She looks at Daisy as if the implications should be clear. Daisy smiles tentatively.

"Amativeness." Mrs. Wexner sighs. "It has taken me into the furthest reaches of the spirit and flesh." Daisy thinks of Mr. Wexner, a vested, corpulent, white-haired man she met once when he came for his wife after a Theosophy meeting.

"He was a soldier in the Great War," her friend says, "A man ten years younger than myself, a boy actually, but our spirits were the two halves of a whole. He did not return and he was not on the list of the dead. It was as if he had been plucked into the ether." Her long fingers twisted upward in the motion of smoke. "You cannot imagine the anguish.

"Ideality made me believe he continued to live. Months, and then a year, and no word—his people had given him up for dead, conducted a service with an empty casket—and still I believed. I believed because I felt his presence. You will understand what I mean, dear Daisy Lou. But did that presence lay tracks upon this earth? This is what I didn't know. How *here* was he? Had he lost his memory in the shellings and did he wander Europe like the wounded knight of the Grail? Had he been captured and had he refused to identify himself and then, at the end, been kept by evil people—a faceless damaged servant of the Hun? I did not know.

"This anguish brought me to the study of spiritualism, its techniques and possibilities."

Her eyes are half shut as she speaks, and Daisy has the odd sense that someone else is lecturing through her mouth. That she has already, in some ways, become the medium she would soon show herself to be.

"I had the privilege, not so long ago, to meet Miss Ada Besinnet of Toledo, Ohio, the famous medium, and we were able to contact my poor boy. The strange part about it, though, was that although he spoke through the personage of Miss Besinnet at the very beginning, he soon switched to me. That is, I began to speak and my voice became very low and it was his. This was when I discovered my small gifts as an instrument."

Daisy can restrain herself no longer. "Where *was* he?" she asks.

"He was dead," Mrs. Wexner says crisply. "However, his spirit had not completed its work on this earth and he continues to exist on the third or fourth astral plane. I have contact with him from time to time. Various kinds of contact, some of it quite…moving.

"He and many many young men are still very close to us, I can tell you. You do not kill eight million boys on the verge of their lives and expect them to leave this earthly existence without a trace." Her face has become genuinely pained. "They were not finished," she says quietly. "They are finishing themselves."

They sit then, unspeaking, listening to the washing rain.

"I know a person who may or may not be dead," Daisy offers. "I knew him in Saint Paul."

Mrs. Wexner studies Daisy fondly. She seems to be more awake now, gets up and looks out the window at the wetness, sits back down, making herself comfortable.

"You know, Daisy," she says, "you must change your name. Daisy Lou is a perfectly sweet name, but it is not suitable for a stage career. It is the name of someone who will always be in the chorus. You know that, of course."

She does this sometimes, has begun to do this as their friendship has progressed. She will suggest that Daisy wear a certain color more often, for instance, or tip her hat at a more intriguing angle. But the suggestion is always that these are incidentals and there could be no possible offense in suggesting them. The suggestion is that she wants the best possible context for Daisy's gift—her voice.

Does she believe in Daisy's voice? Is it actually a distinctive and lovely voice? Mrs. Wexner does not know exactly. It is a fervent and melodious voice—that is certain—and it certainly merits intense training. Beyond that, Mrs. Wexner is content to go on the evidence of the promontories of Tune.

She rises to leave. Then an odd genuine storm develops—sheets of rain, thunder, tumult—and Daisy says again, "I knew someone in Saint Paul who may be alive or dead today. He left under a cloud and I don't know what makes me think he is dead—I have no cause—but I should like to know. He was a friend of my mother's. He was my mother's physician in her final illness."

Mrs. Wexner's eyes close, her head tips forward. The eyes open. Daisy watches her guardedly, watches her place her beautiful long-fingered hands on the arms of the chair. And who knows if anything would have been said had the weather not been so extravagant and fierce? But a big clap of thunder shakes the building, and both women jump. And then Penelope Wexner says, in a strange, listless voice: "He lives. On the frontier. He lives with a group of men." She pulls her closed eyes tighter. "Is it a circus? There is an African animal. A cat, I believe. There are men with bare torsos, like trapeze artists or strongmen. There is a pen, an open cage, a roped enclosure of some sort. He leans on the ropes, calling to something inside."

She says no more.

Daisy is deeply shocked. The vision does not jibe with any she has held in her mind of the haunted Dr. Sheehan. It is too active, too daylit, too imbued with the dust and grit and noise of the present day.

But she believes. She believes the vision, not least because Mrs. Wexner, the seer, does not quite seem to believe it herself. She seems shocked at the words that have come out of her own mouth. She looks chagrined, as if she had thought herself to be thinking silently and found that she was shouting.

She gets up briskly—the storm has slackened—and she departs. Daisy falls immediately asleep and does not wake until the next morning, when the world again sounds hard-edged and dry. She can hear the traffic sounds and policemen's whistles; she can hear bright shouts. She can think—what can she think?—that the young doctor who seemed, one hot afternoon, to be the only person on earth to fully understand her, her artistry and temperament and yearnings—that he is alive out West. The person who knows her best self.

She practices with renewed energy. She will sing once more this week for the man at Aeolian and then he will offer a contract or he won't. She has a new way of practicing. Instead of clasping her hands to her midriff, consciously pushing against them as she has taught all her students to do, she now presses her fingers to the points on her head, just forward of the temples, the protuberances of Tune, and she finds, when she does that, that her voice does not have to seek the proper pitch. She does not even have to be conscious of pitch. She just has it. She knows she does.

Her fingers seem to buzz sometimes, and when that happens, she feels a small trickle of deep comfort. There they are—the manifestations on her boned surface of what lies beneath. She has sung and performed for a decade now. She believes in her talent. But to have actual evidence of it—there is joy in that.

Come forth, she thinks as she runs up and down her scales. Freely show yourself, she murmurs before she jumps into her arpeggios and her warm-up songs. Make me the perfect instrument. Make me the conduit for yourself, she exhorts her latent lovely voice. Send your voice through my throat like the voices of all the beautiful wanderers who float above our shoulders, who drift bravely just beyond the furthest reaches of our sight.

311 W. 88th
New York, N.Y.
Dec. 22, 1922

Dear Jerry, Vivian and little Francis, Maudie and "Tip"—

This will not reach you by Christmas Day and for that I apologize, but I have been absolutely frantic and only now do I get a chance to breathe. The big news is that I have, at long last, signed a contract with Aeolian and shall make a phonograph record within two weeks of the New Year, according to a new manager, a Mr. Higgenbotham. I am so very pleased!!

Mr. Higgenbotham came to the company from Great Britain and brought with him a manner of speaking that is so refined and likable. I trusted his sensibilities the instant I met him and of course I was right to do so. This is what I have worked and hoped for these months and months. I feel that I have never been in better voice, and I owe the improvement, I firmly believe, to the confidence I have come to through my study of Coué, New Thot and the psychical phenomena. Also I believe I have mentioned my spiritual friend, Mrs. Penelope Wexner, who has assisted me greatly in my path to self-knowledge. I have come to believe, with her help, that we greatly underestimate the help and comfort that is available to us through science and the spirit world. She has made a study of the brain organs, for instance, and how the various faculties are reflected on the surface of the skull. Oh yes, I know you are saying bunkum! that is an old idea, that "bumpology." But its only flaw is that it has ended up in the hands of charlatans who are not scientists and who charge money and turn a science into a vaudeville act. That does not mean the idea itself is invalid. On the contrary, it has confirmed for me all my suspicions about my truest nature and has given me the confidence to proceed on the strength of those strengths I own!

I will send you my phonograph record as soon as it becomes available. Pretty soon I will be saying, "I know the new oil king of Montana because he happens to be my brother." And you will be saying, "My sister? Oh, she is indeed the new songbird of New York!"

What do you think about King Tutankhamen's tomb? It is all over the Times and I can't get enough of it. To think that Lord Carnarvon spent *thirty-three* years searching for it and might have given up had he not felt a conviction grow upon him several years ago as to its whereabouts beneath the tomb of Rameses VI! What will be inside the sealed chambers I wonder? The glorious objects in the anterooms make it almost impossible to imagine more. The solid gold sandals and the crowns with the golden serpents and the wonderful throne crusted with jewels. (My friend Mrs. Wexner believes the presence of golden serpents may be ominous because a live serpent of the same type killed a pet canary of one of the archeologists on the very day the tomb was opened.) And the queen's beaded net robes, what do you think of those? The Times said the reason for that fashion was that "when King Zoser, 3,000 years before Christ, was afflicted with an attack of melancholia, his physician ordered a number of the most beautiful women in the Capital to be dressed only in diaphanous bead net robes and to row the King's barge around the sacred lake at Karnak to amuse him." What a picture that brings to mind!

Well my dears, I would love to send you gold sandals and snake crowns and beaded robes, but I am, after all, only a working girl and these small tokens of my affection will have to do.

You wait, Jerry—this slowdown with the oil and the sale of land is temporary and they will boom the field in the spring like you said. You are very likely in the situation of Lord Carnarvon a year ago when he stopped digging temporarily due to illness. He was, at that point, only *six feet* from the stairway to the tomb.

I wish you all a happy and prosperous New Year. I truly believe that 1923 will be the best year of our lives.

Love to you all,
Daisy Lou, soon to be known as
Amelia (my stage name)

III

EVENING
July 10, 1973

IT WAS the multipurpose room of the grade school, a flatly lit, hard-surfaced room filled with long industrial tables for hot lunch. At the front of the room was a raised platform with a podium. Behind the platform and podium was the stage, with its drawn dark curtain.

Jerry and Amelia and T.T. were led to the front table, the one nearest the podium, to sit with eight others they had known for half a century. These eleven were the featured guests, and they felt overexposed because their number was small and the table was long.

There was a large flower centerpiece on the table, mums, with a sparkly decoration popping out of it. The numbers 5 and 0 in something glittery. Jerry slid the centerpiece down to the end of the table because it was something you couldn't see around.

On the beige walls of the room were photos of oil derricks. Of a huge arena. Newspaper headlines: "'Big Fight' Idea Fails to Grow Up." "Dempsey Wins After Full 15 rounds; Surprising Showing Made by Gibbons."

Crepe-paper streamers overhead. A punch-and-cookie table. That unforgiving neon light.

"Feel like I'm in a pen with a blue ribbon on my halter," George McClintock whispered loudly to the others. Amelia gave him her music teacher's frown. George was alone because his wife, Suzanne, had fallen off the bottom church step two weeks earlier and broken her hip. Just shifted her weight a certain way and the shell-like bone cracked and sent her toppling to the cement, where it broke again. She was a feisty little woman whose manner had gotten more blunt as she aged. She kept saying in the ambulance, when they took her to Great Falls to get the pins, "I'd suggest you just shoot me. Easier on all of us."

There, there, the attendant had murmured, bored. We'll get you all fixed up.

"Don't be a fool!" Suzanne had snapped back. "I'm eighty-one years old, you sappy child! I know what happens when an old lady breaks a hip in two places." And, of course, she would be right about the whole thing.

The program began with a welcome by the mayor and a small skit by the fourth-grade class—midgets in gingham and buckskins scanning horizons.

The emcee said the audience was in store for a few speeches, but first he wanted the old-timers to introduce themselves for the record and to comment briefly on their length of time in Shelby, their families, whatever struck them as appropriate.

Good faces, weathered faces. They stood, one by one, crusty and gracious, and said their names and inclined their heads. They said what they had done in their working days, how many years they'd been in northern Montana, where the kids were and the grandchildren. They mentioned a recent vacation, some of them. A child's triumph.

Jerry said his son Francis still worked for the State Department, though he was making noises about early retirement and coming back to Montana. That Francis's son, Don, was, as most of them knew, a radar officer who was shot down on an F-4 Phantom off the coast of Vietnam and that the family was holding out hopes that he would be accounted for now; that he was perhaps alive and coming home.

Daughter Maudie had her decorating business in Seattle and had just remarried—a guy in a management position in the fish business. And Tip was now head auctioneer at the Denver livestock yards and the father of six kids, who could all outyell him.

When the others had finished introducing themselves—Amelia described herself with surprising brevity as a "career musician"—Jerry took the podium for the formal remarks he had been asked to prepare.

He had planned his speech far in advance of this night. He had an agenda. That agenda, that plan, was to defuse any ideas Skiff Norgaard might have about cashing in on the coming oil boom. Skiff sat at the table with Alice, who was bent and shaky-headed, and he watched Jerry with the elaborately neutral face he had turned to him for decades.

Jerry held the sides of the podium tightly with big-knuckled, bruised-looking hands, his only sign of any nervousness. He was, in old age, a slim, slightly stooped man of medium height with a thin thatch of hair that had paled to a rosy white. He wore a stiff shirt with cuff links, and a suit, and high-topped shoes. He put on heavy horn-rimmed glasses to read a few scratched notes in his hand. His face was sere, all the flesh used up and the mouth quite thin and straight.

After messing with the microphone for a few seconds, tapping it with a fingernail until satisfied, he began to speak in a rather strong voice that only occasionally slipped into an old man's plaint.

"I am not a man of extra words," he said. "So I will speak my piece and turn the stage over to the fulminations of my brethren." He swept an arm past the other old-timers in their folding chairs. Amelia smiled and inclined her head graciously. She wore a green velveteen hat with a half veil that screened the top of her face. She had not removed her gloves.

"I have lived in northern Montana for sixty-three years as of May the sixteenth," Jerry said. "I have had my ups and downs like anybody does, but on the whole it has been a good place to be a young man and a not-so-young man and even an old fool with one foot in the grave. My chief regret is that my wife, Vivian, who passed away twenty-one years ago, could not be here tonight to get her own old-timer's certificate and see our fine fourth graders and give me the high sign on when to cut myself off." He drew a finger across the front of his throat, still unsmiling.

He paused then and thought for a moment about Vivian. Everything about the measurement of time had come to seem contrived and irrelevant to him. Twenty-one years was not any kind of measurement of Vivian's distance. She had not been gone two decades in any sense that meant anything. He still smelled her hair, watched her brow furrow, heard her steady breathing in the night. If she were really gone, he would not be trying for a little humor, trying to conjure her beautiful laugh.

"Be that as it may," he continued, "I would like to make a few short statements about oil and Shelby and the field as we have come to know it.

"As many of you know, oil was for many years my ruling passion. Like many others, I was convinced that Shelby sat on the edge of an oil field that would make us all rich, one way or the other. And like many others, I have sat beside many a dry hole and paid taxes on many a piece of worthless land and kept in my possession many a piece of meaningless paper."

He thought of Sharleen Norgaard, at his house this very moment, smoking, playing the radio, running the vacuum cleaner, then cutting those pale eyes to the side while she ran her cool fingers through his records and maps. She had already stolen his gold toothpick. He knew that. He had just noticed it missing that morning.

"What has happened in that field is this, of course. It is a steady producer, but not a spectacular one. It's a factory field—steady and workmanlike. A deposit here, a deposit there—but it's spread out over eight hundred square miles, or twenty-four townships, and so you have to test awfully wide waters before you're likely to hit pay dirt, so to speak.

"I guess we all know how that is. You put all your hopes on a quarter section here, a half section there, but it might be just west, just east, of the quarter section where the oil is. You could think of it as a minefield in reverse. You could run through the whole damn thing and never get a scratch, or you could blow yourself up with one step. There's no surefire way to tell.

"My ultimate point, of course, is that these recent prices on account of the Arabs aren't likely to translate into any kind of renewed interest by the big boys in our area. The field just hasn't proved to yield spectacular strikes. So I, for one, am not going to hold my breath that the big boys will be snooping around anytime soon."

The audience was a little puzzled. Polite and attentive, but they didn't know what to think about this little speech that stated the obvious. And Norgaard seemed oblivious. He might have been sleeping. He had his hand on his pink face and his eyes fixed on his knee. Or closed. It was difficult to tell.

Having made his point about the oil, Jerry moved on to the subject of the big fight of 1923.

"It will," he said, "be an interesting sight to see film footage of that particular day. But before we do, I'd like to remind this audience that I was secretary of the Shelby Commercial Club at the time of the Dempsey-Gibbons fight and that the club was never formally disbanded, so I suppose I am secretary yet. I never got a chance to stand up and read the minutes of the last meeting, which was held about a month after the fight.

"You will remember that things weren't going along too well for Shelby at that time. A couple banks were busted. Mayor James Johnson had lost about seventy thousand dollars, his entire fortune at the time. Of course, he didn't know then that he'd bring in a couple of wells the next year and save his skin once again.

"An unpaid-for arena stood out there on the edge of town where the Arena Motel is now, and that arena was, for those of you who never saw it, the Eighth Wonder of the World. It covered six acres. Of course, it would come down in a few years to salvage the lumber, and that would be that."

He gestured at the clippings and photos taped to the wall. One of the browned photos showed the arena from the sky, huge and outlandish on the edge of a town that was only widely scattered little boxes connected by winding dirt roads, a dozen-tracked rail corridor on its far edge. "Go *look* at the thing," he urged. Then he shook his head, a flicker of a smile on his face.

"Okay, so we're busted. Whole town is. Kearns and Dempsey hightail it outa here with damn near three hundred thousand bucks—*1923* bucks—and we're sitting here busted. All thousand of us."

The people in the larger audience looked serious and sympathetic. But here was an interesting thing. The older people, the old-timers on the folding chairs at the front table, had perked up. There was a look on their faces as if something had finally shown itself and made this evening worth something. Especially the men. They smiled. They whispered to each other. Norgaard shook his head exactly as Jerry did; made the identical small smile.

T.T. Wilkins called out that he still had thirty fight tickets for sale. Cheap. And then Jerry read the telegram that the Commercial Club sent as its last act of business, a few months after the fight. It was addressed to Tex Rickard, the famous promoter, and it said: "Shelby is prepared to offer $100,000 for rematch of Dempsey and Gibbons, July 1924. Anxiously awaiting reply."

The audience laughed and shook their heads.

"We never got an answer!" Jerry said, elaborately at a loss. "We figured the telegraph poles must have blown down. There were some big storms that summer."

The mention of the telegram made the old people laugh louder than they had all evening. Their white heads had tipped toward each other. It was as if they were watching a program everyone else in the audience didn't see; cackling over something that was plain as day, but only to them.

Now it was time for the speech by the young man who used to be Amelia's student, the one who wrote to her. The one named Michael Cage. The one she couldn't remember. According to someone, he made a lot of money with television. He played a part in a sitcom. It was not a big part—he was the neighbor who always came and rang the doorbell—but it was steady and clearly something that would start him up the ladder.

Michael Cage had already done a number of different things in his life. He'd been a waiter in Fiji, a manager of a clothing store, a partner in a failed music company, and, for these past two years, in Hollywood in a sitcom. He also wanted to be a scriptwriter. He wanted to write a movie script about the Dempsey-Gibbons fight. It was a natural. You had boxing, the twenties, high stakes, a famous champion, the West, pioneers, David and Goliath, the whole shebang. So that was his plan, Cage's. He wanted to spend a week in Shelby, really get to know some of these old folks, get a toehold, secure some rights to some lives.

Amelia Malone was still trying to place him. He had come up to her before the banquet and given her a big kiss on the cheek, a loud smooch! She couldn't believe it. He said she was "instrumental" in the fact that he was where he was, and he hoped he could spend an afternoon with her while he was home because he understood that she had a wealth of material about the twenties and the fight and so on. Reminded her that his parents were the ones, down the street, who had helped retrieve all that stuff from her smoldering garage. Wondered if she knew what a treasure trove she had.

She remembered the parents, knew them by sight, of course, knew their names, but she didn't believe this kid could have had any musical talent or she would remember him too. He might have been forced by his mother to take lessons for a year or so. He might have been a fattish sort of kid who couldn't sit still. Or the one who kept a rolled-up comic book in his shirt pocket. Or the one whose sister had a voice with slim potential.

She had been instrumental in his life, he vowed again, saying the words as if they meant anything at all.

So now he was a slicked-down, slim, vaguely handsome kind of fellow. But handsome in that negative sort of way in which there was simply nothing present to make him non-handsome. He smiled a lot. He wore a California suit, almond-colored, and white shoes. No one in Shelby wore white shoes anyplace but the golf course. He reminded Amelia of a game show.

He told the crowd, for starters, that he was mighty proud to be a native of this fine little town, a town filled with history and drama and adventures that do not fade with the passage of time. He said he had nothing but admiration for the brave people now sitting at the front table—he gestured magnanimously and made a white grin in the middle of his tan—who gave up everything to carve out lives on these wide and windblown prairies. People like his childhood music teacher, Amelia Malone, he said with another flourish of his arm.

He said he could only hope that he carried, as his own personal legacy, some of their grit and determination and, yes, their vision too. Their sense of life's inherent possibilities.

Since he quit the ministry and went into dry goods back in the forties, George McClintock had not been averse to a few drinks on social occasions. At the banquet, he was more voluble than usual because he was a little drunk and a lot worried about Suzanne.

He asked Jerry in a normal speaking voice whether he thought it was possible this young fellow would wrap it up before everyone at the old-timers' table was dead.

"You were the people!" Michael Cage shouted. "You were the people"—he stabbed the air before them—"who invited the world heavyweight boxing champion of the world—the incomparable Jack Dempsey—to defend his title in Shelby, Montana, population one thousand.

"Picture it," he said, spreading his hand wide. "A little prairie town in 1923 builds an arena that could accommodate the whole town—*times forty*. And that town raises, not one hundred thousand dollars, and not two hundred thousand dollars, but, yes, close to three hundred thousand dollars to bring the world's champion to Shelby.

"And the fight is fought. And it is a good fight."

There was something biblical in his intonation that was deeply familiar to George McClintock. He thought for a minute about his young preaching self and couldn't quite believe that he and that young person still shared a name, much less a body or a mind.

"Tommy Gibbons, the valiant challenger, stays on his feet the entire fifteen rounds. Fighting Tommy from Saint Paul. He gives the champion a run for his money and gives the audience probably the best fight anybody in the country has ever witnessed.

"It was classic drama, my friends! David and Goliath. The little guy against the big guys and their slick managers and their money. The pioneer West against the urban East."

His other hand was spreading the air now. McClintock expelled his breath loudly. "Picture the big steamers pounding their way across the prairie, bringing all those big-shot reporters—those Damon Runyons and Heywood Brouns—and their typewriters and cameras and sidekicks too," Cage pleaded. "Picture Dempsey's training camp by the historic Missouri River, a camp of rowdiness and color, a camp of men in the wild and roaring twenties. Flappers roaring out to visit in their flivvers. Gangster bodyguards. And then, up north in Shelby, Gibbons and his sweet wife and children in a little green cottage near his workout arena. Gibbons the good guy from Saint Paul. A David, armed with nothing but his grit and his integrity and his fists.

"A townful of people who have put their last dollar on this contest between the underdog and the champion. And as each deadline approaches for an installment of one hundred thousand dollars, the tension, the drama, the stakes rise. As each deadline approaches, we slide closer to the edges of our seats!"

He seemed to have forgotten that he was talking to people who knew all about it. He seemed to be trying to convince someone far away, someone somewhere else.

And he was not done yet. "You were the witnesses!" This with an open-palmed hand to the old-timers' table. "You have the stories and the evidence of the big fight. You do. And you." His finger reached Norgaard, who jerked his head up.

"You, sir," Cage said jauntily. "You, sir, were actually *at* the fight, I believe." He smiled encouragingly.

"What fight's that?" Norgaard said slyly. He looked around disingenuously. "We've had a lot of fights in Shelby. My son Tom was in a half a dozen bloody ones before he was seven years of age."

The crowd laughed, even Jerry.

Cage smiled generously, pretended to be vanquished by wit.

"I salute you," he said, arm aloft. "Our pioneers."

It took some minutes to set up the film. George Shore, who was running the projector, thought he had it all set to go, but the film flew out like confetti when he tripped the switch, piled itself on the floor, and the fluorescent lights flickered on again while the starting and stopping and rewinding was done.

The people at the fifty-year table sat a little lower in their seats than they had when the evening began. Amelia's wiglet and hat were very slightly askew. She had taken off her gloves and was pensively examining the spread fingers of her gnarled hand. A few just rested, in the way that old people do who are no longer revived or entertained by small talk. Jerry pulled a small leather notebook from his vest pocket and flipped back through the pages, searching for a particular notation to prompt his memory.

The room went dark again and the projector light arrowed through it. A little hum ran through the multipurpose room.

Hundreds of people appear on the screen, milling around a big puffing steam engine. Men in hats, straw boaters, move around rapidly. Tom Mix cowboys on horseback. Model T's. Difficult to make everything out because the film is so very black and white. The white hurts your eyes. The black swallows things up.

Dempsey. He is very dark. White shorts and an old dark cardigan. Shiny slicked-back hair. Twenty-eight years old, and his face sags slightly at the edges. A removed look, lowering, unmoving but powerful, like a smoke-darkened idol. He breathes out animal air, slowly. He blinks like a lizard.

And now Gibbons, the challenger, wearing a big figured robe. He looks swaddled in it, like a kid in borrowed clothes. He is alert and wiry as a terrier. There is an industrious ridge between his squinty eyes. Thin lips. He bounces against the ropes, testing them.

Jerry remembers, as he watches, that Gibbons had an older brother, Mike. The Phantom. A middleweight. That Mike was supposed to be the real boxer, the genius, but he lost an eye, flamed out, something. Tunney said one time that he patterned his style on Mike Gibbons. And he used that style to beat Dempsey in '26 and, for good, in '27. So you could say one of the Gibbons boys finally did do Dempsey in, by proxy. It wouldn't be Tom who did it, though.

The camera moves to a group of Indian men in long braids and full headdresses. A one-word caption: "Injuns."

Gibbons has the stupid robe off, a white towel across his shoulders. He is immigrant-white. They pose for the newspaper photographers. Handshake, long freeze. Fists grimly to the chins, long freeze. A breeze blows the towel off Gibbons's shoulders, and he grabs at it angrily. The speed of the film makes everything frantic.

Men mill around the fighters, straw-hatted, frail, and light.

The fight is about to start. Dempsey shoots a cool hunter's look at Gibbons, whose eyes dart up through the shoulders of his handlers.

"It was so hot," Amelia confides to McClintock. "I believe I was terribly dehydrated. I believe the heat made some of those people *rabid*."

It was an unedited, round-by-round film. After the sixth round, after Tommy began to retreat and defend, most of the watchers went into their own thoughts. The evening had begun to seem long.

Smoke wafted up through the arrowing white light. The white heads in the front. The clicking film, so silent. The jittery images. The moments when the silence and the grainy stark images, the naked men clutching each other, took on the look of pornography. Those times when Gibbons clung to Dempsey like a rebuffed, abject lover, as if he had a grief or a desperation that made him do this horrible public clinging and the champion must pluck him off, growl at him, run him into a corner. You wanted to look down at your feet during those paralyzed moments when the muscled, slick-skinned, hand-muffled men held each other like that.

Skiff Norgaard was fast asleep. George McClintock had settled down farther in his seat and had a look of distracted misery on his face because he was thinking of Suzanne in the hospital and the way she would look—so pinched and distant—when his nephew drove him down to see her in the morning.

Michael Cage was jotting numbers now, doing sums and divisions and making columns with the names of different people at the top.

Amelia had her gloves back on and was patting a finger lightly on her bad eye.

Jerry was trying to remember the exact legal description of the piece of land Skiff Norgaard rooked him out of in 1922.

The shadows in the film have grown long and have risen from the floor. The ring is crowded with people and shadows.

Round fifteen. The audience perks up. Gibbons is game. Still game. It is as if he gains something if he can simply diminish the other's win. That's all he can hope for, all he's really ever been able to hope for—that Dempsey won't win easily. And now it's almost over.

The old-timers rouse themselves and watch intently. Something flat, a seat cushion perhaps, sails onto the arena and is plucked away. Towels flap furiously around the fighters' heads and then they are back out there.

Gibbons throws his arms around Dempsey's waist, clinging, and pushes him out of the picture, beyond the camera's eye. The referee follows and disappears.

The crowd at the banquet watches the unpeopled screen—watches one shadow push the other shadow into the ropes. The rope shadows bend with the weight of the phantoms against them, and the crowd leans forward because it seems, now, that something important is happening.

And then the real Dempsey is backing into the ring and Gibbons is pushing him and the referee hops panting beside them,

The next moment, it's over. The bell rings silently and the big arm is hoisted into the air, like something dark and dead.

Fans jump into the arena, lots of them. The fighters disappear. One young fellow walks across the foreground. He is lanky and local. As he passes in front of the camera, he grabs the hat off his head and slices the air with it, disgusted, impatient, tired of the whole fool business.

Several of the men at the old-timers' table believe that man to be themselves. They are so sure, they don't even feel like mentioning it.

The fourth graders took the stage again and sang "America the Beautiful" and "My Home's in Montana."

The emcee asked if any other old-timers had words to say, and Amelia did.

She was by far the most dressed up and made up of all the women. She had the flimsiest shoes, pumps with open toes, and the kind of gloves that went halfway up the forearm. Her crocheted summer shawl and that hat with a half veil.

She walked up to the podium, limping. She had twisted her ankle as she stepped out of the car, and now it had started to swell and hurt.

She spent some time adjusting the microphone. "Can you hear me?" she trilled. "You at the back of the room?" Jerry gave someone a don't-ask-me look.

Amelia thanked everyone for staging such a heartwarming event and thanked Mr. Cage—that's how she referred to him—for his kind and eloquent words. She said the fourth graders had performed admirably, probably because their parents had been so well taught by herself and had handed down a certain musical sense to their offspring. She gave a quick, fleeting little smile when she said this.

The fourth graders' songs, she said, combined with the fight film to make her remember a ballad that a blind soldier sang before the boxing contest, as she put it. It was a very beautiful ballad that is not heard much anymore.

"It was so very hot that day," she said, her voice rising. "I wore a light muslin frock that was tailored for me in New York City—I had only recently arrived from the city, some of you may remember..."

She scanned the old-timers' table and got only one or two verifications—most didn't actually remember how or when she had come to town. One or two consulted their watches.

"And I remember fanning myself, fanning, fanning with a beautiful Japanese fan I had purchased on Union Square in Manhattan for a song, but to no avail! I made a young man in the seat ahead of me put out a cigarette, I recall that as well. And a good thing too. That arena was a tinderbox. Those hot, hot boards, new hot boards with sap oozing out of them—I got a big spot of sap on my skirt—and those young men just smoking and throwing cigarettes around like we wouldn't have all gone up in about two seconds if a fire had broken out."

She paused and tipped her head down a little, as if she had notes in her hand, though she didn't.

"It seemed," she said, "as if the real boxing contest, the one everyone was waiting for, would never happen. They brought out other young men to fight, and one of them became so very bloody I had to avert my eyes. Yes, it's true!" She threw an accusing glance at the audience.

"I began to think I was dreaming. Dreaming that I was in Montana. Dreaming that I was in that huge, that enormous structure, waiting to see Jack Dempsey fight a young man from my hometown and the hometown of my brother Jerry Malone, as it happens." She gestured magnanimously toward Jerry.

"This sense of dreaming, I believe it was because I was seriously dehydrated at the time and didn't know it. You cannot sit four hours in one hundred degrees of heat and keep one hundred percent of your wits about you.

"And do you know, there *were* people who became—well, I call it rabid. Whether from the heat or not, I do not know. One young man in particular, I seem to remember. I heard a pounding behind me in the higher bleachers and turned to see this particular young man *running* down the bleachers in huge leaps. There were not very many people in the bleachers except in the sections nearest the ring. He seemed to have started at the very top, and he came running, leaping down those wooden seats, scarcely slowing to leap through people sitting on the seats—I know because he leaped right past me, leaving a distinct dirty footprint on the edge of my skirt—and he leaped right down to the front row where all the reporters were, most of them from New York City, did you happen to know that? And do you know what he did?

"He stood right in front of them and he yelled, 'Saps!' Shaking his fist right in their noses! 'Saps!' he yelled. And once more—this time to the rest of us, it seemed—'Saps!' And then he walked off very quickly and I never saw him again in my entire life.

"And of course I was nearly crushed to death when the gates were crashed by all those men, and I lost part of my vision as a result, though I didn't know I was going to at the time." She paused to remember something else. "One of the men who crashed the gate was a professional gate crasher from back East named One-Eyed Connolly. He was famous. The newspapermen all knew him."

"Well!" she said briskly. "That isn't what I wanted to talk about, of course." She raised her gloved hand dramatically. It looked floppy, as if a child were playing dress-up. It was a rather long pause. Little coughs in the audience.

"The soldier and the song," Jerry called out.

"I know," she snapped at him. "I was just collecting myself so that I get it right."

"This young soldier," she began, "this blind soldier from the Great War, was from Sunburst, Montana. He wore blue sunglasses, dark round ones, and he sang through a megaphone. I remember thinking, What must it be like to sing for an audience if you are sightless?

"I thought it must be, in some way, like being a blind dancer I heard about. You cannot see what you look like, in a mirror or in the faces of an audience. You just have to send your gift out—your voice—on faith. Try, simply, to make a beautiful sound." Her fingers fluttered a little; lifted in the air.

"Well, that young man succeeded, I am here to say. Even through a megaphone. He had a clear true tenor, a high Irish tenor, and he sang an old ballad you don't hear that much anymore.

"The words I recall as if hearing them yesterday. It is called 'A Piper.'" She began to sing in a high warble.

"A piper in the streets today / Set up and tuned, and started to play, / And away, away, away, away, / On the tide of his music we started away. / The doors and windows were open'd wide; / And all went dancing on music's tide."

Amelia's voice had the appropriate sad lilt. She sang frankly and without haste, and closed her eyes at the end of the verse. At this point, the audience began to clap eagerly. But Amelia was not finished. She lifted her floppy gloved fingers delicately, held them in a gesture for silence, and went on.

"The men left down their work and came; / And women with petticoats color'd like flame, / And little bare feet that were blue with cold / Went dancing back to the age of gold; / And all the world went gay, went gay, / For half an hour in the street today."

Now the old-timers were bending their heads slightly, or cocking them as if trying to hear better. Their eyes were not on her or each other or anything physically present.

When she was finished, she nervously clapped a few claps for herself, then stepped to the side of the podium and did a long low curtsy that must have hurt her twisted ankle, because it threw a grimace of surprise across her face.

Michael Cage jumped up and swept his arm toward her, clapped frantically, then lifted the whole room to its feet with twitches of his fingers, and they all clapped, a standing ovation, and Amelia inclined her head, pleased and unsurprised, and walked carefully back to her chair.

15

Late summer of 1922, and Shelby still had the sound and feel of a town that never slept. At night, headlights ran in a stream from town, north to the field. Men wandered the streets far after midnight, some of them waiting for the bed they shared, in shifts, with others.

The hammers knocked all day and into the night. The big steamers shrieked, pulled into the station, thrummed in place, and a dozen men, maybe more, stepped off with their valises, their orders, their hunches.

New women came too. With the bands that played jazz in the raw new dance halls. With the men. Some were camp followers and looked it. Others were harder to place—so modern and smart and watchful.

A pair of low-cut city shoes, sunk in the mud. A dropped waistline and an eye-hiding hat. A cigarette in a thin black holder.

His name was Sergei Stepov, and he was known as Sam. His English was hissing and heavy. In all seasons except high summer he wore a worsted wool cape that reached nearly to his ankles. Long hair the color of cigar ash combed straight back from a lean morose face. A monocle that wavered in the sun.

No one knew any absolute facts about his past or why exactly they had come to think he was a dispossessed Russian count. But his appearance—his thin imperious nose, his stalking gait, the cape—made the rumor seem true enough. He had a farm east of Shelby, but farming did not seem to be an interest. Most of the time he was in town, leaving his wife and her silent brother to work the place.

Jerry was in Shelby now, every chance he got. He left the girls to mind the treasurer's office in Cut Bank and got on the train or the skidoo and flew to Shelby to be near the feel of oil.

One day in the Red Onion he struck up a conversation with Stepov about Wells's *Outline of History*. Jerry happened to be reading the last few pages over his coffee, and Stepov had, by coincidence, just finished it. A bright blue day with a chill on the edge and Stepov in his cape, even in the indoors.

The Red Onion that day was loud with the boots of men tromping in and out, with shouted greetings and the heavy whine of the door each time a customer came or went. The smoke of cigars and cigarettes floated lazily toward the low ceiling. The thick china clanged.

Soon enough their conversation got around to oil—all conversations in Shelby, that year, got around to oil—and they discovered that they were both familiar with Hager's *Practical Oil Geology*. They could both discuss the field in the language of scientists and mappers, not mere gamblers or speculators. They shared a love of the very idea of oil, its physicality and origins and tendencies, even apart from the question of whether it could be brought up from the ground to fuel motorcars and make fortunes.

Devonian, Silurian, Ordovician, Cambrian, they murmured over their coffee. The Morrison, the Ellis. Anticline, syncline, fault, contact, seepage. Cretaceous, Jurassic, Carboniferous. Virgelle sandstone, pebble band, Colorado shale, blackleaf sandy member, Kootenai, Madison limestone, Jefferson limestone, anhydrite. Producing horizons. Pay zones. Closure.

Stepov was a pure aficionado. He watched the play as he would watch a chess tournament, evaluating the moves, second-guessing the players. He was not part of the scramble, only fascinated, utterly fascinated, by its cerebral nature—the way an idea, an insubstantiality, could create such a fervor. He had seen it before in Russia.

Jerry would put a problem to Stepov. Let's say a fellow could not afford the property just west of the new well, the

Mid-Northern Howling, let's say—pointing at the map. This fellow has to move away from it in some direction and get himself a cheaper parcel or a lease somewhere else. Where would *you* go? Where would you put your rubles, Sam Stepov?

The Russian pondered the map, chin on knuckles. He squinted. Turned the map a degree to the west, a degree to the east. Thought. Tapped the checkered oilcloth with a tobacco-colored fingernail. Put the fingernail on the map and moved it like a Ouija pointer, wanderingly, and then with sudden decision in a crisp circle. These half sections, he said. Somewhere in here. Long chance, but possible. Possible.

Not these? Jerry would ask happily, circling an area to the north and west. Wouldn't this be more likely? More likely maybe, said Stepov. But not more cheap. You want cheap *and* likely. *And* close enough to the play that the big boys will figure you might be onto something and buy it off you just to hedge their bets, eh?

Jerry slaps a bill of sale onto the oilcloth next to Stepov's gaunt fingers. Cash!

The thrill of a new discovery this week—a gusher—from a horizon nobody ever thought would pan out, and now everything has to be looked at differently. The possibilities expand fast, and there is a quick fast burst of frantic buying and leasing. People like Jerry go home with new money in their pockets. Things aren't what they seemed yesterday.

And then they can't help saying to themselves, This is just the beginning. This is how luck feels. This is the verge. It is the perfect thought, the perfect feeling—that you are on the verge, on the brink. It is where we all want to be. Not the moment of deliverance, but the moment just before.

This is the verge. The biggest is yet to come. Say that to yourself enough times and everything that was a question becomes a possibility.

They are sure to boom the field in the spring.

For a while, that is the talk. The real action, the huge boom, is still to come. The rest of the country will hear about this place and come flocking. That is the refrain that thrums among the khakis and smoke and traffic. That winds among the hammers hacking, through the raw young frames of new buildings, houses, dance halls, and the mud and the horses jumping sideways at the pop of car exhausts. Between the lines at the restaurants and the latrines. Across the tired faces of men who spend the days deal-talking, then sleep a few hours in their autos.

Oil, oil, oil. And the best is yet to come.

Jerry spent the money on a sturdy new Hupmobile so that he could tour the oil field without breaking down.

He quit his job at the treasurer's office. He sold three more parcels of land and bought a farmhouse to move onto a lot in Shelby that he had been smart enough to buy a year earlier.

He got ready to move Vivian and the children from Cut Bank to Shelby, twenty-five miles closer to the field. The action.

The all-out boom was coming in the spring. Everyone said it.

Up at 5 a.m. to tour field. Good prospects.

They sent the kids to Clemons's farm for a few days, and he and Vivian took a breather before the move. Took the train through the reservation and up into the mountains.

They pitched the big canvas tent on the shore of Two Medicine Lake. Their low voices around the fire. Heady pine. Cold molten lake. The first frail star. A single big blanket around their shoulders.

In the early light of the next day, they cut walking sticks and climbed Mount Henry. Up and up the long flank, through the baking sap smell, the air still cool at noon on the very edges, and then out of the trees and up, up, above the last scrubby greens to the top. Their hard breathing. Silent resting. Their sweat. Two steps a breath. And finally the top and all those peaks at their feet like a frozen choppy sea. Their names in a logbook inside a tin box. A shared apple and a blanket.

They moved the farmhouse in from the country and set it on a new-poured foundation in Shelby, a few blocks from the school. Blankets on the windows yet. No running water. But they had money from the sale of the Cut Bank house—it sold in two days—and Vivian bought geraniums and a crateful of fuzzy baby chicks for the kids to tend.

The hail came in the night, glass stones as large as English walnuts. They ricocheted off the town roofs and swept in razoring sheets across acres and acres of wheat that had just begun to become gold. The first decent crop in five years was pelted to mulch.

In Shelby, there was the sound of breaking glass in the dark, the sickening knock of pelted rocks.

The hailstones were precisely the size of a baby chicken's head. They flew into the small dirt yard outside the house; hit with a deafening racket on the piece of frail tin nailed to a set of posts to keep the chicken feed dry. They battered the tin sheet onto the ground, where it changed in shape so that it seemed to writhe.

The children peered out the window into the bullet-filled dark. Maudie began to wail and little Tip joined in. Jerry and Vivian urged them all back to bed, wincing at the hammer knocks on the roof. The chickens, the little chicks, will be all right, they said. They have probably found a hiding place.

The sun came up and winked off the balls of ice scattered across the dirt yard. They looked like the aftermath of a celebration, forlorn as day-old confetti.

The chicks were huddled behind the cellar door, some of them. Twenty or so of them quivered silently together, a hummock of gauze. But eleven were further into the yard, lying motionless at strangely even intervals; toppled in their tracks.

The children cupped the silent ones in their hands and placed them in a wicker basket. They are gone, Vivian told them gently. We can bury them in a corner of the yard. No, they didn't feel the huge glass stones break their heads. It was too fast. It was like a bolt of lightning. No, she said, not souls like humans. Maybe some other kind of soul, though. A little chicken soul.

And then one of the chicks opened an eye. And the mourning that the children were easing into, the beginnings of acceptance, shamed them—shamed Vivian too—like a small slap. They had given up too soon.

Even though the eye quickly closed again and resumed its permanent look of death, it was now a mask, that eye. A wink. A joke. And so all the little corpses were placed in the basket, their bodies spaced apart for potential breathing room. They were placed by the stove.

Jerry had to leave. He had business. He had a letter in his pocket he would post to Carlton, urging him to go in with half a dozen other Minneapolis businessmen on a new hotel in Shelby. It was a surefire win, Jerry assured him. They'll be turning people away when they really boom the field in the spring.

When he left the house, his children were huddled around the chickens and didn't even lift their heads as he said good-bye. He walked out into the hammers and the autos and the shouts.

The chick that had opened its eye opened it again an hour later, and the other eye with it. It was late morning now. The hailstones had melted away or shrunk to the size of marbles and peas. The house was very warm. Everyone's forehead began to sweat.

And then the chickens began to stir, all together. An eye opened, and another, and a beak. A small wing poked up. Miniature claws contracted leisurely, like a hand in sleep.

The children screamed with delight. They jumped up and ran around, and Francis made an Indian war cry, his hand fluttering against his mouth. A chick peeped. And another. They're peeping! the children screamed. Vivian came over and peered curiously into the basket. They all began to peep, all but two of the chicks, and those were not stirring at all.

This was now eight hours after the hail. The chickens were frantic for food. The children laughed and shrieked. Francis had a fit of unstoppable giggles and rolled around on the floor, grabbing his stomach, kicking his boots. Maudie ran out to the yard and brought back a tin plate with chicken feed. The chicks were on their feet now, most of them, and they jostled for the grain. They ruffled themselves as if they'd been drenched in water or buried in sand. They poked their tiny beaks into their fuzzy little feathers, officious and brisk.

The sun was high now and the hail was gone. Vivian told the children to put the chicks back into the yard and go outside themselves to play. Before they carried the big basket outdoors, they all gathered for another look at the brood. Two of the chicks still didn't move.

They each ran an index finger over the fuzzy heads of the ones that hadn't made it. Then they placed them gently, matter-of-factly, in the big trash can by the cellar door.

Forever after, Jerry would associate the slowdown, the lag, the beginning of the end of his tallest hopes, with the sound of a wheeze in his own breath: the tightness he thought had left him years earlier.

He thought at first it might be something in the new house. Maybe the chicks. But leaving the house all day changed nothing. The panic-making tightness seemed to be coming back.

Vivian looked at him with deep surprise—it was like a former marriage, this presence. He was familiar with it and she wasn't. He made himself mullein tea, steeped long the way his mother used to do it, but it didn't seem to help.

The end of the summer of 1922. That's when the action began to taper off for good, but no one wanted to see it. That's when deals became almost-deals. Three men instead of eight or nine getting off the train. The signs so slight, Jerry didn't even see them with his eyes or his mind. Only his lungs knew what was starting to happen.

And then, to cap it, his old friend betrayed him.

It was a half section of unturned ground due east of Sunburst—a piece of land that lit up like an electric light in Jerry's mind the minute Stone, the geologist, showed him a new map, a redrawing of the field.

The map, to someone like Jerry who could read it, who could compare it instantly with past versions, showed a small, significant shift of the dome to the east. Nothing huge, but enough to attract the attention, soon enough, of people who knew what they were looking for.

The property was a relinquishment. Jerry could get the surface and mineral rights for almost nothing if he could clear up a few problems with the title at the government land office in Great Falls.

It was morning. A chinook a week earlier had melted everything, then the wind had shifted and frozen it up again, so Shelby was encased in ice. More snow and wind were on the way. People were about, picking their way on the ice in the cold.

A woman, some kind of entertainer with the band at the King Tut, stood at the door smoking a cigarette, wrapped in a big man's coat. Somebody pounded a fender with a hammer, and the sound was bright and jarring.

Jerry hadn't sold anything in a month, but he was smiling now because he would go to Great Falls in the morning, clear up the title, and buy the property. Lease the mineral rights, reserving at least fifteen percent for himself.

He had a strong hunch about this land; his strongest hunch yet.

You play your cards right. You act when the time is right. Bingo.

Skiff Norgaard looked like a farmer even when he was in town. Overalls and that big padded coat. Old-fashioned high-topped shoes. Flat cheekbones and white-lashed eyes. A slow, rocking walk. Thick fingers, thin lips.

He greeted Jerry with a stolid clap on the upper arm, unsmiling, the way he always did. He leaned against the King Tut and rolled a cigarette with his thick fingers and listened to Jerry tell him what a splendid day it was. He nodded his head slowly, the way he always did.

He listened to Jerry talk about the morning's oil gossip: who's going to do what, and where, and when. "Ya," Skiff said. "That Gladys Belle well, it sounds like a big one. Ya, it's a heck of a field—so big, so shallow. What's it gonna shape up to be, a guy has to wonder."

He listened to Jerry tell him he would be on No. 43 to Great Falls in the morning. "Business at the land office, Skiff. Business that can't wait.

"Why can't it wait?"

"Sorry, pal," Jerry said. "Mum's the word."

But a secret is a heavy thing to carry.

"The land office," he repeated.

They smoked for a while. Jerry turned to his friend. "This is it, Skiff," he said fervently. "This is really it. This is the big one. The goods."

He unrolled the map under his arm and held it up on the wall.

"I ain't been following the play," Skiff said. "What are you seeing here?"

Carefully, Jerry traced the previous version of the structure. Then he ran his finger around the new edges.

"Farther east," Skiff said. "They're guessing farther east."

"A matter of days," Jerry said. "They'll be leasing, and they'll be leasing for big money."

Skiff's heavy index finger went to a small red *x* on the eastern edge of the big oval. "Seems like a guy with some extra cash might want to put it here," he said.

"Hmmm," Jerry said, his voice full of happy mockery. "By gosh, you might be right."

Skiff Norgaard's big mittened hands on the wheel of his Ford, not two hours later. He squints through the flurrying snow. A rutted, hazardous seven hours on the road. Off it once, near Brady, but two fellows get him going again. The snow stays light enough. He makes it.

Skiff Norgaard drives straight to the land office and pounds with his big mittens on the door at 4:55. Flexes his big fingers slowly. The clerk scowls, casts elaborate glances at the tocking Elgin on the wall.

A quick title search and a conclusion. Skiff's fingers around the pen. A check. The big rigorous signature.

A meal at the hotel, where he will stay the night, driving away in the morning, just a few minutes before the arrival of the next train from Shelby, with his friend Jerry Malone aboard. His hands rest on either side of his plate.

He has the quiet look of someone who has just delivered bad news.

Norgaard's signature, its up-and-down rigor, the ink thick and for all time on the page. Below it, the clerk's time stamp—11 January 1923—and above it the legal description of the property.

The Great Falls land office dim and only frailly heated by the big potbellied stove. Wind battering the walls, pushing small rivers of frigid air beneath the frosted glass door, to trickle around the feet.

Jerry is stiff with the cold, the trip. But his excitement, until this moment, has kept the icy air at bay He has, since rising in the night, felt fueled. His fingers have quivered slightly. His heart has thumped against the wallet that is going to buy him the highest kind of luck.

Now it all stops. His heart, the heat. He stares at the paper anchored with the signature of his friend, Skiff Norgaard. The paper that says Skiff Norgaard has, since yesterday afternoon, owned the best hunch of Jerry's life.

He and Francis haul water on a sled in the moonlight to the new house with the blankets on the windows. Jerry is quiet these days since the discovery of Norgaard's treachery. He hopes he won't hear that someone wants to drill there. He hopes nobody will care, ever, about that property.

As he and Francis pull the sled together, he listens to his breath leaking a little on the edges.

Francis sold a marble that day for fifty cents that he had bought for a quarter. Then an oilman paid him a dollar to stand in line for his mail. He is flush, Francis is.

There is a buoyancy to the family yet. Things always slow down in the deep winter, Jerry heard Vivian tell a friend. They'll really boom the field in the spring, she said.

Maudie rode with a little friend in the friend's father's car, out to the oil field. They returned after dark. The little friend stayed over and they chattered long into the evening, fired by the lights out there on the prairie, the lonely industrial whine of the big pumps.

Vivian has not mentioned Seattle in months.

Skiff Norgaard leased Jerry's hunch to Standard Oil of California for $5,000 and a big bonus and a fifteen percent cut. In the early spring of 1923, they hit oil, a gusher, and Skiff gathered in his money and bought a few wheat farms north of town.

Skiff would have a long run of luck after that. He would escape the hailstorms, weather the Depression, keep his son out there working, acquire more land and more machinery. By the 1960s, he would be a millionaire a few times over and still farming.

They never spoke again after the winter of 1923, Jerry and Skiff, though they belonged for the next half century to the same Lions Club and ate lunch in the same cafés and took their families to the same Fourth of July picnics and sat in the same auditorium at their children's school graduations and piano recitals.

The Norgaards always had the biggest, newest automobile in the county, even during the dirty thirties.

The land business was slow, mysteriously slow, that winter of '23. Jerry had holdings, every cent in land or leases, and no one was buying. Why? He couldn't fathom it. Everything about the field seemed promising, worth a risk, a try. *All my ships out to sea.* But it was as if the field had somehow become a blind spot in the public eye.

It was so far away, so crusty and blank, that country. Like Canada. The rest of America just didn't see it. And his best hunch had been yanked out from under him.

The sudden stillness of that winter, the sense of an arm with a hammer raised in the air and then frozen. The feeling that the place was going to stop, become a frozen scene of a boom town, applauded by all.

The way men like Jerry felt themselves become aimless. It was like going every day to a movie that never started. Taking a seat, folding the overcoat, clearing the throat, and then nothing.

The feeling that the course of the river has shifted. You are the frozen part, but you can hear the channel running. It's not far away. People like Norgaard, the ones who made the last big deals, were in the channel, moving. Pole-rafting; hair back in the wind.

Twenty-four below, and Shelby huddles into itself, glitter-iced, smoking. A hard white sun. Gleaming naked buildings.

Puffed up, empty oil news in the *Tribune*. Getting ready, getting ready. Anytime. Nervousness. Too much time to think.

Jerry sits alone in his freezing cement-walled office. He just wrote a rent check for it and is furious. Seventy-five dollars. It's about what he's got left to his name. Gouged, he feels. And then he has just heard a rumor that Norgaard bought another place and sold it the next day for a pile. Doesn't have the heart to check.

He spends the day indexing oil and gas journals. Seventy-five dollars. Shivering under his overcoat in a stupid, drafty box of an office, his maps spread out before him, the one he showed Norgaard with the red *x* on it. He shivers with fury and the cold. He feels caught in a poker game he can't leave.

A big party was going on in the rest of the country. Swells were waving their dough around and having a big time while little Shelby stood outside the tall windows like a waif, yelling about some black stuff that was spouting up through the lawn.

A shudder of wind hits the building. He is in a basement room with a high window well. He sees only the feet of people walking past. The blowing snow above his head like racing clouds. He is freezing and stiff. Joints won't move. Can't go home, because he would have to say there was nothing doing, except that a deal just fell through that he'd been counting on to pay his office rent. That they were almost out of money. That the office was useless because no one stopped in; there was no reason.

He thought of the warm treasurer's office in Cut Bank. How, this time of day, the two girls would be making tea, pulling the blinds against the cold. How the new treasurer would have things to do, another hour's worth of things to do, and then the Closed sign and another day with pay.

The Silver Grill smells like cigars and fried meat. Smoke from the stove, smoke from the pipes and the Little Queen cigars. The smoke of people waiting, heating up. And nowhere for it to go, because the small oily windows are sealed against the cold. The smell of men who haven't had baths in many days. The smell of sleeplessness and bootleg and no luck.

He closes his burning eyes for a moment. He can hear the almost-imperceptible wheeze at the edge of his breath. He moves nearer a poker game in the corner, jostling shoulders, holding his breath against the low stench.

Five men, all out-of-towners, slap down their cards, tip back their chairs. Whiskey fumes float from their coffee. Chas.

Thomas, the doodlebug man. The man with the leather spats, the geologist. Two real estate birds from Canada. A stranger in a long driving coat.

As he watches them, Jerry feels again the envy he carries for certain kinds of men—the jaunty and reckless; the loud and wild and womanless. Slapping cards down. Pushing in large bets on weak hands, bluffing like kids. There was a kind of grace in it, a kind of decisive recklessness that was similar to the way the best stockmen worked a herd of wild horses.

Maybe it was simply their momentum. The way they seemed to expect good and bad and triumph and reverse, and always a crisis, a crisis created if it wasn't there, the pure forward movement making each setback smaller because there were so many of them.

They were wild men but they weren't passionate men, because they could not die of hope as he was beginning to feel he could. Hope deferred.

They did not get sick hearts, these men. They were buoyant, elastic, hearty, alive, without conscience or scruple. They made burghers out of the men who were already here, who had weathered it, stuck it out, made a life, made children. They made cautious burghers of men like Jerry Malone, who felt every penny he had just put down for a bad cup of coffee.

He intends to stay a half hour, then go home. Have a cup of coffee and listen to the talk and maybe ask Olson if he wants to reconsider on that lot option. But he stays because it feels like a hub, as if something is going on. He orders a piece of pie.

The Monroe kid is there with his newspapers, and Jerry asks him to tell Vivian he will be home in an hour or two. She will think it is business. That he is making a deal. And she might be right. He should just stay, see what comes up. A dozen loud men in a café, and now someone has brought out some hooch, and another card table has been set up. It is dark. The wind has increased, and the thought of going out in it is awful. Something has torn loose on the roof, a wire for the sign maybe, and it is smacking the side of the building.

The first group of poker players disbands. One of them mimes a gun to another one's head, then scoops up a pile of change, and they all move in a pack to the door, headed to wherever the women are.

And now the people left in the room are, with the exception of two men eating silently in the corner, all from Shelby. They have known each other since that first Round Lake picnic, that first summer when their hopes were so simple and extravagant.

They glance around at each other with the bored, familiar expressions of siblings around a dinner table.

They talk long into the night. Shout some. Drink a little. Seven of them. Five are in real estate and doing nothing. The one with a newspaper reads a small item aloud.

Montreal offers to hold Dempsey fight.

They talk about publicity stunts, getting the attention of the boys with the money. The place turns quiet for a moment. You can hear the hiss of a steam kettle back in the kitchen, slop tossed out the back door into the kind of night that nearly freezes it before it hits the ground.

Laughter. A pencil and some doodling. Another roar of laughter and another round of drinks.

A slammed door and 3:00 a.m. and two men walking through the breath-grabbing night, its stars like speckles of glass.

The depot, the telegraph operator.

The men laughing one last big laugh, tired, the stunt done—and the bleeps begin to run along the country's wires toward the windowless office of Mr. Doc Kearns in New York City. It is addressed to Kearns's fighter, the heavyweight boxing champion of the world.

"We are prepared to offer you purse of $200,000 to be paid $50,000 upon signing of contract and balance when you enter ring for fifteen round championship fight against

Tommy Gibbons July 4 in Shelby Montana Stop. Please wire acceptance."

Campbell's big gusher hit the newspapers on the ides of March, 1922. A year later, on the ides, Jerry and the other promoters stand on the site of the huge boxing arena to be built just west of town. The last grand stunt. Does anyone feel a flicker of coming disaster? Does anyone wish it were another day?

The photo. Jerry stands on the end, a slight, suited man of thirty-five years, right arm cocked, cigarette. Unsmiling. Thirty-two of them. All in shirts and ties and city hats. All but the man in the puttees. The one with the little terrier and the silk pajamas. He stands next to Jerry. His hat has a higher crown than most. He is tall, rangy-looking. Dark shirt, dark ties, insolent stance. The jodhpurs. The boots and puttees. He is the only one who is not looking at the camera. His gaze is off to the side, over the tops of the other men's heads.

Stepov, the Russian count, is not in the photograph. He has taken up farming and chess.

16

The costume is actually two American flags arranged over her everyday chemise. They were delivered in a large box with the spiked crown and the torch, both papier-mâché.

She folds one of the flags and pins it around her waist, adjusting the hemline so that it falls to mid-calf. The second flag must be draped over one shoulder, leaving the other bare. There is a pencil drawing in the box of the way the costume should look. This look will require slipping off one strap of the chemise and pinning it out of sight. She considers altering the style to a more modest one. She has never actually worn a dress with one shoulder bare, and she tries to think of it as a classical style, like that woman in the French Revolution painting whose nakedness in the midst of battle is high and pure.

She knows, however, that her audience this evening—the members of the Bonhomie Club—want "patriotic entertainment," as the man put it. And that her bare shoulder falls in the entertainment part of it, not the patriotic part. Along with the knee-length hemline in the little drawing, but that is where she really must draw the line.

She completes the pinning, dons a star-spangled sash, and turns herself slowly in the mirror, left and right. Her bare shoulder, so white, looks like a chilly child's. She touches it protectively. It's a blustery April day. She wonders how she is expected to cover herself against the raw little wind when they come to pick her up. Her coat flung like a cape around the drapes. That will have to do.

So there she is, standing in front of the mirror, dressed in a pair of American flags. She tries on the crown. She holds the flimsy torch aloft.

Lelia told her about the job. Less than two hours of work for ten dollars at a well-established club, and they will come to get her in a chauffeured automobile. She will hoist the torch, smile her heartiest, and nod graciously at the pianist. He will play a brief, stirring introduction and then she will sing "God Bless America" and take requests. They might sing along, the men. It will be an enthusiastic crowd and they will applaud her and perhaps thank her in a way that brings another round of applause. And then they will bring her home again in the car, ten dollars richer.

She has opened the window to air the flat. Lelia smokes all the time now, always with a cigarette holder, which she holds at ear level between puffs. One of the holders is crusted with small rhinestones. She calls that one her "after-five."

She goes and comes and Daisy never really knows when to expect her, though Lelia does faithfully come up with her part of the rent.

Daisy and Lelia have not been speaking during the past few days, since their exchange about Mr. Higgenbotham, the Aeolian person who gave Daisy reason to believe she might soon have a record contract. Lelia laughed in the hardest way imaginable, and she said, pretending to be solicitous, her hands on Daisy's shoulders, "Daisy Lou," she said, "*Mr.* Higgenbotham is a fast-talking little cherub whose days at Aeolian are numbered, to put it nicely. You believe Mr. Higgenbotham, and you are putting your money on a lame horse. That test record was your one phonograph recording, my darling. Believe me." She herself is giving up whistling for something she calls cabaret performance.

Daisy hears heels clicking on the sidewalk two stories below and recognizes them, or thinks she does. She jumps back from the window and peers carefully. Yes, it is Penelope Wexner. It is, of course, her distinctive brisk step. She seems to be out for a stroll with her new dog, a Welsh corgi Daisy thinks is grotesque. She can't believe someone of Penelope's taste and style would see beauty in an animal so squat and infelicitous. It shakes Daisy's faith in her friend somehow that she—a spiritist, an aristocrat, an arbiter of taste—could proffer affection toward an animal named Marconi, who tended, when at rest, to drool on the toe of one's shoe.

They are mounting the steps to the building. The doorman will let them in.

Daisy cannot have Penelope Wexner see her in a flag. She cannot tell her she is going in a flag to a hall by the river to climb up on a platform and sing patriotic songs for the Bonhomie Club. The simplest explanation, put to words, flushes her face red, puts splotches across her bare shoulder.

She walks very quietly and carefully to a closet, opens it by inches—the heels are knocking down the hall now—and places herself inside the closet behind Lelia's perfumed and smoky clothes. Clothes that smell like jazz.

Penelope Wexner knocks on the door and calls out her name in a cheerful voice. She raps again. Daisy can hear Marconi snuffling, scratching at something. And then she can hear her friend chatting to the dog as if he were a snide friend. "Where could Daisy Lou—excuse me, Amelia—*be*?" she asks the dog in a rather loud, rather mocking kind of voice.

"Why would her window be flung open so wide if she weren't at home?" The dog snuffles louder.

"I know! She has *jumped* and they have hauled off the remains. Poor sweet dear!" This, followed by a warm chuckle. And then the heels clacking back down the hall, trailed by the dog's whispery claws.

Something in that small episode washes Daisy with bleakness. She closes her eyes and leans against the back of the closet, fighting a quick urge to weep. What is it? That her friend Penelope, who is supposed to be so tuned to emanations, cannot even divine that her friend of these months, her close spiritual friend, is within a few yards of her? That she laughs with a fat corgi about Daisy Lou jumping out of a window? That she could even conceive of such a joke?

All of that, yes. And something more. It is as if, hearing her friend's voice through the door, through the clothes, she hears it filtered to some kind of essence. And the essence seems, for the first time, frivolous, silly, even a bit pathetic. She feels the way she does at a moving picture show when the image, jumping around and fuzzy, is adjusted by someone up there in the room that emits the ray of light—and the picture becomes hard and clear. There is something in what she just heard that makes Daisy think about that.

How very long this day would be! Daisy could have had no idea.

She finally stepped out of the closet and made the last adjustments to her garb and sang the songs of her program quietly to herself, listening to her phrasing, making sure she made clean attacks, especially in the case of the high notes in the anthem. She consulted her clock and went downstairs, covering herself with her coat as best she could, to wait for the car. She put the torch in a large shopping sack with her music and the spiked liberty crown, hoping the sleepy old doorman wouldn't pick this occasion to ask questions. Already, she wanted it over with.

The automobile was fifteen minutes late and it was driven by a chauffeur who wore no uniform, nothing more than a white shirt with the sleeves rolled up. He spoke with a cigarette in his mouth, amiably but in the accents of a street hawker, Daisy thought. He was very young and provisional-looking.

The car was mud-spattered and was not a terribly large one, as she had expected. It didn't even have a hard roof, just a black cloth one that didn't fit any too tight. She sat on the front seat next to the driver, the cramped quarters requiring some adjustments with the crown and torch. She made sure she had her sheet music. She always brought it for the pianist so she could be sure that her numbers would be played in the key that best suited her voice.

The driver was overly solicitous at first. He put her coat up higher on her shoulders before she stepped in, and she could feel the warmth of the end of his cigarette, too near her neck, and his dry fingers brushing her bare shoulder.

He was a fast and competitive driver, tooting the horn often and squeezing exuberantly into minuscule spaces in the line of moving traffic. Daisy tried to ask him some questions—how long had he been associated with the Bonhomie Club; was this an annual patriotic event? He knew nothing. He grew distracted. He began to seem like what he was: someone hired off the street for the day.

They arrived and Daisy's hopes climbed, because a rather nice-looking man in a suit presented her, on the spot, with an armful of red and white roses. They were a little the worse for wear, but roses nevertheless. And they had her photo taken then for a newspaper, the man presenting the roses to her, she giving them back, he giving them to her again, and the flashes flashing all the while, until she saw nothing anywhere but small cold flares.

Shall we talk about the rest of the evening? We already know, don't we? Maybe it's enough to see Daisy up there in her flags, trying to make her voice heard over the growing din. The cheers, even some coins thrown at her feet. Or the half hour she stands outside in the gritty breeze, waiting for the boy to come around in the car, her coat slipping off her shoulders because she can't hold everything—the roses, the music, the crown, the coat. Maybe we see her hail a taxicab and the way the people inside it crane their heads and point and laugh as they pass. Or Daisy mistaking another car for the one that is supposed to come for her and running toward it, the flags flapping.

Would anyone have dared to tell her then that the club launders bootleg money, and processes bets, and that this annual event, trotted out for the papers, is a sham and most everyone knows it? That her money may or may not be in the mail?

The driver finally appears, surly now to the point of muteness. A whole life seems to have passed for him since he dropped her off. Hopes raised and dashed. Prospects appearing and winking out. Who can know?

Daisy has perhaps hoped that he would cheer her, deflect the grief that she knows is about to settle in. But he hasn't a shred of heartiness. He is no ally.

They ride through the streets and he curses obstructions as if there were not a lady within miles. Daisy occupies herself by imagining what could have happened to him since they parted, but comes up with blanks. She begins to hope it was very bad, whatever it was.

In her flat, she tears off the flags, screaming a little at the pins, throwing the material in a ball in the closet, the old roses in the trash.

Lelia is gone, of course. She has left a note that if so-and-so comes by, tell him to jump in a lake! These shards of another life show up all the time now. She has anchored the note with one of her cigarette holders, the peacock-green one, and left a faint whiff of something that Daisy imagines is gin.

Now she lets the entire day wash over her and around her—it sounds like mocking applause and a friend's suddenly silly voice and motorcars—and she says to herself, in a new voice, When, my dear girl? When are you going to step into the cold light of day?

Enclosed in the letter is a blurry newspaper photograph of Daisy Lou receiving roses from a portly grinning man. She looks quite jazzy and pretty, they think in Montana. The children keep the photo in an old book and show it to their friends. This is the one who made the phonograph record, they say, and then they will sometimes play the mended record again and examine the photo of Daisy being handed roses like a queen and her face a pretty heart-shaped one and her hair so stylish. What is she wearing? one of the children wonders. It appears, Jerry says wearily, to be the American flag.

April 20, 1923

Dear Jerry, Vivian and children—

Well the daffodils have made their annual appearance on the strip of earth that borders my building, a harbinger I am sure of bright days to come! How exciting it is to read in the New York papers about Shelby, Montana, and the Big Fight. I tell everyone my own brother was instrumental in arranging this extravaganza, and though I don't know that I approve of boxing, I know it is considered a manly and character-forming pursuit among many decent people, and so I shall withhold my judgment on that score. It thrills me, I must say, to be related to people who live in a small village that is on the front page of the New York Times! Even Lelia was impressed. Do you think the money can indeed be raised? There is no small amount of skepticism on the part of many newspaper reporters here, but then they are a hard lot, I believe. I have met some of them personally in my work and see nothing to dissuade me from that judgment.

For my part, I believe you can accomplish whatever you firmly set out to do and so I do believe that Mr. Jack Dempsey will indeed defend his world championship in Shelby, Montana, on Independence Day. And why should I not?

I have been busy as busy can be with my musical career. I am hoping Aeolian will see fit to make a phonograph record of my voice alone, without the presence of whistlers, and I am told it is a distinct possibility. However, they have seen fit recently to dismiss a Mr. Higgenbotham, an extremely artistic person and my staunch ally, and so I do not know what that portends. It is a crushing loss to me, as he had rare musical sensibilities and a

Perfect Ear, all combined with Business Sense—a rare combination in this world!!

It is not easy sometimes in the city with so many people scrambling for opportunities. The photograph enclosed was an event in which I was chosen over many many others to perform, at least three singers I know have asked me how I was able to get the job altho, of course, it is only to make ends meet and does not fairly represent my aspirations. It was not an altogether satisfying event but live and learn.

I believe you mentioned that you have a radio station in Montana. Do you indeed? I ask this because I know that radio stations are starving for live entertainment, professional singers in particular. They have all those hours that they must fill with sound and so this has opened up many new career opportunities for musicians and—think of it!—a person can sing over the radio waves and reach audiences that number in the thousands and are sitting by their receiving sets hundreds and hundreds of miles away!

I ask about Montana because it occurs to me that there cannot be very many high-caliber musicians in such a place and that I could perhaps offer my services on a short-term basis and have a visit with you and Vivian and the kiddies too. What do you think, Jerry? Carlton writes that he will not miss the Big Fight and so perhaps we would have the first reunion of the three of us since Mother died. Wouldn't that be glorious?! I have in mind a radio program that would be beautiful and appropriate, I feel.

Of course, I should only be able to stay several weeks, as I will very likely go to Europe in the early fall to study with Professor Lino in Milan, who is an intimate associate of my dear friend Penelope Wexner. Mrs. Wexner says it is essential that I achieve finish to my voice and that Professor Lino is the undisputed master in that aspect of performance. She insists on paying for the study and the trip—her husband is a very wealthy financier—but I have told her I cannot accept a gift and shall only consider a loan, to be repaid at the earliest possible opportunity.

Isn't it terrible about Lord Carnarvon? That a mere bite from a mosquito should cause his death and just when he was on the *verge* of the culmination of his life's work. It is too cruel!!! To think that, after thirty-three years searching for the tomb of King Tutankhamen, other eyes shall be the first to gaze upon the king's remains in the innermost recesses of the tomb. One cannot help thinking that the tomb perhaps has a curse upon it. Mrs. Wexner says it assuredly does and that the first sign of it occurred last December when the pet canary of one of the excavators was killed by a serpent. Lo and behold, the very same kind of serpent was wrought in gold in the crowns of the statues inside the grave! Of course, I would be inclined to dismiss this as coincidence had I not heard a speech by Sir Arthur Conan Doyle only recently here in Manhattan. He said there are indeed spirits of the killing type and that he knew of a British journalist who contracted typhoid because he did research on a curse attached to a mummy in the British Museum. Sir Arthur said an evil elemental might have been brought into being by Tutankhamen's spirit and caused Carnarvon's death. He said an elemental is a built-up artificial thing, an imbued force which may be brought into being by a spirit mind or by nature. He said it exists of itself for a specific purpose and is not procreated. This seems to be a possible explanation for the untimely death, I believe. Lord Carnarvon had simply gone further than the spirit of the dead king could allow. Yet, how could he have known that he was "trespassing," I should like to know? It seems such an unforeseen disaster, and so chilling too!

Well this has turned into a small book. Write me with all the inside news about the Big Fight and I shall send you clippings from the papers here. Also, please do not forget to check about the radio station.

Your loving sister,
Amelia (my new name.)

17

It was quiet that morning, suddenly quiet after ten days of steady rain. Shelby came out of the night peach-colored and steaming, the only sound the drip, drip off the eaves. A pretty sun climbed a June sky.

They had promised each other, he and T.T.—the first rainless day, and they would put the kid in charge of the refreshment parlor and take the local to Great Falls.

They would go to Great Falls, do some real business if they could, and see Dempsey, the brute, in the flesh.

It was the kind of morning that made you think the whole thing might work out, after all. Maybe it was possible. Maybe there would be no more faltering, no more dramatic showdowns over the money, and the thing would come off and the new arena—planked high over six acres—would actually fill up with paying customers.

They wanted to see Dempsey work out because they wanted to confirm an idea they had of him.

This was a fighter who had not been fighting. Fifteen minutes of actual ring time in the last five years—add it up!—and the rest of the time hanging around Hollywood with movie stars and swells. Letting them stuff him with frog legs and gin fizzes. Babes and greasepaint and trips to Europe, but not a fight since Carpentier. Doc Kearns, Mr. Slick, couldn't manage to find his champion a white man to fight. And said champion therefore sits around and goes soft and contented, and that is the end of the hound in the belly.

They wanted to see this for themselves.

T.T. sits on the depot bench smoking a huge cigar, hat pulled low. His loopy mustache has turned solid gray though he is scarcely into his thirties.

He is reading the oil news in the *Tribune*. Promising. Maybe. Soon. That is the language now. Has been for a while. And now everyone finally knows it for the code it is. Nothing is happening.

But T.T. still thinks the fight will change that; will bring the rich boys in with their motorcars to look the field over, chat it up, get some idea for themselves of the possibilities. This day has made him as optimistic as he ever gets, though you would only know it by small touches like the cigar. Or the way he gets up now and stretches, facing the rising sun and the flashing tracks.

They sit together, waiting for the train. A few shouts reach them. Those revelers who never sleep. The all-night denizens of the King Tut, the Green Lite, the Cabin. The ones who outlasted the imported dance bands. It was as if a huge radio had transplanted the sounds of the rest of the country right to Shelby. You imagined the musicians, these early mornings, propped sleeping in their tuxedos, to be wound up at nightfall: the night pulling them to their feet, the hands pulling the horns to their mouths, the horns pulling the city sounds out of the air.

People will be up soon and moving through the rosy mist. Rumpled. Hungover. The boys from the big papers back East. The local kids running errands for the strangers. The self-appointed cops with their big fake badges, strutting the boardwalks. Cowboys on horses. Indians in headdresses. A lady phrenologist in a gypsy costume and sensible mud-ready shoes.

By now, the fans should have been stepping off these trains for a week of revelry and spending and playing at being in the Wild West. But it is still mostly drifters, grifters, minor entertainers who are disembarking at Shelby.

The only people arriving are the ones who hope to make money off the thousands still to come.

Shelby, so soaked for so many days, exhales damply and gathers itself and gets busy again. The muffled hammering, the huffing saws, come into the open air. Tar paper is tacked to plywood. Signs are painted, hung to dry.

Ten days to go, and the last concession stands are going up. Everyone is selling something: Gibbons ribbons, miniature oil rigs, cowboy hats, chocolates.

Jerry and T.T. have converted Jerry's basement office into a refreshment parlor. They got the ice cream in and a gross of blue sunglasses too, and then the rain began. So, of course, there was no business. No one wanted to venture down eleven slick steps to a basement room called the Cavern to buy ice cream or sunglasses.

Maybe today, though. Maybe it will get hot and the Monroe kid will sell some ice cream to somebody. More likely, he'll give it out to his pals.

But today you can say, There's still time. And this is only a half-brained little booster venture, anyway. A very temporary sideline.

Over east, the peaked green roof of the house where Tommy Gibbons and his wife and three young boys are living while he trains. And beyond the roof the monster arena, exhaling in the new sun. Waiting for its forty thousand fans. Just waiting now.

There is a child's wagon on the step of Tommy's house, filled with rainwater. A bird feeder hanging from an eave, covered with sparrows. Soon Tommy will come blinking out of the front door, a cup of coffee in his hand, tousling the head of one of his boys. While his wife fixes him a fighter's breakfast, he will sit on the step and breathe the rainless air, a pleasant-faced burly young man with rosy cheeks, a pug boxer's nose, a mangled ear, knobby finger joints.

He will sit on the step, squinty-eyed, moving his gaze over the ramshackle little town, the glittering tracks that are supposed to bring all the people to the fight of his life.

He will feel the previous few years in his bones—fifty fights to Dempsey's four—and will know again, in his body and mind, that this is his highest and last chance to be something other than a professional opponent.

Six weeks in this wind-battered, rain-battered, sun-battered little town, and he has begun to show the strain. Everything by a spit and a hair. A crisis a day. Fight's on. Fight's off. Backers have the money. Maybe not.

Why would a dozen men in a town of one thousand people think they could raise $200,000, in the first place, and then $300,000 when Kearns jacked it up? It was a miracle when they came up with the first third. Selling their fool heads off, peddling tickets all over the state, sending their emissaries out in a little roofless airplane to carry the word.

And the second $100,000, by the very skin of their teeth. Zooming around the state in the plane, two of the ticket-peddling zealots, and the thing crashes and they're lying in plaster in the hospital. Mayor Johnson putting up every single asset, his life's work—at least $50,000 and probably a lot more—and the rest kicked in at the eleventh hour by some money fellows in Great Falls.

And the whole thing still uncertain, less than two weeks before the fight, because Kearns—the icy-hearted fop—won't guarantee that his fighter will fight. Not until he's seen the last dime.

And yesterday the head money-raiser resigns. Nine days, now, to come up with another $100,000, unless Kearns relents.

Tommy has a tired, stubborn look on his face. He was exhilarated and ready when he arrived. Now he has the weary look of the kid who has fought over his head all his life. The look of a kid whose brother, The Phantom, always led the way.

By afternoon, though, he will be game. He will have himself together and he will give another show for the fans—sparring, dipping, sweating, showing his stuff. And they will love him, as they always do. They will watch him, cheer him on, the hardworking, true-hearted, knotty-muscled fighter from Saint Paul. The family man. The underdog.

This, he tells a reporter, is the opportunity of my lifetime.

In Great Falls, the trees along the avenues are a young green. The hotels, the theaters, look newly washed.

Jerry has some very appealing land offers with him. Parcels to tempt the representatives of the oil companies. Good deals, truly. They could never do better, and he wouldn't even be taking the offers around now if he weren't so short on money.

T.T. waits for him at the hotel, smoking another big cigar in the wingbacked lobby chair, looking like a businessman at rest while Jerry makes the rounds.

T.T. is sleeping when he returns. Hat tipped down over his eyes, cigar cold in his hand. Jerry's face is set. The last guy actually laughed out loud. One of them referred to "that circus" and said he heard that Tracey, the head promoter, had washed his hands of the whole fight. One of them thwacked him indulgently on the back and told him to go back to Shelby and try to make some money any way he could.

Shelby was off-limits. The field was off-limits. Nobody was going near the place until this fight was over, or aborted, or whatever was going to happen. Not until it was history, and all the adventurers had moved on, and you could get a clear siting on that piece of country.

Go home, one of them said. Go home and ride this little show out, then check back in and we'll see where we are.

T.T. had met a high roller from Denver in the lobby, and he got himself and Jerry invited up to the guy's room for a few drinks after lunch. The stuff was concocted and poisonous, probably boosted with cocaine. A few sips, and the lips and tongue began to go numb. Jerry put the shot glass down carefully and lit a cigarette, his head already light, his mouth reluctant to form words.

T.T.'s initial cheerfulness had seemed to turn into something more frenzied. Perhaps it started when he met the Denver swell. Or when he saw Jerry's face after he'd made the rounds to the oil guys.

T.T. was talking loudly. He drew a little flask from his vest and the high roller filled it with the cloudy white stuff and the three of them took off in a shiny Suiza to the Dempsey camp, north of Great Falls at a huge abandoned roadhouse on the banks of the Missouri.

The Denver guy—he said he was in town on unspecified business and was staying for the fight—drove furiously. They bounced and thumped and careened along the road, the driver goggled and intent and smashed.

T.T. loud and whooping. Jerry in the back, trying to fix on the horizon, hold himself steady until the rotgut had done its worst.

A bad narrow road, still puddled from the long rains. The glint of the river. An occasional grove of river trees. T.T. and the Denver guy yelling back and forth above the roar of the car. It'll happen, they assured each other. That fight is gonna happen. Confidence! the Denver guy screamed. You got to say the money is there, whether you know or not. You don't falter. Faltering is death. No faltering, no maybes. A big maybe, and nobody gets on those trains. Not if they think they're traveling toward a Big Maybe.

It'll happen, T.T. yelled again. There's $200,000 in the coffers, or that's what they're saying.

And another $100,000 due in a week, Jerry called out from the back. Where do you suppose that's coming from?

They would have talked slurred talk about the fights of the past, including the one that put little Goldfield, Nevada, on the map. They would have discussed Gibbons—told the Denver guy how tenacious and strong their boy was, how ready, how fit. How he had never been knocked out. Never. How Dempsey, the slacker, the brute, might be in for the surprise of his life in eleven days. He might!

Big talk. A kind of dedication to bluster during that ride because that's what seemed to be called for. Confidence.

Yes, some trains had canceled. Yes, some reporters were saying it wasn't going to happen—that maybe there wouldn't be a fight. Well, they were wrong. They were dead wrong. The arrogant, second-guessing bastards.

The heavy curtains in the Denver salesman's hotel room. The pattern on them and how it did not bear a long gaze. The smell of the booze, its nuances of rat poison and rubber and the terror of dentistry.

The mad drive through the mud, along the wet grass, and under the glittering leaves of the big cottonwoods. The shouts of the men in the front. T.T.'s wildness that day. His last real wildness.

They got stuck three times, extricated themselves, sat on the running board to drink a few more shots. Jerry had one more—he was way behind them—and he felt the alcohol settle at the front of his head, right between his eyes like an ice cube. It burned. It felt like a light, so strong that it made the world too bright to look at. The bright prairie, the metal of the car. Even the Denver guy's goggles and the phony diamond on his thin hand. All of it too harsh, too shaky and bright.

And so, in some ways, the camp was a relief. The light had to make its way down through the leaves.

There was a dim, crepuscular, shrouded feel to the place.

They stopped the car in long grass and walked into what had once been the grounds of the roadhouse and beer garden. The big stone house where Dempsey was headquartered, a clearing around it, a training arena on the edge of the clearing, all of it rimmed by the big cottonwoods.

People milling everywhere. Something dreamlike about them. Maybe it was the booze. But they seemed to move without hurry. A languor. As if all of them—the floozies, the followers, the sparring partners, the sightseers from town—had all been here for days. That this was where they lived.

The grass was damp, and that made it flicker more.

Some floozies played cards under a spreading tree. They shouted tinkling insults at a group of passing men who had the low-hatted look of slickers with guns under their vests.

Chickens ran loose.

Somewhere, perhaps inside the thick walls of the stone house, someone played a saxophone.

A waist-high man with a large head rocked past them, leading a wildcat cub on a leash.

A woman with a torn stocking took the leash and tied it slowly around a slim tree. The cub's collar was made of rhinestones.

The dwarf picked up a water bucket and made his metronomic way toward the practice ring.

The ring was situated at the bottom of a slope and the slope was covered with spectators, all hats and the low hum of voices. Some stood, a few handsomely dressed women among them.

On the far side of the crowd, two huge men with the planted look of bodyguards shook their heads slowly at three young women in filmy dresses. One of them handed one of the bodyguards a picnic hamper. Their postures were flirtatious and supplicating. The prettiest of them pointed toward Dempsey's big stone house.

The man bent his head over the basket and pawed its contents. No, his head shook. No.

One of the girls hit him playfully on the arm and they all ran off then and jumped into a motorcar—one of the girls at the wheel—and it popped, popped away, sliding a little on the turn. The bodyguard pawed some more. Pulled something out and smelled it. Closed the lid and tossed the basket over his shoulder as if it were an apple core.

All those people, but there is something intent and hushed about them, They preside somehow, they have control. The tenders, the sparring partners, the handlers—they are slickers, men of the world. In Shelby, everybody's a kid.

It seems to Jerry a time and a place for competence, worldliness. But T.T., usually so reserved and watchful, has gone completely nuts on the booze. Jerry doesn't want to be with him. T.T. goes off with the Denver guy to see a bear in a cage and then to stand smoking and waiting on the banks of the Missouri. Jerry watches T.T. from a distance: T.T. and the Denver guy.

T.T. sweeps his arm toward the waters of the Missouri. He sways back on his heels. His hand chops the air too many times.

Some Great Falls sports say they are watching Dempsey fight now because there is no way he will ever fight in Shelby. The money isn't there. The Shelby guys are bluffing. It's a huge mess, and Kearns isn't going to bring his fighter forth until he's got the whole works. And there is no way that a bunch of yahoos is going to come up with $100,000 in a week. Come on.

They think they'll get it in the gate receipts, someone says. They think Kearns will forgive the July 2 deadline and let them come up with it at the gate, the final payment. All those trains rolling in with all those people with all that dough.

All those trains! A low hoot. They're canceling right and left! And the tickets? They're going for ten dollars now. They'll be five tomorrow, and those rubes will be tackling people on the Fourth, begging them to take one for fifty cents. You wait!

That arena? The spectators? A few peas at the bottom of a soup bowl! *If* the thing comes off at all, mind you.

Their self-satisfied chuckles. The growing rage in Jerry—pure violent chagrin. Like the time he was a child and someone pinned a donkey's tail to the hem of his Sunday jacket and he walked around like that, in his own house, even his parents hiding their giggles. What a betrayal. His mother stopped the nonsense, but not before she let him walk around for a few minutes wondering about his brother's red face, his sister running in giggles out of the room, even his kindly father, dropping his face down behind the newspaper to hide a broad grin.

That moment when he discovered the joke. It felt, the rage, like this.

He thought of his makeshift ice cream parlor, the ceiling dripping.

Smug, smug they all are, under this dappled light. Waiting for their champion. But you look around at this scene and think about Gibbons, the tendons tensing, his white iron-muscled legs, and you think, Maybe.

You look at a bobcat tied to a tree with a rhinestone collar around its neck, and the bear, and the buzzing, complacent decadence of the place, and think, You may be surprised by an underdog. You think it with fury. There is some sense of fatal leisure about this place. It has grown hot now, and the flies buzz and a few people on the edges of the crowd on the hill have stretched out on their backs, hats over their eyes, waiting for him. The champion. Dempsey. Blackie Jack.

Two men in ice cream suits smoking together near the makeshift ring. Epicene, slim, in their light-colored clothes. Hatless, their hair slicked to a patent shine.

Kearns, someone said. On the left. He leans forward, the one who is Kearns, to hear a question. Makes a throat-slitting motion. Throws back his head to laugh.

I hate him, Jerry thought. I hate that monster-hearted con artist.

Johnny Dempsey, someone says. The one on Kearns's right. The older brother.

A hand in a pocket, a posed slouch, a face, eyes, that even from a distance are too avid and weary. A nervous dandy.

The dope fiend, someone explains. Jack's Hollywood friends got him hooked. Oh, yeh, everybody knows. You hang around here and you know. Maybe Kearns keeps him supplied. Part of the deal. You pump up the champ. You sedate his monkey-ridden brother with the slim slouch, the moving eyes.

These people are jaded, complacent. Dempsey will be the same. He will be the beefy version of those two fops.

But then Kearns snaps to and Johnny fades off and something is happening, and Jerry feels fear in his throat because here he comes.

That big dark body and his way of walking toward a ring, the sullen, swinging walk. William Harrison aka Kid Blackie aka Jack. The Manassa Mauler and his handlers.

Jack.

His lean, knobbled father, Hyram, scurries behind the boys, green light rippling across his white-stubbled face. Johnny has reappeared, looking too alert and helpful.

Dempsey has a secret brine that he uses to tan his skin, make it leather that will not cut. He is very dark. All of him. There are purple pimples on the backs of his big thighs. He calls a greeting to someone. His voice is eerie and high, the voice of a boy.

It was supposed to be practice, but a lot of people in this crowd had been here before, had watched one of these sessions among the dappled light of the river trees, and they were intent and unsmiling. They were not the joking, easy men who watched Gibbons train in Shelby.

Jerry caught sight of a land agent he knew from Great Falls, and waved. The agent nodded curtly, his eyes quickly back on the ring.

Dempsey was always forward, on his toes. He leaned into it, always the aggressor. There was a kind of competent violence to him. He seemed to have a killing switch inside him, and whenever he went into the ring, the switch went on and there was no reprieve. It was never practice. Other people could say it was. Dempsey himself could call it sparring. But it was always a fight.

Jerry saw this. He also saw T.T. on the far edge of the crowd, gesturing. He ignored him. Something in the booze had hopped him up, and Jerry had seen it before. Seen guys swill some of that stuff down and go loony. Raving. He had never seen T.T. this animated. He tried to ignore him. T.T. embarrassed him—a dipsy kid at a hard man's game.

In the sixth round, the sparring partner, a Pittsburgh heavyweight named Jack Burke, landed a punch that cut the leather skin over Dempsey's eye. The crowd buzzed, not so much at the blow but at the look it brought. Not surprise or shock. Just cold killer rage. As instinctive as a cat's drawn-back eyes. And Dempsey moved in then with a left hook, followed by quick rights to the ribs, and Burke was down on his knees. As he staggered to his feet, Dempsey lobbed another left, and Burke fell forward, to grab him in a clinch. His face was pulp and blood. His nose was broken.

Jerry closed his eyes. He could hear Dempsey's fast volley to the back of the neck, the punch you kill a rabbit with. He could see, even behind his closed eyes, the agonized orgasmic expression on Burke's face.

When it was over, Burke managed a ghoulish smile. Dempsey grabbed his partner's hand and smiled his first smile of the fight. He was panting and serene. Then he did a strange thing. He brought Burke's arm to his mouth and bit it, lightly, affectionately. The crowd whistled and clapped their relief, and the sparring partner limped off toward the big stone house.

There was more. It was as if the afternoon accelerated after that and Jerry has just snatches. There was a birthday cake—it was Dempsey's 28th birthday—and it was hoisted, flaming, into the ring between sparring sessions. The champion, a sweater over his shoulder, scooping out a bite with his taped fingers. A mournful, off-tune rendering of "Happy Birthday." The fading light and the beginnings of the rain clouds in the west.

The blow that broke the jaw of another sparring partner, the seven-foot giant, Ben Wray. The sound of it. The way Jack continued to bounce on his toes, tipped forward, alert.

Johnny Dempsey, the brother, picking the gaunt fingers of his father from the arm of his impeccable, pin-striped shirt. Johnny Dempsey in some kind of fervent discussion with T.T., who was clearly so smashed Jerry knew he had to get him out of there. He was weaving, throwing his arms around, laughing, pounding a fist on a tree, fishing some bills out of his pocket.

The first big drops of rain and—hours later, it seemed—the train in the dark and the streaming rain back to Shelby. T.T. had finally sunk into a half-lidded silence. He was sobered.

Rain in sheets, the train burrowing through it, clacking, hissing. Jerry's cheek against the window. A feeling of absolute, end-of-it weariness. A mild, detached vision of the ceiling of his refreshment dungeon oozing water, plunking it down on a pair of sunglasses.

T.T., trancelike, examines the watch. It has scrollwork on the silver case that looks like figure eights on ice. The numerals are large and ornate. It is old. Maybe valuable.

Johnny Dempsey sold it to him for four dollars. Made the deal spontaneously, enthusiastically, as if he'd just thought of it and why hadn't he before? Such a good, reasonable idea, to pull someone else's silver watch out of his pocket and offer it to a drunk stranger for the price of some bliss.

18

On again. Now it was on again. Twenty ghostly investors were each ready to hand over $5,000 to save the honor of Montana. The last $100,000 by July 2, tomorrow, and the fight was on. It was a go.

Who were these men with the money? Did anyone know? Did anyone really believe in them?

Twenty lifelong friends, the banker Stanton says stoutly. Friends of Montana. The new fight czar, Major Lane, nods agreement. Lifelong friends. For the honor of the state.

And the train finally hauls them out of Great Falls—Stanton and Major Lane and some of the other boys—away from the mess of the last few days: the shouts, the lost tempers, the drunken exhausted reporters floating between rooms, carrying messages, waiting for a yes, a no. Kearns holed up in his room—the brutal little prig—holding out. Not an inch, not an inch. I'll take my fighter to Cleveland, to Montreal. We don't have to fight here. We don't have to guarantee anything. You come up with the money—the final $100,000—and *then* we guarantee he will fight.

Did Stanton and Lane think they had the money? Or did they only know they had to claim they did, true or not? Get it out in the newspapers—it's on!—and the thousands would crank up their autos, step onto those waiting trains, and Kearns would feel them coming, forgive the deadline, and get his last pound of flesh at the gate.

For a day, today, it didn't matter if the lifelong friends and their money existed or not. The idea was to celebrate the idea of their existence, to get those people coming to Shelby—and yes, the sun was out now and the weather would be dandy—get them *moving*, and then how could there be such a pressing need, even for Doc Kearns, to see the full amount up front. He had his $200,000. The rest was surely on the way.

Shelby was drying fast, the sky was blank and spanking, the fight was on again, and the kingpins were arriving to claim and celebrate the twenty ghostly friends of Montana.

A brass band met Lane and Stanton's train. The big tuba caught the morning sun in its big bell and hurled it playfully into the eyes of the gathered crowd. Did they all believe Stanton had the pledges? Well, they acted as if they did. It was a day for the motions of believing.

So play Sousa. Welcome the new fight czar. Welcome the banker Stanton. Smile at the newsboys, strike a pose for the photographers, dust off the epaulets, and blow. Conjure those thousands of fans out of their lidded baskets.

The big glinting tuba, the old uniforms and sad shoes. The hammers again and a last round of real hope—it did feel real if you thought quickly about it and then about something else—and so people are walking the streets and honking their auto horns and horses are dashing around and there is a new energy, the sun helping because it is a sun that looks as though it will stay. Straw hats, boaters, everywhere. Reporters sending their stories beep-beeping across the wires, that, yes, the fight will happen in three days, the money is said to be there, Shelby seems to have pulled it off.

We didn't doubt it for a minute, the local folks are trying to say as they hawk and yell and spread their souvenirs with a flourish. You boys are the doubters, they say, jabbing fingers at city vests. And if it was up to you, this fight would have been a fizzle weeks ago. But it's not, is it? It's a go, and how can you say the tens of thousands are not on their way?

The porter bends to place the metal stepping-off stool on the ground. The hatless band conductor stands poised, baton in the air, watching over his shoulder. A woman appears at the door and, behind her, vests and cigars, Major Lane and his entourage. The drop of the baton and "Hail to the Chief." The porter ready to assist the disembarking. But they don't move, because the woman doesn't move and she is first.

She pauses on the step, glancing around. She has come all the way from New York and the trip shows itself in the lavender crescents under her eyes, but she is alertly turned out in a traveling suit and city shoes and a close-fitting hat with a feather that curves so that it seems to cup her jawline.

She has a heart-shaped face, a slim figure. She carries an old water-stained valise. Her skin has not wrinkled but seems only more fragile, more tissuey than the last time we saw her. Also, a new bob and a small red mouth, a little blurred.

She has the contained look of someone who always travels alone.

The band is exuberant and slightly out of tune and very brassy. She does not move from her step. Major Lane catches sight of someone out in the crowd and leans over her shoulder to slash a greeting in the air with his cigar.

She surveys the crowd helpfully. She casts a frantic smile over her shoulder, but the man there just gives her an encouraging nod. The porter extends his hand.

She takes it and steps onto the metal stool, where she stands again, unmoving, because the band sound has surged. They are looking at her, playing at her. She smiles again. A drummer smiles back. She looks around again for Jerry—there he is, trotting down a side street, late—and she decides for one wild pleased moment that this is all for her. That her brother has arranged this for her. It is what a person like Jerry *could* arrange, out here in the West, where everybody is everybody's friend, comrades together in the hardship of building something from scratch.

And in that wild pleased moment she raises her hand high to the band—now a piccolo player has lowered his piccolo to smile at her too—and steps off the metal stool to the ground of Shelby and sinks into a wide curtsy, which makes more people smile and laugh, and a little boy on the edge of the band begins to clap wildly and that is the moment Jerry rounds the corner to meet his sister, here all the way from New York.

She had not aged in four years, Jerry thought. Only faded slightly. Everything about her seemed slightly blurred, though it could have been her pastel dress, its soft modern material, or her new short hair, or the indeterminate red mouth. She was city pale, but unwrinkled, except perhaps for the merest cobwebs at the corners of her mouth and eyes.

Yes, she looked like a woman who had made a phonograph record. There was some kind of assured mockery in her bow to the band, he thought. And her clothes had a lilt that had been absent four years earlier. She looked as if she would know slang; had tried cigarettes; had booked passage to Milan.

Up close, though, her eyes were slightly too wide and rapid. Her shoes were very old. Her valise was shabby. When she opened her purse to tip the porter who brought her belongings, she rustled her fingers past a small paper package, and Jerry smelled stale chicken.

They loaded everything into the Hupmobile and drove slowly up the long shallow hill to the little frame house. She chattered, of course. She craned her neck around and exclaimed. How wild and open it was! Like a mining camp! How beautiful the countryside. The lakes of water she had seen on the grass, stretching forever, covered with strange, long-legged birds! Such a rain there must have been.

She blew her nose vigorously and pushed the wadded handkerchief up her sleeve. Their mother's habit.

She showed him the little towelette from the dining car that you got to keep.

She said she hadn't wanted a berth anyway, because her artistic temperament made her one of those people who need very little sleep. It had gotten worse over time, but then that gave her more hours of the day, didn't it?

The Hupmobile popped and roared and slithered up the road, still gumbo here and there, and she patted the doors and shouted her admiration for its color—so beautifully tawny—and its stalwart character.

At one point, her voice dropped out altogether, though her lips kept moving, and when Jerry looked harder at her, she smiled brightly at him with her little crooked mouth.

They made her a bed in the washroom and hung a flannel cloth across the door between it and the kitchen. In addition to the valise with the big watermark on it, she had a rather large trunk with frayed straps.

She began to unpack her things, the flannel cloth pulled back so she could talk to the family, gathered cautiously, curiously around the kitchen table. The children were unusually quiet. They watched her as if she had stepped out of the moving pictures.

Inside the valise were two dresses, sundries, another worn pair of shoes. Inside the trunk were several packages wrapped in brown paper and string. Most of the trunk was empty.

One of the brown packages held sheet music—two operas she must memorize. She pointed to July 20 on the big wall calendar, the date she must, sadly, return to New York. Her patroness, Mrs. Wexner, had booked her passage to Milan, where she would study with Professor Lino, who had launched any number of opera careers.

She carefully draped her meager clothes on three hangers and placed the hangers on a large wall hook. Seated around the table, they all watched her. She had refused help. She wanted to chatter and be busy, and there was something in that wanting, or perhaps simply in the fact that she moved in a room behind a drawn-back curtain, that made them feel they were watching a stage show.

She drew each package out of the trunk with a flourish, placed it on the cot, unwrapped it carefully. The first three held small gifts for each of the children—a tiny replica of a Sopwith Camel for Francis, a miniature tea set for Maudie, and a slate with colored chalk for Tip. Then a cookie jar fashioned like a crowing rooster for the house, for Vivian and Jerry. And, for all of them, a paper packet full of sugar cubes from the train.

She unwrapped several other packages and placed the contents carefully, side by side, on the covered wooden crate that served as a bedside stand. A stoppered blue bottle. A knotted piece of satin cord. *The Wanderer of the Wasteland* by Mr. Zane Grey. A book called *The Hidden Words.*

Mr. Zane Grey, she explained, was very religious and mystical, in addition to being an authority on the West.

She patted the two books and sat on the edge of the cot, finished, hands folded in her lap.

"Is she going to stay here always?" whispered Maudie, pointing to the articles by the bed.

"Oh, no! I will be gone"—whoosh, her hand arrowed away—"in less than a fortnight."

"What's a fortnight?" Maudie asked.

"And now," her aunt said, "I must request something. My name henceforth is Amelia. That is the name I have chosen for the stage and for my life, and I must request that you use it." She smiled brightly. "I don't even hear the name Daisy Lou anymore. It's uncanny!"

Vivian got up from the table. "A fortnight is two weeks," she told Maudie.

The stoppered blue bottle. It had a label fixed around it with a piece of string. The glass was a beautiful blue, pale and clean as flax.

"It's cheap," Amelia told the children, who were now on the floor of her little room. "I bought it from a man for five cents. But the bottle doesn't really count. What counts is what is *in* the bottle." She read her own label as if she had forgotten. Her loopy extravagant handwriting.

"It says..." She squinted fervently. "Why, it says, Comet Dust!

"I caught this dust from Halley's Comet, in nineteen and ten. I held this bottle aloft just as Halley's Comet, the most important comet there is, passed directly over my head. This was in New York City, on the banks of a very important river."

"What did the comet look like?" Francis asked. "Was it a fireball like the sun?"

"I believe it was," Amelia said. "If I had seen it, I could tell you. As it happened, the sky that night was obscured by a dense layer of clouds. An extremely dense layer of clouds. We had hoped—my friend and I—that the comet would at least be visible as a kind of moving light behind the clouds. But no, it wasn't. However, it was there. The scientists had performed their calculations, and they knew, to the *minute*, when that comet was passing over our heads. So we knew it was there. We simply couldn't see it." She shrugged cheerfully.

"One of those very scientists suggested that we trap the comet dust. I got the bottle from that scientist, in fact, and followed his instructions for dust trapping, to the last detail."

She showed them how she had raised her arm high over her head. She froze her empty hand, the thumb and first two fingers grasping the air daintily, and she very slowly moved her wrist in the minutest of motions, making adjustments for the most efficient snaring of the dust. Her face took on a very solemn look, and her eyes were fixed on the drying rack across the room.

"Four minutes, exactly," she said firmly. "That was the method." She dropped her hand. "And then, quickly! the stopper." She plunked the imaginary stopper into the imaginary bottle. "And there it is." She gestured to the little blue bottle on the orange crate.

"What does it *do*?" Francis asked.

"Well, it is not supposed to *do* anything. It is just supposed to *be*. You see, it is the dust of an event that happens only once every seventy-six years. The comet comes around and then it moves far, far out into the heavens, farther than you can ever imagine, but then it comes back. It travels in a large circle. It takes seventy-six years to go around the circle, but at the end of seventy-six years, there it is again! The very same comet.

"The dust is saved, trapped, for good reasons." Her voice was very firm and definite. "Let us say another comet just happened to appear in the same year Halley's returned. If the dust from that comet proved to be different from the dust in this jar—different in kind—why, then we would know it was not the real Halley's. It would be an impostor!"

"If it was a spectacular comet, I wouldn't care," Francis said.

"Why, silly, you would indeed! We all care. We want to know that there are constants in the universe. Also, there is this. The comet's tail has magnetic properties, and it gathers up the very essence of the world it passes near; the things we can't see. By analyzing the dust at a later time, we can apprehend what we couldn't have apprehended at the time. Emanations. Celestial tunes."

The satiny green cord with the knots in it? That was so she could move through her Coué chant. "Every day and in every way I am getting better and better," she instructed the children.

This irritated Vivian, the Catholic. "Me, me, me," she said in a low voice to Jerry in the kitchen. "Never *us*. Never *Thy* will. Just me. Give me."

It was uncustomarily bitter, and Jerry felt called upon to defend his sister. "If not 'me,' who else?" he asked her. "Who is going to accomplish your life for you?" His tone was heavy. There was the weight of his early instruction in it.

After supper, Mr. Clemons came by in his automobile for the children. He took the children away to the farm until the fight was over, because Shelby had become no place for children. Francis balked and pleaded, to no effect, and he left with a furious face.

And so, yes, it is July 1 and Daisy Lou has arrived and now she is Amelia.

They sit at the table that night, the three of them. Three people, still young, though Vivian's hair is beginning to gray at the temples. She has it smoothed back, still long, and she has a line between her eyes. Jerry has his strafed look still, and the brusqueness. But something about the hopes of the last four years have also left their mark on him. He seems more present, more avid, than he did.

In some odd way, the three of them feel themselves to be collaborators. There is something clandestine, maybe dangerous, in the air. Perhaps it is just that the children are gone. Perhaps it is the telegram that arrived that day from Carlton, a panicky order to Jerry to sell, get rid of, get *something*, for Carlton's share in the new hotel. SHELBY A BUST, he said. TRIP CANCELLED.

He hadn't seen the latest news stories, they decided. He hadn't seen that the fight was on again. That it would go ahead as planned.

Yes, there was something about to begin. Vivian examined Amelia, fixed the name once and for all in her mind, noticed the details of her clothing, her hair, her mannerisms. Didn't like her. Didn't like her frivolity and shallowness and effusions. She always thought that when people made a huge to-do about their surfaces, they had little or nothing underneath.

Amelia. Where had she come up with that?

She watched her sister-in-law flutter her hands, talk at Jerry. He listened stalwartly. Vivian thought of flashing trolley cars on a city street, and the smell of roses, and the luxury of a quiet house. Of the way her brother George didn't talk very much, and how comfortable that had been.

Waking in the night, Vivian hears Amelia padding back and forth across the floor of the washroom. She hears her murmuring. She listens to the faint horns from the Green Lite and the faint explosions of the autos that seem to crawl around now throughout the night.

She wakes later and there is only deep, exhausted breathing from the washroom. A small sleeping whine like a child's.

19

July 2, the deadline day, began with Jerry rushing out early, rushing down to the refreshment parlor in the damp-walled basement. To his ice cream and sunglasses. The room was very dim. He had to keep two kerosene lamps going, even with the rain gone and the day becoming hot and bright. He took a small can of red paint with him and painted over the black arrow on his sign, the arrow that pointed down the crude steps to the basement. Now it was harder to ignore.

It was chilly down there, chilly enough for a heavy sweater. He retrieved a few blocks of ice from sawdust in a far, cool room and packed his ice cream and waited.

Back at the house, Amelia embarked on her vocal exercises, using a tuning fork to gain her pitch. Vivian baked bread. The exercises—the earnest, trilling soprano voice—made her knead the dough more violently than she had to. Light sweat broke out on her arms like a surprise. Not because the voice was terrible—it was no worse than anyone you heard on the Victrola or on the radio programs, really—it was just...steady. There was drudgery and piety in it. The weight of labor; a weight that transferred itself to the listener. She washed a sinkful of towels and hung them on the line in the new sun. Inside the house, the voice marched dutifully up and down, avid and empty. The ping of the tuning fork. Up a third. The mannered upward march.

She punched the dough down, it gasped, and she made loaves and put them in the oven, the voice now repeating and repeating a short passage in Italian. She swept and washed the kitchen floor. She removed the loaves, washed her face and patted rose water on her neck and repinned her hair and changed her dress and pulled back the curtain.

"Amelia," she said briskly. "It's time to show you around."

She wrapped a loaf of bread to take to Jerry for his lunch, cut a piece of cheese to go with it. Amelia put on her best dress and requested a cup of tea.

She stood on the front step, sipping, and surveyed the scrub grass, the random rutted paths, the haphazard presence of small houses down the long slope that ended in railroad tracks, the depot, the row of low businesses like a carnival midway.

"This," she announced to Vivian, "is absolutely beautiful, this place. Oh, you think I am making a mockery, but I mean beautiful in a spiritual sense.

"Oh, that may not be the Woolworth Building," she said, waving at the two-story square that was the school. "And that may not be the Taj Mahal," she said with a mysterious, dismissive wave at what seemed to be the rim above town.

"But *that*"—she squinted at the arena waiting on the edge of everything, huge—"that is a Miracle of the Modern World! Can you deny it? No, you cannot."

"I have never tasted such tea," she said, holding the flowered cup aloft. "Perhaps it is the altitude, or the bracing air." She sniffed long and hard.

"How did the poet phrase it?" she mused. "'Stepping westward seemed to be / A kind of heavenly destiny.' Well, he is exactly, precisely right!

"To me, even the humble aspect of the buildings, the mud, the frontier hurly-burly down there"—she waved in the direction of town—"speak to me of fortitude and faith, of the ordinary man getting out there and going for broke! Oh, how could you know how wonderful this is for me to see, Vivian, after the hardness, the corruption of the city?"

There was a silence. Vivian had been wrapping the bread, listening, gazing at her sister-in-law's silhouette through the doorway. She felt she should applaud now.

"Yes?" she prompted politely. No answer. She joined Amelia, who had closed her eyes, the teacup pressed to her breastbone. Her lips moved. Then, as if on cue, her eyes snapped open.

"I personally knew a young man who was cut down in cold blood by mobsters," Amelia said reverently. "In broad daylight."

She clarified herself. "That's not when I knew him. That's when he was cut down. In broad daylight."

She sipped the last of her tea. "Well, that's when I knew him too. In broad daylight. We were just friends. He was not a beau, is what I mean to say."

She gazed intently at Vivian. "He was conscripted by evil men and could not extricate himself, and he was cut down in the prime of life." She drew a long breath and closed her eyes. "The wick of his being was snapped."

They put on their hats and descended the long shallow hill, walking along the edge of the track, where the mud had dried. The day was brash and blue and becoming noisy with autos, shouts, and manic birds.

"The faith!" Amelia exulted, flinging her hand again toward the arena on the edge of everything. "It is like the Roman Colosseum. It is! If a thousand people could decide to build something like that, think what a million of the same sort of people could build. Why, they could build something that would cover the entire earth!"

Jerry was out of the light, down in his cellar, behind his counter. A teenager was there too, one of the Wilson boys, the one with a grieved face of acne. He was scooping out ice cream for another teenager, and Jerry was telling him to charge two scoops for a mess like that. It was dim and shadowy down there, a peculiar murkiness that the kerosene could not chase away.

Vivian plopped the wrapped bread on the counter.

"Charge him anything you like," she said cheerfully to the Wilson boy. Jerry looked at her curiously, with irritation. She had a sturdy smile on her face. Her voice was sturdily cheerful.

"It's off," Jerry said flatly. "That's the leading rumor at the moment, anyway. The twenty lifelong friends didn't materialize. That's what one of the newsboys told me."

"Give him two scoops," Vivian urged.

That was only one of the rumors on July 2. They were already scuttling blind and fast through town. Rumors that the whole thing was off. That it was on and Kearns had agreed to take what he got at the gate and call it even. That Dempsey and Kearns had left Great Falls with their $200,000 as soon as they heard that the rest wasn't coming. That Gibbons was in seclusion. That he wasn't and he had given a little speech about putting your best foot forward, and nothing attempted, nothing gained.

By late afternoon, when the sun began to make the shadows long, those with blocks of tickets would begin to hawk them, their mournful cries like birds. Fifty-dollar tickets for thirty, for twenty, for five.

By midnight or shortly after, a second round of rumors would give serious chase to the first, and word would finally come to the Green Lite and the King Tut and all the other lit-up joints that Kearns had agreed to take it over. Get his last pound of flesh at the gate. That was the deal. Shelby learned about it from the wire services.

When the rumors first began to run around, when they made their insect presence felt, everyone knew what that meant. It meant the tens of thousands would not come. They would hear that it might be off—reporters were filing stories by early afternoon—and they simply would not come. Or if they were already on their way, they would turn back, because why would anybody come to Shelby, Montana, if the fight was a bust?

This, then, is what everybody in Shelby knew by the time they'd heard a second or third rumor. That the thing was a bust, whether it happened or not. This is what Jerry told Vivian and Amelia.

It simply didn't matter, now, what exactly came to pass.

When Jerry heard the first rumor at ten o'clock, he walked very casually to the bank and retrieved all the money he owned—$400. By two o'clock, there was a small run on the bank, and within a week it would close its doors.

By two o'clock, Jerry and Vivian and Amelia had eaten bread and cheese in the Cavern. They had scooped themselves ice cream cones and helped themselves to pairs of blue sunglasses and locked the Cavern and ascended into the sunlight of the afternoon.

They passed Stepov in his cape, and Jerry introduced his sister. The news of the fight rumors had not deflated her. In fact—and this would be something to wonder about later—the news didn't seem to deflate anyone right away. For the next forty-eight hours, Shelby would muster a strange kind of energy: the stylish kind of energy that is unconstrained because it is without hope.

Amelia examined Stepov with delight, stepping back to take him in, his monocle, his cape, and she said urgently:

"I have to tell you, Mr. Stepov. You live in a town that is truly beautiful. Spiritually beautiful. And in country, I might add, that is beautiful, inwardly and outwardly.

"The water I saw, coming into this country! It lay in great golden pools on the grasslands, and there were birds of every imaginable variety, pelicans, I think, or cranes. The noblest and loveliest of birds. Oh, it thrills me simply to see it all again in my mind's eye, that glossy water and those flocks and flocks of birds, more birds than I could ever have imagined in one place.

"And the brass band at the station, of course. I bowed! I thought the band was for me!" They all laughed, even Stepov. "This is a valiant town," Amelia insisted. "So bold. To take such a risk! To put on such an extravaganza. To live with these days and days of agonizing doubt—yes? no?—but to *keep on*, with some style too. Oh, I am...what is the word? Not charmed. Something stronger than charmed. Deeply impressed.

"I feel privileged to be here," she said, shaking Stepov's hand again. "I am dumbstruck, sir."

The vendors began to sell their popcorn and hot dogs to each other. The lumberman who provided all the unpaid-for boards for the arena drove slowly down the street with a big sign on the side of his car: I BUILT THE DAMN THING. The shopkeepers, concessionaires, visitors, ambled to the curb to watch it pass. They shook their heads. Most of them laughed.

Jerry and Vivian and Amelia, their sunglasses on, walked slowly down the street, past all the establishments, taking them in as though they were all tourists.

The Days of '49, the Red Onion, the Silver Grill, the King Tut, the Black Cat, the Blue Mouse, the Chicken Coop, the Green Lite, the Log Cabin.

Shelby wanted to be Wild West, so it tried to be a cowboy movie. Tom Mix in *Chasing the Moon* was showing at the theater. And Mix himself was coming to the fight. He might be filming. He wanted plenty of Indians and cowboys around. This meant that the man who had the wit to sell big movie sombreros was doing the best of all the concessionaires.

Shelby wanted to seem colorful and Western and lively. Also jazzy and clever and nobody's dummies.

Red, black, blue, green. Attach it to onion, cat, mouse, lite. Whimsical, fun, modern names. Light and sassy, with liquor in a special room in the back.

All of it required a diligent casualness. The need to be flippant enough to get people to spend money that you desperately needed. It was like calling to an animal whose death would keep you from starving. It was difficult to be light-voiced. To look as if you didn't care.

A saxophone player in a tuxedo passes Miss Lorena Tricky, a girl trick rider in huge woolly chaps. A young fellow wearing a tin deputy's badge clops horseback past Heywood Broun, obese, pensive, scribbling in his notebook. A fortune-teller with a long chiffon scarf, cherry lips, sagging jowls, many rings, scurries across the street and drops one of her scarves. It is handed back to her by a man carrying foot-high oil derricks in a box.

A skinny man with a pencil mustache, shouldering a big camera tripod, rests it for a minute against a large poster—a poster of the human head divided by dotted lines into regions of propensity. The tripod tip rests, an armless marker, on the region of Tune. A painted arrow points down the street to the phrenologist's tiny shack, wedged between two stores, suddenly there one day like a toadstool. Another poster advertises the Knight and Day Wild West Show, two performances a day, and there atop a mane-flowing horse is the cowgirl we just passed in the flesh, her spurs the sound of ice cubes in a sturdy glass. In the poster, she is chapless—wears a kind of bathing outfit, a trapeze-artist outfit, in fact—and clings to the back of a running horse with her bare feet, her lasso roping the entire sky.

An oilman in jodhpurs stalks past a kid hawking near beer. A drunk reels out of the soft-drink room of the Sullivan, bowing elaborately to a young girl who runs toward the mercantile, sent by her mother for a can of lard.

Two middle-aged Blackfeet men pad past in moccasins, elaborate beaded buckskins, swaying feather headdresses, war shields. They take off their headdresses and place them carefully in the rumble seat of a Model T. One of them bends to crank the starter. The other places his braids behind his shoulders and dons large driving goggles.

Esmerelda the fortune-teller, a fat woman with paste-jewel rings on her index fingers, sits in her little wooden box and knits something that looks like a baby blanket.

Everyone is in costume. Even the local people, the local men and women and kids, seem costumed. It is a moving picture lot for now, and they are playing "locals."

An empty frankfurter stand.

Mangy dogs at the kitchen door of the Red Onion.

Near the end of the street, two barkers with megaphones. Girl shows, they say. A Big Girl Review at the King Tut. Also Tom Howard, the funniest comedian in America.

The afternoon performance at the King Tut Castle was called "The High Cost of Loving." Fifty cents at the front door. A quarter more at the top of the stairs.

Part of the dance floor was staked off as a stage. Through the open window at the back of the stage area, you could see the railroad tracks in the early dusk, and now a freight train gliding, bumping, coming apart, regrouping.

A girl named Patsy Salmon sang something.

A comedian made a joke about cowboys and gin.

The train cars crashed and the whistle shrieked.

Jerry and Vivian and Amelia watched the entire performance from a bench in the first row. The sun was slanting in the window behind the heroine's copper-colored hair. They left their glasses on.

Amelia tried to engage the phrenologist in a discussion. She was a middle-aged woman with a turban on her head, and she didn't want to talk. Amelia pressed fifty cents on her and invited her to run a finger over her head. She guided her. "You see. Ideality," she said, resigned. "That has been the undoing of me, I fear."

Vivian began to laugh. She laughed right out loud.

The phrenologist was Susan Watkins—the second wife of Lem Watkins, who had come out to Montana the year they did and farmed north of town somewhere.

They stopped at the King Tut. The women had lemonade for ten cents and Jerry had "lemonade" for twenty. Six couples moved around the floor. A sign offered five-cent dances with any of ten beautiful women. Amelia told them that she wished she had written down everything Sir Arthur Conan Doyle said about King Tut and the death of Lord Carnarvon. She said she would charge at least twenty cents to dance with any of the men she saw on that floor.

One table in the King Tut was filled with men and women in identical safari outfits—jackets, hard-brimmed hats, trousers tucked into boots. They roared with laughter. They signaled for service.

Another table of strangers wore neckerchiefs and brilliant cowboy boots.

The Fitzgeralds and the Smiths from Cut Bank sat at a third table. The men wore rumpled suits, the women, pretty dresses and hats. The rest of the tables were empty.

They walked up the hill to the house. The mud had dried. Amelia was finally silent, though she looked around with an alert, almost rapt, look on her face.

"Did you happen to go to the bank?" Vivian asked, as though she didn't care very much.

"Yes, I did," Jerry said. "We've got what we've got. It ain't a fortune."

The stars were coming out in the purple. Vivian thought she had not seen so many for years, not since her days out on the grass in her shack. A breeze had come up. It blew various smells at them. Cut hay. Horse dung. Sweet prairie grass.

The arena grew larger. It looked mysterious and huge in the half dark.

"Would it be round from above?" Amelia asked.

"It's eight-sided," Jerry said.

"Hmmm." She seemed to be trying to remember something. She hummed a small tune as they walked, and it sounded quite lovely.

She said, "Ixion? Do you remember Ixion from school? Mr. Graham, the classics man with the beating cane?"

Jerry said he didn't, or only vaguely.

"Ixion," she said. "He wanted too much. He wanted Hera, Zeus's wife. For punishment, Zeus put him in the center of an eight-spoked wheel and set him turning for all time.

"You *must* remember Mr. Graham, Jerry," she urged. "He made you get the asthma. He was one of the worst in that respect."

20

It was dawn and the world existed on its own terms, breathed its own breath like a huge resting animal, the first human scurryings only gnats on its back. The first wheels, the first feet, skittered across the surface of something broad and deep where the birds were and the wind; also the sounds of grass moved by wind and the black molten hum of whatever it was that might be below.

There were many birds then, and at dawn they were a beautiful roar.

A splash of thrown wash water. The sight of it arcing silver from a door. The muffled thwap of someone beating a rug. A cough.

The autos and the moving feet begin to sink in and raise dust. The dust thickens and the noise too—the dogs, the cars, the concessionaires. By seven, eight o'clock, there is shouting and firecrackers. Automobiles shrouded with alkali dust lurch spectral into town and move aimlessly around the rutted tracks between the buildings and around the edges. Montana cars, mostly, with signs on the sides: SHELBY OR BUST.

Down the street from the Malones, Mrs. Torgerson stands over a hot stove in a stifling kitchen, making candy for her husband to take to the little stand he has hammered together over by the arena. She has been up since three, stirring the burbling stuff, because her brother-in-law in Great Falls owns a bakery and he sent her the expensive sugar out of pity and the kindness of his heart.

She is a stout bent woman in her fifties, exhausted now and wringing wet. She is making meringues, and she bends over each cooling batch and presses walnuts into the sticky white pieces, walnuts she shelled the night before with her arthritic fingers blazing, and droplets of her sweat fall on some of the candies but she keeps at it. She takes no shortcuts. She makes beautiful candies for her silent husband to box up and take to his little stand, where they will fall out of shape and gather flies that Torgerson will bat at, the smell of the sugar cloying and stupid almost as soon as he begins to bark through a cardboard megaphone.

Candy! he will scream furiously at the crowd. Sweets!

A group of big-shot reporters and photographers will pass by his booth, not long before the preliminary fights, and one of them will call out in that nasal back-East voice of theirs, "Hey, sport! Got any candy to go with them flies?" And then he'll take a swig out of a small silver hip flask and offer a mocking conciliatory swig to Torgerson and that's when Torgerson will leap out at him and get his arm broken by a wildly swung tripod.

Then he will have to go home, the candies abandoned, all that valuable sugar, and wait until the day ends so he can find Doc Nelson and get his arm plastered. All afternoon he will sit in his oven of a house gulping spoonfuls of his wife's tonic, listening to the distant roar of the crowd in the arena—the roar of a poisonous ocean is how it will begin to sound to him through his pain and the sugar smell in the house and the odd whinnying of his horse out in the corral and the deep breathing of his exhausted wife, who sleeps upright in a chair on the porch, head on hand, her mouth absolutely sad.

An almost-imperceptible insect whine grew louder and began to fill the air. A small plane wobbled into view over the top of the rim. It was roofless, with two men inside, front and back. The noise became deafening. Horses bolted and whinnied. Dogs howled like coyotes at the sky thing.

Stunters had been harrying the skies ever since the rain stopped, and this was only the first one of the day.

The plane wavered screaming over the hilltop and began to circle Shelby like a drunken bird, buzzing low over the arena. It seemed then that the day declared itself.

Cars began to switchback slowly up the ridge and park themselves, noses toward the distant arena. Their drivers would watch a tiny fight for free. North of the railroad tracks, tendrils of smoke rose from a modest circle of pitched tepees. The eleven autos in Camp Nok Out sputtered around a space staked out for three thousand, kids and wives at the wheels, practicing their driving.

An auto lurched ahhhooogahing onto Main from the east, a bathtub lashed to its roof. The tipsy plane buzzed Main, and more horses bolted. A temporary marshal with a tin badge dashed around on horseback, pointing directions at drivers who ignored him. He turned his finger to the sky and shot at the plane.

The dust thickened and climbed.

Jerry emerged from his refreshment parlor to stand in the daylight by his street sign. He called out in a mild, embarrassed voice: Ice cream! Sundries! Five ringside tickets to the big fight! He'd sell a fifty-dollar ticket for ten. A passerby grinned at him and said a fellow was selling them over by the arena for five. He put the tickets back in his vest pocket and dipped his handkerchief, for a nickel, into a bucket of cold clean water that a kid was taking around. He held it to his forehead. Over his nose. He heard the wheeze on the edge of his breath. Such dust! Not such dust since the bad, bad summer of 1919, when it seemed to crawl its way into everything. Such gagging, vehement dust.

A horse-drawn cart sleep-crawled down the street, dispensing oil to settle the dust. The smell of oil and the smell of dust—the smells of his time of highest trying. The smell already of piss.

The milling. As the town filled—not forty thousand by a long way, but four thousand, five thousand, six thousand, and still the No. 2 from the Twin Cities to come—as it filled, as the streets grew dense and slow with people and vehicles and horses and moving vendors, it was as if a huge slow spoon stirred it all, set them all milling. For the few hours before the arena gates opened, at noon, everyone moved aimlessly, tirelessly, circularly, stirring up the oil-sprinkled dust, peering into booths, into the doors of the Black Cat and the Log Cabin and the Green Lite. The cafés were crammed. People hung over eaters' shoulders, waiting for a seat. The lines to the outhouses were long.

Shortly after eleven o'clock, the sun now high and white, the shape of the stirred crowd began to change, elongating on one edge toward the arena a half-mile away. Slowly, almost as if in a dream, the walkers walked and the drivers drove, slowly, steadily, in a long row toward the huge bowl.

Two women in knickerbockers leaned their heads together under a single wide sun umbrella, reading something in a newspaper.

The Calgary Scots Band warmed up behind the livery, and the epic wail of bagpipes began to float out into the shouts, the popping exhausts, the wisps of piano music, the drone of the stunting planes, the whinnying of horses, the futile splash of the watering wagon, the cowboy yodels, the clank of photographers lugging their big tripods, the barks of concessionaires hawking model oil derricks, Help Build Shelby buttons, flavored ice shavings, Japanese parasols, binoculars, near beer, miniature boxing gloves, green Go Gibbons hatbands, and fresh oil paintings of Indians and sunsets.

Dempsey's train has arrived from Great Falls. There is a great bustle, boys running everywhere, jostling. The train goes past the depot, continues for a full mile, the boys gasping behind it on the tracks, running all the way in that white sun.

A clot of fervent disembarking men hustle a tall dark shadow into a Ford that speeds toward the arena.

A ragged man with a black hat and a long yellow-white beard sits on the tracks with a sign: LORD GOD, WHERE ARE YOU?

Shaggy little parades make their way ringward. A group of Blackfeet in full war regalia emerges from the pitched tepees and walks slowly in the intensifying heat, the leader carrying an American flag.

A man in an army uniform, drunk, snips all his unsold tickets in half, bowing briefly between snips as if he is cutting one town ribbon after another.

All day there was popping. Firecrackers. Buckaroos firing six-guns. Automobile exhausts. Frail pops that skittered across the back of the big breathing animal.

The arena, that day, belonged to the animal. The people climbed long stairways to its rim, then they climbed down its blank face toward the ring. They looked, when they had finally all arrived, like leaves at the bottom of a teacup, sand in a large shell. They shadowed their eyes like sailors and scanned the empty slopes.

The house is strangely quiet without the children. Vivian and Amelia wear their good dresses and are talking carefully when he comes in to change his soaking shirt. They have been invited to Rachel Zimmerman's to hear an opera on the wireless and, after that, for those who are interested, the prizefight. On the airwaves.

Most of the wives will be there.

Amelia has been arguing politely in favor of the fight in the flesh. She herself has no particular love for the sport—she expects the bout to be brutal and short and undoubtedly bloody—but the thought came to her in the middle of the night that this was a historical event, and she cannot, today, seem to believe otherwise. She feels that when she is in Milan, when she is back in New York, she will feel terrible that she has missed a historical event that occurred directly under her nose.

She hadn't known she felt like that. She had wanted to visit her brother and his family before embarking for Europe, and she had, of course, wanted to see a frontier town in a state of excitement, yes. But she truly hadn't cared about witnessing the actual bout—not until the middle of the night, when a voice came to her and said, Do it.

She asks Jerry to tell Vivian that respectable women will be there. He says he doesn't know what's respectable and what's not. Some of them are wearing knickerbockers and pith helmets and buckaroo outfits. The city ones are. But what does that mean? You tell *him*.

He says this to Vivian, hoping for a wry remark, an opinion, anything. For weeks, she has seemed simply to be waiting. Good-naturedly, mildly, unreachably. Waiting for the spectacle to be over, Jerry thinks.

She has been very even, very patient, like a midwife in a chair. Rarely has she raised her voice or even talked about it much—the strangers, the noise, the wild stories in the papers. Rarely has she even raised her voice to the children, who have been agitated and quarrelsome, though she snapped at Francis when he made a fuss about being sent to the farm. Otherwise, she has been oddly serene in a way that Jerry feels as anger.

She is biding her time, he thinks. The prizefight will be over in a matter of hours. The town will empty. Amelia will go away. The children will come in from the farm. School will start. And then she will turn to him, and she will say, We have to stop this. We are adults. We have children. We have to be done with stunts.

Now, though, she just smiles and shrugs, and again it is unnerving. It is as if she has a voice in her head that is dispensing consolations to her, urging her to have patience—with this town, with this visitor, with her own husband.

He shows them the tickets, fans them out like a deck of cards. They make Amelia adamant that she must attend. He doesn't care. It is all the same to him.

Vivian begs off, mildly, with a smile. Jerry goes into the bedroom to put on a clean shirt. Vivian watches him from the other room; watches him put on a clean shirt for a debacle. A slim man who has for a year and more hoped as few people have hoped, gotten up at five o'clock in the winter dark to sniff out the main chance, to stake his claim to something big in his life, to do everything he can do to tap into extraordinary luck. And it hasn't worked.

He looks to her, at that moment, like the loneliest man on earth.

For these many months Jerry has reminded her of Francis, when he was one year old and thought he could fly. He thought he could fly because he always got caught when he pitched himself headlong off one end of the sofa toward the adult in the middle. She will always remember her child's face the day she sat on the step shelling some peas, and he pitched himself forward off the top step, past her shoulder before she could stop him. All she caught was a small face that flashed pure eagerness, and then that face scraping the graveled ground. The absolute shock in his eyes before he began to scream and the way the eyes continued to look bruised for so many days while the big scrapes on his nose and forehead scabbed and healed. There had been something of that flying eagerness in Jerry this past year or so, ever since the oil.

Now, though, he is quiet in the next room, putting on a shirt, five tickets in his pocket that he'd bought with those eager eyes for $250 and would sell for five dollars apiece if he could. He was putting on a shirt to take his chattering sister to the big fiasco.

She sees the back of his white shirt and she goes into the bedroom and takes her big-brimmed hat from its nail on the wall. She puts on her walking shoes. He squints at her—even inside, the day seems too bright for him—and she sees him as she saw him one day in the rain not so long ago, in his ice cream parlor, waiting for a single customer with a look of complete depletion and surprise.

"Say hello to the ladies for me," he says politely.

"I'm going with you," she says. "I hear you have some tickets to that hullabaloo on the edge of town. I hear you could let me have a ticket for a good price." He looks at her quizzically. "I hear this is a once-in-a-lifetime event," she says.

"That last part's right," he replies with a small smile. "We couldn't take two of them."

Amelia must stop at a number of concession stands along the way to the arena. She wants to find just the right item to engrave this visit on her mind forever, to remind her, in Milan, in New York, wherever her life and career may take her, that she has been here on this day, in this place, at this spectacle. This opera, she calls it.

She holds her parasol close to her white face and it gives her a shrouded look, as if she speaks from a cowl. They stop at a little stand that sells green Gibbons ribbons. And one that sells large metal pins that call Shelby the Fastest Growing City in the Country. And one that sells green sunshades and small fight pennants. And one that sells latticed wooden oil derricks, about a foot high, with *Shelby, Montana, site of the Dempsey-Gibbons championship prizefight* painted in small imperfect black letters around the bottom. This is what she must have. The derrick.

She makes Jerry carry it because she doesn't think it looks right for a lady to carry an oil derrick. As they walk with the slow crowd through the roiling dust, he lets it hang at his side, as if he doesn't know his hand is there.

Inside the arena, the dust was gone, and everything—the endless rows of pine boards, the people who filled the bottom of the huge saucer, the reporters and their typewriters at ringside, the boys selling soda pop and seat cushions—all of it was unbearably clear and bright. Bathed in white light. Too clear, too peeled.

The sap smell of the new boards mentholated the air. The place was wildly bright because most of it was empty. The empty reaches, like sand or snow, seemed to grab the sun and throw it down on the people, the fans, who sat like tea leaves at the bottom of the huge octagon.

The men wore straw boaters. The women, scattered here and there, wore the bell-shaped cloches of the day. Green sunshades went on. Sunglasses.

A reporter touched his typewriter keys for the first time and yelped.

Another one made a loud remark about wide open spaces.

The Calgary Scots Band, high notes wailing above a prehistoric drone, made its entrance and began to march slowly along the top tier of seats, miniature figures in kilts. The Ladies from Hell, Jerry called them. They played "The Campbells Are Coming."

A portly man brought a box of sandwiches to the reporters. He wore a gray linen suit pin-striped with red, a white hat with a plaid band, and a green eyeshade.

A boy of about ten, all alone, marched in with the stub of a fifty-five-dollar ringside ticket and took his seat behind the reporters. He watched their fingers and scanned the crowd.

A man jumped into the ring and shouted through a large megaphone that smoking articles must be extinguished. A lick of flame, a gust of wind—yes, the wind did reach inside the bowl, a clean breeze—and the whole place would go up. And what a way to die. Incinerated at a misbegotten spectacle. It would be as ignominious as choking on an overeager bite of food.

Two stripped men climbed into the ring and a small bell rang and they hit at each other until one knocked the other cold in the second round.

A fife-and-drum corps played "You're in the Army Now."

The Blackfeet, the men in headdresses, walked in and took their seats in a block near the ring. Some of the women carried children. For a moment or two, Amelia saw them as they must have appeared to the first Europeans—huge dazzling birds stalking their own planet.

Amelia announced that she had been thinking about the booth with the Gibbons ribbons. That she must have one and she was afraid they would be sold out. She would simply go get one. There was time. She and Jerry argued a little—he said it sounded rowdy out there—but she must have one, and she would simply whisk out, get it, and be back before they knew she was gone. She had a very strong feeling the ribbons were going to sell out, and she had learned, to her sorrow, not to ignore such feelings.

A gun was fired somewhere outside the white bowl and the sound of it drifted over the top and settled on them. And then the whining plane wavered again over their heads, its shadow racing across the bleachers.

A man in a flannel shirt and spats yelled through the megaphone, and two more muscled, stripped men climbed into the ring. The bell sounded, small in the air, and they leaped at each other.

Amelia left, the stub of her ticket in her hand, walking very straight and graceful, parasol aloft, away from Vivian and Jerry, up the aisle to the very top of the arena where the stairways from the outside came in.

The movie men began to climb onto parapets that jutted from the bleachers halfway up the side of the bowl. They hunched over their big cameras like crows, waiting.

Amelia climbed the stairs beneath them, slowly. She seemed to glitter in the heat.

The boxers pounded each other, lips drawn back. They clinched and staggered. A round ended. Another began. Blood began to flow down one man's face and drop onto the arena floor. By the eighth round, when the referee called it a fight, the cut man's eye was a slit plum on the surface of his face.

The man at the gate told her to be careful. She said she was coming right back. He suggested she stay inside. She shook her head and walked through, her parasol clearing a small space around her, her ticket inside her glove.

The gate was built into a wire fence that ran all around the arena. Men pushed against it; hung on it as if they were caged. They cleared a path for her—she had her city stride, her decisive city step—but they filled in behind her. They yelled. "We'll come in for ten bucks! We'll come in for five!" And a few of them screamed, "We're coming in now!" though nothing happened for a few more minutes.

It was chaotic outside the arena. Stifling dust. The yells of the men. Children and dogs darting between the taller forms. The heat of a broiling afternoon in July. Firecrackers and running boys. The wire fence glittering its teeth at the bilious crowd.

She scurried to the little booth, her linen handkerchief over her nose, sweat trickling out of her hair and down her face and neck. She plunked down her quarter for the ribbon—there were many ribbons left, and the vendor had no words for her, hardly a look. He was also selling opera glasses.

Back at the fence, in the span of a few minutes, the mood had become acrid. One of the gatekeepers shouted that Kearns had ten-dollar tickets, and he pointed somewhere down the long fence to his right. The marshals on horseback, riding up and down the fence between it and the men, were now holding packets of tickets aloft, offering them for ten dollars.

Amelia collapsed her parasol and tried to make a path for herself between the sweaty shouting men. Excuse me, she said. She retrieved her ticket and clutched it, hand high. Excuse me, and she zigzagged toward the gate she had exited because she knew the keeper would remember her. People were now partway up the fence, hanging on to it. The noise had grown so that she could scarcely hear her own imploring politeness.

She smelled horse. One of the marshals loomed near her on a tall speckled animal. A soda pop bottle flew through the air, just past the horse's ear. The horse snorted and ran sideways, knocking into the milling men, and it seemed that that was the moment when something broke loose. Someone might have shouted "Let's go," or perhaps it was just a yelp of pain from someone stepped on by the shying horse, knocked over maybe, but it was then that a cracking sound could be heard and the mournful whine of bending wire. A section of the fence dropped to the ground.

Amelia felt at first as if she had been lifted off her feet, lifted by the elbows and rushed forward. Then her feet hit the ground and they were moving frantically, trying to keep the rest of her upright. Shoving bodies and screams and panting. Someone stepped hard on her foot. She grabbed at the cloth of a shirt in front of her. A strangled voice screamed in her ear. She dropped her parasol and the ribbon. Her arms flew wide for balance and she grabbed at an arm. She couldn't get her breath. She heard her own yipping shrieks through the pounding feet.

Something that stung like a hot cinder flew into her eye. Her hands flew to her face. Blind, she felt the rushing bodies push her forward for a few moments, then she fell among their knees and feet, then she was crouched into herself, hands across her face, the flailing legs passing her, passing on. The shouts too.

She blinked inside her dark hands. She gulped air and coughed. Someone put a hand under her elbow and lifted her to her feet. He pointed at a bent blue hat in the dirt, and she nodded. He picked it up and poked at it and handed it to her. She coughed. She blinked hard. Her left eye watered and stung.

She slowly dusted off the hat. The feather was bent at a right angle. She snapped it off and dropped the feather in the dirt. She surveyed the front of her dress and smacked the dust out of it the best she could. There was a rip in her stocking. Her foot throbbed. The Gibbons ribbon was not in her hand. She decided not to look for it.

Everyone seemed to be gone now. Everyone was in. She could hear distant shouts and the thud of feet on boards.

The man gestured, a question, toward the interior of the arena. She nodded. They walked in and he tipped his hat and was gone.

Strangely exhilarated, she scanned the arena and, yes, it was fuller, but it was still mostly space. The crowd—all those clambering feet, those shouts, those thousands—had pushed inside. Everyone moved freely down toward the ring, and they still reached only halfway up the arena's long slopes.

She picked her way carefully down the steps, excused herself daintily as she stepped over feet until she reached Vivian.

Jerry had gone to look for her. He had heard the stampede and run out to find her, and now he was coming back, his face anxious and then, when he saw her, relieved.

She smiled. She was fine. Her heart was hammering. Her eye got scratched and her clothes certainly gathered some dust—she batted again at her dress—but she was fine. The eye hurt in the light and she squinted it closed. Jerry handed her a pair of sunglasses.

It is almost time. Some have been sitting in the sun for hours and have turned pink. The vendors have jacked soda pop up to twenty-five cents. A bald man on the other side of the ring dumps a bottle of water over his head.

A search is on for a stool. The stool is missing from one of the boxers' corners. There is some scurrying around. The shadows are beginning to lengthen.

The announcer, the man in the heavy flannel shirt, gives a man in a soldier's uniform a hand into the ring. He walks him to the center and calls out that he is a sergeant who was blinded in the Great War.

The sergeant is a slim man in his early twenties, clean-shaven. He must have kept growing after he enlisted, because his arms are too long for his uniform. He has a megaphone in one hand. He wears round blue glasses, and he turns his head slowly, side to side, scanning with his ears.

The announcer takes his hand from the soldier's arm, leaving him to float in the center of the ring. Crackles of applause, some shouts—this is a foot-shuffling, testy, sun-stunned, distracted crowd—and he moves his head again. His face is very narrow and smooth. His mouth is mild and quizzical.

What does he think is out there? Where does he think he is? How can he possibly imagine where it is that he stands? How he is the center of a structure that reaches halfway up the sky. This is a twenty-four-year-old from Sunburst, Montana, blind since July 21, 1918. He saw the Eiffel Tower, but he never saw anything like this.

He bows. He makes a smile, then he makes it go away, and he raises the megaphone to his mouth. A sweet, high tenor drifts out of it, stripped by the amplifier of all nuance. But still it is high and sweet, just a natural gift that appeared in a farmer boy in Sunburst like his first eager, jagged teeth. It is that natural.

What happened to him in the Great War? Mustard gas? A blinding light? Trauma?

He makes the gestures of someone who sees. A hand drawn slowly to his heart. A gesture toward a sunrise on a spring day. The sightless eyes following something beautiful through the air, leading the way. A hand behind an ear, as if listening for something new in his own voice.

The megaphone points there, and then there. He moves slowly around in a circle, sending the voice outward. It seems that the megaphone is pointed for quite a long time right at Jerry and Vivian and Amelia. He seems—they all would have told you this—to be singing directly to them.

They are listening, their hands in their laps: A young man in his thirties, in a suit and a starched white shirt and a straw boater with a sunshade. The mottled, freckled hands of a redhead. Pale dry red hair beneath the hat. A face green from the shade. Legs crossed. Arms folded. A model oil derrick near his foot.

Next to him a woman wearing an unfashionably wide-brimmed hat, a pretty straw hat with a wilted flower in the band. Long hair drawn up under it. Glossy drawn-up hair, beginning to gray at the temples. A round sweet face. A careful smile because she has lost a tooth and they don't have the money for a new one. Her Sunday summer dress, blue, and heavy black shoes for walking in a town without pavement. She seems not to hear the young soldier, though it could be that his voice or the words have pushed her into another place in her mind.

And next to her a young woman with a mussed bob, a battered hat, a rip in her stocking, and blue sunglasses. She is listening intently to the singing soldier. Her dirty gloves are clasped in her lap. She is stock-still. She is blinking back tears.

The soldier finishes and bows deeply. He places the megaphone on the ground, tapping it to make sure it is there. He bows again, flings his arm out in stylized gratitude for the applause, lifts his face and flings his hand toward the empty upper reaches of the arena. And then he is led away.

There is a pause, during which the sun pulls itself closer to the arena and its sweltering occupants. Programs are fanned frantically across faces. Some stand, hoping for moving air through their clothes. Hats sit atop handkerchiefs that have been draped over heads, over necks, desert fashion.

And then the boy who came in alone and sat in a fifty-five-dollar ringside seat—the young boy who walked in by himself—stands on his seat. He screeches. It is like a blast of trumpets. Here he comes! the boy shrieks.

He stands on his toes and points at a group of men walking tightly together toward the ring. The crowd whirls. The stern-faced strangers advance. They are packed tight around a taller one. His large dark head floats above theirs, a smoky idol.

And it is time.

21

It seemed that the town began to evaporate almost as soon as the final bell rang and that dark arm was hoisted into the air; that the arm in the air was almost an act of nature, a signal for the dismantling to begin.

The bell rang, so faint it was almost inaudible, and the big arm went up, and almost at that very instant nails were pulled screeching out of boards. Souvenir oil derricks went into cardboard boxes. Fortune-tellers wearily unraveled the chiffon from their heads. Gibbons ribbons went flying into the big barrels of garbage. Traveling ladies tore up their murky, aromatic cots.

All those wooden and cardboard signs—rentals, admissions, entertainment, refreshments—were stacked for kindling. On top of one pile, a piece of cheap scenery showed a cottage in rose time. Another pile waited to be loaded onto the back of a rattling truck. A trunk of costumes. A megaphone. A Tom Mix sombrero. All of it waited to be lifted and moved away.

The dust. Huge clouds of it. The sun a wound in the sky, the way it looks when grass is burning somewhere, when trees are burning somewhere else. All that movement and all that dust. Wet rags over the nose and mouth. The long, irritable snorts of the deputies' horses. A flung bottle, rolling down the boardwalk, stepped over by all those moving feet.

A briskness to the day now. Everyone on the move. That small tinkling bell, and then everyone to their feet and bent forward and moving out of the arena and into the already-emptying town.

The trains shrieking away, the first an engine and caboose carrying Mr. Doc Kearns and Mr. Jack Dempsey and their quarter of a million plus.

And as the day darkens, the wobbling lights of the automobiles aim themselves out of town. Frail wooden walls topple over. More nails squeal out of wood. A saw huffs through a board. Covers are flung off cots. Bedrolls rolled and hoisted. Feet. Wheels. Another howling train, weary musicians in the window, smoking.

Autos, trains, carts, horses, pulling all the people out of Shelby in long strands, their shadows long on the grass.

And then, as the moon begins to rise, the dust falling wordlessly to the ground, settling. The moon becomes tall and small and loses its first orangeness, to shine hard and white and electric. Down on Shelby.

On its scattered frame houses. Its narrow one-story, two-story buildings along Main. Dark now, all of them, except for the Green Lite and the King Tut. They are small, too, but their windows are warm orange and small shouts come out when the door wedges open for the figures that go in or out. Small shouts and the sound of a clarinet.

The last big night at the Green Lite, the King Tut.

And yes, clearly, that is Amelia's slightly wavery voice now, in front of the band. She is singing "Baby, Oh My Baby," and there is wild clapping for her because there is wild clapping for everything, and she has a particular light of her own tonight, so new to town, and the way she knows how to move her hands, to make the right gestures, and the way her eyes seem to glisten, almost to overflow, while she smiles.

She is loose and jazzy because she is not trying to be excellent and she is leaving in a few days.

T.T. Wilkins leans against the wall, arms folded, watching her as if she might suddenly scurry out of sight.

The band stops and there is the sound, over in the corner, of coins thrown across a wooden floor. Laughter. Mayor James A. Johnson in his suit and walrus mustache, with his big pockets turned inside out, the white linings like windless sails. In another magnificent arm-flinging gesture, he throws his last coins. That's it boys, he roars. That's seventy thousand, give or take.

T.T. Wilkins offers Amelia a clean white handkerchief for her eye, which has grown scratchy and red. She says it will be better in the morning and she appreciates the handkerchief. They have a small stilted conversation. It comes up that KDYS radio in Great Falls has issued a plea for professional singers. It comes up, also, that the piano player at the Orpheum has been suffering fainting spells and must have absolute bed rest for a time.

Amelia thinks to herself that men in the West have a quality of inward strength that shows itself in a nonreliance on words. And honesty too. No false flattery to see what they can get.

A few of the fight boosters huddle together. They are just back from Williams's auto out back, the rumrunner pleasant and silent as he took their money.

One of the men, slightly older than the rest, has his finger pointed to the sky and is declaiming. A flutter of doubt, he intones. That was the demise of the whole deal. That second payment. Fatal to be late, boys. Fatal to be late.

Somebody suggests another telegram. Shelby offers to stage a rematch, stop. Shelby prepared to offer $100,000 for rematch, stop. Three of the young men pull their long pockets out of their pants and let them hang empty. This has become the badge of the night. Two of them are laughing so hard they can't get their breath.

Someone says solemnly that Stanton's bank is going to fold. Where did he get that money for the second payment, anyway? He thinks that people aren't going to reach a conclusion that makes them run for their last few bucks? The two laughing men break into new peals of hilarity.

Vivian and Jerry realize they haven't danced together for months. They don't do the new fast dances, but this is a slow one, a drifty one, and there they are, gliding around the floor. They feel giddy, exhausted from the endless day, ready to keep going, though, because this is the circus, and the circus will be gone, all gone, at dawn.

They know they will not have a night like this again. They could not have said why they are so sure, but they are, and there is in it a mixture of mourning and relief.

Every now and then, Vivian tosses her head back for a long look at her husband. She studies him and he studies her back, and then they hide their faces in each other for a moment and then straighten up and dance like ordinary people. Sometimes they smile, amazed at the day they have come through. Amazed at each other and the day and the place. They are travelers leaving a dire and exotic place, never to return, and they feel the moment of savoring that comes just before something is sure to disappear forever, that moment before a shocking country is left forever behind a river bend.

Everyone is giddy and strange and reluctant to close the day. The men walking around with their empty pockets flapping. Amelia so wild and good-humored and suddenly uncareful. The roars of laughter from the huddled men in the corners. Fewer and fewer strangers as the night goes on. They have filtered away to the King Tut, or onto the train, or even into their motorcars, to drive through a night that is flooded bright with the moon.

Amelia and T.T., Vivian and Jerry, walk home at three o'clock in the morning. Through Amelia's left eye, the moon has grown smeary on the edges. She thinks she sees a shooting star, two of them.

The moon bathes the little town, the narrow rutted streets. It gives everything a shadow.

Some of the people in automobiles have stayed to camp under the white moon. They will leave at daybreak. Their cars are in circles, like covered wagons. They dream of drunken airplanes.

The moon gives the arena a very large shadow and turns it silver and timeless as a dead lake. A huge shallow bowl of silver. A man-made wonder of the modern world.

A tiny figure sleeps inside that huge silver bowl. A crazy man who hopped off a freight car, a tall black hat in his hand. His name is Jeremiah, the name he gave himself the day he unhooked the curled talons of the devil from his wrist. The day the scales fell from his eyes.

The first thing Jeremiah noticed as he limped through Shelby was a playbill for something called the King Tut. It said: "Thorns and Orange Blossoms," "The Tie That Binds," and "Which One Shall I Marry?" The messages seemed telegraphed directly into his brain. They seemed to sum up everything there was to say about life on this earth.

The second thing he noticed was the huge wooden bowl on the edge of town. Transported by God. He shied from it, making his way onto a bench above the town so he could see it from above. An octagon, each side as long as a city block. The sides dipping toward a small sacred square in the middle. Eight sides. Eight spokes.

That is where he lies now, a tiny figure bathed by the white moon. In the very center, wheeling in atonement for all eternity.

And Tommy Gibbons in the little green-roofed house. His eyes are closed too. He, too, lies splayed. His wife—his young first wife—presses cool compresses to the yelping bones of his face. A Blackfeet war costume, his honorary membership, is draped over the foot of the bed.

He listens to the faint squish of the compresses and his son's breathing in the next room.

The moon flings its white light down upon it all. The town. The huge molten arena on its edge. The railroad tracks like fallen ladders across the grass.

IV

22

222 Defoe St.
St. Paul, Minn.
Sept. 27, 1927

Dear Jerry,

Enclosed please find most recent tax statement on the Yates place. I would like you to sell that property for me if you find a buyer at five dollars an acre. I do not think it at all likely the oil play will go in the direction of that farm and, in fact, I am now of a mind that the field has been greatly overrated and I can do better things with my money. I believe life insurance—not fire or marine insurance—is the way to go for me. The early signs have all been promising—I have drawn up three policies during the past week alone—and I find that life insurance, particularly the writing of monthly income policies, is something that engages my talents to the fullest. I have been so successful at this early stage that I am writing a small book about monthly income insurance. I began it a month ago and am nearly finished. It seems to flow directly from my head onto the page, and I find I have to make only the slightest corrections the second time through.

The writing of this book, forcing as it does the contemplation of the entire philosophy of life insurance, has helped me view Family and Posterity in a new and richer way. As I mentioned a few months ago, the best decision of my life was to return to my neglected marriage and children. I say "neglected" with a full measure of remorse and regret. However time heals all wounds and we are, I can report, a family again with mutual goals and mutual respect, clean habits and a go-getting attitude.

My insights along these lines of marriage and family make me very concerned about Daisy Lou, that she is making a big mistake regarding Mr. T.T. Wilkins and will live to rue the day. I cannot, for the life of me, make sense of her objections to him. They seem frivolous at best, and then there is the matter of a divorced woman in a small town simply striking out on her own with no rhyme or reason. And the legal procedures with her name. Can't you talk some sense into her?

Ruth and I have had but one significant argument in the seven months since we were reunited, and that involved my decision to attend the Dempsey-Tunney rematch in Chicago. She views boxing as a barbarism, as what decent woman doesn't when all is said and done. However, I felt compelled to attend because I had a sixth sense of the outcome (I am using the bout in my insurance book as an example of science and strategy prevailing over the impulsive and prideful instincts) but, more importantly, because a number of business prospects would be on the special trains from St. Paul and it seemed a good opportunity, in the leisurely and intimate atmosphere of a train car, to explain to them the advantage of life insurance policies. (I proved my theory by selling the three monthly income policies.)

Well, you should have been there, old boy! More than one hundred thousand of us paying a couple million for the privilege. Made Shelby's "extravaganza" seem a schoolyard fight, you have to admit. I had one of the best seats, just a few rows from ringside, and I can tell you the newsboys did not capture the immaturity of our man Dempsey at the moment of truth. He *had* Tunney! The man would never have made it back onto his feet in ten. But Dempsey's problem is—and I go into this in some detail in my book—that he will not go by the rules or by strategy. He is a creature of instinct and emotion, a barroom fighter still, when you get right down to it. He just hovered around like a big panther that has had a whiff of blood, until the referee pushed him into the neutral corner and started counting. By then, of course, Tunney had the extra seconds and up he got. And of course he is a man who uses his head and plots his moves and thinks of the long picture, so he knew exactly what to do for the rest of it. Retreat, retreat. Make Dempsey a maddened bull, wear him out, and bingo, that's the end of a champion.

I can tell you there was a lesson in it all for me. Strategy, strategy, and a cool head. That is the ticket! Along those lines, I hope you and Vivian will take a few minutes to read through the enclosed policy. It is a draft of course and subject to amendment and refinement.

It is not pleasant to contemplate a future in which Vivian might be left a widow, but I believe some planning now can prevent heartache later. I'm sure you remember Father's sermon about the Prophet Elijah who was sent by the Lord in a time of drought to ask sustenance from a poor widow. And how her generosity produced the miracle of an endless barrel of meal and an unfailing cruse of oil. I take this lesson to my book and say: "Life insurance ministers to widows and, thru life incomes, brings to them the cruse of oil that never fails, and the barrel of meal that never wastes. The greatest tool in the hands of life underwriters today is the monthly income for life. That is the barrel of meal. That is the cruse of oil that continues to flow so long as the widow has need."

Please give that idea some thought and give the enclosed policy your fullest attention.

Ruth and I and the boys send you all our very warmest regards.

Carlton

The book was put out early in 1928 by an insurance publisher in Indiana. Two copies, taped together and apparently unopened, lay among the soggy letters and logbooks, the browning photos, that the firemen carried out of Amelia's smoking shed. *Monthly Income Insurance and How to Write It.* That's the title. Carlton's name beneath. Inside, a dedication: "To the mother of my children, who stands out as the highest type of womanhood for whose protection the great institution of life insurance exists, this book is dedicated. Were it not for such women, there would be no life insurance."

Odd that this is the only real letter there is from Carlton. The telegrams stuttered across the wires to Jerry during the oil fever, but no letters—not that survive. Just this single, aberrant version of a man steeped in temporary rectitude.

For two years, Carlton drank no spirits. He joined the Lions and Odd Fellows and moved back in with his first and only wife and children. He applied himself to the vocation of life insurance, a profession for which he felt sincerely talented.

> Chapter X: Personality in Life Underwriting
> There is probably no vocation where personality counts for more than it does in the field of life underwriting. What makes up personality? Many things go to make it up, and among the first of these is manner and charm. It might be said that good manners, a clean-looking well-groomed body and a happy disposition are the open sesame to any office, to any society…
>
> Another quality of mind which makes a personality glow is vision. There is a great difference between vision and dream life. The man of vision is the man who makes his dreams come true, who doesn't just live in a dream life. He is the man who is a worker, a builder, who can never rest content until the vision of his own or another's has been worked out from the blue-print into the actuality of the building itself. There is a magic in vision that carries men on to great achievement…
>
> Then, too, imagination helps an underwriter to draw a picture for his client of the estate he has created and what it will do for his family, of the lack of sufficient income

> to accomplish his life's objectives; not in cold financial statements, but in a real human way that will make him see the need, expressed in terms he will understand, and therefore realize how vital a thing it would seem to him were he to be confronted with the fact that he was today to take the journey to that undiscovered country from which no traveler returns. And this is no faraway picture! To those who have spent only a short time in this great business there have come personal experiences showing the tragedies that occur so quickly in this modern day of rapid transportation. In spite of improvements in safety devices, in spite of preventive medicine, the human life is a frail thread that may be snapped in a moment.

She had left in the middle of the night while Carlton slept off a two-day drunk and another financial reverse. Fitzi—the tearoom hostess who took him away from Ruth in the first place and for almost six years ran with him through his booze, his money, his schemes that panned out and then didn't pan out. And when the IOUs piled up high enough and the headwaiters began to feign ignorance and when Carlton began to make a single Havana last a few days—a puff here, a puff there—well, then Fitzi ran off with someone in exactly the same way she had run off from a husband with Carlton.

So many times Carlton had imagined the sucker who came before him, the husband ghost who enhanced his and Fitzi's boozy recklessness. The mournful cuckolded presence that fueled them.

He couldn't stand to think of himself as that person, as someone providing an enabling image of aloneness and sorrow-drowning, and that is probably the reason he created someone entirely new. A sober family man, a seller of life insurance policies. Someone who could never be abandoned by a calm and worldly woman with blonde hair and sequined shoes. He would be someone with prospects, with the ability to make himself anew.

He has lost some weight, five or ten pounds. He is, if not lean, certainly solid. Good color. High-colored as always. Still with a pinkie ring and a propensity for a good cigar. But, otherwise, he has the trussed-in look of someone trying, minute by minute, not to misbehave.

He earnestly types his book in a room off the kitchen. The teenagers do their homework on the dining room table. Ruth quietly places things in cupboards.

He wonders when he will stop hating the clarity, the bright tin feel of sobriety.

He thinks he has embarked on an unremarkable and patterned life at last. He decided to do it, and he did it. He has peddled a new self to an old self.

Ruth is a handsome woman and not as bitter as might be expected. He honestly appreciates her. But it is the other woman he summons in order to perform his doleful conjugal duty. He summons Fitzi with her extravagant laugh and lazy eyes, smoke winding from a crimson mouth.

There is a difference between vision and dream life. He knows that, but he can't stop the dream life. He can't stop the moving picture inside his head—the movie of himself, sober and wealthy and smooth, walking into a nightclub where a frayed Fitzi dispenses hat checks. Or his name on the financial page of the *Chicago Tribune* and Fitzi, hungover, smeary, dropping her forehead into her hands to weep. His photo in *American* magazine, in an expensive suit, above a respectful interview in which he explains his great success—a combination of cool strategy, a financial plan, hard work. A prudent accumulation of capital, which enables, finally, one last big risk. A calculated, sober, muscled risk.

And afterward, Fitzi, sequined and humbled and sardonic, accepting the little blue flame from a lighter with his initials tooled in the gold.

23

It is a small, low-ceilinged room off the kitchen. A kind of mudroom that T.T. built on. It is very dim, with only one small, smeary window. He has not run the electricity there, so even on a bright day you have to take an electric torch or the kerosene lantern in there to find anything. She doesn't like to linger there. She'll walk through it, out the back door to the clothesline, say, but she doesn't like the tight cold feel of that place.

A workbench runs along one side; shelves and drawers along another. Hooks on the third for T.T.'s mackintosh, spare auto chains, an old high-cantled saddle. Nothing in the room is painted. Heavy iron tools hang above the workbench, grim mysteries. The floor is cement.

It is T.T.'s room, dark, low, smelling of iron and sawdust and motor oil. Every time Amelia enters it, even after four years, she feels like a prowler.

She needs something. She needs a hammer. She hung a pretty picture on the wall of the front room—a cheap print of a cottage in rose time, but it did brighten the room a little—and she has noticed that the nail is sagging. It seems urgent to replace it, anchor the picture. She doesn't want to take it down and wait for T.T. to do it, because she doesn't want the wall bare and disheartening all afternoon.

So she is looking in the mudroom for a hammer. A huge one with a ball peen hangs on the wall with the other tools, but she is hoping to find a smaller, more manageable one in a drawer. Four years, and she has never opened any of those drawers.

They are heavy and a bit warped. Hard to move. The first is full of horseshoes and strands of barbed wire. Different kinds with different barbs, some innocent, some torturous.

The second drawer, a deep one, contains old cans of poison. For rodents, for moles, for grasshoppers. Some of it has trickled out of the corner of a cardboard package, the mice poison, and gives off a smell of chemical death. The drawer is low enough for a child to reach. Not that there are children in the house or ever will be. But a neighbor child could wander into the room, a visitor's child could toddle into the mudroom while the adults are eating pie around the stove and dip fat little fingers into the stuff in the drawer, yes?

He must move those poisons, she thinks with a wave of vehemence and distaste. What a self-centered, witless thing to do! Stuff a drawer full of poison, an unlocked drawer the height of a very small child. Did T.T. Wilkins forget that he had once had children of his own? Did he think himself responsible only to himself? Did he never stop to consider that his own thoughtlessness, his solitary way of moving through the world—arranging his things to suit only his own convenience—that such an attitude could harm someone else, even kill someone?

She pushes the big warped drawer shut, struggling with it, hitting at it with the flat of her hand.

The next drawer slides easily. It seems to have been oiled. This one is a relief because it is an ordinary junk drawer, a drawer of odds and ends. A ball of string, tacks, oily receipts, a small box of pennies, a few rags.

She stretches her hand carefully toward its dim recesses, patting delicately for a shape like a hammer, and lands on something flat, cool, and smooth. She rests her fingers on it for a moment, moving them to feel its cool roundness and slide it forth.

It is a pocket watch. A pocket watch with Roman numerals on its face and scrollwork on the silver like figure eights on ice. The face is cracked. She traces the lines with a cool and terrified finger, lingering.

T.T. said he got the watch from Johnny Dempsey, not to be confused with Jack.

Johnny was the brother, a dandy in a bow tie with the curved slouch of a pretty boy. Johnny was also a dope addict. Everybody seemed to know it. And if you didn't know it, you might have suspected some kind of monkey riding on the guy's shoulder. He moved his eyes around too fast, as if a single slip would do him in.

Johnny came up to T.T., that day at the training camp on the Missouri, and offered to sell him a watch. A good one. Given to him by a friend and never lost more than a minute a year.

Jack Dempsey hung around with Hollywood swells after he finished off Carpentier. He lived the good life, and Brother Johnny came out to hang around and ride the champ's gravy train, and some swell hooked him on dope. Everybody knew it. Everybody knew, too, that someone in the champion's crew, his entourage, kept Johnny supplied. A trainer, a doctor, who knew?

Johnny. He's why Dempsey lost to Tunney again this year. What finished him off. Two months before the fight, Johnny the junkie finally goes over Niagara headfirst, so to speak. Shoots his wife, who's trying to leave him. Shoots himself.

They had a mountain lion with a jeweled collar at the Missouri camp. Johnny led it around. Twitchy little guy but likable enough. Came up to T.T. and struck up a conversation and, at the end of it, offered to sell the watch cheap. Pure silver. Never more than a minute.

Got dropped a few months later on the concrete floor of the mudroom. Stopped. Forgot about it.

She watches his mouth grind pot roast, watches him swallow.

She thinks about the girl at the movie theater who takes tickets. A girl infatuated with picture cowboys and derring-do. Four years ago, barely married to T.T., Amelia listened to the girl tell her, in full admiration and awe, that T.T. Wilkins once told one of those snake-waving preachers to get out of his way, and when the preacher didn't, he pulled him off his wagon and throttled him until he was dead. Dragged him off to a coulee and dumped him for the crows. The bad summer of 1919. He and Skiff Norgaard.

Amelia hadn't believed it for a minute. She laughed when she told the story to Jerry. The girl was notorious for her fantasies. She claimed she was a descendant of Pocahontas and wanted to give speeches about that fact to the Lions Club and the high school.

Jerry laughed too. He told her that the preacher had had it coming. That T.T. and Skiff knocked the loony out cold and laid him next to a water trough so he'd have a bit of rusty water when he woke up. Put his tall black hat over his eyes. That the preacher and his horse and sheep wagon left town at dark when the traveling was cool.

Jerry said T.T. should have beat up Skiff—probably would have, if he'd known that Skiff was going to do him in. Buy his land off him, then refuse to sell it back when T.T. finally saved the money from his town job. There you have grounds for a beating.

The watch in the drawer is some kind of explanation for what Amelia has come to grieve about T.T.—his flat taciturnity, his brusqueness and rough hands. His refusal of tenderness in any of its forms. His disdain for the amenities. These are not the qualities of a man leathered by great hardship, she decides. They are the qualities of a man without imagination.

That pocket watch had been through a struggle. It had been damaged.

She thought of its cracked face—that was the only face she could bear to see for the moment—and she put her own face in her hands, sitting right at the dinner table across from T.T., and she sobbed, one last time, for all that had receded from her.

It's your eye, Daisy Lou. It's your eye, Amelia. It is your eye that has caused you to panic.

Jerry is so reasonable these days. He has stopped by to see her on a night when he knows T.T. is bowling. They sit at T.T.'s old, gouged table—Amelia has arranged doilies over some of the marks—and have a cup of tea. Jerry wears a Boy Scout neckerchief because he's scoutmaster and has just come from a meeting. A late-autumn thaw has turned the snow and ice into water that drips down the windows.

It is not my eye, she says. It is my illuminated sense of my mission on this earth. She actually says those words.

The eye, according to that young doctor in Great Falls, is gone for good. It has finally blinked out. Four years of infections and salves and compresses and potions. No surgery because Amelia wouldn't allow it, hoping always for the next treatment to work. She has removed the last patch and the eye looks out onto the world now, blue and milky; cauled and blank.

It is not because of my eye, she repeats. Though, even as she says it, she remembers a night, a few days after she arrived in Shelby, when she and Jerry watched the silk train pound through. How they stood near the tracks with a few others and simply watched the train the way people will watch the ocean. It was the thing that moved fastest on the earth. That was the reason people watched it. That and the idea of the cargo encased by its black windowless body. Bolts of silk from the Orient, bound, roaring and unstopping, to the factories on the other side of the country.

They watched the light on the caboose get smaller and smaller. It was a warm night, and they watched until the light was a pinprick and then gone. That's what the loss of her eye had felt like. A disappearing silk train.

She and two other married women from Shelby took the train to Great Falls and saw *The Jazz Singer.*

Sound on the screen. Voices coming out of their mouths. How paltry it all seemed to Amelia. What a disappointment!

Amelia at the movie theater in Shelby, filling in for the piano player. She uses no music; couldn't see it anyway in the dimness. Not with her eyesight. She wears her best dress and a small gray hat. Her dressy black shoes, the walking ones hidden, mud-clumped, behind the piano.

Since arriving in Shelby, she has learned to improvise. To some extent, at least. As the picture flickers huge and silent above her head, she keeps her fingers playing. Themes are her secret. She has memorized piano passages for the seven themes she ever needs for a moving picture: love, sorrow, contentment, fire, apprehension, flight, and triumph. Plus an all-purpose transitional pattern that basically involves sustained chords in minor keys.

She glances quickly up at the screen, judges like lightning what is going on, and plays the theme until it seems that something else has begun to take place. Music, to her, conveys so much more than the tinny human voice, talking. Than words. Music tells you more than what is going on. It tells you how to feel about something.

She feels the same way about talking movies as she does about Lindbergh. A man now crawls into a plane and flies for thirty-three hours, alone, and he lands in France. The thought appalls her. It makes France so close and ordinary. Europe should never be anything so casual. It should be a place at the end of yearning and travail. Everything is too close now. She feels that.

These things happened: her eye, the talking movies, Lindbergh. They perhaps predisposed her to her decision. But it really was the pocket watch. The scrolled pocket watch of young Dr. Sheehan from Saint Paul. Or its twin.

It really was the pocket watch. When she found the disc of it, shining and battered in that dark drawer, she saw that she had taken a dire turn away from what was best in herself and the world. She had abandoned her ideals, her artistic solitude, for life with a man who was distant and ordinary.

And so, on the day of November 11, 1927, she did three things. She borrowed $500 from her brother Jerry and arranged to rent a newly empty house, just down the street from Jerry and Vivian's house. She put an ad in the newspaper for voice and piano students, with an offer to teach the third child in a family free of charge.

Then she walked slowly, in a light snow, down to the courthouse, and there she filed a petition to have her name legally changed. The last name would revert to her maiden name. The first name would make legal and permanent her stage name. Daisy Lou became, forever, Amelia.

24

It is a five-year diary, five years to the page, a few lines for each year. The year 1923, running along the tops of the pages, shows Jerry's handwriting large, fervent, jubilant, despairing, erratic. The entries at the bottoms of the pages, the entries for 1927, come to us in a small neat hand.

The tops of the pages seem to waver with tension and hope. A man on a cliff in a high wind. The bottoms are grounded and safe. The man with his sleeves rolled, raking a lawn.

At the end of each month, space for a short summary.

May 1923: Made no money. Town property going stale on acct. of the Fight. Started getting ready to put in ice cream parlor.

Drop to the bottom. *May 1927: Wettest month in 50 years. Lindbergh flies NY to Paris. Started dieting and took off 6 lb. since 10th. Francis got a pony at Cut Bank but hasn't brought it down yet. Cancelling machine installed in P.O. Agreed to take on Boy Scouts.*

Flick the pages. There at the top: *July 1923: The Big Fight pulled off a fizzle and lost a lot of money. No business whatsoever. Just about out of money. Daisy Lou staying on.*

But drop only to the bottom. *July 1927: Splendid month. Put on Boy Scout concession the Fourth of July. Got $500 from Big Six syndicate on lease. Took small trip via Butte to Kalispell. Weather good.*

Dieting and a steady job. A job as postmaster. Postmaster and scoutmaster and taker of vacations in the summertime. The oil field just an oil field, a steady and unspectacular producer. A little lease money here, a little there. No more gushers, no huge surprises.

The vacation is lovely and calm. A high green Montana summer, and the car works all the way. Maudie and Tip stay at a friend's farm north of town. Francis is off to a Boy Scout camp on Flathead Lake across the mountains.

Jerry and Vivian drive and picnic and talk. They camp at tourist camps. The glow of campfires and the silhouettes of the heavy purple mountains. Do they feel themselves to be entering on the long, calm, ordinary time of their lives? If so, it feels, at this point, like relief.

They make the long loop, stopping to fish at any stream that strikes their fancy, roasting hot dogs, dedicating themselves to recreation in all its available forms.

They pick up Francis at camp and he is sunburned and wears a beaded headband with an eagle feather in it. He has swum every day in the glacial lake, out to a splintery dock, his heart burrowing away from the shocking water like a frantic dog. He has learned five dirty jokes and watched a team leader kill a snake and stoutly smeared calamine over his bug-bitten skin. He has made the leather headband and, in wood carving, a beautiful replica of the *Spirit of St. Louis.*

That is actually what Francis became consumed with at the camp. The rest went on around him and he went through the motions, like the terrible swim to the raft, when he had to. But he really lived the entire ten days for that airplane. He worked on it every available moment and kept it in the cook's kitchen at night, safe on a high shelf in a box.

At twelve, Francis is a tawny, gangly, fast-growing boy. He is earnest and pious and adventurous and idealistic. He has a shock of glossy chestnut hair that falls over his eyes, and a handsome, good-looking grin. He has a kind of cavalier, careless look—an ease and humor with other boys—that belies his intensity, his bursts of fervor.

He has, in the past, been fervent about religion—for six months, through a long winter, he served daily mass in the frigid little church at 5:30 a.m. He was fervent about his aunt Daisy, waiting, waiting for her record to arrive. And how he wept when it arrived broken and had to be patched!

He is fervent about horses and has bought one of his own with his newspaper money. (He also uses his paper money to buy his mother roses on her birthday.) And now he is fervent about Lindbergh. Impassioned by the man and his feat.

He loves the man. Lone luck personified and triumphant. He thinks there could be nothing finer and more exciting that a human could do. Crawl into a machine shaped like a bird and propel yourself, alone inside the bird, across the Atlantic Ocean. The propellers gobbling the air.

The thought is an absolute counteractant to the heaviness of his near adolescence.

He wants to be a hero. He doesn't see the point of life without heroics.

He wants to be a flier. He feels the wish as destiny.

Francis highest in his room on mentality test.

The wettest month in fifty years and that wide country in May is beautiful in its fleeting green. The farmers smile. Even when their autos stick in the gumbo, they heave with good-humored vigor until the machines are extricated and chugging off again through the sweet drizzle, past the lime-colored wheat, the pretty prairie grass.

Vivian has big boxes of geraniums on the front steps, out from under the eaves so they will be watered by the showers. The flowers are red and plump. The steps are newly painted, bright yellow. A silver bicycle rests against them.

Inside, a new couch and chair. Crisp checked curtains.

Shelby has become mad for clubs. Jerry joins the Lions, becomes executive vice-president. He plays basketball at the Men's Club. There are card parties and dinner parties and, in the summer, big cookouts down by the river. Tennis when it's not too windy. Dances. The Mr. and Mrs. Club.

Vivian plays bridge once a week. Every woman she knows plays bridge, and they stay out, routinely, until midnight, 1:00 a.m., 2:00 a.m. It is their turn and they take it.

The town is busy, busy, the way a child is who has badly scared himself by running away from home and comes back wanting nothing but routines: the blanket, the story, the food in the right places on the plate.

There is some peace in all this. (*Lovely day. Put up ten gallons of root beer.*) The children have grown tall and present and active, and their parents' eyes have swiveled slowly away from the world of their own concerns to those of their children, on the specifics of their children's days.

They require politeness and rigor inside the house, in the schoolroom, but give the kids the outdoors for their own. Francis and his friend Phil will ride their horses twenty miles, twenty-five miles in a day, anywhere they please, and if they aren't home by dark, well, they have bunked with a rancher or farmer and will show up the next day.

Maudie and five other third graders join the older kids on Sneak Day and walk seven miles to the Marias River in June for a swim. They're home by dark, sunburned and giddy, and their parents welcome them calmly, give them the routine speech about not skipping school, put them to bed.

They like their children to claim the country this way; make it familiar and theirs. It helps to wipe out those couple of years when Shelby seemed to contain an occupying army. It encourages them in the idea of adventure.

Spoke at the Men's Club on P.O. system.

They will squint out the windows at Shelby, passengers on the Great Northern; squint out into the dawn or the late afternoon, through the sideways snow or the sun, because they remember: This is where the fight was. This is where they held the thing.

It would never be an attractive little town. It would always have the look of a too-skinny kid with a few teeth knocked out. Rakish, unkempt, spare houses scattered like thrown dice across the flat, up the side of the ridge, north of the tracks where the shacks stood in their uncut weeds. It seemed to defy the idea of fame, this town.

But yes, this was the place, and so you looked around for some sign as the train huffed impatient at the depot. And were there revelers straggling out of bars and dance halls? Were there celebrities, speculators, bootleggers, hawkers, reporters, fortune-tellers, grifters walking those streets? Not in your wildest dreams.

Was there a wooden saucer bigger than Madison Square Garden? For a few years there was, out there on the edge of town, the evidence. Then it was torn down. After that, not in your wildest dreams.

There was just a very small, very quiet little rail town with edges that frittered out onto a huge swelling prairie. The child's-primer light of dawn. A young mongrel dog on a baggage car, ears cocked. A curl of smoke from a small café across the way. A man in overalls stepping across the tracks, black lunch pail swinging. A man in a business suit swinging a mailbag onto a cart, wheeling it away toward a low brick building that flew a flag.

Lovely day. Lions Club. Got Tunney-Dempsey returns and won $35 on same.

V

MIDNIGHT

As THE two old people talked in the blue light of the television, shadows came into the room and sat on the end of the couch next to Amelia's feet, in the rocker, at the table in the next room. One stretched on the floor, feet crossed casually, arms behind the head. One lounged against the doorjamb.

A July breeze that smelled of cut grass drifted through the open window and nudged the shadows and swirled among them. Everything remained—the shadows, the sweet breeze—when Jerry turned off the television and flicked on a warm table lamp.

He tipped back his chair and thought with a small leap of happiness about homecomings and oil.

Amelia said she felt better than she had in days, more relaxed. She could feel her ankle healing by the minute. She said she felt as though the hands of a very gifted and spiritual healer had been laid upon her ankle. When she said that, she thought about the letter she wrote to Penelope Wexner in the late summer of 1923 to say that she would be staying in Shelby; would not be traveling to Milan. She thought, rather, about the reply.

It was a telegram that did not try to save money. MY DEAR DEAR AMELIA, it said. YOUR POWERS OF IDEALITY HAVE CLEARLY SURGED TO THE FORE IN A MANNER DIFFICULT TO ANTICIPATE STOP I HAVE CONSULTED MADAME DE PLANTE THE FINEST SPIRITIST IT HAS BEEN MY PRIVILEGE TO MEET STOP SHE SAYS YOU HAVE CORRECTLY JUDGED YOUR ROLE IN THIS LIFE STOP YOU SHALL ENABLE OTHERS STOP THIS IS A PRIVILEGE STOP YOURS VERY TRULY MRS. PENELOPE WEXNER.

The shadows nodded. A car thundered past, sped on, screeched, faded, and then the night was quiet again.

"I used to watch my best student, Virginia, roar off after her lesson in a motorcar," Amelia said. "It broke my heart, the frivolity of it. The waste. She chose a young man over her talent." She thought for a moment. "Saint Paul. Not here. Virginia lived in Saint Paul. She may live in Saint Paul to this day."

She adjusted the ice bag and wrapped herself closer in the blanket. "More likely Virginia is dead," she answered herself matter-of-factly. "They all are."

Sometimes at the pond where they swam after church, large birds appeared in the trees. Crimson and turquoise, they moved through the filmy leaves, or perched and watched. When they flew away, wings thumping the air, their wind lifted the hair of green-eyed gypsies who roamed the jungle and made campfires at dusk.

Francis's young son, Donnie, was somewhere in that jungle. And the boy Penelope Wexner lost in the Great War. All the lost ones. They were making their way, exuberant, back to the pond.

"I was surprised that I was able to recall all the words to the song I sang this evening," Amelia said. "I was very pleased with myself, if I do say so myself."

"You were in very fine voice the day of the prizefight, if I recall," Jerry said. "That evening, when we all went out. And you sang with the dance band that looked like desert sheiks."

"Exactly like those men you see now on the television," Amelia said. "Those Arabians." She sat up on the couch. "What did I sing? Oh, I am trying to recall what I sang with those sheiks. Something about love, I'm sure of that. Or stardust perhaps. Or the moon. Probably the moon."

"Bright as a torch that night."

"I could see the shadows of the blades of grass that night."

"Vivian said she could see through her fingers. That the light went right through the skin."

For Maudie's high school graduation, in the middle of the Depression, Vivian ripped apart her own wedding dress and sewed her daughter something that could have come from Lord & Taylor. She had never learned to like sewing, but she cut the material fearlessly with the long shears. The kids were all at a dance. Vivian's face was flushed. Her hair was prematurely white but still full. She cut the pattern and pinned it to the pieces of material. They listened to the radio. He made popcorn and they ate it out of a single bowl. She washed the grease from her fingers and sewed two new long seams in the new dress, then put it aside, hidden from Maudie, because it was getting late. They tamped down the stove—a spring storm had changed from light snow to washing rain—and she sat on his lap and put her hand on his cheek and smoothed his eyebrow with the tip of her thumb and ran her thumb lightly across his mouth.

Vivian showed him an oversized, elaborate Easter card from Carlton. He said he had "taken a position" in Dempsey's restaurant on Times Square and talked every day to the champ. His handwriting was cramped and shaky. Carlton's children, a lawyer and a fashion buyer, said they had heard he was in California. They hoped he was alive and on his feet.

Carlton was one of the shadows. They let him stay, hoping he would just doze.

The shapes of their parents were there too. Their mother wore a white nightgown. Their father was a boy in a preacher's frock. Mrs. Wexner, imperious, stood by the window. Suzanne McClintock read tea leaves. Skiff Norgaard snooped around in the kitchen. Vivian, of course, sat in the other big chair, and the children were in from the cities. Their children too, including the missing Donnie—gaunt, medaled, triumphant. On the bed, stretched out as if returned from a long trip, the young Dr. Sheehan slept, hands across his chest.

"I feel strangely happy," Amelia announced. "The way I did, sometimes, as a child, when I didn't want to sleep because I would go away from that happiness."

Jerry brought her another blanket and a glass of water for her teeth and propped the pillows. He led her into the bathroom and left her to go about dismantling herself. Her knee had developed an odd twinge. She wished she had a handsome cane with a gold knob on the top.

Amelia removed her dress and girdle and jewelry and put on a robe Jerry had brought her. She decided to leave her wiglet on so she wouldn't shock him too much.

Jerry went into his office and turned on the goosenecked desk lamp. He chuckled to himself. "Norgaard." he said. "I would like to see his face when that forty-dollar oil starts chugging out of the ground." He bent eagerly over his papers, making notations, penciling *x*'s on his map, smiling shyly from time to time. "You wait, Norgaard!" he crowed, stabbing the air.

Amelia, back on the couch, called out that she was very grateful for Jerry's hospitality. Then she called out that she hoped T.T. knew which cupboard she meant for the kibbles. Then she had Jerry come in and pull back the curtain and turn off the light so she could watch the night outside. She had twenty-thirty vision in the undamaged eye and could see plenty when there weren't distractions.

Jerry went to bed, closed his eyes, and saw the film again, stark and grainy.

He seemed to see it better in his mind's eye than he had on the screen. He could see how young the fighters were and how hot the day was. How Dempsey, fighting, is beautiful and forward-tilting, like a ship's figurehead. Always forward and dancing lightly during the pauses. Springy and cruel. His shoulders as muscled and sleek as a big cat's. The long thighs dark against white cloth.

Gibbons is planted and scrappy. Defending. His back is knotty. He jabs at Dempsey like a brave kid poking a coiled snake with a stick. He hitches his trunks nervously, making him, each time he does it, too human and alert.

In the corners between rounds, black umbrellas flare, collapse. The flick, flick of white towels fanning. Clapping hands that flock upward each time Gibbons lands a blow. The quivering shadows of ropes and men when the two fighters move outside of what the camera is able to see.

Sometimes Dempsey lunges at air like a dog, because that is simply what he lives to do. Provoke. Attack. He is like bad weather.

Gibbons comes back. Again and again. He can't be knocked over. The clapping hands ruffle upward like birds.

He might be a rich man by the time young Donnie steps off that big plane. He'd pick up the boy in a big town car and take him to the rest of them, and Francis would laugh the way he used to, because his flying son was finally home.

The nurse would say something different. She would say Vivian was dressed and anxious to be going, and he would whisk her out of that white place, off to a little town out West that had the sound of trains and wind.

Junegrass, slender wheatgrass, blue grama.

If they couldn't afford a tree, they would decorate a big tumbleweed. Francis would laugh helplessly at his own jokes and Daisy would clap the hands of her big china doll.

There would be entertainment. Twins singing "Red Wing" and then Daisy-Amelia singing "Baby, Oh My Baby" with the sheiks. Suzanne McClintock, her hip healed, telling fortunes.

His mother's hand would sweep the hair from his forehead, and his breath would come a little easier.

Outside, the wheat would climb high. Unblown. Well-watered.

Oil would gush out of the kitchen sink and they would all roar their approval, thousands and thousands of them, while

Dempsey staggered, grabbed, fell—knocked out cold. They'd take him to a room at the Arena Motel, and then they'd have a big party at the Green Lite or the King Tut. They'd laugh all night. No one would go home until dawn.

Amelia sat up awake long after Jerry went to his bed and sank into his rich sleep. She watched the night like an owl, calm and alert. Stars were everywhere, and they made her remember the night she and Lelia went looking for the comet. How she had felt the low electric presence of the comet.

She heard Lelia out there in the dark, warbling very quietly. And then the warbles dropped away and a clear, high soprano voice remained. It stayed for a while to sing portions of Amelia's favorite songs—songs like "Life" and "Vale" and "A Spirit Flower"—each one conjuring a specific scene. She saw herself leaning across a long florist's box to kiss the face of a young man named Furey. She saw summer light arrowing through gauzy curtains onto a horsehair couch and a girl's white lap. She saw sweltering bagpipers escorting a blind tenor up a slope of white-pine steps.

After a while, the singing stopped. Amelia raised her hands to clap and saw that the moonlight went right through her skin.

In the far darkness, she recognized the swimming pond of their childhood. It had frozen and was almost too bright to gaze upon. Figure eights swirled across its surface, made by the winking blade of her own confident skate. It etched the glassy pond, threw up a little shower of crystals that fell to the earth with the sound of distant applause.

She closed her eyes, then opened them again and adjusted her blanket and her ice bag.

She sat back and watched the rest of the night move slowly through its colors, black to deep blue to lavender with fire on the edge, and she listened to the calm exhalations of everyone around her, and then she slept.

MORNING
July 11, 1973

Amelia rose from the couch very early and went to the door to see the day. It was a calm and delicate morning, all pastels, and the birds were a torrent of music.

She felt absolutely rested, very light on her feet, though she could have slept only an hour or so. If Jerry made money from the oil, they would go on a cruise, or perhaps to Seattle to see the *Aïda* production with the real elephants. She clearly had the stamina for it.

Her ankle felt much better. The swelling was down, though it was still tender. She took two more of Doc Mineaux's pills for energy.

She thought about going back to the couch until Jerry woke. Then she thought, This is a new day, and she inserted her teeth and repinned her wiglet and looked out the door again. There was no one about, not even the paperboy or a dog.

She examined her dress. It was not the one she wanted to wear that day—it was all wrong for this particular day, and wrinkled too—and so she folded it and put it on the arm of the couch, her girdle tucked discreetly beneath it. She placed her hat on top of the dress.

She found Jerry's long coat in the closet and put it on over her underthings. She put on her gloves. In the corner of the closet, she found a tinny curtain rod to use for a cane.

She sat down for a little while to gather her thoughts. She drank a glass of water and took another pill.

She would go home and write a letter right away to the people who put on the old-timers' banquet, telling them what a perfectly beautiful job they had done. She would write a follow-up letter to the parole board on behalf of the young man who set fire to her storage shed, this time including a few programs from her musical performances to give them a better idea about her credentials.

She would also get all her letters and photographs in order for the boy who wanted to make the moving picture about their young lives, that Michael Cage. She'd choose a piece of music that he could use as an overture to the film—she believed formal overtures should be reinstated—and she'd choose it with great care and sensitivity. An orchestral piece that conveyed the appropriate combination of apprehension, sorrow, and triumph.

Her feet were too swollen for her little black shoes, but she didn't need shoes to walk three blocks. She left them neatly next to her folded dress and her velveteen hat.

Verdi would be meowing, and it was time to get an early start on this day.

The world is absolutely new. She walks through it. Her painful ankle feels like nothing more than an annoyance, a piece of furniture that must be stepped around. A part of life. As she does every morning, she searches inside herself for her soul, and finds it hammered and dented but still there, still glowing like comet dust.

She begins a list in her head of some of the highlights of her life. For Michael Cage. She will need pencil and paper and a long, uninterrupted day. She hopes he will wait until tomorrow to call. That he gives her the necessary time.

She walks slowly because she is thinking and because her knee now has a sharp little pain in it too. Her head feels as if it rides the air, some distance from her body.

She leans a little more on the curtain rod and decides to walk in the street, where there is more room. Then she decides to go back up on the sidewalk. She sits resting for a few moments on a low brick wall, her coat open to the cool morning because no one is about.

She watches the breeze ruffle a honeysuckle bush so that it looks like a sea of tiny clapping hands, and then she thinks about the clapping hands in the prizefight film—how, watching them, she had heard again the cowboy yodels for Gibbons and then the way the Blackfeet had picked up the cry and turned it into a thing that soared straight to the sun. One of those high, true notes you hear only two or three times in a lucky life.

She rises, buttons her coat the best she can, and walks again. Now she is not sure whether the new pain is in her knee or her hip. It has grown rather urgent. She will rest for a while when she gets to the house. Have her tea.

There he is, Mr. Verdi, in the window. Waiting for her. She waves to him and turns to cross the street.

The bone of Amelia's hip has an old lady's porosity. Over the decades it has thinned and grown delicate. A crack the size of a filament appeared in that ancient, chalky bone when she twisted her ankle, and it has been moving slowly along the slope of the ilium for an evening and a night and an early morning.

It does not zig or zag but follows the same horizon, an inch and a half below the surface of her soft, tired skin. It runs minuscule between the limestone cliffs of that world, sending false clues to its whereabouts via nerves that refer the pain to her knee. She would tell you most of the pain came from her knee.

She stands on the curb, leaning lightly on the frail curtain rod, and waves again at her vigilant little cat. He disappears from the window to meet her at the door.

She reaches with the curtain rod and plants it just beyond the curb. In the corner of her eye, she sees the sun glint off a metal roof at the bottom of the long hill. She smells the sweet prairie, a freshly mown lawn, the honeysuckle bush. In the far distance, she hears the cry of the No. 2, the train that brought her here.

As she steps off the ledge, the rod begins to bend. She tightens her grip, one foot in the air, and the rod sags more abruptly, yanking her hand like a headstrong child.

Her eye frantically and futilely tries to gauge the distance to the street. Her arm flies up for balance and the curtain rod clatters to the ground. Her heart flails in its cage.

And then Amelia is leaving the curb. And for a moment that seems to her as long and short as life itself, she feels herself to be perfectly poised. She is motionless and soundless on the crest of a high turn.

There is time in the world for her to spread her arms as wide as they will go. Time to raise her old eyes to the light that is raining on them, and to begin a low hum at the bottom of her throat.

And then she is on her way. Everything about her is wildly alive. She leans into what is about to begin, and the sound from her mouth joins the climbing wail of the No. 2.

Acknowledgments

THE AUTHOR is particularly grateful to the following: the Corporation of Yaddo, the Thurber House, the Montana Historical Society, the Marias Museum, Ron Levao, Steve Lott at The Big Fights, Inc., Curt Noltimier, William McNamer, Megan McNamer, Leonard Wallace Robinson, Patricia Goedicke, Kate Gadbow, Kitty Herrin, Andrew Wylie, and Terry Karten.

Readers' Guide for

One Sweet Quarrel

Discussion Questions

1. What does the title mean? What is a "sweet" quarrel? Who is the quarrel with?
2. Why do you think McNamer didn't have this novel move from past to present in chronological order? What does the novel gain (or lose) by her decision? Did it add or detract from your enjoyment of the novel?
3. What would have been lost, or gained, for you as a reader if the novel had been set in an imaginary location, rather than a real place?
4. If McNamer had chosen to tell the story from one point of view—Carlton, Daisy, or Jerry's—who should it have been? Why do you think she chose to tell it from an omniscient narrator's point of view?
5. Why did Daisy leave T.T.?

Suggestions for Further Reading

If you enjoyed the Montana setting of Deirdre McNamer's *One Sweet Quarrel*, try these:

Debra Magpie Earling's novel *Perma Red* takes place on a reservation in Perma, Montana, and relates the heartbreaking story of the beautiful Louise White Elk and the two men who love her.

I thought about Jonathan Raban's *Bad Land: An American Romance* all the time I was reading *One Sweet Quarrel*; this award-winning nonfiction is an account of the history of homesteading in eastern Montana in the first three decades of the twentieth century.

The Girls from the Five Great Valleys by Elizabeth Savage, one of the forthcoming Book Lust Rediscoveries, features five teenage girls growing up in Butte, Montana, in the 1930s.

James Welch's devastating novel, *Fools Crow,* is set on the Blackfeet Indian reservation in Montana; it depicts its characters' struggles to find a balance between their traditional way of life and the white world that is rapidly encroaching on the tribal lands.

With a time frame roughly similar to both Raban's history and *One Sweet Quarrel*, Percy Wollaston's memoir *Homesteading* is the story of his parents' attempts to make a home on the Montana prairie.

If you want to read more about homesteading and are willing to leave Montana as a setting, take a look at these:

Elizabeth Corey's *Bachelor Bess: The Homesteading Letters of Elizabeth Corey, 1909-1919* complements Gloss's novel (below), as it's about a single woman trying to prove up a homestead in South Dakota as shown in the letters she wrote home to her family in Iowa.

Honey in the Horn by H.L. Davis won the Pulitzer Prize for fiction. Like *The Jump-Off Creek* (below), it takes place in Oregon in the first two decades of the twentieth century. As one reviewer said about this coming-of-age novel, "It's a rollicking good story."

Bethany and Wade Cameron, the newlywed couple at the heart of *The Edge of Time* by Loula Grace Erdman, leave their home in Missouri to homestead in west Texas in the 1880s.

Edna Ferber's *Cimarron* tells the engrossing story of a young married couple who settle in tiny Osage, Oklahoma in 1899, right after the land rush began.

In Molly Gloss's *The Jump-Off Creek,* we meet Lydia Bennett Sanderson, a widow homesteading in the Blue Mountains of Oregon in 1895. It's a wonderful novel about the West that doesn't make use of any of the tropes of Westerns.

Joanna L. Stratton's *Pioneer Women: Voices from the Kansas Frontier* is a marvelous nonfiction account of what it took to succeed at homesteading: luck, courage, and determination.

About the Author

Mark Bryant

A native of Montana, Deirdre McNamer grew up in Conrad and Cut Bank. In addition to *One Sweet Quarrel* (a *New York Times* Notable Book of 1994), she is the author of the acclaimed novels *Rima in the Weeds* (winner of the 1992 Pacific Northwest Booksellers' Award), *My Russian* (a *New York Times* Notable Book of 1999), and *Red Rover* (winner of the 2007 Montana Book Award from the Montana Library Association, and named a Best Book of 2007 by *Artforum*, the *Washington Post*, the *LA Times*, *Bloomberg News*, and the *Rocky Mountain News*). She teaches creative writing at the University of Montana.

About Nancy Pearl

Nancy Pearl is a librarian and lifelong reader. She regularly comments on books on National Public Radio's Morning Edition. Her books include 2003's *Book Lust: Recommended Reading for Every Mood, Moment, and Reason*; 2005's *More Book Lust: 1,000 New Reading Recommendations for Every Mood, Moment, and Reason*; *Book Crush: For Kids and Teens: Recommended Reading for Every Mood, Moment, and Interest*, published in 2007; and 2010's *Book Lust to Go: Recommended Reading for Travelers, Vagabonds, and Dreamers*. Among her many awards and honors are the 2011 Librarian of the Year Award from *Library Journal*; the 2011 Lifetime Achievement Award from the Pacific Northwest Booksellers Association; the 2010 Margaret E. Monroe Award from the Reference and Users Services Association of the American Library Association; and the 2004 Women's National Book Association Award, given to "a living American woman who...has done meritorious work in the world of books beyond the duties or responsibilities of her profession or occupation."

About Book Lust Rediscoveries

Book Lust Rediscoveries is a series devoted to reprinting some of the best (and now out of print) novels originally published between 1960 and 2000. Each book is personally selected by Nancy Pearl and includes an introduction by her, as well as discussion questions for book groups and a list of recommended further reading.